MY LAST KISS

BETHANY NEAL

SQUARE
FISH

FARRAR STRAUS GIROUX
NEW YORK

Dedicated to my grandma Hall for keeping me stocked with Barbies well into my twenties. Thank you for balancing my karma so this amazing journey could begin.

SQUARE
FISH

An Imprint of Macmillan
175 Fifth Avenue
New York, NY 10010
macteenbooks.com

Square Fish and the Square Fish logo are trademarks of Macmillan and
are used by Farrar Straus Giroux under license from Macmillan.

Square Fish books may be purchased for business or promotional use.
For information on bulk purchases, please contact the Macmillan Corporate
and Premium Sales Department at (800) 221-7945 x5442 or by
e-mail at specialmarkets@macmillan.com.

Library of Congress Cataloging-in-Publication Data
Neal, Beth.
    My last kiss / Beth Neal.
        pages cm
    Summary: "When a seventeen-year-old girl dies and can appear to her
boyfriend, she learns that her death may not have been an accident, and must
delve into her past to face all the decisions she made that led to her last
kiss"—Provided by publisher.
    ISBN 978-1-250-06300-7 (paperback)   ISBN 978-0-374-35129-8 (ebook)
    [1. Death—Fiction.   2. Love—Fiction.   3. Mystery and detective stories.]
I. Title.

PZ7.N249My 2014
[Fic]—dc23

2013033521

Originally published in the United States by Farrar Straus Giroux
First Square Fish Edition: 2015
Book designed by Elizabeth H. Clark
Square Fish logo designed by Filomena Tuosto

10   9   8   7   6   5   4   3   2

LEXILE: 770L

MY
LAST
KISS

MY FIRST KISS

HOW OLD WERE YOU when you had yours?"

I leaned my hands on the sun-warmed railing of the old covered bridge and hung my head low so Ethan wouldn't see the corner of my mouth twitch the way it always did when I lied. "Sixth grade," I answered.

"Really? I didn't kiss anyone until eighth."

I smiled a little to myself. "Who was it?" I pressed onto my toes, squinting against the summer sun, so I could see the family of brown bats that roosted between the wooden beams under the bridge. My best friends, Aimée and Madison, and I spent almost every night that summer before freshman year on Aimée's roof watching the bats flap and dive in the indigo sky as we debated whether or not the food would be better in the high school cafeteria come September.

"Layla Moore," Ethan answered.

I jerked my head up and grinned at him. "You made out with Lay-me Moore?"

He held up his hands. "She wasn't like that in the beginning of the year, and we only kissed once behind the dugout after baseball practice."

"Ooo, behind the dugout," I teased. "Were you in uniform?"

He rolled his eyes and crossed his arms. "All right, I told you mine. Now tell me yours."

"Some other time." I turned my head and watched the river babble below us. A heady summer breeze that smelled of honey-dew and grass blew my skirt flat against my thighs.

"Oh, come on. It can't be that bad."

It was worse, way worse. I was finally hanging out with a cute guy—alone!—and I'd lied so massively that I couldn't even think of another lie to get out of it.

"Okay," he started, "I'll guess." He bent down and leaned his elbow on the railing so he was eye to eye with me. "He definitely goes to our school, because you're scared I'll know him."

"I'm not scared," I retorted, trying to hold together a decent poker face, but I couldn't stop smiling. Every time I met his rich umber eyes my mouth curled up uncontrollably.

He squinted at me. "I definitely know him. Let's see." He tapped his chin. "Was it Luke Newman?" I shook my head. "Mica Torrez? Drew Ridelle?"

"It's not any of your friends."

"Hmm." He thought a minute. "If you don't tell me, I'm going to spread a rumor that you kissed all those guys in sixth grade before they had their braces off."

"Mica never had braces," I said. "And you'd never start a rumor."

He shrugged. "Yeah, I suck at lying. Besides, rumors are lame."

He opened his mouth to say something else, then started over. "When I was little my grandpa used to tell me this story about the river. He said if you looked into the reflections from the sun long enough the water would reward your patience with the face of your true love."

"That's a sweet story. Have you seen your true love's reflection yet?" I asked playfully.

He held my gaze long enough to paint a blush on my cheeks. "I've been very patient."

I glanced down at the water, hoping to catch a glimpse of what he saw. And there it was, a wavy version of him reflected beside me.

He wrapped his arm around the crossbeam between us and leaned out past the railing, peeking back at me. "You're lying, aren't you?"

My heart jumped into my throat. "About what?" I stared at the shiny spikes of golden-brown hair sticking up from his forehead. If I met his eyes, I'd probably confess everything. Ethan had that effect on me. I wanted to tell him everything about myself. I wanted him to know me better than anyone else did, even Aimée, who I'd known since we were embryos.

"You're not going to tell me some other time, are you?" he asked.

An airy, relieved laugh escaped my lips. "Doubtful."

He leaned closer, and my eyes moved to his lips. I'd never really paid attention to boy lips before. I was used to my own full, glossy girly lips. His were uneven—full on the bottom and chiseled on top—and they looked dry.

"So you're a woman of mystery then?"

I wasn't sure which word caught me up more, *woman* or *mystery*. Either way, I didn't answer and I didn't look away from his lips.

He tilted his head toward mine, and a slow rush of heat spread through me. When his lips touched mine they weren't dry; they were soft and warm and the kiss was everything I'd never thought to dream a kiss should be. It only lasted a moment, but the tingling in my toes and low in my stomach lingered.

When he pulled back, I answered his first-kiss question. "Ethan Keys."

"What?" he asked softly.

I pressed my fingers to my giddy grin and shook my head. "Nothing."

"You used my last name. I thought I was in trouble or something," he said, and laughed. I did too.

He took my hand, and I was certain, in that moment, that I would never kiss anyone else for as long as I lived.

1

IT'S SNOWING OR MAYBE it's raining . . . no, it's snowing. I can feel the wet flakes gathering in the corners of my eyes, melting down my cheeks like tears. The warmth from the sun I felt on my face only an instant before is gone. When I blink, the only things I see are blotchy white bits of trees and clouds and lights. Where are those lights coming from? I stumble onto my feet and my legs feel Jell-O-y, like I've been swimming for a really long time and now the ground feels too rigid.

I take one step and suddenly my whole body stings. I fall to my knees and clutch my middle. The worst pain I've ever felt invades my limbs, like when your foot falls asleep except it's my entire body and it's epically stronger. I'm screaming and gripping my sides, writhing in the fluffy white snow. And then the pain stops; as fast as it came, it stops. Filled with relief, I do a quick once-over of my body. I even pinch my arm to check if I'm dreaming. How dumb is that?

I manage to open my eyes enough to see a silhouette standing above the waterline among the trees in Dover Park. He—at least I think it's a he—is staring at me, but not at *me*, me. He's staring at the bloody, twisted mess of me on the rocks along the riverbank.

Why are there two of me?! And how did I get in the river?

I run toward my Other, mangled body. I *must* be having a nightmare—but it's like there's a force field around me. I sort of melt into the air, then get flung back. I land on my butt in a massive snowbank at the water's edge, waiting to feel the cold from sitting in waist-deep snow.

A jagged chunk of ice floats by, sparkling in the early-morning moonlight.

I still haven't felt the cold.

The silhouette is talking now. I hear him, but the words are muffled as if he's talking underwater. I press my hands to the sides of my face and squeeze my eyes shut, concentrating. His voice comes clearer . . . He's telling me he didn't mean to.

Mean to what?

Now he's telling me this isn't how it was supposed to go. This is *her* fault.

Is "her" me?

I open my eyes to check if he's talking to *me*, me. He's not. I look at my Other body, broken and folded in ways a body should never bend over a mound of gray rocks. In one of my Other hands I'm holding something, maybe a piece of paper, but I can't see it clearly. Snow piles high again around my eyes and my cheeks and now on my shoulders. It comes down, harder and harder, until I feel buried in it. I can't even see it and I'm *buried* in it so deep that I can't breathe.

Slowly a thought creeps in, settles in the front of my mind. It tugs at something I feel like I know but can't quite remember. I open my mouth to speak it, but I don't see my breath the way I should in early March. I glance up at the silhouette. He's crying or maybe he's yelling; either way, I can see his breath.

I'm not breathing. I don't need to. The words float past my lips like a rehearsed chorus: "I'm dead."

2

FOR FOUR HOURS I've been trying to remember how I died. It's not going very well. No matter how hard I think, I can't bring a single memory of last night to mind. It doesn't help that I'm standing next to the biggest distraction in the world: my body—my Other body. God, that's weird to say. I want to scream or cry, but nothing feels real to me. I keep thinking if I can just get back inside my own flesh, all this will be over. I'll wake up from this creeptastic dream and everything will go back to normal.

But I can't.

The force-field thing is getting stronger. I don't even melt into it anymore. I just smack against it. It's like my own body is rejecting me. It makes me feel horribly unwelcome in this sterile dark room, but where else am I supposed to go?

Finally, a woman enters the room. She's wearing a surgical mask and a long green medical coat over her matching scrubs.

"Excuse me, Doctor, can you help me? I—" She switches on a light above Other Me, and my words catch in my throat. Harsh fluorescents flicker, illuminating a room I've only seen in episodes of *Buffy* until now: the morgue. I stagger back away from the metal table I've been standing next to since 1 a.m. My eyes jump from trays full of glistening tools to industrial-looking scales and sinks to the tile floor with a wide drain in the center. I pull my arms in tight to my sides, terrified to accidentally touch anything in this place.

The woman starts examining all kinds of embarrassing, totally exposed body parts. I want to reach out and stop her, hit her hand away and scream that she has no right to touch me, but I'm paralyzed where I stand. She jots down a few notes, then pokes and prods at my right ankle, then pinches my knee.

"Careful, I—" I start to tell her about the tender bruise above my knee that I got during ballet practice last week, but by the time the words are out they don't seem important anymore. Nothing does except getting my body back.

Another woman walks in. She has a clipboard. "What do we have today?" she asks.

I glare at her. It's bad enough one person is violating my naked body. Plus, she asked her question like I'm the breakfast special on some morbid menu.

Coat Woman answers, "Miss Cassidy Haines joins us in her seventeenth year."

"Only seventeen?" The woman tsks and sets her clipboard on a small table near one of the sinks.

"And for only three days. According to the report, she had a birthday on Thursday," Coat Woman says.

It's infuriating the way she says my name and talks about me. Especially since I can only see her dark-as-molasses brown eyes and wide, arching black eyebrows above her surgical mask while she sees *all* of me.

She continues. "Seems the darling couldn't keep her head above water this early morning to bear another year."

So that's how I died; I drowned. The stillness in my chest is an eerie reminder that I have no memory of my lungs seizing and burning for oxygen.

"Do you know anything else?" I ask her, but it's more out of blind habit than to get an answer since neither of them has acknowledged my presence. Still, without thinking, I step forward, anxious to hear even the smallest detail about what happened to me.

Coat Woman doesn't answer. Instead she asks the other woman for a tool that looks disturbingly similar to the X-Acto knives Mr. Boyd lets us use in Art class and starts slicing into my body on the table.

I jump back and cry out, "No!" I instinctively clutch the spot above my breastbone where her blade cuts, anticipating pain and blood will burst across my chest, but not one drop of red beads up on me. Or on Other Me.

"Stop!" I shout at her. "This isn't right—I'm not supposed to be here for this." I wave my hands in front of her face and let out a scream that should shatter the lightbulbs.

She asks for a sharper blade.

Suddenly it dawns on me: No one can hear me. Or see me. I guess I expected they couldn't—disembodied at the morgue and all—but there's something about the casual, almost cheerful way Coat Woman asked for that knife that hits me hard with awareness of how unreal I truly am.

My floaty limbs feel heavy. The abrupt sense of loneliness is like nothing I've felt before. It runs through me like blood used to in my veins. I look down at my body, desperately hoping for some small spark of recognition, some link to click back into place connecting us.

As Coat Woman's incision travels down to my navel and the phantom pain ebbs away, a slow realization spreads through me. That body—my body—doesn't belong to me anymore. We aren't connected. I'm alone in this sterile horror show. My hands fall and dangle loose at my sides.

When Coat Woman lifts her knife to make a second incision, a drip of some kind of terrible fluid splatters onto her latex glove, and it's all I can take. I run out of the room.

The quiet of the hallway settles in around me. It feels right, how it should be. The hallway is empty, but, strangely, I don't feel alone anymore—far from it. I can sense everything and everyone all around me. It's like the whole town is *in* me. Like I could do that *I Dream of Jeannie* head-bob thing and magically appear anywhere in Crescent Valley.

I'm desperate enough that I try the head bob. When I look up and I'm not at my oldest best friend Aimée's house—the last place I remember being alive—I start to hyperventilate. My chest heaves and I feel like I'm gasping even though I'm still not breathing. I clamp my mouth shut mid-inhale; it doesn't affect me one bit except maybe to lessen how spastic I look. But what does it matter anymore what I look like? I wasn't hyperventilating; I can't.

But how can I still exist if I'm . . . dead? Because that's what you are when you stop breathing, right? When you leave your body behind?

A tidal wave of emotions rises in me and crashes down against my insides. I don't want to be disconnected from my body, my life. I want to live it, but I'm pretty sure I no longer have a choice.

What did I do to deserve this? Why is this happening to me?

No answers come, no spirit guides mystically appear, like in movies and in books, to help me understand how to deal with the part of dying where you, well, don't.

What am I supposed to do now?

My skin feels like ice as the pain from before comes back in sharp jabs. I bend down and brace my hands on my knees, closing my eyes, wishing for the pain to stop, for this to start over, but with instructions this time.

Maybe I'm supposed to stay with my body. Maybe I did something wrong. I need to get back to her—to me.

I run for the room where Other Me is and throw open the double doors. The two women don't turn from the large stainless basin they're scrubbing their hands in, side by side. Other Me is still on the metal table, but I look different. I look like someone gave me reverse Botox, then stitched me up for Dr. Frankenstein to experiment on.

How long was I in that hallway?

I gaze at my lifeless, marked body for a long time. The longer I look, the more I think I might throw up. I cover my mouth to hold back vomit that never comes. Even though I'm horrified by the sight of my corpse—that's the only word for it now—I can't resist the urge to try one more time to make contact.

My toes bump against the force field as soon as I'm within reach. I push against the dense air as hard as I can, but the resistance increases the closer I get to my body. My hand snaps back, and I frown. I want her back—I want my body back! But all I can do is helplessly look on. As I do, the invisible barrier slowly materializes into a shiny film that's bubbled around the table. My mind is numb, trying to process so many unbelievable bits of my new reality.

I spread my fingers wide, refusing to give up, and focus on reshaping and pulling apart the film. It's no use. There's no edge for me to grip or even any texture to let me know if I'm making progress. I gaze longingly at my layered auburn hair, splayed out on the table, wishing I could move a swath of curls that's coiled around my left ear. They took out my rosebud earrings. The sight of my empty piercings burrows a woeful hole inside me. I've never felt so sad about something so small.

I position my left hand so it's next to my lifeless hand resting on the table. Neither of them looks like it belongs to me.

When the women are done washing, they come back to the table and cover Other Me with a sheet. Panic hits me when they switch off the light and leave the room, because I can't see my body anymore. Nothing is anchoring me to this world, this life. I'm just suspended in darkness. I spin around, calling for them to come back. The doors swing in their wake, jutting into my shoulder twice until the swing loses momentum. I realize then that when I burst into the room, I didn't throw open the doors at all. I went *through* them.

Snow gathers around my eyes again, and I decide it must be tears since it's impossible for it to be snowing inside. Although it's also impossible that I'd be standing in a morgue staring at two sets of my hot-pink nails. I close my eyes and try to remember how I got here, how I got to the river, how I stepped out of my-self and broke every rule that was supposed to be unbreakable.

My icy skin turns molten as the heat of last night returns to me. I can see faces: Madison and Ethan and Aimée. Someone else. It's Saturday night and we're in Aimée's ginormous back-yard standing in front of a roaring bonfire. My trio of junior girls is drinking vodka and Sprite with Jolly Ranchers—jolly vodies as Aimée calls them—that are turning our clear drinks fruity colors: cherry red, apple green, grape purple. The colors are so vivid it's like I'm there, in that moment, HD instant-replay memory-style. I can smell the smoke and feel Ethan's gentle arms as they wrap around me from behind.

He's next to me the entire night. Then he's not. Then I'm alone. Then I'm not. This part plays out in segmented bits, as if someone scratched the DVD of my life.

When I open my eyes, the lights are on again and the woman with the clipboard is back with an unfamiliar man in a dark blue uniform and someone else that I instantly recognize.

Oh no, Dad is here too.

He's crying. I've never seen my dad cry before. I thought he was going to when my little sister, Joules, was born, but he didn't. I want to hug him so badly. A surge of need and fear consumes me. I run to him. I run right *through* him! The prick of a thou-sand needles attacking me from the inside out nearly drops me to the floor.

"Cassidy, baby," Dad says. His voice breaks my heart—even if I no longer have one, I feel it crack and crumble inside my chest.

Now I know I'm crying. I leave the room again. I can't stay

16

and grieve my own death with my dad, not when part of me still lives.

I pass by an old man coming in the front door as I run out into the blizzard that is swirling up snow in little tornadoes around the parking lot. I look down, half expecting to see the flakes breezing through me, but they're glancing off my skin. I lift my arm to capture a handful, and for a fleeting second, I can see a million tiny rainbows dancing in each individual flake in my palm, and the hollow hum of the wind is the only thing I hear.

Then the world comes rushing back to me in dull grays, and I'm running again.

Before I know where I'm running to, I see the riverbank. My feet stomp slushy puddles and freezing water splashes my legs as I cross the park. Wait, it hasn't rained in days and the snow on the ground is dry and frozen.

Then how did my legs get wet?

I swipe at the spray and come up with wet palms covered in leafy debris and bits of ice. It's river water dripping from my fingers, as if they are fleshy faucets. As wetness seeps into me, spreading an eerie chill across my skin, I see Aimée's tall white house through the trees on the other side of the covered bridge. The whitewashed planks that make up the bridge's walls are fissured and shadowed. The threat of the wind rustling the gaunt branches seems to be enough to blow the bridge right over. It's a vague remnant of the sanctuary it used to be for me. I stare across the partially frozen water, trying to remember what the bridge once was, but my vision starts to blur. I blink, bringing it back into focus for a brief moment.

The bridge isn't sunny and bright the way it was that day with Ethan. Did I dream that? No. It was real—Ethan and me reflected beside each other that day.

This bridge is where I had my first kiss and . . . I'm pretty sure it's where I had my last.

BREAKUP

DID YOU HEAR THEY'RE breaking up?"

Sugary grape vodka goodness slid down my throat, warming my chilled bones as I straightened the Birthday Princess tiara that Madison bought for me (and that I really didn't want to wear since my birthday technically already happened two days before), halfheartedly eavesdropping on the girls behind me. It was warm for this early in March, but it was still March. The heat from the bonfire couldn't reach me at the drinks table, so I took another sip to warm up.

"Who?" the other girl asked.

Girl number one lowered her voice. "Birthday girl and E."

My head reflexively jerked toward them so fast that my tiara flew off into the snow about a foot away. I dropped to my hands and knees half looking for it, half hiding so they wouldn't see me.

"Omigod, Carly, you can't call him E."

"His friends do."

"But you're not his friend."

"Friend of a friend then."

"You aren't that either."

"Could be real soon. He'd make a certain non-friend *so* jealous," Carly said with a giggle that made grape-flavored bile clog my throat.

"Can you please get over Mica already? Besides, Ethan seems so sweet. He would never cheat."

"I heard that's why they're breaking up. She had some meltdown and he cheated or she cheated—something. Anyway, point is, there's trouble in paradise, which means he's soon to be available."

"Happy birthday," Madison singsonged as she walked up beside me with Aimée. I sprang to my feet so fast I almost spilled my drink on Madison's furry white boots. She jumped back with a yelp, and Carly and the other girl stared at me in stunned horror.

"Someone's jittery." Aimée reached out to steady my drink and slid her hand into my coat pocket to borrow my watermelon lip gloss the same way she did at least six times a day. I didn't bother playfully swatting at her hand like usual. "Isn't this surprise snowfall so festive?"

"Who are those girls?" I pointed an accusing finger at Carly and her friend as they skittered away into the crowd around the bonfire.

Madison brushed her long bangs down so they shaded her eyes as she sipped her green-apple jolly vodie through a bendy straw. "Dunno. Why?"

"You made the guest list," Aimée reminded Madison while she returned my lip gloss and zipped my pocket.

Madison fluttered a hand at me and Aimée. "I'm sure they're just freshman tagalongs. What's the big?"

"Never mind." I looked around me. "Have you guys seen Ethan?"

Aimée started to motion toward the bonfire, but Madison interrupted her. "Just saw him go inside with Drew. Ice or something."

I pushed past them without another word and made a beeline for the house.

Aimée called after me, "We made you a birthday s'more. There's a candle in it and everything." I didn't answer, didn't even really process her words. She added, "Stay with your girls!"

I twisted to give her an apologetic wave and saw Caleb Turner and his stoner crew huddled in the back corner of the yard. They were *not* invited guests. Without thinking, I changed course and marched up to him.

"What are you doing here?" It came out sounding a lot more get-out-of-here than I meant, but considering what I had overheard from those girls, it was merited.

"Hi," he replied with his standard laid-back smile.

Three weeks ago I would've rolled my eyes, three days ago I would've laughed, now I wanted to forget he existed. "Seriously? Hi? That's what you say after I specifically asked you not to come?"

He shrugged. "It's rude not to say hello to the host, don't you agree?"

I glared at him. "I'm not the host, Aimée is."

"That should be interesting, but okay. Where is she?"

I put a hand on his chest to stop him from walking toward the drinks table. "What have you been telling people?" I must have looked as enraged as I felt because his circle of guys quickly dispersed, snatching up their twelve-pack of cheap beer on the way.

Caleb answered, "That the Beatles are more popular than Jesus?"

I glanced over my shoulder to make sure no one was watching before pulling him behind a thick oak tree. "Get serious, Caleb."

"Y'know I don't do serious." He flashed a coy grin at me.

"What about Thursday at your house?"

His cool exterior faltered for a second. He looked away from me and reset his expression. "That wasn't serious, that was inebriated."

A ball of rage burned in my belly. "I'm surprised you can pronounce a word with so many syllables," I spit at him. He looked at me like I'd trampled over his second-grade crepe-paper piñata (which I had, accidentally, back when he was my seat partner in Ms. Peterson's class), and his eyes glazed over with visible resignation. An apology started to rise up my throat. I swallowed it.

"People are going to believe what they want, Cassidy."

"Especially if you give them a reason to talk," I accused.

"What do you want from me?" He held his hands out, palms up.

"The truth!"

He pulled his stupid smile back up. "That's not what they pay me for."

"Can you be serious for one minute? You might not care what people are saying about me, but I could lose everything."

"Dees?" I peeked around the tree and saw Madison standing with her head tilted to one side like a confused, drunken puppy. She thrust a red plastic cup into my hand. "Twinsies photo op— you and me." She tucked my hair behind one ear so our hair matched not only in color but in style too, then snapped a picture with her camera. When she spotted Caleb, her head tilted farther to the side, asking a million silent questions.

Fabulous. Now I'd have to think of a lie for why he was at my party. For a brief moment, I thought about telling her everything. Then she opened her mouth.

3

I LOOK DOWN AT MY HAND, blinking when I realize the red cup is gone and I'm holding someone else's hand instead. But it's not Madison's or Caleb's. These fingers fit snugly twined between mine, like they were meant to puzzle together. Only one person's hand fits in mine so perfectly.

Ethan's.

I want to wrap my arms around him and pull him close so I can see his gorgeous face, but sharp stabs burn through me when I move. As the pain slowly subsides, I realize I'm not outside anymore and it's not last night. I'm back to reality—or, I guess, the present would be more accurate. And my mind is full of impossible questions that keep me from him.

Did I have a flashback? Blackout? Out-of-body experience? I guess, technically, everything is out-of-body for me now, but how did that happen? It's like I dissolved into a parallel dimension where Saturday night is still running on a constant loop and I relived a small portion of it. It didn't feel like a repeat while it was happening though. I wasn't even aware this reality—the one where I'm dead—existed. I was in that moment, seeing it through my own eyes as if it was the first time I'd experienced any of it.

I look down at my legs to see if they're wet like they were before whatever just happened to me happened. From what I can see in the dim room, they're not. I'm wearing the cream-colored corduroy miniskirt and leggings topped with my puffy lavender coat with silky faux-fur trim around the hood that I wore to Aimée's last night. My rhinestone horseshoe necklace is even around my neck still. Lot of luck that brought me. If I'd known this was going to be my outfit for eternity, I wouldn't have worn leggings. At least I have on my favorite black suede Mary Janes.

My eyes move to the familiar blue-on-blue striped wallpaper and pictures of me taped to a square mirror over a dresser that holds a fish tank I helped set up. A sense of calm fills me, washing away the confusion.

I'm in Ethan's bedroom. He's sleeping with his arm hanging over the edge of the mattress, and I'm sitting on the floor next to his bed playing with his fingers.

"I can still touch you!" I let out a tiny squeal of joy. I squeeze his hand tighter, just because I can, but my moment of relief disappears when I realize he would've woken up by now if he could hear me or feel me. He doesn't seem to notice when I walk my fingers up the inside of his forearm, a gesture that would have him doubled over with ticklish laughter if he could feel me. I drop my head.

Being here is a cruel joke. One second I'm walking through

doors and invisible to everyone and the next I get to feel Ethan's warm hand again only to realize it's a one-way street. I'm not real to him or anyone anymore. I know that has to be true, but I don't go through him like I did my dad, and there's no pain. Maybe it's foolish, but I can't help thinking there's a chance he can see me. Maybe I'm not alone after all.

I weave my fingers between Ethan's again and squeeze even harder, hoping he'll respond this time. My skin looks like porcelain, almost iridescent, compared to his.

Sadness swells in me. I wish I could dismiss this as a dream, but seeing my body like that—mangled on the rocks and crushed and gray (a person should never look *gray*)—was way too macabre to be one of my dreams. My subconscious is more along the lines of I'm-in-class-and-have-no-idea-what-the-assignment-is, nothing freaky. Crushed, gray death stuff didn't come from my subconscious, it came from another place entirely—a place I have no control over: the past.

Every inch of me seems poised to realize my purpose here, but I have no idea what it is. It's like I'm wandering through a thick mist on a cliff, rushing toward the inevitable drop-off, at a complete standstill. And the memory of those girls talking about me at the party was so *real*. Can I do that with any moment from my life? Is that what happened before, when I came to in the river; was I remembering my first kiss with Ethan? Can I go back and see how I died?

As terrified as I am to relive that moment, I have to know. I close my eyes and cross my fingers behind my back: *HD memory machine, please show me last night when I drowned.*

Nothing happens.

I shake my head, frustrated. I shouldn't be here. I should be inside Other Me at the morgue, passing on to heaven or merging with Mother Earth—whatever it is that's supposed to happen when you die. But I'm not.

Why?

Am I a ghost, a spirit, a lost soul? I'm certainly not human anymore. Humans breathe.

Something still pulses inside me though, something new I didn't feel at the morgue, not quite a heartbeat, but something that connects me to this world, to this place. To Ethan. It anchors me to the dark blue carpet under my Mary Janes, holds me unsubstantially to Earth. It has to mean something, me being here, not moving on.

I search my mind for a reason why I fell into that specific memory and magically transported to Ethan's bedroom afterward. I mean, I get that seeing Aimée's house might have sparked the memory and since I was on my way to find Ethan in it I ended up here with him, but I'm not accomplishing anything. Aren't ghosts supposed to have some sort of agenda? I really hope mine isn't to haunt my boyfriend's bedroom. That is way too clichéd.

Ethan rolls to his side, bringing his face inches from mine. The pulsing in my chest speeds up to a staccato beat and my mouth curls into a smile. It's faint but my bones and flesh seem to solidify, and I don't feel floaty or cold next to him.

He makes me believe I'm . . . almost . . . alive.

I cast away that dangerously hopeful thought and look up at Ethan, deciding to take advantage of what time I have left with him.

His lashes bat against the sunlight breaking through the

curtains. He yawns, then tucks his free arm under his pillow. I press my fingertips to his eyelids and wish that I could hold them shut forever so this moment would stay with me. Or better, that I could fall into a deep sleep with him and awaken to reality because this cannot be it.

I pull my hand back and close my eyes so I don't have to see him stare straight through me when he wakes. Then a gentle whisper of a touch brushes my wrist and moves my hands away from his face. The pulsing hiccups into my throat and pounds behind my ears the way I remember my heartbeat doing when I was alive.

He can't actually be touching me. Can he?

I squeeze my eyes more tightly shut because I'm sure I'll slide right through him if I open them. His thumb draws circles on my palm, and my skin vibrates under his touch. The sensation travels across my shoulders and down through my chest. His other hand finds my neck and I let out a quiet sigh. When he encloses his hands around mine and presses my fingertips to his cheek, my eyes fly open and I see him. Asleep.

I pull my hands away and slump against the foot of his bed. He'll never touch me for real again. I'm not even sure what *I* felt was real.

I back away from his bed and tuck myself between his desk and the wall, forehead rested on my knees, eyes shut. I should leave before I plummet into full wallow mode, but I literally can't think of anywhere else to go. It's like the rest of the world doesn't exist. Maybe Ethan's bedroom is my afterlife prison—no, prison isn't the right word. I want to be here with him, but I feel like there's no way out, no choice.

I listen to him get out of bed, leave the room, return five minutes later, and climb back into bed. His cell phone rings. He doesn't answer it. Finally, after ten solid minutes of it ringing, he picks up and Mica's deep voice comes through the line so clear that it's like he's in the room. Mica says, "Don't hang up."

Ethan hangs up without a word and curls his legs close to his chest, then starts to cry. I've seen Ethan cry before—unlike my dad. I know I have, but . . . the memory of when I did is missing. Watching him fall apart like this, reminding me of what I've lost, is unbearable. I pull the first happy memory I can grasp to the front of my mind.

I'm in my driveway, on a chilly spring afternoon, prancing through the steps from my first ballet recital. My pigtails are swooshing back and forth against my cheeks, whipping me in the eyes with each pirouette. That was the year my mom made me cut my hair up to my chin because I got Bubblicious stuck in it. I refused to stop wearing it up even though the ends were too short.

I squeeze my eyes shut at the memory of my four-year-old self's pigtails whipping me again, holding tight to the moment, savoring the simple ability I always took for granted: being able to remember. When the air shifts and coldness rolls over me, I know I'm no longer with Ethan.

4

A TREE-LINED SUBURBAN STREET slowly comes into focus. I would know it anywhere even if it is blanketed in a layer of fresh snow.

How did I magically teleport—ghost-a-port?—to my street?

I chalk it up to my ghostly powers, which I seem to have absolutely no control over. I pass a beige ranch house and turn to face the yellow two-story house across the street.

The mailbox my mom hand-painted with daisies and happy vines looks like it could collapse at any moment with the weight of snow on top of it. My mom is always trying out things like that to warm up our Midwestern existence. Her new sky-blue Beetle is parked crookedly at the end of the driveway with skid marks behind it in the snow. It's the kind of parking job she makes when she's late, which is almost never.

Inside, Joules's figure skating crap is piled on the stairs. I step over it even though I'm pretty sure I wouldn't have any problem passing *through* it. At the end of the upstairs hallway, I stop in front of my bedroom. The door is cracked open just enough that I can get inside.

I lie on my bed and shove my head under my tie-dyed pillow—if that's possible—refusing to believe any of this is real. Now that I'm home in my own room everything can go back to normal. I can wake up from this tripped-out walk-down-memory-lane dream and forget all the morbid parts at the morgue and the river. I stay in bed with my head hidden until I hear frantic voices across the hallway. My parents' bedroom door is closed, which muffles their actual words, but their conversation is quickly replaced by sobs.

My ten-year-old sister pushes open my door and stands with her mouth hung open like she forgot what she was going to tell me. Joules's blue eyes rove my bedroom, pausing on insignificant items like my black wrap sweater hung on the corner of my full-length mirror and my dance bag overflowing with crumpled tights and leotards that I'll never wear again. Before I realize her face is flushed and tear soaked, she's gone.

From the hallway I hear, "Joules, honey, what are you doing awake?" Mom's voice is jerky and full of sniffles.

"I was just waking Cassidy up."

What's left of my heart rips right down the middle: half comfort—Joules has been playing backup alarm for me since she started kindergarten—and half anguish.

Mom replies, "Waking her up? Joules, you can't . . . Oh, honey." The sobs are full volume outside my door. I'm indescribably grateful I can't see through walls the way I can walk through them.

"She's still in there, Mom." Not the thing to say. Mom breaks into hysterics.

Dad's soft voice attempts to comfort her, and they must go downstairs because the scene fades to silence. Deafening silence. The kind of silence you hear at a rock concert between sets. It doesn't fit because it's a rock concert; it's supposed to be loud. Whenever Mom and Dad talked, for the past few months at least, it was like Metric was holding a sold-out show in our living room. It's weird hearing their quiet murmurs to each other now.

Joules is standing in my doorway again.

"Morning, Cassidy-dee." She whispers her standard wake-up call in a voice too low to be my little sister's. "Mom says everyone's staying home tomorrow. No school the entire week."

One time we missed school—for Dad's great-aunt Meryl's funeral—and Joules was so thrilled you'd think we were going to Disney World, not Mueller's Funeral Home. But she doesn't sound happy about the time off now.

She looks right at me. A tiny sprig of hope takes root inside me.

"Jouley . . . can you see me?" I hold my breath—or press my lips together the way I would if I had breath to hold—and wait.

Joules tries to smile a little, then leaves.

I sit up and look around my bedroom. Everything looks exactly as it did when I left for Aimée's yesterday, right down to the pile of rejected outfits next to my closet. Maybe Mom crying in the hallway was part of my dream and I'm finally awake. I flex and point my toes; they feel real enough. I do the same with my fingers, then start to pinch my arm again, but I stop myself and decide to go all out. I punch at my alarm clock. I've always wanted to smash the incessant killjoy anyway. My fist goes straight through the entire nightstand and I almost fall off my bed with the momentum of the empty punch. My shoulders slump as my sprig of hope shrivels.

When I look up, I notice I left the top drawer of my dresser open. I wonder how long it will stay frozen like that, with a polka-dot sock dangling off the corner. I wonder whose responsibility it is to take care of my socks, my furniture, everything in this room that has been mine since the day my parents brought me home from the hospital. Sadness wells in me, thick and agonizing, knowing that it will not—cannot—be me.

I stare at the spot my sister just vacated. Why am I here? I keep repeating that question, but it never gets any easier to answer. This being-a-ghost thing sucks. If I don't figure things out soon I'm converting to poltergeist.

I think back to the countless trite ghost movies I've seen. It takes more effort than it should to recall them. In almost every one there's a reason the ghosts stay on earth, unfinished business of some sort that no one else can accomplish. And it's usually from the day they died.

I focus every ounce of my energy on remembering the birthday party Madison and Aimée threw for me last night; it comes back to me in waves of sounds and smells and sensations.

The bonfire warms my legs, but my feet are cold because I'm standing in two inches of snow. I hear laughter and water rushing, then buzzing silence that vibrates between my ears.

I rake my hands through my hair, shaking my head to clear the piercing sounds.

Ethan's face appears behind my eyes. He looks so mad or sad,

33

maybe confused. I want to race back to his house, but Joules just walked into my bedroom and sat in the center of my sun, moon, and stars rug. I can't leave her. She sets her Hello Kitty backpack down and pulls out her math book. She opens it and unfolds her assignment, staring blankly at the page.

I slide off my bed and sit cross-legged next to her. "Why are you doing homework? You should be honoring my memory by eating an entire carton of Mooney's blue moon ice cream or something." I laugh a little even though what I said isn't funny in about twelve ways.

Joules gets a determined look on her face and starts where she left off on her assignment. Her pencil keeps poking through my knee as she taps it on the corner of her book.

I point to number three and say conversationally, "You forgot to carry the one," forgetting how unseen, unheard I am. Her pencil stops working on number five and she reworks her answer for number three.

"Jouley!" I put my hand on her arm. She doesn't seem to notice as it slides right through her sweatshirt.

An intense tingling sensation numbs my arm—it's the same pain I felt when I walked through my dad at the morgue. The deeper my hand sinks into her arm, the harsher the tingling pricks become. I jerk my hand back, leaving behind a trail of glittery dust in the air between us. I lift my hand to marvel at the dust and realize the dust *is* my hand—or was. I grasp at the tiny particles, desperately trying to retrieve them. They slowly settle into whispers of lines until I can see my fingers again. I gape at my re-formed fingers, turning my hand over to make sure they aren't going anywhere.

Joules moves her hand so it's *in* my lap, and I flinch as it sinks down to the rug. My eyes fix on her fingers underneath my leg as she taps her thumb in the center of one of the yellow stars on the rug. My floaty flesh surrounds her solid limb like water capturing a stone. I ignore the stinging pain for a moment, but it quickly grows too harsh to bear and I have to scoot out of her way.

She starts singing the song we made up on the car ride to Mammoth Caves National Park when I was eleven and she was four. My parents always took us to "educational" vacation spots like that. Mom said she wanted us to visit all fifty states together. "The Haines family takes over the country one vacation at a time." So corny. So Tessa and Rodge. The car rides were always the best part. Joules and I used to share a seat in the back of the minivan and stick Post-its on the forehead of our older brother, Shaw, while he slept. Girls versus the only boy.

I made it through fourteen states. This year was supposed to be Iowa. My chest clenches at the thought of them going without me, and then tightens further when it dawns on me that they'll probably cancel the trip.

I hear crying again, this time from downstairs. Joules resets her determined face, stands, and walks to my closet. She rummages through the pile of clothes I'd decided not to wear to Aimée's and picks up my red cardigan. She holds it to her chest and runs her fingers over the sequined trim. It's way too big for her. She's always been small for her age. We both have willowy frames thanks to Mom's side of the family, but since Joules is so short it doesn't work quite as well for her. She has the same auburn hair I do but hers is curlier.

One side of my mouth inches up as she presses onto her toes and does a small pirouette. She looks like a younger me when I used to try on Mom's cocktail dresses.

Mom. I haven't seen her yet.

I instinctively move for the door, but the memory of my dad crying at the morgue stops me.

The windows do that subtle *whoosh* thing they do when the front door is slammed. "Mom, Dad?" Shaw's deep voice carries up the stairs. He arrived home from college on Thursday just in time for my birthday dinner. He must have slept at one of his friend's houses last night like he usually does when he's visiting for a weekend.

Joules snags a tissue from my dresser and dabs at her glistening eyes, surprisingly grownup-like. She folds my cardigan into a small square, stuffs it into her backpack, and hurries out of my room. I follow too.

At the bottom of the stairs, Shaw wraps Joules up in this full-body hug that lifts her off her feet and makes the whole room seem safer. I rush down the stairs to be near him.

"Where were you?" Joules asks.

"At Jay's," he answers. "Where's Mom?"

A muffled cry-hello sounds from the couch in the living room. Shaw doesn't set Joules down as he walks toward Mom. "My phone was on vibrate, sorry. What's going on? What's the emergency?"

Mom doesn't answer him. She's looking fixedly at the flat screen mounted above the fireplace; it's not even turned on. Shaw looks with her, as if the black rectangle holds some infinite wisdom, until Dad comes in from the kitchen. He spills the tea he's made for Mom all over the coffee table when he sets it down.

Shaw asks again, "What's the emergency? What couldn't you tell me over the phone?"

Dad folds and unfolds his arms, then stuffs his hands into his pockets. He pulls them back out as he clears his throat and says, "Your sister"—his eyes flick to Joules for a second—"our Cassidy, is gone."

"What do you mean 'gone'?"

Dad averts his eyes. "She . . . she's dead, son."

Shaw sets Joules down and looks between her and Mom and Dad. He doesn't start bawling like Mom or get the shakes like Dad. He just stands there. Total disbelief on his face. Then he asks his newly downsized family, "How?"

Silence. Rock-concert silence, again.

I feel like I'm the one who should answer his question, but my voice won't work. My mind isn't circulating information on that topic at this time. All systems failure.

"She fell," Joules says. Shaw doesn't ask any questions about where I fell from or how high it was. He's perfectly silent. Everyone is.

5

I'M AT THE RIVER AGAIN. It's frozen over solid now. I could easily walk across it to Aimée's backyard without it splintering, but I don't. Instead I take the bridge, pausing at the entrance where the split-poplar planks meet snow-sprinkled yellow grass.

Hazy rays of late-afternoon sunlight blanch the tawny surface of the boards as they creak in the wind. As I cross the bridge, I'm assaulted by a fractured montage of memories: Ethan turning to walk away from me, me staggering on the heels of my Mary Janes in the dark, a bottle pressed to my lips, lips pressed to my lips . . .

I gasp and throw my hand over my mouth. I don't remember why or when any of those moments happened. Suddenly, I'm halfway across the Coutiers' acreage, the bridge quiet behind me, and I see Aimée in one of the third-floor windows, staring out past the river to Dover Park. I haven't seen her in that window seat since she found out she didn't get into the high school summer program at Brown University last year. It's her life-has-ended-I'll-never-get-over-this spot.

My pace quickens as I go inside through the garage and up the back staircase to the bonus room that we call the playroom. I pass through the door and rush to the window seat at the far end.

Aimée's eyes flick toward me, giving me the smallest glimmer of hope that she can see me, but then they lower to the Berber carpet that's littered with wads of tissue. She's shaking her head and wiping mascara streaks off her cheeks. It's so her that she's wearing fresh makeup the day after her best friend died. Her long brown hair is tied up in an intricate bun too. She looks absolutely flawless except for the black tears.

"Meems." I say my nickname for her.

She shakes her head harder and chokes on a sob.

"Oh, Meemer." She cowers against the wall when I sit next to her, and for a second, I wonder if she can at least hear me. "Please stop crying. It's not what you think. I'm here." My hand hovers slightly above her shoulder. I'll shatter into a million irreparable pieces if I have to watch my hand pass through her, and then there's the debilitating pain.

A strangled cry bursts out of her chapped lips. "I shouldn't have let you leave," she murmurs. "I knew things were messed up. I knew . . ." The words are muffled by tears.

"Knew what?" I ask, leaning forward.

She doesn't say anything else for a long time, simply cries more. I look around the room filled with board games and stuffed animals from our younger years and see a box of tissues next to the king-size air mattress we used for sleepovers. I consider bringing her the tissues, but I'm not sure I can pick up things and figure now's not the time to test my tactile limits.

She mumbles something unintelligible, and I ask, "What?"

"I think I need therapy," she says, as if answering me. Her go-to response for explaining what's bothering her lifts my mouth into a wistful smile. "Talking to myself is clearly not helping me deal." She makes a dramatic gesture toward the heavens. "It's Sunday. Maybe I should go to confession."

"You're Jewish, Meems."

There's a knock on the door. "Aimée?" Her sister, Bridgette, peeks her head into the room. She's only two years younger than Aimée, but right now she seems unusually small. "Mom says it's time to come down for dinner."

"It's only four o'clock," Aimée replies.

Bridgette changes the topic. "Do you want to come down and watch a movie with me? It's that old one with that actor you like. John Krasinski or whoever."

"His last name is *Cusack*. John Krasinski is from *The Office*. Besides, I'm not the one who likes old movies, Cassidy is." Aimée's voice trails off.

"That's right," Bridgette says quietly. "So do you want to come to my room and watch it?"

Tears flood Aimée's green eyes. "I don't want to watch a movie right now, Bridge." Her voice shakes with the effort to sound like she's not falling apart.

"Come on, it could help—"

"Not now," Aimée says firmly, cutting Bridgette off. Bridgette leaves.

I ask, "What happened at the party, Meems?"

There's another knock on the door. "Tell Mom I'm not hungry, Bridgette," Aimée shouts.

The door opens a crack. "Aims? It's—"

"Mads." Aimée exhales a relieved breath and gives Madison a long hug, then holds her at arm's length.

Madison keeps her eyes on her shoes. "I wanted to come over sooner, but my dad said I needed time to grieve alone or some psychobabble BS."

"How are you?"

When Madison finally looks up, tears spill over her stormy blue eyes. "This is totally my fault," she confesses.

Aimée lets go of Madison's arms and waits.

Madison's layered hair swooshes across her shoulders as she shakes her head. It's dyed the same auburn color as mine, but her strawberry-blond roots are starting to show. "The party was my idea. If I hadn't made such a big deal and—"

"No, Mads, I planned the party with you. I hosted it." Aimée sinks back down onto the window seat. "It's my fault too. I knew something was off with her, and I thought a party would cheer her up, but I had this feeling . . . I knew."

"Knew what?" I ask again, starting to get frustrated with being ignored.

Madison presses her lips into a tight line. She turns to look out the window. "There's no way we could've known she'd jump into the river."

"Jump?" I snap my head to look at Madison. "I didn't jump."

Aimée's thin eyebrows scrunch up. "You think she jumped?"

"I didn't!" I insist.

"She was alone and the police said they found a bottle of

booze floating next to her. I mean, what else could've happened?"

Aimée looks sideways at Madison with a crazy-intense expression. "An accidental fall is more logical in that scenario than suicide, and the fact that the police are even considering that her death was intentional makes me seriously question their ability to solve any case. Besides, how do we know for sure she was alone?"

"They found a note. I guess it was pretty obvious she meant to—" Madison stops. "You look pale, Aims. How much sleep did you get last night?"

Aimée continues as if she didn't hear Madison's question. "Is that what everyone thinks?"

"I didn't write any note!" I yell, but then I remember seeing the piece of paper crumpled in my body's lifeless hand when I came to on the riverbank. Could that have been my suicide note?

"It's what my dad heard from his buddy who does psych analysis or something for the police department."

"Well, it's not true," Aimée replies, staring hard at Madison.

"We weren't there, Aims. There's no way of knowing."

"*I* know," Aimée says brusquely.

I give her a grateful look for sticking up for me.

"Sorry. I didn't mean to . . ." Madison drops her head. "You're probably right. Everything was a huge accident."

I'M STANDING ON THE ROCKS where I found Other Me. The frustration of not being able to remember what happened Saturday night is even stronger now that I know the accepted cause of my death. I couldn't have jumped. No way would I give up on all my hard work at school and ballet and on everyone I love—on myself—like that. But if everyone starts to think I did, they're going to make up reasons for why, stories that could damage more than the integrity of my memory. Someone has to know the truth. Someone alive must know what happened to me.

I stare at the spot between the trees in Dover Park where the silhouette stood. I can hear the muffled voice and see the tall shadow looming over the rocky bank of the river, but I still can't make out a face.

I rub my temples, watching the sun set on this bizarre day, trying to remember. I was supposed to be celebrating my seventeenth birthday yesterday, not dying. How did my night take such a horrible turn?

A lone leaf drifts down from a skeletal tree, landing on top of my shoe. Suddenly the weight of snow presses on my arms and legs as if I'm sinking in quick-snow even though there isn't a single flake floating in the sky. This cold burden is for me alone.

I stare at my leggings. My eyes widen as the gray turns a mottled black, spreading like spilled ink from my ankles up to my knees.

Not again! I fight against the pull, terrified that if I fall into the past again I'll never make it back. The puddle I'm standing in rises until my entire body is icy and my eyes can't focus through the wavy film covering them. Trying to clear the film, I blink and then I'm gone.

TEMPTATION

MRS. WIRLKEE WAS DRAWING a diagram of Maslow's Hierarchy of Needs on the whiteboard as part of her explanation for our semester project. She told us it would be worth a quarter of our grade, but I was only half paying attention. After the fight I had had with my mom that morning, I couldn't concentrate on anything. I needed to think about happy things, things that would distract me, like the biggest party of the year being thrown in my honor, courtesy of my two best friends.

Aimée's parents would be out of town during my birthday weekend, so Madison convinced Aimée to host one of her bonfires to celebrate even though we lived in Michigan and spring hadn't exactly sprung yet. Madison was busy inviting everyone we knew and everyone we wanted to know. It was still three weeks away, but I was already picking out outfits. I wouldn't have to avoid my favorite corduroy mini, seeing as Mom wasn't home to tell me it was too short to wear out. Guess there's a silver lining to my family's dysfunction after all.

A paper airplane landed on top of my purple-and-brown Pumas as I rubbed my neck to loosen the lump forming in my throat. I bent down to pick up the expertly folded note. The double folds of the wings looked impossibly straight. Inside it said: *Wirlkee looks smokin' today.*

I looked up at Mrs. Wirlkee's size-eighteen hips enclosed in a pair of too-tight Wrangler Mom jeans and peeked over my shoulder to find the sender.

It was Caleb Turner. I'd known him practically my whole life. We had playdates together in kindergarten, and he was the only boy who came to my first boy-girl swim party back in seventh grade. I had the biggest crush on him after that, but he started hanging with his older brother's stoner crew that summer. We hadn't talked since.

He was grinning at me and nodding his head suggestively. I shook my head and mouthed, "No way!" like the three years of silence between us had never happened.

He wrote something quick on another prepared airplane and shot it my way. I reached under Alicia Westing's desk to retrieve it. It said: *Jealous?*

I snorted, and Mrs. Wirlkee cleared her throat followed by a stern "Miss Haines." I shoved the notes inside my binder and pressed my lips together, stifling a laugh.

After class, Caleb met me at the door. "We should be partners for this psychological-studies thing."

"You mean psychological strategies?"

"Yeah, that. What do you say?"

I clutched my books to my chest. I didn't want to hurt his feelings, but I couldn't be Caleb's partner for several reasons.

Although I was a little curious about why he'd decided to join the land of the sober and talk to me again. "I don't want to get stuck doing all the work. Sorry," I added quickly, realizing how snobby that had come out. He didn't seem to notice.

"Guess you forgot how I got us an A on our simple-machine project."

"That was fourth grade, Caleb, and your mom built most of it. She probably won't be available to help out on this one."

He pushed a lock of floppy blond hair out of his eyes and turned down one side of his mouth. "Doubt any tools will be required for a Psych project, so living with my dad shouldn't affect our grade."

The lump re-formed in my throat. I opened my mouth to ask him what it was like splitting his time between two houses since I'd probably be finding out soon, but I waved a hand at him instead. "I didn't mean—it's just, you hardly come to class."

His frown turned into the easy smile that I remembered from elementary school. "Well, I'll have to start attending regularly so I don't let down my partner." The way his voice shook when he said "partner" stirred this urge inside me to hug him. "Sorry I got you scolded by Wirlkee, but you looked like you could use some comic relief. Something up?"

Yes, I answered in my head, *an Everest-sized something that you're probably the only person I know who would understand.* Out loud I said, "Okay. I'll be your partner for the project."

He nodded at me like he knew I would say yes all along; I kind of did too. "We should get together this weekend to work on our project," he suggested.

I started to tell him we should stick to in-school partnering, but he interrupted me. "Wanna ditch second and go sledding?"

A laugh burst out of me. "No." It felt so good to laugh after the world-shattering morning I'd had with Mom that I laughed again. Caleb was right. I'd needed some comic relief. "Who goes sledding in March anyway?"

"Oh." He held his hands out and lowered his voice. "Let me clarify that 'sledding' means smoke a jay."

I elbowed him in the ribs and teased, "I'm not that kind of girl."

"You could be." He winked at me.

I turned my head away and pulled on my bottom lip to hide my smile. "No, I couldn't."

"You sure?"

"Cassi." My head snapped up when I heard my name. Ethan jogged down the hall with his backpack slung over one shoulder. "Ready for Español?"

I flicked my eyes at the guy to my left as I hugged the one on my right.

"Hey, man." Ethan gave Caleb a guy nod.

Caleb nodded back, uncharacteristically quiet. My heart was going an inexplicable fifty thousand beats a minute. I couldn't decide why I was suddenly so anxious. Or maybe I just didn't want to admit why.

"I'm gonna split, Cassidy," Caleb said casually, like there'd been no notes and no invitation to share illegal substances. "Go do some sledding." He held two fingers to his mouth, waggled his eyebrows, and spun on his heels to leave.

"What was that about?" Ethan asked, escorting me down the

47

hall with an arm around my shoulders. It felt like a bag of bricks. "There's hardly any snow left on the ground."

"I hear there's a storm coming," I said quietly.

"What?"

"He's in my Psych class." I tried to imitate Caleb's casual tone.

"I'm surprised he even knows his schedule." Ethan chuckled.

I stopped and crossed my arms. "What's that supposed to mean?"

Ethan turned to face me. "He's a total pothead, Cassi. Everyone knows that."

"He's not that bad. I wouldn't call him a 'pothead.'"

"Didn't you see that little smoky gesture he made back there?" He pointed with his thumb. "He's probably tokin' up right now."

"Maybe it's his way of dealing with stuff."

"What kind of stuff?"

Family stuff. Stuff you would never understand. I shook my head. "Nothing. Never mind."

"Plus, I heard he's on probation for breaking and entering."

"That's a dumb rumor. You don't even know him." It came out shaky and defensive. I never spoke to Ethan like that.

His eyes widened at my unexpected response. "Well, I know his type."

"His type?" A knot twisted my stomach. What would Ethan think of me if he knew my family had become as broken as Caleb's?

"He's bad news," Ethan added.

"Who's bad news?" Madison bumped my hip with hers as she joined us.

I avoided Ethan's confused expression as I changed the subject, asking Madison, "Did you finish the guest list yet?"

"I still have a few strategic additions to make, but it'll be ready in time. The only snag will be if it snows, but don't you worry, Dees, your party will go on, snow or shine."

"Sounds like it'll be a celebration worthy of its guest of honor." Ethan kissed the top of my head.

Without warning, Madison held her hands up and started talking animatedly about her plan to score drinks for my birthday party. It involved her ample cleavage, Harlot Red lipstick, and her cousin's expired driver's license.

Ethan told her, "If anyone can convince a third-shift party-store employee to sell to a minor with a questionable fake, it's you."

Madison smiled at him, blushing slightly at the compliment. They went back and forth on strategies to make her look older. I was thankful for the interruption. The conversation Ethan and I had been having was going nowhere good fast.

"So will you?" Madison asked me.

"Huh?" I shook myself out of my thoughts and looked questioningly at her.

"Will you walk me to class?"

"Um." I glanced at Ethan. "We have Spanish on the other side of the building. Why do you need me to walk you?"

"Because Drew can't keep his hands off me today."

"Guess you guys are on again?" Ethan said.

Madison nodded and rolled her eyes. "Must be Tuesday."

"You know, if Drew wasn't my friend," Ethan replied, "I'd be obligated to tell you that you deserve better."

She brushed her bangs down over her eyes. "He means well. I'm just not feelin' it today. So what do you say, Dees? Pretty please walk me. Ethan can cover for you with Señorita Cope, right?" She peeked up at Ethan through her bangs.

I could feel him watching for my reaction, but my eyes were glued to the floor.

"Of course. I'll tell Cope that Wirlkee kept you late," Ethan said.

"See?" Madison tugged on my elbow, coercing me in the direction opposite to where I needed to be headed. "He does everything for you. You're *so lucky.*"

"He does not," I protested.

"But I would if you asked." Ethan pulled me back to him and kissed the back of my hand, then lifted my arm above my head and spun me out toward Madison. "I love watching you twirl." The uncomfortable tightness in my stomach loosened some.

After we turned the corner, Madison asked, "You okay?" I nodded, purposely avoiding her concerned eyes. She adopted a lighter tone. "So, are you budding up with the little-stoner-that-could again?"

"No," I said too loudly.

"Oh. I saw you guys walk out of class together, thought maybe it was middle school all over again." She paused. "I heard he's still into you."

"That's ridiculous," I replied automatically.

She leaned away from me so she could study my face. I bit down on my twitching bottom lip. "Are you sure you're feeling okay? You missed ballet yesterday. Is it—?"

"It's nothing," I interrupted her. There was no use trying to explain about my parents to her, or to Ethan and Aimée for that matter. *Their* families were perfect. "I guess I've been tired or something."

"Well, studio was torture without you there. We learned a new eight count that is going to be the end of me. I swear Madame Tourand's sole choreographical goal is to break one of my hips so I won't be able to perform in the recital."

"She's only trying to motivate you. She can tell when someone's heart isn't in it." I gave her the same questioning eyebrow raise I always gave her when the topic of ballet came up, silently asking why she continued dancing when she clearly hated it.

She ignored the gesture as usual. "Want to come over tonight so I can teach you? It's an excuse to get out of your house," she offered.

The idea of my house being a place to avoid struck a pang of sadness in my heart. "That's okay. I'm sure I'll catch up pretty quick tomorrow."

"I know you will, but I'm worried about you, Dees."

"That's because you're a good friend."

"Takes one to know one." She shook her hair away from her face, stopped in front of her classroom, and drawled in her most baby-sweet voice, "Thanks for being my escort."

As she air-kissed me on both cheeks, I couldn't get Caleb's easy smile out of my head. When I opened my eyes, Madison was staring at me. I hadn't realized I'd closed them.

"You better rest up before your birthday party," she said. "It's going to be unforgettable."

6

I BEND AND FLEX MY LEGS to make sure they're not still melting or whatever it is they did right before I was pulled into that memory. A sharp sting punctuates each movement, so I stop even though the numb tingling sensation spreading through my limbs doesn't seem to be going anywhere anytime soon. After a few labored blinks, my eyes slowly focus on the jagged line of the snow-covered riverbank below me. My feet are angled in first position—heels together, toes pointed out—making the tips of my Mary Janes hang over a broken, unguarded portion of the covered bridge.

How did I get up here?

That self-preserving instinct that should tell me to jump back to safety doesn't kick in. Guess a ghost doesn't need that instinct.

I run my hand over the cracked edges of the broken wood on either side of me, sliding through where splinters jut out. This must be where I fell. My eyes move to the river and the spot on the rocks where my body landed, then back to my feet. My shoes are scuffed and there's a tear on one of the heels. I poke at the broken strap on my right shoe with my left toe. I'm surprised by how torn-up they look; they seemed in good enough condition when I put them on yesterday. The shadows shifting in gnarled patterns against the frozen water below impel my feet to scuffle farther over the edge.

For a moment, I try to remember what it felt like to plummet from this height. Am I capable of such a drastic leap? A gust of wind jerks the yellow caution tape stretched across the broken rail back and forth with a clipped, harsh *clap* that snaps me out of my river-induced trance.

In a blink the damage to my shoes is gone, along with any insight about that night. Confusion and guilt from that last memory consume me. Why was I defending Caleb Turner? Bigger question: Why was I flirting with Caleb Turner? I have to be remembering wrong.

I want to believe that, but the subconscious doesn't lie.

I force the Caleb-flirting memory away by swapping in memories of flirting with Ethan: mussing his hair so the spikes stuck out in a silly way, stealing his Doritos at lunch, nudging his shoulder as I passed his desk in Spanish.

Suddenly, I'm in his bedroom. I don't know if it's that ghost-a-porting thing I did earlier or if I merely ran so fast, so distractedly, that I arrived before I knew I'd left. Right now, I don't care.

I spin around, scanning the room. His bed is empty, covers pulled to one side. His laptop sits unplugged on his desk. I can't remember the last time I saw that thing powered down. The shirt he was wearing this morning is balled up on the floor next to his hamper. He's not here.

I blow through the door, ignoring the weirdness of literally going *through* it, and go up the basement steps. The whole house is still. His parents must be asleep. I check the kitchen, then walk into the living room where his golden retriever is curled up on the floor next to the glass-topped coffee table.

"Where's Ethan, Wendell?" I ask.

A faint rustling sound disturbs the quiet. Wendell tilts his head toward the hallway and whimpers. I rush to the noise— my feet moving impossibly fast—and halt in front of the den. The burgundy leather couch is covered with wrinkled flannel sheets. There are two empty glasses on the end table and a half-eaten plate of toast on the floor.

I pull my eyes away from the makeshift bed and see Ethan standing at the wall of built-in shelves. He's holding a vinyl copy of *In Rainbows* in one hand; the other hand is hovering over the needle of his dad's old record player. There's a second of muffled scratches before the thrumming piano chords start.

The pulsing in my chest that's stronger now that I'm near Ethan morphs into a pinching pain that causes tears to spring to my eyes. He's staring at the album cover, tracing the lines of text like they're the lyrics to the song. Our song. The slow, soothing rhythm fills the room and awakens months, years of kisses and touches and I love yous. They swirl around me, transporting me to the past, to my life.

Before I can think to fear the possibility of dissolving through him, I reach for his arm and sigh when the expected pain doesn't come. Instead I feel revived and buzzing with warmth. My iridescent hand looks so unreal resting on his bicep. His shoulders tense and he reaches to lift the needle on the player, but something stops him.

"Cassidy." His voice is so quiet I'm not sure I heard right. "Cassidy," he says again.

I squeak out, "I'm here." His face is turned away from me, jaw clenched like he's holding back tears. There are so many things I want to say to him, to ask him, but I stay quiet because saying them to deaf ears seems like the saddest thing in the world—sadder than his breaking our promise and listening to our song without me.

He turns with a raised hand that knocks mine off his arm. I gasp, savoring the heated rush his touch ignites. He props his elbow on one of the shelves and lets his head crash into his palm. His face tilts toward mine, and I wish more than anything— even more than to be alive for real again—that he would kiss me. That I could feel his soft lips and taste the spearmint flavor of his breath. That this whole messed-up day has been a dream and I will be awakened by his kiss. I close my eyes, hoping, waiting . . .

"You're dead."

I open my eyes and the heat drains from me. Ethan's backed into the corner with his fists pressed to his forehead.

Did I imagine touching him again?

"You're not here. You're dead." He repeats it like a mantra.

"I am here, Ethan." My voice catches.

He shakes his head and digs his fists in deeper. "Stop!" he yells. "I can't—you can't be here. It makes me . . . it means I'm . . . I'm hallucinating."

I look over my shoulder to see who he's talking to, but no

one's there. I stare at him until he looks up. "Ethan? Can you . . . can you see me?"

He slams the heel of his hand into the wall. "Stop that!"

I look around the rustic den to see if maybe Wendell has wandered in. He hasn't. I walk toward Ethan with slow, measured steps. "Who are you talking to?"

His umber eyes lock steady on mine even though the rest of his body is trembling. He answers firmly, "You."

My mouth drops open and I freeze midstep. He's not supposed to answer me. I'm supposed to be invisible. I stare unblinking for what feels like an eternity.

He coughs a humorless laugh, shaking his head. "I'm crazy, straight-up certifiable."

"No." My arms ache to reach out to him, but I don't dare. "I—I'm real . . . ish."

He narrows his eyes at me. His trembling lessens. "I don't believe you. My mind created you because I miss you too much."

"No, Ethan, I'm here." His thick eyebrows scrunch into a tense line. "Okay," I continue, "tell me to do something."

"What?"

"If I'm a figment of your imagination"—I stumble over the words—"you'd be able to control me, right? So tell me to do something."

He thinks a minute. "Levitate."

"Something I can do," I harrumph.

He takes another minute. "Sing the school fight song."

A sob-laugh bursts from my mouth. I shake my head. "Uh-uh. You know I despise all fight songs on principle."

"Holy crap." He backs away from me with one shoulder

anchored to the wall and stumbles onto the couch. "How . . . is this possible? You . . . I *touched* you—you touched me!"

I reach for him but his stunned expression stops me.

His eyes roll up and down my form, deciding whether he believes what he sees. He leans forward, rubbing the sides of his face. "How?"

"You're the only person who can see me. I've been home and to the morgue. I saw Aimée and Madison. No one noticed me. Only you."

"You were at the morgue?" There is so much pain in his voice—pain that I caused.

"I didn't mean to . . ."

He looks at me with an unreadable expression. "Mean to what? A lot went down last night. Might want to be more specific." I cringe at his gruff tone.

"You're mad at me." He was. I remember that. At the party, we fought. But what about?

"Does that matter anymore?" Neither of us says anything for a long time, and the melody of our song fills the space between us. "Why didn't you stay with your body?" he finally asks.

I meet his eyes and the only thing I want to say is *I came back to be with you, I stayed for you.* But I have no friggin' clue why I stepped out of my body, and lying to him seems impossible.

I drop my head and see his toes curled into the plush taupe carpet. His feet are bare. I wonder if he's cold. For once, I don't feel cold, not around him.

I take a tentative step closer as he opens his mouth to say something.

"Ethan, sweetie, are you still awake?" Ethan's mouth snaps

shut at the sound of his mom's voice. He throws me a frantic look, then rushes out of the den.

I hear his mom tell him he looks tired and that he should try to sleep in his own bed. Mrs. Keys is one of those concerned moms who are always worried her kid isn't getting enough of some random vitamin she read about. My mom used to be like that. Lately she hasn't been home enough to notice my vitamin consumption or much of anything else.

I wait a few minutes after the door to his parents' bedroom clicks shut, then slowly step into the hall. Ethan's leaning against the wall at the far end near the kitchen with his arms and legs crossed.

"So . . . you're a . . . ghost?" He tests out the word.

I don't answer. What do you say to that?

He squints at me like I'm a really faraway billboard he's trying to read. "If you don't say something I'm going to assume you're not real."

"I am real, Ethan." My voice comes out a whisper.

"I was afraid you'd say that," he mutters. "You were in my bedroom this morning, right?" I nod. "I thought I was—"

"Hallucinating," I finish.

"Yeah. Still kinda do." His expression turns curious, and he slowly strides toward me. He reaches out a cautious hand and gently grazes my cheekbone with his fingertips. A warm sensation spreads through me and over to him. I can see it in the way his muscles respond. He feels it too.

He exhales a long breath. "You *are* real."

I lift my head to meet his eyes because I'm not sure if the my-girlfriend-is-a-ghost realization has freaked him out more or calmed him down. We gaze silently at each other for an immeasurable amount of time. I'm afraid to speak, worried I'll break the spell. His warm fingers explore my collarbone and neck as he leans closer.

I want to close my eyes, lean in to him, and kiss him like it's the first time, but my eyes won't obey. They drink him in: the slight peach coloring under his sun-kissed complexion, the square line of his chin, the deep tawny color of his eyes that picks up the golden highlights in his brown hair. There's a subtle change in the set of his jaw and he blinks, dissolving the moment.

"This is incredible. I thought I was never going to see you again and now after everything . . ." He backs away. "I must be going crazy."

"You're not crazy. I mean this"—I gesture to my iridescent body—"being a ghost is crazy, but it's not in your head."

"Says the apparition that only I can see."

I start to laugh. There is absolutely nothing funny about this, but I can't hold it in. I'm too relieved that he can see me to worry about whether my reaction is appropriate. I place my hand over my mouth. When I look at Ethan again, he starts laughing too. We yuk it up for a few seconds, but the silence hangs heavy once we stop. The pulsing in my chest picks up pace. I press my hand over the spot that echoes the beat of my long-gone heart.

"Why are you here?" he whispers.

"I don't know." I look away from him because he deserves a better answer than that, but I don't have it. "Do you know"—my voice wavers—"what happened to me?"

"I wasn't on the bridge when you fell, Cassi."

"Who was?" I ask eagerly.

His voice hardens. "You tell me."

"I . . . I can't . . . I don't . . ."

"You don't remember?"

I shake my head. Ethan peers skeptically at me. He used to believe everything I told him, no question. What changed?

"Why—" I start to ask about the argument I vaguely remember having with him less than twenty-four hours ago, but I chicken out. No matter how much I want to know, the prospect of the answer terrifies me. "Why are you sleeping in the den?"

"You." His expression shifts and his mouth inches up into a rueful smile. "I kind of thought you were haunting my bedroom."

I open my mouth to tell him I'd thought the same thing, but another thought strikes me. "Do I have a reason to haunt you?"

The look in his eyes makes me instantly regret asking. "You think I . . . ?"

I slump to the floor a few feet away from him with a sigh. "I have no idea what to think, Ethan. I don't even know how I died, and now I'm back and no one can see me but you. There has to be a reason I'm here, otherwise it's a massive waste of cosmic energy." I push my hands through my hair, gripping at the roots. "I wish I could remember."

"Why'd you do it?" he asks.

"Do what?" I meet his eyes. Does he think I jumped on purpose too?

He opens and shuts his mouth like he's not sure what to say. "Why'd you go to the bridge?"

I want so badly to answer his question, do whatever I can to make this easier for him, but I don't have any answers. I'm so overwhelmed by his question and by the lingering heat of his touch that tears fill my eyes.

His face gets steely for a moment, but it doesn't last. "Don't cry."

It's an impossible request. My emotions are in overdrive. Fear and sadness and relief and confusion and guilt clash in a post-mortem mess.

"Cassi, please."

A new round of tears falls. He's the only person who calls me Cassi.

"Please don't. It makes this so much harder. Don't . . ." He kneels in front of me and captures my face in his hands. I'm not sure, but I think I hear him murmur, "Go."

Don't go.

He inches closer—impossibly closer. His breath, warm on my lips, stirs up whispers of kisses that will live forever in my memory. As his hands slip from my skin, the warmth ebbs and murky river water drips down my sides, pooling in my shoes.

No, no, no! Not now.

I get to my feet and step away from Ethan before the water can overflow onto him. I'm scooping up handfuls and tossing them away, but the flow gains and gains until I'm so drenched I can't feel the cold anymore.

Stay, I tell myself. *Stay with Ethan.*

I strain to see him through the deluge, but it's too late. I'm already gone.

SCHNAPPS

WE HAD SCARSOONIE'S CLASS together in seventh grade, remember?" He smiled at me with dizzy eyes.

My eyes were dizzy too and it was dark on the bridge, so I couldn't quite make out the rest of his features, but his brown eyes stood out. He took a long drink of peach schnapps and handed me the bottle. I hesitated for a second, but I was so cold and nervous I'd do just about anything to calm my shivers.

I shouldn't have worn these stupid thin leggings, I thought, and took a small sip. Of course, they wouldn't be a problem if I was inside with Ethan. I took another, longer sip.

"I sat one row over behind you," he continued. "I loaned you about twenty pencils that semester."

I laughed. "That's because Mr. Scarsoonie refused to grade anything but graphite." I made quotes with my fingers and almost dropped the bottle. He took it from me, looking concerned that it would spill. "It's sorta a rule of mine to only use pen."

"Green pen." He pointed at me with the bottle.

My eyes widened in surprise that he knew such an obscure detail about me. "It's a preference."

"Teachers hate that crap—green pen. It's like their old eyes can't handle the contrast ratio."

I almost spit I laughed so hard. "Contrast ratio" seemed to be the funniest phrase in the English language and laughing released the anxiety wringing my stomach.

He offered me the bottle again, but I shook my head. "I'm good . . ."

Moonlight reflected off sparse patches of ice floating on the river below, but the bridge was black. He nudged my arm with the bottle and smiled encouragingly. His teeth looked glaringly white in the shade of the covered bridge.

"Seriously"—I waved my hands at him—"no more."

He guzzled the rest of the bottle and chucked it off the bridge. It made a hollow *ding* when it hit the snowy riverbank.

I looked over the railing to see where it had landed; it was floating in a thawed puddle. "You're gonna have to go pick that up. Aimée's parents will erupt if they see a bottle of booze on their property."

"She has parties all the time," he said dismissively.

"They don't know that." I squinted at him. "What did you say you wanted to talk about?"

"I didn't."

When I turned around, he was practically on top of me. My smile dropped. "Hey, bubble space much?" I forced out a short laugh, trying to downplay my nervousness. I shoved him away and crossed my arms tight over my chest.

"Are you cold?" he asked.

"I'm fine." I tucked my hands deeper into the fluff of my lavender down coat, taking a step away. He mirrored my step.

His lazy smile warped into a crooked grin. "Sure you're ready to rejoin the party? You seem a little on edge. Anything you need to get off your chest before you run back to E?"

"What do you want?" I asked flatly.

His eyes narrowed at that. "What's the matter, Cassidy?"

I took another step away, glaring at him, as he slurred something else. The heels of my Mary Janes hit the railing when he placed his hands on my shoulders.

"I don't—you know I—I," I stammered. "We should go back."

He nodded, leaning closer. "Right, we should go . . . or . . ."

"Yes," I whispered hoarsely. The adrenaline running through me made my throat dry.

"Yes?" He arched his eyebrows.

I opened my mouth to tell him to stop, but nothing came out.

7

SHADOWS LOOM SO THICK in front of my eyes that the numbing sting in my arms and legs that always seems to follow a memory is the only thing that lets me know I'm back in the present. But the pain is nominal compared to the residual anxiety I feel. Aimée's suspicions were right; I wasn't alone on the bridge, but what I saw wasn't the whole story. Pieces were missing, buried deep in my subconscious. I struggle to regain the use of my hands to rub my eyes clear.

As I wade in the haze, I try to recall the tenor of his voice or some small gesture that will let me know who I was with, but the harder I try to remember, the faster the light creeps in, bleaching out the murky bits I have to work with.

Once my eyes refocus, the first thought I have is of Ethan. He saw me! But he isn't here.

My house is as silent as the night outside its darkened windows even though everyone is sitting together on the sectional in the living room. Dad's clicking through the three hundred channels we get, but the TV is on mute because Mom is curled up next to him with her eyes closed. He's rubbing slow circles on her back and glancing down at her lovingly. I gawk at my parents cuddling. I can't remember the last time I saw them hug or kiss, much less touch, besides bumping into each other between the toaster and the kitchen table.

When I first introduced Ethan to my parents almost three years ago, my dad teased that he and Mom had met in their freshman year in high school, too, which made me feel like I was on track with some predestined plan. However, in the past few months, I'd heard my parents argue over everything from who forgot to pay the water bill to which brand of paper towels was more environmentally friendly. The more they argued, the less I believed I was on track with any sort of plan.

Joules is sitting with her legs spread in a V, stretching while she does more homework: Social Studies this time. Shaw is slumped next to her, aimlessly thumbing the dial on his iPod. The whole family's together now that I'm here.

I walk past Joules's side of the couch and make a motion with my hand like I'm flicking her ponytail. With my eyes closed I imagine the smooth, slightly crunchy texture of her moussed curls. The gesture feels so automatic, so normal. I hesitate at the ottoman where Mom's feet are daintily crossed at the ankle. Her breath is shallow and steady as she sleeps. I could reach out and . . . I keep my distance. After the dust-pain thing that happened with Joules and Dad, I won't be attempting to touch anyone who can't see me anytime soon.

Mom sniffles and shifts so her head rests in Dad's lap. He switches the remote to his other hand and combs his fingers through her long curls. His eyes have purple shadows under them; so do Mom's and Shaw's. Joules is the only one in the family who doesn't look like the living dead.

Ha! So funny, Cassidy. Undead humor. Lame.

The phone rings, and Mom jolts awake. Joules picks it up from the coffee table.

"Hello? . . . No, this is Joules Haines. May I take a message?"

After she hangs up, Dad asks, "Who was it?" His voice is a gravelly whisper.

"Someone named Mr. Mueller. He said for you to call him. I wrote down his number." She tears off a corner of her homework and hands it to Dad.

He rubs his stubbled face. "Joules, I needed to speak with him. He's the funeral home director."

"Oh." Her entire face frowns, even her button nose looks sad. "Mom told me to take messages unless it was Grandma calling to tell us when her flight arrives."

Mom sits up. "I only meant to screen calls from the reporters."

Dad turns so Mom can see his disapproving expression. "We can't avoid them forever, Tessa."

"There's no reason we should feed into the media's exploitation of our daughter's drunken suicide."

Joules breaks in. "Cassidy didn't do that to herself."

I give her an appreciative look. "Thanks, Jouley-bee."

"That's kind of you to think of your sister, Joules, but we can't be sure of that."

"Then how can you be sure I'm wrong?"

"She can't," Dad answers flatly.

Mom purses her lips and leans back so she's crammed into

the armrest, not touching Dad. This is the parental duo I know. I kind of wish it didn't, but their arguing comforts me somehow. "I'm only saying this is difficult enough to deal with in private without involving the media."

Shaw exhales a loud breath, pulls out his earbuds, and stares up at the ceiling. "It was just a phone call. If you two are going to go through this every time the thing rings, we should unplug it."

"And what about the school?" Dad says to Mom as if he didn't hear Shaw. "The sooner we pick up her things, the better."

Mom gasps like he has personally insulted her. "Why don't we all go over there first thing tomorrow morning, Rodger? We could contribute to the assembly on teen suicide."

"Jesus." Shaw stands and paces the room with disgust visible on his face.

Dad turns his head away and grinds his teeth.

"I'll clean out Cassidy's locker," Joules offers in a tiny voice that still manages to sound stronger than our parents' yelling. "Shaw can drive me. Right?"

Shaw gives Joules a weary head shake, then slips out the back door. Mom reaches for him weakly, silently calling him back. He shuts the door behind him.

Dad sighs. "No, Jouley, you don't need to do that."

"But I know the combination. Cassidy told me once and I never forgot."

Mom and Dad exchange strained looks, and Mom moves to sit beside Joules. "Aimée already offered to do it. You stay here with us, okay, honey? Your dad can call Mr. Mueller back tomorrow and the school can wait."

"Tessa—" Dad starts back in, but Mom cuts him off.

"They can wait. Everyone can goddamn wait." The words get caught in her throat. Her head falls into her hands and she starts to sob.

I know I should feel bad for her, but I'm too disappointed in her for falling apart in front of Joules and accepting that I'm capable of taking my own life. She should know me better than that. She's my mother.

Something visceral tugs me away from her, away from my house. It pulls me through the back door the way my brother left. I follow Shaw's footprints in the snow across the backyard and through the thicket of trees separating my house from the next subdivision. I'm sort of glad it's pulling me to him, like he needs me to comfort him instead of the other way around like it used to be.

I stop where Shaw's tracks end and follow the faint buzz of music echoing among the spindly, leafless trees beyond the trail. I tiptoe toward the sound even though I could stomp and scream and Shaw wouldn't even blink.

He's sitting cross-legged on a small hill that's somehow managed to stay clear of snow, shivering because he didn't bother to grab a coat when he stormed out of the house. His dusty brown hair is longer than I remember, but then again, he hasn't been home in over a month—busy at college, avoiding the daily scream fests between Mom and Dad. He lifts two fingers to his mouth and sucks in until the end of the cigarette he's holding burns red. Smoke billows around me as he exhales.

"Shaw!" I yell without thinking. My brother does not smoke! Guilt fills me. I'm sure this is a grief-induced habit, caused by my death. Then he exhales perfect donuts of smoke that probably take years to learn how to do, and I ram my hands into my hips, shaking my head.

I'm mad even though I have absolutely no right to be—the transmigratory have no place to judge—but this is my National Honor Society older brother. My community-service role model. This is vice-less Shaw. Maybe he wasn't any of those things after all. Maybe that's merely how I chose to see him.

I climb up onto a fallen log that's propped diagonally above where he's sitting, dangling my feet beside his head, and let the sounds from his headphones clarify in my ears. I recognize the high-pitched vocals. It's an older band—from when Mom and Dad were in school—that he always used to listen to in the car when he drove me home from school or wherever.

He finishes his cigarette, snuffs out the butt, wraps it in a tissue, and stuffs it in his coat pocket. There's the environmentally conscious public policy major I know. Another shiver shakes him, but he doesn't head back to the house. He remains sitting, bobbing his head to the beat of his music.

I saw him here once before, the summer after he graduated high school. Aimée and Madison and I were in a Wicca phase—don't ask—so we spent a lot of time in the woods under the tree house my dad had built me in second grade, lighting candles and pretending to believe we could bewitch Will McPherson into asking out Madison. We were lying in a patch of heather, pointing out pictoric clouds, and Shaw showed up all puffy eyed. His girlfriend had broken up with him because she was going off to college in California. We hid so he wouldn't see us. I remember promising myself I would never break a boy's heart like that.

Images of flirting with Caleb in Mrs. Wirlkee's class flood

my mind: passing notes, deciding to put my hair up so I'd have to turn around to search for a hair tie in my backpack when all I really wanted was to catch one of his casual smiles directed at me. I shake the images out of my head, refusing to believe they're real.

After what seems like hours, Shaw stands and walks up the trail toward the house. I wait for the pulse that drew me out here to urge me to follow my brother again. Instead I feel it yanking me in the opposite direction, farther into the trees. I jump down from the log I've been sitting on—float is more accurate, actually. I fall with the grace of a feather. I raise one pointed foot to my knee as if I'm balancing a fouetté rond de jambe en tournant. It hasn't occurred to me until now that I probably weigh about as much as a feather.

My feet stop, from some predestined will, in front of a towering maple tree. It's the one that holds my tree house. I lift my hand to the worn slats of the handmade ladder that's nailed to the trunk. My initials are still visible on the bottom step. I trace the uneven letters with my finger: CEH. Above them, on the next step, I trace the letters CAT. Cat? Placing my thumb over the capital A, I realize they're initials too. I yank my hand back when I remember whose: Caleb Aaron Turner. My best friend when Dad built this for me.

My hands sink into the tree as I attempt to climb the ladder, and I stumble through it, barely catching my balance on the other side. I let out a small laugh because this reminds me of the first time I used the tree house. I had my mom call Caleb's mom to invite him over, and he dared me into rock-paper-scissoring to see who got to climb up first. I was so mad when he won, until he turned to tell me how easy the ladder was to climb and fell ten feet to the ground.

When I straighten, I'm standing inside the tree house. I peek out the window, wondering how I managed to get up here without climbing, and see a pair of black Vans dangling over the ledge. I pull my head back inside and glare at Caleb. "Why are you up here?"

He responds by swinging his feet. I stare at his untied white laces tangling in the breeze, wondering why he asked me to be his project partner. I draw my eyes away to check out the tree house.

It's been years since I've been up here, but it looks exactly the same. The milk-crate tables and the ratty old striped rug in the middle of the oblong space. Even the drawing I made of two dogs dancing *Swan Lake* is still tacked to the wall behind the paper airplanes that Caleb hung from the roof with my dad's fishing line. The floor is littered with damp leaves, but other than that, the place is in pretty good condition. I kick at a pile of brown leaves and wonder if Caleb's responsible for how well kept my tree house is.

I bend down to examine a Tic Tac container that's fallen out of his hoodie pocket near the undisturbed pile of leaves I kicked at. It's full of white ovals that are just flat enough to distinguish from the fresh mints that should be inside. He picks it up, flicks open the top, and pops a handful of pills into his mouth like they're candy.

"I take it those aren't prescribed to you," I chide. "You have to be kidding me that you came up here to get high while I'm—"

"You should have gone home early," Caleb mumbles, interrupting me.

"When exactly are you . . ." My mind strays mid-sentence, distracted by images that fade before faces reveal themselves. A chill rolls down my arms. His brown eyes turn black, then blue like mine, and I can't be sure which color is true because they're all blending in the water dripping from my hair.

Caleb closes the top of the Tic Tac container and the *click* echoes through the woods like the *clap* of an oar on rough tides. It carries him away. Then it's cold, and he's back. And I'm . . . I'm not dead yet. But I want to be.

CHEATER

THE MAIN THING I THOUGHT about that entire afternoon was how cold it was in Caleb's house. His mom was out of town for I don't know what and he was supposed to be staying with his dad, so we would have to kind of sort of break in through a loose screen on one of the kitchen windows.

He told me all this while Mrs. Wirlkee gave us "project planning time" (meaning she was behind in grading and needed her own planning time). I'd switched desks with Brent Foster so we could both sit next to our project partners. I'm sure for completely different reasons since Brent's partner had a binder full of work sheets and notes while my partner was cracking jokes.

"Sounds like you're pretty good at staging break-ins," I teased.

"Nah," Caleb said, waving a hand, "but my mom's gotten pretty good at calling the cops instead of parenting."

"Is that why you're on probation?"

His expression hardened for the slightest moment, then he

switched to his usual jokey tone. "Don't believe everything you hear, Cassidy."

I clearly didn't. A small voice in the back of my head had been telling me to stay away from him for four days now, ever since he asked me to be his partner.

"So," he started, "my mom has these killer frozen éclairs at her house. We could munch while we work on *el projecto*."

I laughed at his add-an-*o*-to-the-end-of-any-word-and-it's-instantly-Spanish jargon. "Are you bribing me with food?" If he was, éclairs were the way to go. They were my absolute favorite. Especially the frozen kind. I used to bring a box into elementary school for my birthday treat every year and, later, over to Madison's house on Friday nights for our end-of-the-week chow-downs—until she got cut from freshman dance team tryouts for not being able to do a full split on both legs. Convinced the "failure" was based on costume size, her mom put the kibosh on sweets after that. The joke was on Mrs. Scott though because Aimée started hosting vodka-fueled bonfires to fill the Friday-night void.

I couldn't believe Caleb remembered my favorite snack.

He leaned over the front of his desk and did a slow examination of my every curve. I adjusted my hair to cover my hot cheeks and crossed my legs away from him.

"Doesn't look like food's your Achilles' heel, but all girls love chocolate."

"That's kind of a sexist remark," I snapped, but it was flirty fire. We'd been teasing each other like that the entire week in Mrs. Wirlkee's class. I tried not to think how Ethan would feel about it.

Caleb folded his arms on his desk and rested his chin on top of them. "I suppose the same goes for dudes—and dogs. My dog *loves* chocolate."

"You're not supposed to give dogs chocolate. It kills them." I uncrossed my legs and turned forward in Brent's desk.

"We need to work on our project, partner." The words drifted past my ear. Caleb's desk creaked as he leaned closer.

I pressed my hands to my chest to slow my breathing.

"My place or yours? Doesn't matter, but I have éclairs." He laughed quietly, and whatever part of our flirting was innocent disappeared when his cheek brushed my shoulder.

"Yours," I breathed into the back of Brent Foster's head. He half turned, then realized I wasn't talking to him.

"Solid. I'll see you at three."

I have no idea why I agreed to go to Caleb's house after he so clearly laid out the fact that we'd be alone and more eating would take place than actual work, but I did. He was my friend. We were partners for a school project. That was it.

That was what I kept telling myself: he was my friend. That was it.

His mom's house was tucked in a neighborhood that bordered the athletic fields behind the school. I knew exactly where it was because we used to have playdates there in elementary school while our moms drank white zinfandel and complained about our dads.

I offered him a ride home since we were going to the same place and it made some sort of backward sense that if everyone saw me giving him a lift home that's all it would be. But he insisted it was quicker for him to walk. He was right. When I pulled into his driveway, he'd already sneaked inside through the window and opened the front door to tell me to park around the corner and walk through the side yard. That should've been a massive red flag.

Hide your car? Wake up, Cassidy! Adultery 101 rearing its slut-bomb head.

But I didn't even think. I simply got back in my car and parked along the curb three houses down.

"Sorry about making you move your car, but my mom has the neighbors watching the house while she's away, and I'm not supposed to be here today." He took my backpack and tossed it on a wooden rocking chair near the door.

"Seems a little paranoid."

He muttered, "Not enough," but I ignored it.

The house was different from what I remembered. There was hardly any furniture in the front room and the country geese figurines that I used to beg Mom to put in our house when I was little seemed tragically out of date and tired. The decor clashed like nothing else with Caleb's neon hoodie and sagged skater jeans. I remembered us playing Guess Who? in here and Caleb acting out the voices for each character. His brother would always walk by right before Caleb was about to win and call out who was on his card, but we never cared. It was more about being silly than winning. It didn't feel like that innocent place anymore.

"I don't think I've seen the inside of your house in about four years," I said.

"You and that friend of yours were at my last party. Thanks for saying hi, by the way."

My mouth formed a surprised O. "We only stayed for, like, five minutes."

"You still could've said hi."

"Same to you."

"It was *my* party. It's just rude not to say hello to the host," he said sarcastically.

I cracked a small smile. "So we've agreed to always say hello to a host."

He tilted his head and looked at me out of the corner of his eye with an easy smile. "Mandate of the party gods."

"Mandate?" I laughed. "Like you follow any rules."

He waggled his eyebrows at me. "Only my own."

My lingering smile rendered my eye roll ineffective. "It was Madison's idea to go to that party anyway. It's not my fault that we didn't stay long enough to say hello."

"Your friends hate me. Why would she want to come here?"

"They don't hate you. They just don't get you."

He was reaching for my hand to pull me toward the basement door, but tensed when I spoke, gripping my wrist tight enough to make me pull it back. He stood staring at his empty hand still bent in a hold on my invisible wrist. I started, but he opened the basement door. "Shall we?"

I eyed the dark staircase and sneaked a peek at his face, but it was shadowed by the door. "Let me get my bag."

"Whatever." He laughed in this way that made me realize I had no idea what he was thinking, but the totally strange thing was that not knowing made it feel inexplicably right to be there, with him.

As I followed him down the basement steps, I could almost

see a cloud of smoke emerging under the low paneled ceiling and hear laughter and clanking bottles fill the narrow space: the sound track of the party gods.

I sat on the futon in the back corner because it was the only place to sit. Caleb picked up a remote from the low table at the foot of the stairs where the keg had been at his party and aimed it at the stereo. Bass vibrated between my ears so low I couldn't make out any lyrics, only the deep rolling beat.

He walked toward the futon. My eyes flicked up at him when he stopped in front of me. His hair was dangling low over one eye, and when he saw me looking he tucked it behind his ear all shy-like. My stomach did an unexpected flip.

"I thought there were éclairs involved in this," I said in a shaky voice.

He held up his index finger. "One sec." He sidestepped into a small room near the stereo and came out with a frosty box of chocolate pastries, tossing it on the futon. "See? I produce."

Rubbing my thumb over my horseshoe necklace nervously, I looked down at the box. I could feel the chill wafting off it.

He sat on the other side of the box and stared at me until I met his eyes. "So," he started.

I blurted, "I need to be home by five."

He gave me an amused look. "You got here, what, two minutes ago and you're already talking about leaving?"

"I—I wanted to let you know how much time we have to, you know . . . like, work and stuff."

"Okay." He was quiet for a minute. "So why do you have to be home so early?"

"My sister has a figure skating competition to qualify for

regionals, and it's going to be stressful for her because our parents are—" I pressed my lips together, thinking of sitting in the frigid stands with my immature parents while they argued over whatever the dysfunction du jour was. As much as I loved watching my little sister glide across the ice in her velvet dress like a snow fairy on a mission, I would've done anything to get out of sitting through that.

"You know what?" I turned to face Caleb. "They probably won't even notice I'm not there. And I kind of don't care if they do."

Caleb gave me this unbelievably understanding look that I had no idea what to do with. So I sat there, quiet, rubbing my necklace until the metal felt hot between my fingers.

The silence was unbearably awkward. I thought of a million different things to break it—pulling out our project rubric, stuffing an éclair in my mouth, complaining about the bass making my ears bleed, leaving—but I didn't do any of those things. We sat inches from each other, staring, lingering, leaning closer. *He* leaned closer, completely calm, completely confident that that was what I wanted, without having to ask. My pulse matched the beat of the bass line, fast and hard. Of the million things I could have done to break the silence, I did the one that never crossed my mind.

ETHAN IS SHAKING ME BY THE SHOULDERS, trying to bring me back to the present. I know it's him because the warmth of his touch is melting the iciness inside me. I pry my eyes open and will my arms to move, hoping I'm not a puddled mess.

"Cassi?" The low song of his voice fills me with relief as my fingers find his hand and squeeze as tightly as I can manage. "Are you hurt?"

With considerable effort, I shake my head.

"Are you sure?" As Ethan dries the corners of my wet eyes with his thumb, I realize he wasn't shaking my shoulders; he was trying to still them. I'm crumpled on his bed crying so hard every inch of me is trembling.

Like an electric shock, the memory of Caleb jolts me. The deep vibrations of bass-heavy music, the frost from the éclairs box prickling goose bumps up my legs, Caleb's steady eyes. I pull away from Ethan and stand, backing away from his bed.

"What's wrong? Did I do something?" he asks.

You didn't do anything. But I did, or might have. I'm torn between wanting to remember more and wanting to forget everything. I part my lips to explain, but it's like my mouth doesn't know how to form such hurtful words.

Ethan reaches his hand to me, then draws it back. "Where did you go?" His tone has a tinge of accusation.

"I . . ." It takes a couple seconds for me to get my thoughts straight. "I'm not sure exactly." I pause to think how to describe my transportive memories. "I keep having these intense memories, or, actually, they're a lot more like out-of-body flashbacks or something. I have no control over when they happen or what I remember . . . I think. But they're so *vivid*—like I'm reliving them. One second I'm here and the next, I don't know. I kind of . . . melt into the past. Literally."

"Yeah," Ethan says emphatically, "I saw that. If I didn't think I was crazy before, that sealed the deal."

I look away, feeling embarrassed that he saw me melt. "I told you. I'm really here."

"Doesn't mean I'm not crazy."

The shock on his face fades and the pounding in my chest steadies to the pace of a normal heartbeat. It's such a relief being near him that I let myself forget about Caleb. At least for now.

I search Ethan's face for a reason why he's the only person who can see me. *Why Ethan?* I ask the unseen parts of the universe that brought me back to him. No answer. Guess that's not how this whole ghost thing works.

I glance at his clock. It's 2:40 a.m. I ask, "Why are you up so late?"

He laughs a short laugh, probably at how absurdly casual my question is. "Couldn't sleep, so I decided to work on conjugations for that test we have—" He shakes his head. "Well, that *I* have next week. I was trying to clear my head, or occupy it." His eyes flicker and he shakes his head again.

"What is it?"

"You mean besides the fact that I can see down the hallway through your belly?"

I tuck my hair behind my ears, embarrassed again.

"It's like you're here and real and I've touched you, but your skin looks like pearls—see-through pearls." He walks to where I'm standing, lifts my hand up to his desk lamp, and rotates my arm. Faint glimmers of refracted light cast a sheen of iridescence on my pale skin. The colors move in unpredictable patterns like a graceful, spontaneous dance I wish I knew the steps to.

"Yeah, I am kind of a freak show now, huh?"

"No." He pauses. "You're beautiful."

An image of Caleb's cheek brushing against my shoulder, dangerously close to my face, invades my thoughts. I slip my hand out of Ethan's. "Need any help with the conjugations?" I ask, trying to change the subject in such a pathetically obvious way that it makes his amazed expression go flat.

He slams his Spanish textbook shut and shoves it across his desk, nearly knocking over the lamp. I cringe when he grumbles, "Wasn't planning on making this a study date."

"In the den earlier . . . you didn't think I was real?"

"I didn't think you would come back."

I absorb the verbal slap. Based on my last memory, I deserve it.

"I'm sorry I showed up out of nowhere like this—and left the freakish way I did before." I sigh. "Where else am I gonna go? Home is . . . You're the only one who can see me, so . . ."

He turns his head and stares at the window. The blinds are closed. I don't want to think about what it means that he'd rather look at a dusty panel of white vinyl than at bizarro Ghost Me.

I focus on the fish tank sitting on top of his dresser and the hum of the filter. His house is full of normal nighttime noises like that: the furnace kicking on, floorboards creaking in the room above his, a bathroom door opening and shutting. My house has lost its normal.

The tetras swim in and out of the plaster coral reef, passing by each other, grazing fins as they wobble through the filter bubbles. Their existence seems simple, automatic, and easy. Whereas mine seems so complex right now that I can't even move. So I don't. I stand next to Ethan's dresser and stare at his fish, embracing the normal.

"Before—" He stops, clamping his mouth shut. I stare at the inches between us that seem more like miles or days, wondering if he knows anything about Caleb and me, if he knows more than I remember. "I said some things. I was a jerk."

His words surprise me. "I thought you handled the whole ghost thing pretty well, actually."

He shakes his head. "That's not what I mean. The things I said to you—"

"I don't remember anything jerky being said in the den." Nothing I didn't deserve anyway. I force a small smile at him to hide the growing guilt I feel.

His face scrunches up like my smile is blinding him. "Not in the den . . . before."

Suddenly, I realize what he means by "before." I wave my hands at him. "Whatever it was, it's done."

He nods, but it doesn't seem like he agrees. His eyes flit between me and the fish. Back and forth, back and forth, back and forth. It's making me dizzy. Then slowly, hesitantly, he reaches his hand out and brushes his fingertips along the back of my hand. I turn my palm over and his fingers whisper against my new skin. My eyelids feel heavy and the sigh that flows out of me draws him nearer.

"How are you not freaking out right now?" I ask.

"Believe me, I am." His eyes are wide with awe. "This is unreal."

I can't take my eyes off his fingers on my arm. I don't want to blink. If I do, this might all disappear. Everything feels so evanescent, as if one wrong move would thrust me back into Other Me and I'd never see him again. My airless breath catches in my throat because I've already made that wrong move. I'm not even supposed to be here now. I'm dead, clinging to the "living" world by some unexplainable phenomenon, and I still haven't figured out why.

"Ethan." I wait for his eyes to lose their dazzled glaze. "Why do you think I'm here? I mean, why do you think I didn't stay with my body?"

"How would I know?" The accusation slips back into his voice.

"I figured since you're the only person who can see me, your opinion might be relevant. Madison said . . ." My voice trails off. "Do you believe what the police think?"

He fixes his eyes on the fish tank and angles his body away from me.

85

I step in front of him, forcing him to look at me. "You have to know I would never do that."

He mutters something that sounds like "I hope not." He doesn't mention the note. I wish I could remember what it said.

"I think I'm supposed to do something while I'm here. It doesn't make any sense that I'd be given a free pass to haunt about and chill with my boyfriend. And it's completely frustrating that I can't remember the party—well, more like most of the past few weeks." And the stuff I do remember I don't want to know. "Why do you think I stayed?" I ask again.

He stuffs his hands into his pockets, thinking. "Only you can know that." There's something in his voice I can't place, a wavering that hints he knows more than he's saying.

"Does it make me the worst ghost ever if I don't have a clue?"

He holds my gaze for an indeterminate amount of time. Then he lightens his tone. "You're my first ghost. What do I know?"

"I'm your first? I feel honored," I half joke.

A smile breaks across his face. "Always will be. First everything. No matter what comes between us."

"Like death?"

His eyes sink to the floor. "Yeah. Something like that."

9

ETHAN TOLD ME I COULD SLEEP with him in his bed like I used to when his parents were out of town, but I said no. The invitation seemed loaded with meaning I couldn't decode. It's never been easier to shack up—invisible, hello!—and I can't bring myself to do it. Not just because I don't sleep either. I'd lie wide awake next to him for all of ever, but I can't shake this feeling that he's upset with me—for the argument I can't remember? For dying on him? For Caleb? Plus, my being here is so unfair. What is he going to do, putt around his basement with his dead girlfriend while the rest of the world rolls on aboveground?

As guilty as I feel though, I can't deny I've been enjoying our alone time.

He stayed up with me most of the night, holding my hand and asking me questions about being a ghost. He finally succumbed to sleep an hour before his mom came down to check on him on her way out to work. It was the first time I was relieved when someone didn't see me.

Once Mr. and Mrs. Keys have both left, Wendell pads down the basement steps and nudges Ethan's hand with his snout. When Ethan doesn't awaken, the dog curls up on the floor next to the bed with a dejected sigh.

I look at him and say, "I know the feeling." His tail swishes from side to side, barely missing my leg. I sit next to him and hesitantly brush my palm along his bushy golden tail. The slight tickling sensation actually feels like light hairs brushing my palm instead of needles destroying my insides. Promising, even though he didn't seem to notice.

I pull my hand back and stare at his snout. It's his bliss button. Rub one finger back and forth on that dog's nose and he lets out a low groan of pleasure. It was kind of embarrassing when Ethan and I first started going out, but after we got to bliss-button status ourselves, it became an inside joke. If I was going to get a solid touch through to Wendell that was the spot. When I suck in a long, albeit airless, breath—I can't help the calming habit—I realize that the unmistakable dog smell Wendell always carries with him is missing. I lean closer and still don't smell anything, not even the bayberry candle that keeps Ethan's bedroom from smelling like boy.

I can't smell.

Infuriated that I've been reduced to four and a half senses, I make a deliberate poke for Wendell's shiny black nostrils. Instantly, needles stab at my finger.

"Ouch!" I shake my wrist until the glittery particles of my freakishly disembodied digit settle.

Ethan sits up in bed and whips his head from side to side. "Cassi? What's wrong?"

I sigh. "Sorry. Guess I've gotten used to people not being able to hear me."

"Heckuva wake-up call." He yawns.

"I was trying to pet Wendell."

"Did it work?" His voice is high and excited.

"Not so much." I scoot across the floor and lift myself up onto his bed.

As if sensing how much I need to feel real, he rubs the sides of my arms from wrist to elbow with his fingertips. It feels *amazing*. "What did you remember last time when you . . ." He doesn't finish.

I move away from him and avert my eyes.

"If you don't want to tell me—" He holds up his hands. "Never mind. I get it."

I don't deserve his understanding or the warmth of his fingers on my icicle arms. I'm starting to think it was better when I didn't remember anything.

When I don't respond, he changes the subject, hardly managing to hide his frustration. "You know, I bet Wendell is aware you're here even though you can't touch him." He reaches under the bed and tosses a grimy tennis ball out his door. Wendell hops up and chases after it.

"Wait." I hold my hands out. "So you think Wendell knows I exist even though he can't see or feel me? How?"

Ethan pulls the covers back and stands to retrieve the slobbery ball Wendell just dropped in front of me. He lobs it underhand up the stairs, and Wendell leaps after it. I'm momentarily distracted by Ethan's navy blue boxer-briefs. They're the only thing he's wearing. I start to regret not spending the night in his bed until the unnatural pulsing in my chest reminds me why I didn't.

"Yes," Ethan answers. "I think he knows you exist, it's just—" He shakes his head. "Never mind."

"What?"

He hesitates. "It's sort of out there."

I put my hands on my hips, looking annoyed, which takes considerable effort since I'm still swoony over his abs. "I'm a ghost, Ethan. Can't get much farther out there than that."

He exhales, long and loud. I lean forward, hoping for a whiff of his breath even if it's sour, morning scented, but there's nothing. I frown.

"Okay," he says, probably thinking I'm disappointed at his reluctance to explain. "I think he knows you're in the room because he can smell you in the way that animals can smell fear and stuff. A dog's reality is in scents." As if on cue, Wendell trots back into the room. "No smell, no you."

"That's ironic." Ethan gives me a curious look that I pretend not to see so I won't have to explain about not being able to smell. I tilt my head to the side and glance down at Wendell gnawing on his ball. "So he's operating on some sort of doggie sixth sense, but why can you see me?"

Ethan grabs a T-shirt from the floor and tugs it over his bed head, then steps into a pair of loose pajama pants. Watching him dress sends this enlivening crackle-surge through me. "You said I'm the only one who's seen you since—"

"I died," I finish for him so I won't have to hear him say the words.

His Adam's apple slides up and down his throat as he

swallows. "Right. Are you absolutely sure no one else can see you? Maybe they were ignoring you because they thought they were going crazy or something." He sits next to me on the bed.

I turn his face toward me with one finger on his chin. Feeling his scratchy stubble is the most amazing sensation in the world. "You're not crazy. And I'm sure. I screamed my head off in the morgue and no one even looked up."

His throat works through another hard swallow. "So I'm the only one." His voice sounds thick, worried, but under that I can hear something else. Something prideful.

Sunlight shines through the part in the blinds and draws a stark white angle across his bedroom. Ethan takes my hand and holds it up, watching the sun dance off my pearlescent skin. His pulse races under my fingertips.

"Does your whole body shimmer like this?"

"Haven't peeked under the clothes," I respond, trying to keep things light.

"You should," he says excitedly. My eyes widen. "Er, that's not what I meant."

I press my lips together. "Fair is fair. I got to see you half naked this morning." I attempt to push my sleeve up my arm, but my hand slides over the top as if my clothes are painted on. I shake my head and say, "That's embarrassing."

Ethan tucks one leg underneath himself as he turns toward me. "Maybe you're not concentrating enough." His voice is eager, curious.

I shrug and say, "It's possible." But before I even finish the sentence I'm dreading that it's not possible. I can tell Ethan's working up the courage to try for the zipper on my coat. Fear fills every part of me. Embarrassment and regret mix with fear as I imagine him reaching for my coat and passing right through it, right through me like Joules did.

I reach around him for his pillow. My hand predictably slides through the blue-gray cotton case. "This is beyond frustrating."

He thinks a minute. "Maybe you have to want to touch it."

"What are you talking about? Of course I want to touch it."

Ethan cocks an eyebrow. "It's a pillowcase, Cassi. Doesn't exactly prompt intense desire." I give him a wry smile. "Think about it. If you want something bad enough, you can almost always accomplish it."

"What about flying?" I say sarcastically.

"I got you back from beyond death. I think that's a little more impossible than flying." We're both quiet, absorbing what he's said.

After a long minute, he opens the drawer of his nightstand. Inside is his cell phone, some pencils, a wrinkled to-do list, and a Band-Aid box that only he and I know is filled with condoms. "If you could talk to one person besides me right now, who would you call?"

"Aimée." It comes out so automatically it surprises me.

"Try to dial her number."

I look from his cell to the Band-Aid box, wondering which one offers a greater incentive to touch. Another enlivening surge courses through me. "This is dumb. Aimée doesn't need a post-mortem prank call."

"I'll do the talking if she answers." He opens the drawer farther. "Try."

I meet his eyes. His expression is the same as Joules's was the day she learned how to ride her bike without trainers. The hesitation I saw there last night is nearly gone. I look back at the drawer. The phone seems a million miles away. "I can't do this, Ethan. I've already tried."

"Cassidy." Ethan has this way of saying my name that makes me feel up for anything: a math test, strip Uno, shots of hundred-proof liquor, Rollerblading. Anything.

"Okay, I'll try, but I'm not making any promises."

He nods. "Think about something specific you want to say to her. That might help."

I slowly lean toward the open drawer. Aimée's tearstained cheeks are the only thing I see when I reach for the phone. I imagine my fingers wrapping around the plastic rectangle and dialing her number of their own will, then my mouth forming the words I would say—the confession I'd make. I extend my index finger to start dialing but then yank my hand back.

"What happened?" Ethan asks.

"I—I can't . . ." *Say what I need to tell Aimée in front of you,* I finish in my head.

"You didn't even try. What are you afraid of?"

I don't say, *I'm afraid that if it worked and Aimée picked up I'd have to listen to my best friend cry over the phone, which is indescribably worse than in person.* Instead I say, "I didn't make any promises."

He says something under his breath that sounds sort of like "Yes, you did." He picks up his cell and tosses it to me. He purses his lips when it lands between a fold in the sheets, under my leg. We reach for it at the same time and there's this suspended moment where our hands touch and all the years of good and bad memories between us fall away and it's just us: two inseparable beings.

"We'll figure this out," he says as some footnote to a thought.

I want to tell him that I don't deserve his help, but his hands slide to my hips, across my waistline to the small of my back, and up. His fingers twist into the soft curls at the nape of my neck, making it impossible to resist leaning in to his touch. My fingers slowly trace a line down his arms, then guide his hands to my hips. My skin starts to tingle and burn in all the right ways.

I shift so I'm up on my knees and gently push him down onto his bed. My hair cascades around our faces as my hands slip under his T-shirt. Responding to my advance, Ethan wraps his legs around my ankles and rocks against my hips. Airy moans of pleasure escape my lips as I tilt my head so our noses touch. We're so close now that I can almost taste his breath. I want to kiss every inch of him, slow and deep, to prove that he's the only person I was ever meant to kiss.

Abruptly he pulls his hands away and untangles his legs from mine. "I shouldn't have done that."

"I didn't mind," I say, sounding out of breath.

I don't drop my gaze from his eyes. I'm sure my afterlife mission isn't to hook up with my boyfriend—especially after what I just remembered about Caleb—but I can't ignore the allure of his touches. Besides, I don't actually know what happened with Caleb. I came out of the memory before anything really wrong happened. Still, I have this itching feeling that I did something I shouldn't have.

"Didn't you feel that?" I whisper. "My hands moved your shirt."

"Cassi, you didn't move my shirt."

"Then how come I can feel—" I look down at my hands on either side of his rib cage, not *under* his shirt but *through* it. "Oh." He rolls out from under me, but my hands reach instinctively for him, holding him close so we're lying face-to-face. "Didn't you feel that rush though?"

"Yes." His expression softens into something between longing and apprehension.

I bite down on my lip as I move his hands to my hips again. "Don't you want it, like, so bad that nothing else seems real?"

"Yes," he murmurs, looking down at my lips.

Then kiss me! I silently beg with the same fevered anticipation I had for our first kiss and about twenty hundred thousand times more lust.

His hips press against mine and my entire body awakens. Being this close to him kick-starts my heart. My chest rises and falls with deep, quick breaths. My lungs fill with air—real air!—taking in every enlivening bit of this moment. I wonder if this is how I would've felt if I'd been shocked back to life on those river rocks by paramedics. Revived.

The tension in Ethan's muscles lets loose and his hands explore every part of me that isn't bundled in my clothes. I melt into his embrace, his lips temptingly close, until an image flashes behind my eyes. A hand on my neck—different hands gripping my shoulders.

Pain starts at my feet—stinging, burning cold—then seizes my lungs, stills my enlivened heart. The absence of that brief whisper of life is worse than if I'd gone a century never breathing again.

This time I'm the one to push away. "This can't be why I'm

here, Ethan." It takes me a while to get the words out, and they sound harsher than I intend.

"Then what is?" He sits up and swings his feet over the side of the bed, leaning forward with his elbows on his knees.

I stay on my side, clutching my middle. I grit my teeth, hiding how much pain I'm in. "Do you really think we're supposed to pretend like nothing's happened?"

Ethan shakes his head and pushes his hands through his hair. "Is that what we're doing?" The question hangs between us.

He absentmindedly runs his fingers over the silver buckle on my shoe. Each spot he touches reveals a new tear in the leather. Suddenly, the heel splits down the center and spills out freezing cold water. I sit up with a jerk and gasp. My hands grope at the comforter to contain the pool, but it's already flooding over the edges of the bed, drenching the carpet.

"What's wrong?" Ethan asks me. "Did you lose something?"

My hands are still pawing at the covers, melting through them. "Can't you see . . . my shoes . . . ?"

Ethan's eyes dart to the frayed strap on my right shoe and back up at me. I hear him say, "Again?"

I reach for his worried face, but a familiar voice telling me to relax stops me. My raised hand drips icy water down on Ethan as I melt away.

MY FUTURE BOYFRIEND

RELAX, DEES." Madison popped the last bite of her second Twix into her mouth, carbo-loading before she got home and her mom reduced her calorie intake to skinless chicken breasts and steamed asparagus. "Your parents already said you could spend the night at Aimée's."

"But they don't know she's having a boy-girl party. You know how my dad is about boys."

"Then don't tell him," Madison replied, like it was the most obvious solution in the world, pulling back her natural strawberry-blond hair into a long ponytail.

"You could whine to your mom about your dad and get sympathy permission," Aimée suggested. "You know, pit them against each other. That always works with your parents."

I grimaced even though she was right. Maybe *because* she was. I pointed a finger at my chest. "Worst liar ever, remember?"

Madison shrugged. "So leave the boys part out."

"That's the same thing as lying."

Madison lowered her new sunglasses, which matched mine but covered half her face, and peered at me over their tortoise-shell frames. "You have so much to learn. You are beyond lucky you have me." She hugged me tight, squeezing out a giggle. Madison always knew when I needed a laugh.

Aimée reached up to pluck a heart-shaped leaf from the purple-blossomed tree we were walking under as we turned onto her street. "Listen, you have two full days to figure out a way to break it to your dad that boys live in the world. We're high schoolers now—or almost—and soon every party we go to will be boy-girl." She spun the leaf between her fingers, pointing it at me. "Which, by the way, is why you should stop saying 'boy-girl party,' Dees." She winked at me, and I shoved her. True to form, she stumbled off the edge of the sidewalk, dumping her back-pack. Aimée was the only fourteen-year-old in America who carried a fully stocked backpack around in July.

As we waited for Aimée to gather up her things, I practiced my turn-out by running through the basic ballet positions. I pressed my left heel into the arch of my right foot, forming third position.

"Besides," Madison started, "how else am I supposed to meet and fall in love with my future boyfriend if we don't have this party?"

"I'm sorry, who are we talking about?" Aimée asked in a teasing tone.

"Yeah, Mads, your list of future boyfriends is hard to keep track of lately."

Aimée stifled a laugh as Madison thrust her arms out, very

melodramatic. Aimée's teasing increased with each name Madison mentioned. Before long, Madison's naturally rosy cheeks were painted a furious shade of red.

I stepped in, playing peacemaker. "Ethan Keys." I repeated the last name Madison had said. "He was in our English block. He's friends with that hockey player who made out with that girl in the rink locker rooms. You know him, Aims. He's cute."

I nudged Aimée with my elbow, and she hooked arms with Madison, silently apologizing for giving her such a hard time. "Ethan, yeah, I can see how you'd think he's cute."

"Um, duh!" Madison almost yelled. "It took me five days to work up the courage to ask him to come." She turned to me with a devilish expression. "I invited your future boyfriend too."

"Who?" My eyes bugged out in surprise. The idea of Madison setting me up made my stomach churn.

"Caleb Turner," she drawled suggestively. I pointed my left foot, shifting from third position to fourth and then fifth.

Aimée bumped my heel with her foot, interrupting my nervous habit, and groaned. "I thought you were over Caleb."

I bent down and picked up one of the heart-shaped leaves from the sidewalk as we resumed walking. They were sprinkled across the neighborhood. Someone's tree must've thought Valentine's Day came late this year. I bent the leaf in half. "I can't talk to him anymore. He's so . . ."

"Greasy?" Aimée offered.

"I think the PC term is herbal," Madison said jokingly.

Aimée came back with, "I think it's the *herb* that's making him greasy." They both giggled.

I shook my head, unfolding and refolding the leaf until it cracked at the center and split in two. "Don't be mean. He's going through a lot right now. I feel bad about ignoring him this summer."

"I'm sure his new friends have kept him busy," Aimée said. "*He* ditched you. Don't feel bad about it."

I nodded even though what she'd said wasn't entirely true. Yes, Caleb had started hanging out with a new group of friends who were "less than desirable," as Mom would say, but we'd been friends since kindergarten. I felt racked with guilt for letting our friendship waste away, but every time I even thought about calling him, my throat tightened up. I knew his family as well as I knew Aimée's or Madison's. I didn't want to think about what going to his house would be like once his mom or dad moved out. Two Christmases. Visitation rights—it was too scary. Especially since my parents fought as much as, if not more than, his.

"He probably won't even show up," I said, knowing Caleb would have plans with his other friends, the ones who actually talked to him.

"Then you can meet someone new," Madison chimed in, her voice high and optimistic.

"Maybe even cute Ethan," Aimée added with a tinge of sarcasm that was meant for Madison. She didn't seem to notice, suddenly lost in a far-off thought.

Aimée fished her house keys out of her backpack and started grilling Madison about how many people she'd invited. I wandered across Aimée's yard, mesmerized by tiny spots of black wobbling in the late-afternoon sky. They danced like drunken birds in a fog, dangerous and free.

"Dees?" Aimée's voice broke my trance.

"You have to see this," I called to my friends, eyes still locked on the spectacle in the sky. "What is that?"

"Bats," Aimée answered. "My dad said they've roosted under the covered bridge."

"Ew!" Madison squealed.

Aimée scoffed. "Bats are a sign of good luck."

Madison turned her head to give Aimée a proper are-you-nuts look. "Says who?"

"Roughly 30 percent of the world's population."

"You're such a nerd." Madison flicked her extra-long ponytail in Aimée's face. Aimée swatted it away.

"Let's watch them from your roof tonight," I suggested. Something about how fearlessly the bats dove toward the trees lining the river fascinated me. I couldn't turn away.

"That sounds awesome," Madison said, shifting her opinion of the bats on a dime. Aimée rolled her eyes at how blindly Madison agreed with me. "I'm up for livin' on the wild side," Madison continued, "but if either of you falls and breaks your neck, it's not my fault."

"If anyone's falling, it's from me pushing you," Aimée joked.

"Ha-ha." Madison stuck out her tongue at Aimée. "You're just jealous I have dibs on the *cute* boys."

"We'll see."

We watched the bats a while longer, dipping and diving in their dance until *thwack*! One of the bats crashed into the hipped roof of the old covered bridge. The three of us gasped. Aimée grabbed my arm so tightly it hurt. I glanced between my two best friends so I wouldn't have to see the poor wounded bat flapping its last breaths into the grass.

Aimée shared my frozen expression of shock. Madison was staring unflinchingly at the bat, crying behind her sunglasses.

10

UNDULATING SHEETS OF WHITE mask my vision. I do a frantic check of my limbs to make sure I'm still here in my semi-alive state. Two arms, two legs; I appear to be whole. My eyes slowly focus, revealing the rolling landscape of Dover Park. Flawless white snow covers every pebbled hiking trail, every bench. When we were younger, Joules and I used to toboggan down these hills. They seemed a lot bigger back then.

I let out a relieved sigh because when you're a ghost who can't keep her grip on the present, ubiquitous white sheets of light are terrifying. That is, if you want to stay a ghost. I'm still not sure I do. Then the crisp outline of the covered bridge reveals itself and the memory I just had comes rushing back.

The party we were talking about ended up being when I had my first kiss. I'd told Ethan about the bats that Aimée said were good luck, and he asked me to show him their roost. Once we were alone, he told me about his first kiss and he became mine.

As I approach the bridge, the image of two fourteen-year-olds sharing an innocent moment blurs and reshapes into an elongated shadow crawling up the slatted walls of the bridge, creeping into and invading the happiness I used to feel here.

The darkness bears down on me, calling me. I squeeze my eyes shut, willing my legs to a sprint across the bridge, fighting the draw of the shadow so I can get to Aimée's house on the other side of the river without being swallowed by its darkness.

I don't want to lose myself in another memory. I want to see my best friend and make sure she's okay.

Of course, she's not. She's still in the playroom, but it's worse than before. The wads of tissue are gone. Her makeup, a blow-dryer, and her bedazzled red hairbrush are set out in a perfect line on the counter in the en suite bathroom. The spring collection of her wardrobe is hanging on the rack, organized by color, where we used to store dress-up clothes. She's sitting on the edge of the air mattress giving herself a French manicure with sparkly white tips.

This is bad. Hyperorganization is Aimée's supreme coping mechanism.

I sit on the floor next to her. "You need to leave this room, Meems. It's been—" *A day and a half* I finish in my head. It's been a day and a half since the party . . . since my death. I'm not sure if I'm shocked because that timeline seems too brief or because it seems too drawn out.

I lean my hands on the air mattress. It doesn't move an inch, mostly because I go through it. Aimée coats her left pinkie nail with a clean line of white, but her hand trembles as she dips the brush back into the bottle of polish balanced between her knees and it tumbles to the floor.

"Son of a—" She rights the bottle and fumbles with a box of tissues, then throws the box across the room when she finds it empty. Her head drops into her hands, ruining her still-tacky polish job. "Crap!" She shakes her hands in a weak attempt to dry the polish and wilts onto the mattress.

I've never seen her so distraught. I want to clean up the spill, but after a morning of experimenting, I know I won't be able to manage it. Besides, it would freak her out if the stain miraculously disappeared.

"I'm coming in," Aimée's sister, Bridgette, announces. Her long, straight hair is the vanilla to Aimée's chocolate. She's the only member of Aimée's family with blond hair, but she resembles her sister and mom so closely in every other way it's obvious she belongs in the Coutier clan. She nudges Aimée's shoulder. "Are you sleeping?"

"No." Aimée's voice is thick with tears.

Bridgette pulls a minipack of tissues from her back pocket, not noticing me sitting on the floor two feet away. "Here."

Aimée accepts the offer, wipes her eyes, and rolls onto her back. "Did Mom send you up?"

"No. I was worried about you. Everyone is."

"What were people saying at school?"

"You know, how Cassidy was nice to *everyone*, almost to a fault."

"Gee, thanks," I mumble.

She continues. "They miss her or at least are pretending to. It was the longest Monday *ever*." She lies next to Aimée. "The most random people came up to me and said how sorry they were."

"I bet."

"What?" Bridgette and I both ask.

"What did they say about how she . . . ?"

"Nothing. It's mindless gossip."

"Tell me."

"You asked for it." Bridgette sits up on her elbow. "Well, I heard some guys saying she tried to go skinny-dipping in the river and froze, which is downright ignorant to suggest. Then Kristy London started telling everyone she saw Cassidy throw up at a dance once because she was bulimic and that's why she committed suicide." Aimée and I simultaneously object, and Bridgette holds up her hands. "I know. Don't worry, I set her straight." Bridgette shakes her head. "Most people are too freaked to talk about it much though. Something like that could happen to any of us, you know?"

Aimée doesn't answer, but I can tell she's working something out in her skeptical brain.

Changing the subject, Bridgette says, "You will not believe the assembly they had today. Principal Dewitt was all robot voice: 'This is a sad, sad tragedy that has wounded our flock.' I hate when he refers to us as his little mascot children." Bridgette rolls her eyes. "Student council threw a fit that it was only fifteen minutes long and basically a PSA for suicide prevention, so they petitioned to hold a real memorial later this week. Nancy Yeong asked me to, quote, 'urge you to return' in time for the assembly. I told her to shove it."

Aimée sits up and states definitively, "I'm going back tomorrow."

"What, to school? Are you ready? Do Mom and Dad know?"

Aimée waves a hand. "You can tell them."

"You don't have to come for the memorial. That was just Nancy being Nancy. No one expects you to come back before the funeral."

The funeral. *My* funeral. I hadn't even thought about it. My thoughts go to mush contemplating how I'll soon have no body to claim. Will Ghost Me cease to exist when that happens? Will I be left in limbo on Earth or will my spectral flesh fade into nothing? There's no way of knowing, but the life I lived will be reduced to rumors and lies if I don't uncover the truth in time.

Aimée stares at her botched manicure for a long second, then squares her shoulders. "I'm going back."

There's no arguing with Aimée once she's made up her mind and Bridgette knows that well. "I have diving practice before school, but I can skip so we can ride together," she says.

"I'll be fine," Aimée says, shaking her head.

Bridgette hesitates. "You're not going back so soon because . . ."

"Because why?" Aimée asks in a challenging tone.

"Nothing. As long as you're ready." Aimée gives her sister a that's-what-I-said look. Bridgette clamps her mouth shut and steps over the nail polish spill on her way to the door. She turns back to Aimée. "Are you coming down for dinner later?"

Aimée shakes her head. "No time. I have to get ready."

"Okay. I'll bring up a plate for you." Bridgette probably assumes Aimée meant get ready for school, but I can tell by the fire in her green eyes that's nowhere near what she meant. After the door closes, Aimée texts Madison something I don't see. Five minutes later, Madison calls her.

"Did you tell your parents?"

"Yeah," Madison's high voice sounds from the receiver. "And

Doctor Daddy said he 'believes it's too soon, but everyone grieves in their own way.'" She imitates her dad's clinical tone. "You know the drill."

"But you're still coming back with me, right?"

There's a quiet moment. "Are you sure this is a good idea?"

"No," Aimée replies, "but we have to do it for Cassidy."

Something inside me churns. What are my girls up to?

NIGHT IS MY FAVORITE TIME NOW. With everyone asleep, it's easy to pretend that's the reason nobody sees me or talks to me.

Aimée didn't eat one bite of her dinner. The tray Bridgette brought up around eight o'clock is still sitting on the toy chest near the door. I stay with her until midnight, when she finally allows herself to sleep. As I leave, I have every intention of going back to Ethan's, but hearing Bridgette talk about the assembly at school reminded me of my mom and how upset she was about the school exploiting my death.

I find myself crossing the south end of the park, winding through the worn-down paths among the trees, crossing streets, then passing more trees until I'm in my backyard.

Through the sliding glass door in the living room, I can see my dad reclining on the sectional. An involuntary smile lifts the corners of my mouth. I was hoping he'd still be awake, the family's resident night owl. Knowing that I, too, prefer the night now, I feel something warm and welcome unfurl inside me; I am somehow closer to him now than even when I was alive. Then I see my mom and an instinct not even death can squelch invades me: vigilance.

As soon as I pass through the door, the argument begins, as if they were waiting for me to arrive. "We should make this decision as a family," Mom says.

"What decision?" Dad asks, his hands raised. He's already given in—given up? "There's no decision to be made. What's done is done."

"Well." She paces between the coffee table and the fireplace, twisting her hair into a loose chignon the way she always does when she's upset. She starts again. "Well, we need something to tell people."

"I thought you didn't want to answer questions from the media."

"I'm not talking about the media, Rodger. I'm talking about *people*—friends, co-workers, the rest of the family." She narrows her eyes at him, one hand extended. "Have you heard anything I've said?" Before he can answer, she throws in, "You never listen to me."

"I am listening, Tessa, but you make mountains out of mole-hills."

"That's only because you never have an opinion on anything. You sit back and wait for me to take care of it."

Dad rubs a hand over his forehead and sighs. "You always have your mind set on a solution before you even consult me, so what would you have me do? Disagree so it can turn into a fight?"

"It's already a fight!" Mom places a hand over her mouth, too late to contain her outburst. Dad's eyes dart up the stairs toward where my brother and sister sleep.

My parents have had this exact same argument at least fifteen times. Fighting about fighting. Nothing has changed but the trigger. Last time it was Shaw's tuition money, this time it's my presumed drunken suicide. It's not the issue that matters, but their underlying impulse to disagree with each other. They lack their usual heat, though. The frustration seems choreographed; they're simply going through the motions because they don't know what else to do.

I wish I could give them an answer, throw the truth down onto the coffee table between them so they wouldn't have anything to debate, but the truth isn't here, in my home. It's being kept hidden by someone I thought was my friend.

11

THREE DAYS AFTER MY DEATH, school seems exactly the same as it was last week. I don't know what I expected, but morning announcements and Mr. Clarkson passing back homework isn't it. No one's crying or asking for a pass to the counselor's office or even wearing black. Bridgette said everyone missed me so much. Sitting in my assigned seat next to Madison in third-hour Trig, I can't tell.

Mr. Clarkson pauses at Madison's desk and lets her know she has until Friday to hand in the weekend problem set that was due yesterday. Somebody mentions my funeral is on Friday and he adjusts the turn-in date to Monday. He glances at my desk, then continues up the aisle.

Madison slips her cell out of her vest pocket and texts under her desk. I lean over to read: *3rd hr w/o her is brutal! Cnt stay here!*

A response from Aimée silently pops up: *U have to bump into him after class. Just 15 more mins.*

Madison's fingers tighten around her cell as she types: *OK*.

"Who are you supposed to bump into?" I ask her.

While her phone is out she checks her missed-calls log. I don't expect to see any since she always answers her cell on the first ring, but there are several from Drew, which isn't that surprising if they're in one of their off-again bouts, and one from a number I don't recognize. She stashes her cell deep in her gold purse, then pulls out the blue folder that we share for Math. Madison and I have inexplicably shared a math class every year of our academic lives together. In sixth grade she suggested we alternate weeks of homework because "you don't look fate in the mouth when it smiles at you." She even changed her handwriting so it matched my wide looping cursive. Last week was my turn to do the problem sets. I wish I had a way to tell her they're sitting on the top shelf in my locker.

Madison has started working on the first problem when Kelsey Flink one seat back passes her a piece of notebook paper. It's the problem set with a red check mark in the top corner. Madison turns around and gives Kelsey an expectant stare. Kelsey points to a seat one row over. Ethan's best friend, Mica Torrez, flashes Madison one of his million-dollar smiles and holds out his hand in a *you're welcome* gesture. Madison half smiles and quickly turns back around. She's still going to have to do the work. Everyone knows Mica gets jock-exception grades.

She spends the rest of class folding his assignment into halves until it's so small it fits into that minipocket on the front of a pair of jeans that's good for pretty much nothing. With one finger, she slides the paper into her pocket, making it disappear.

After the bell rings, Mica catches up to Madison in the hall.

"Thought you could use a break on the assignment. I got full credit, so you should be good with copying my work."

Madison yanks the straps of her backpack tight down over her shoulders. "Thanks."

"Have you heard from E at all?"

Madison's cheeks drain of their usual rosy tint. "Ethan doesn't really call me. Why?"

"I called him a bunch of times, but he didn't pick up." His expression turns reproachful, and he rubs his forehead. "I was wondering if he was avoiding everyone or if it was only me."

Madison sharpens her gaze on Mica for a brief moment, then seamlessly shifts back into friendly conversation. "I'm sure he's only laying low for a while. I guess I wouldn't want to talk to anyone if I were him."

"You kinda are. You and Cassidy were inseparable. Why'd you come back to school so soon?" He searches her ashen face. It's like his eyes are staring right through her to me.

"Madison?" a girl with a high blond ponytail yells from across the crowded hall.

Madison brushes her long bangs across her forehead, hiding her eyes, and pretends not to hear the girl. "Gotta go," she tells Mica in a rush. When she turns to leave, she bumps into the girl.

"Madison." The girl pauses to take a breath. She looks strangely familiar. "Didn't you hear me calling you?"

Madison pinches her cheeks to call back some color and turns with her best fake smile plastered on. She nods at Mica. "We were talking."

"Carly, hey." Mica gives the girl a nod, and she blushes like she's been hit on by him before and fallen hard. One of many.

I'm surprised he hasn't given her a wink or one of his other play-boy trademarks.

Wait. Carly? I look back at the girl, studying her face, remembering her waterfall ponytail. She was at the party with another girl I didn't know. They were the ones I overheard talking about Ethan and me breaking up.

"What do you want?" Madison asks, still fake smiling.

Carly reluctantly pulls her eyes away from Mica's face. "Oh, I just feel so bad about what happened at the party. I hope you know I—"

Madison cuts her off. "Thanks for letting me know you feel bad."

"I *do*. Don't you?"

"Everyone feels bad about what happened to Cassidy," Madison retorts.

I glower at Carly. "But not everyone is strapped with the guilt of spreading rumors about me right before I died," I say, even though I know she can't hear me.

Madison continues. "And I could do without the constant reminders from people *I don't even know* who feel *so bad*." She makes finger quotes around the last two words.

"But—" Carly's eyes dart between Madison and Mica, then to the floor. "Got it," Carly says, sounding ashamed. "I better get to class."

As soon as she's gone, Mica says, "Bet you're in for a whole day of that."

"I expected worse." Madison groans. I offer her a sympathetic smile.

"Then why'd you come back?" he asks a second time.

Madison mutters, "It wasn't my idea."

"Maddy?" Drew steps up between Mica and me.

"Madison," I correct him automatically. Every guy we know—except Ethan—inexplicably calls Madison Maddy and she hates it. Not that she'd ever risk upsetting prospective suitors by telling them.

Drew lobs his arm around Madison's shoulder and leans in to kiss her. "You didn't tell me you were coming back to school today. I would have given you a ride." Inside his khaki-pants pocket, he jingles the keys to his vintage BMW. The silver coupe is about as old as my dad, but Drew takes care of it like it's a priceless antique. He shows it off constantly.

"That's sweet," she says in the same cheery, detached voice she always puts on for him. He smiles like he doesn't notice how much more excited he is to see her than she is to see him. This is a rehearsed dance between them and they both execute the steps flawlessly. Madison trips up at the end though. She shrugs away from Drew.

"I called you last night," Drew says to Madison, still taking hold of her hand, adding with a sad laugh, "and a few times on Sunday."

She presses her fingertips to her closed eyes, feigning tiredness for the reason she freed her hand from his. "I haven't been sleeping very well. I lay awake wondering what Cassidy was thinking about right before she . . ." When Mica clears his throat, Madison looks up with a start. She fluffs her bangs down over her eyes like she's hiding from her own thoughts. "Anyway, I took some NyQuil to try to get some sleep. I must have slept through your calls. Sorry."

"You're forgiven as long as I'm invited over tonight," Drew tells her with a suggestive grin. When he leans in for another kiss, she gently pushes him away, but she does it with a smile so his ego doesn't get bruised.

She checks the clock on her phone. "I'm going to be late to class."

"See you tonight?" Drew asks.

Madison gives him a noncommittal nod. She looks at Mica before leaving. "Thanks again."

For a second, Drew watches her walk down the hall, his shoulders tensed, then turns to Mica. "What was she thanking you for?"

"Chill, man. I just gave her some homework to copy."

"Good," Drew says quietly. He pushes his longish curls back off his face. "She left awfully quick though, right? You noticed that too?" Mica starts to reply, but Drew rambles on. "I didn't mean anything by what I said. I was only trying to take her mind off things."

"That's not going to happen anytime soon."

Drew nods twice, real quick. "You're right. I should give her some space. I mean, she probably needs a few days to get over everything. I should've waited to talk to her—let her come to me. Or not." His voice rises at the end like it's a question.

I peer at him out of the corner of my eye. No wonder he and Madison are so on-again, off-again. He's the most indecisive person ever. This is definitely a side of him I've never seen.

"Dude," Mica says in an exasperated tone, "do you not see who she's talking to over there?"

Remembering Aimée's text, I snap my head to see who Madison bumped into. Her back is to us, but I can tell by the way her hands are flapping about that she's trying to be friendly. Still I can't see who she's talking to.

Mica's hands ball into fists at his sides. A low growl rumbles in his chest. He's clearly bothered by Madison talking to whoever is over there. The anxiety spreading across his face piques a memory I can't quite grasp. It makes me wonder if he knows what happened to me. Was he there? I can't even recall seeing him at the party, but he must've been invited.

When Madison starts down the hall again, finally off to her next class, I get a good look at who she was talking to: Caleb, who is still sitting on the floor, head propped against the wall. Mica communicates something silently with Drew and they stride toward Caleb.

"Nice black eye," Mica says to Caleb. "What'd you do, run into your bong?"

Caleb slowly lifts his head, until he sees two varsity hockey players standing over him. He staggers to his feet, but he doesn't seem intimidated by their size. Something else has him spooked.

He says, "*She* came up to me, okay?"

Mica laughs darkly at Caleb's urgent tone. "We're supposed to believe that?"

"What did she say to you?" Drew asks in a calmer voice.

Caleb answers, avoiding looking at Drew's face, "I don't speak neurotic. Sorry."

Mica shoves Caleb. "Wrong answer."

"She wanted to know if Cassidy talked to me at the party, okay?" Caleb straightens his bright blue hoodie, disheveled from Mica's manhandling.

"And?" Mica shoves Caleb again.

Caleb glares at him and says mechanically, "I was high that night. I don't remember."

Mica laughs again, looking over at Drew. "He doesn't remember. Maybe I'll take credit for that shiner then, if you don't remember how you got it. Give the other eye a waxing so you'll have a matching pair."

Drew pulls Mica back. "Relax. We're good here." He stares at Caleb. "Right?"

Caleb opens his mouth to make some comeback, but seems to think better of it. He gives a jerky nod before pushing between Drew and Mica to leave.

Mica lets out a low whistle. "You've got saintly self-control, dude. I was gearin' up for an off-ice tag-team brawl."

"You should rein in that impulse. It'll mean trouble," Drew says, still watching Caleb.

"Like I'm afraid of that," Mica jeers.

"You said you saw him hitting on Cassidy Saturday night, right?"

"Yeah." Mica clears his throat, his amused expression shifting. "I saw them together."

"I can't lose Maddy like that."

"What, to him? Never, man."

Drew slides Mica a knowing look. "To anyone."

"Well, I don't think you need to worry about Stoner Boy." Mica gives Drew a chummy pat on the back. "With that pot he smokes, that junk kills your libido, y'know? Plus, I think if you were going to lose her it would have been after one of the four hundred other times you guys broke up." Mica lets out an awkward laugh when Drew glares heavily at him. "I'm joking. She's probably out of it because of Cassidy." His expression goes serious. "I am too."

"Yeah, I was wondering what would make you think your homework would be helpful to anyone."

Mica knocks Drew on the shoulder. "You're a real prick, you know that?" Drew smirks, and they walk toward the gym.

I stay put, wondering why it was so important to Aimée that Madison talk to Caleb. Does she think he had something to do with my death?

I make my way toward Aimée's fourth-hour class, hoping she'll do or say something that will clue me in to what she's trying to uncover. As I turn the corner into the science hall, familiar voices trickle into my ears. I stop and turn to look at the perfectly solid wall in front of me, concentrating. I place my hand on the rough brick and allow my fingertips to slide through, then my arm and shoulders and chest until I'm completely on the other side. I have to hop to my left quickly because Aimée is pacing the narrow passage between the bathroom stalls and the sinks and is headed straight for me.

"We could pull him out of class," Aimée suggests to Madison, who is sitting atop the big heat register. "The attendance office is signing passes for anyone who needs grief counseling. We could say it's for that, then talk to him ourselves."

"Judging by his nonresponse earlier, he's not going to agree to counseling."

I look between my two best friends. "Are you guys talking about Caleb?"

"People love getting passes from Guidance." Aimée taps her smudged nails on her folded arms. "Most people," she adds, because she would be completely annoyed if she had to miss a lesson on cell splicing or whatever it is they learn in Advanced Bio for something as inconsequential as a counseling session. I'm actually shocked to see her here instead of in class, even given the circumstances.

Madison replies, "Sure, when it's for something regular like going over college applications. Not when it's to talk about a dead girl." She slouches against the wall with her knees bent close to her chest. "I can't believe I said that." Tears gather in the corners of her gray-blue eyes.

Aimée's expression steels, as if the words she's about to say are a necessary pain that will inevitably lead to a gain, like a tetanus shot. "What did he say when you talked to him?" Aimée asks, all business.

"Not much," Madison tells her. "He was pretty self-medicated."

Now I'm positive they're talking about Caleb.

Aimée rolls her eyes. "I can't believe he was high at eight-thirty in the morning. I'll never get what Cassidy saw in him."

"We don't know anything about it. Maybe she really was innocently working on a class project with him."

"Yeah, maybe I was." Part of me hopes saying it out loud will make it true. But there's something in Madison's voice that tells me she doesn't believe it any more than I do.

"Why would she keep working with him from us if nothing

else was going on? And why did he crash her birthday party? How did he even know where I live?"

"Everyone knows where you live, Aims," Madison counters.

Aimée finally stops pacing and squints at Madison. "You know what I mean. Why are you defending him?"

"I'm not!" Madison shifts uneasily and lowers her voice. "I'm sticking up for Cassidy."

Aimée focuses on her hands, chipping away the flaws in her manicure. "That won't bring her back."

"Neither will making up some explanation for why she jumped."

Aimée purses her lips. "The point is, she didn't jump. And I'm not making anything up, Mads. I saw her and Caleb talking at the party. If we can piece together what happened in her final hours, we might be able to prove her fall wasn't on purpose."

"I don't know. You might be overthinking this," Madison says. "Dees was acting really strange lately."

I turn to her. "I was?"

"I mean, buddying up with Caleb Turner," she says as if answering my question. "Then wandering off to the bridge alone in the dark like that. Maybe the police are right. Maybe she wanted to . . ."

"Don't even go there." Aimée rushes to my defense. "Dees wasn't suicidal—you knew her as well as I did. How can you even suggest that?"

"I'm trying to make sense of everything like you are, but . . . I—I don't know if I can do this, Aims." Madison's head falls into her hands, hiding her face behind a tousle of shoulder-length waves the same auburn as mine. "This is too much."

Aimée blinks back tears, squares her shoulders as she leans on the register, and puts an arm around Madison. "She was our best friend. It's our duty to find out the truth about what happened to her." Her strong voice clashes with the pained expression she wears. She blots her eyes dry with her sleeve just before Madison looks up.

"But—" Madison sniffles. "How do we know it wasn't an accident? That's what you said yesterday. She was drunk and it was icy. An accident makes sense. Why couldn't it have been an accident?" She sounds like she's trying to convince herself.

"There's something off about that note, but the police ruled her death a suicide without doing an investigation." Aimée looks up at the ceiling. "I know this is a lot right now, and maybe no one else is involved, but I can't believe that note was meant as a goodbye. The police have to be misinterpreting it. And if we don't find out the real story behind it, they will file away her case for good. She'll become a statistic, a name used to warn kids not to drink by the river." She swallows down the tears thickening her voice. "I can't let that happen to her. I won't."

Tears roll down Aimée's cheeks. I reach out for her, but Madison hugs her before I can make the attempt. I'm happy they have each other, but I can't help feeling jealous, too. We're not a threesome anymore; they're a duo.

"That's not what I want either," Madison says softly.

"Then help me ask around. See if anyone talked to her while she was on the bridge, if they saw anything."

"Aimée, I—" Madison clamps her mouth shut. "I'm sorry. I want to help you, but . . . I need this whole thing to be over."

Aimée pushes off the register and starts digging in her messenger bag for something.

Madison watches her for a moment. She says, "I think I'm gonna go home early."

Aimée stops digging, clutching her red binder.

Madison pulls a tube of lip gloss from her pocket and hands it to Aimée. It's bubble gum, the only flavor Aimée hates more than my watermelon. She takes it without looking at Madison and rolls it over her dry lips.

"My dad's gonna have a big bowl of I-told-you-so waiting for me at home," Madison weakly tries to joke. "Are you staying?"

Aimée purses her newly glossed lips, hiding her disappointment in Madison's decision. "I think someone should."

12

AT LUNCH, our friends keep the conversation light and laugh extra-loud at anything Aimée says that could be considered remotely funny. They answer her questions about what the last thing I said to them was and how I seemed. Everyone falls for the mourning-best-friend-looking-for-closure act, but Aimée's perfect outfit and sleek French braid give her away to me. I notice the stiffness in her back and the intense look in her eyes as she scrutinizes each classmate who walks by. And, to be honest, I am now doing the same. She's not looking for closure. Not yet. Not until she gets the answers she's looking for.

"Aimée, hey." The girls at our table turn their attention to Mica, smiling and batting lashes at him. Except Kennedy Grange. Mica let her down easy last week after she broke up with her boyfriend for him, and, by the looks of it, she hasn't gotten over that yet.

Aimée narrows her eyes at him, studying his face. "Hi," she finally says, a careful smile inching up the corners of her mouth.

It's kind of impossible not to smile at Mica. Even when he was intimidating Caleb earlier he looked cheerful doing it. I have this theory that that's why he's such a good hockey player. The opposing team doesn't expect a baby-faced Hispanic kid to have such a fierce competitive streak.

"So you and Maddy came back today, huh?"

"Madison," Aimée and I correct, but Mica doesn't seem to notice. He watches her curiously, like there's a script to this conversation and she's gone off book.

"How you two holdin' up?" He looks past Aimée, probably expecting to see Madison sitting next to her, but she's not here. I am.

Aimée glances over her shoulder and gives herself a split second to fall apart. No one else sees it but me. No one senses how in-over-her-head she feels. I want to squeeze her in a hug and not let go until I'm real enough that she can feel it.

"Fine," she lies. "But I'm on my own this afternoon."

Drew walks up right when Aimée finishes. "What happened to Maddy?" He sounds concerned, but his expression looks annoyed.

"She wasn't feeling well," Aimée answers in the cold, vague way that we'd both taken to using with Drew. We had good reason. At least once a week I had to cancel on Ethan to comfort Madison when Drew stood her up. I seriously don't know why she puts up with it. She has one of those round cherubic faces that could land her a Neutrogena ad, curves that—despite what her mom thinks—work in her favor, and a social-butterfly personality. She could do much better than hot-one-day-cold-the-next Drew.

When the bell rings, Drew hurries out of the cafeteria with

his cell clasped in his palm, texting with his thumbs. Mica nods at Aimée and his mouth relaxes into the coy smirk he usually reserves for freshmen who still think it's worth detention to wear skirts that break dress code. He seems relieved they're alone.

"Walk ya to class?"

Aimée stands with her tray. "Listen, I don't have the energy to shoot you down today, Torrez. So let's skip to the part where you tell me I'm a tease and leave me alone."

"I'll carry your books for you," he offers. Aimée turns to him with a vicious glare. He holds up his hands. "Sorry. Most girls think that's sweet."

"Most girls lie to boys they're attracted to."

"So you're not attracted to me?" He smirks again.

"I'm not most girls."

Mica's eyebrows arch as he follows Aimée to the row of trash bins near the exit. "Aimée, come on, this isn't my usual flirting gig. You don't have to play tough. I know you don't want to be alone right now. Let me walk with you."

She pauses with her tray poised over the bin, deciding. "Have you talked to Ethan since the party?"

"Nope." The playboy shine disappears from his voice. He stares at Aimée with a look so full of unidentifiable meaning that I start to feel like I'm intruding on a private moment between the two of them. I guess I am. "Cassidy really did a number on him."

"It's not true about her committing suicide, and I intend to make sure everyone knows the truth."

"You know what that is?"

"Do you?"

126

Mica thinks a minute. "From where I was standing, she was unstable that night."

"That viewpoint wasn't on the covered bridge, now was it?"

"I was inside your house with Drew when she fell, if you're fishin' for my alibi."

"You offered that up pretty quickly."

"Always eager to please. Anything else you'd like from me?"

Aimée scrutinizes him with her eyes, then dumps her tray of uneaten chicken nuggets and leaves the cafeteria.

Mica doesn't follow. He stares down at his shoes, clenching and unclenching his fists until the second bell rings. After he leaves, the cafeteria clears out, but conversations still echo off the walls. *She was totally drunk . . . I heard she froze to death . . . Who kills herself over a breakup? I mean, really?*

I'm alone now in the center of the round room with the lies my classmates told like they were facts. I can't stay here. I need the comfort of my best friend even if she can't see me.

When I get to the gym, I pass through the girls' locker room to the mirrored exercise room where our dance class is warming up. I take a stance in my usual spot at the wall barre behind Aimée, in front of Madison's empty spot, and shadow her exercises through rond de jambe. At the beginning of the semester, I begged Aimée for the fiftieth time to sign up for dance with me and Madison. She'd finally caved despite her natural talent for tripping and falling over her own feet. Maybe it's my imagination, but she seems steadier than usual in her movements, her turn-out and form improved. I, on the other hand, feel like one of the hippos from *Fantasia*. The graceful ease I spent years in a dance studio perfecting seems to have escaped me.

The class moves to the center of the floor to practice arabesques, but I stay at the barre, stubbornly trying to revive what used to be second nature to me. It's not that easy with heels on. I try to convince myself that's why my feet feel like foreign objects, but I know it's simply one more *alive* thing that I've lost and desperately want back. I push down the rising chill of sadness inside me and will my limbs to respond, but I can't concentrate. My classmates' voices keep creeping back into my mind. After misstepping for the umpteenth time, frustrated not only by my lacking footwork but also by the skewed way my classmates think of me now, I stomp my foot into the wooden floor—and the room is suddenly empty.

Is class over already? How long has it been? I rush to the locker room and follow Aimée into the hall.

Her braid is still perfectly flyaway-free and her makeup is flawless. You'd never know she had just spent thirty minutes working out. She pushes open the exit door and snow breezes inside, dusting the speckled tile floor. She tightens her houndstooth scarf around her neck, ducks her head, and steps out into the cold.

"Hey again."

Aimée's head snaps up a second too late as she bumps into Mica, dropping her messenger bag in the process. "Sorry. I'm not usually this clumsy."

"Actually, you always are, Meems," I say, finally feeling a small bit of the comfort I expected from seeing her.

Mica picks up her bag and hands it to her with a smile. She snatches it away from him, clutching it to her chest. He chuckles. "You don't have to be embarrassed about falling all over me. I'm sure you must have used up your coordination in dance class."

"How did you know—" Aimée straightens her scarf, collecting herself. "What are you doing here?"

"I had conditioning with the rest of the team."

"Ah, yes. Varsity sports allows two hours of Phys Ed. I'm sure you boys are getting a stellar education with that rule in place."

Mica shrugs. "So are you going to let me walk you this time or do I have to start begging?"

Aimée takes a step back. "Stop it."

"Stop what?"

"Offering to walk me to class, flirting with me like this is any other ordinary day. I'm not in a fragile enough state that you can break me down and finally get me to agree to go out with you, so you can give it up."

Mica doesn't answer right away. "You honestly think I'm concerned about hooking up after what happened on Saturday night?" he asks.

"You told the police you were so drunk you didn't remember anything about Saturday night. Why so melancholy about it now?"

"How do you know what I told the cops?"

"Why haven't you answered my question?" Aimée retorts.

Mica starts cracking his knuckles one at a time. "Cassidy was my best friend's girl. No matter how much I drank that night, what happened to her got to me, a lot. It— I only want to make sure you're okay."

"Still breathing," Aimée says sardonically.

"Weird how that makes you feel like scum now, huh? Mrs. Fitz said that's called survivor guilt, or something."

Aimée asks, "You went to see the counselor?" Mica shrugs

with an uncharacteristic hint of self-consciousness in his dark eyes. Aimée's expression is unreadable for a moment. She's not giving anything away to him—or me. "At the party, where did you last see Cassidy?"

"Um, by the bonfire, I think," Mica answers in an unsure voice. "She told Drew and me that she was going to get a refill of her drink and never came back."

"How did she seem to you? Happy, depressed, distracted, stressed out?"

"She seemed drunk, Aimée," Mica admits. "Exactly like I was."

An image of my shaking hand wrapped around the neck of a bottle of peach schnapps, the bottle Madison said was found floating next to my body, the bottle whoever was on the bridge with me threw into the river, flashes behind my eyes. I was definitely drinking at the party, but was I drunk enough to forget everything that happened?

Aimée studies Mica's face for a second and then starts walking. She doesn't stop him when he falls in step beside her. "So," he starts, then he loses momentum.

Aimée sighs. "It's all right. No one knows what to say to me now. Let me fill in the blanks for you: You're very sorry; you want me to hang in there; and if there's anything you can do for me—"

"Pretty ballsy of you to come back so soon," Mica interrupts.

Aimée glances at him out of the corner of her eye. "Haven't gotten that one yet."

"Sorry." Mica shakes his head. "What I meant was, most people would be a wreck."

"I think we established in our last chat that I'm not most people," Aimée responds with a smirk that quickly falls, like it was too heavy for her to hold up. "I wasn't doing anyone any good sitting around at home. I function much better when I have a task to accomplish."

"Task?" Mica pinches the bottom snap on his varsity letterman jacket and snaps and unsnaps it a couple of times. "What, like homework?"

Aimée tugs on her scarf. "That would qualify."

Mica steps in front of her to open the door to the main building and pauses with his hand on the handle. "What are you doing after school today?"

I look in shock at Aimée. "Wow, he really has no shame, asking you out right now."

"Why?" She peers at him.

"Same reason I wanted to walk you to class," he says plainly.

Aimée thinks a minute. "Don't you have hockey practice?"

He shakes his head. "Got suspended from the team last week."

"What, too much time spent in the penalty box?"

"Yeah, actually. Guess I need to watch my temper." Mica bends down and tilts his head so he's looking right at Aimée. "How'd you know that?"

Aimée's pale cheeks flush. It's subtle, but I can see it in the awkward set of her shoulders: Aimée's flirting.

"What happened to 'I vow never to be a member of the Torrez Band of Skanks'?" I ask her, pulling a direct quote from the Book of Aimée. I know she won't answer, but I can't resist teasing.

"I pick up Cassidy's sister from figure skating on the days she has ballet." Aimée slaps a hand over her mouth like she's chiding herself for saying my name so casually. I want to tell her it's okay, but I know it's not, not to her. And she can't hear me anyway. "I used to," she corrects herself. "So I've seen the way you play."

Mica nods, looking equal parts proud and regretful. "The life of an enforcer."

"An enforcer?"

"That's what they call the guys who skate . . . defensively. Drew's my partner in crime."

"I bet he is," Aimée deadpans. "Doesn't that hurt your chances at landing a scholarship?"

Mica shrugs like it's no big deal, but everyone knows a hockey scholarship followed by fast-tracking to the NHL—preferably with a stone-cold puck bunny by his side—has always been Mica's dream. He'd do anything to achieve it.

"But colleges can't scout you if you're suspended, right?"

Mica shrugs again but doesn't answer. A quiet moment passes. "So are you free tonight?"

"I think I'm going to be booked up for a while."

"Gotcha," he concedes, starting to open the door, but he shuts it again. "Hey." Aimée looks up, curious. "Do you have your cell with you? I could give you my number, you know, in case one of us makes a fool of themselves in front of someone who's totally out of their league and needs to be talked down." He winks at her. "Not that that would ever happen to me or anything."

Aimée coughs to cover the tiny laugh that sneaks past her lips. I'm so relieved to see her smiling that I almost say yes for her.

"I don't bring my phone to school."

I eye the zipper pouch on the front of Aimée's messenger bag where I know she keeps her cell. She doesn't trust him, which makes me wonder whether I should.

"Well, to be safe." Mica grabs her hand as she opens the other door, the one he's not holding shut, and jots his number on her palm before she can pull it back.

Aimée yanks her hand away, but her lips are pressed together suppressing another smile. As soon as she's inside, Mica jogs off to whatever class he now has less than two minutes to get to.

I catch up to Aimée, and we walk side by side through the doorway to her Physics class. My right shoulder disappears into the door frame and reappears on the other side. Aimée glances at her palm as she takes her seat.

"Has Mica finally worn you down?" I hesitate next to her desk and scan the room, double-checking my invisibility. Everyone looks predictably bored. No one sees me. "Ethan's gonna flip when I tell—" I stop myself.

My instinct is to run a round of no ways with Ethan about our best friends' might-be romance, but once I see him I won't be able to pretend I didn't remember a potentially breakup-worthy incident with Caleb. It was near impossible for me to lie to Ethan when I was alive; there's no way I'm capable of such masterful posthumous deception.

I push my hands through my hair and sit on the corner of Aimée's desk. Her elbow pokes through my leg when she opens her red binder. I move closer to the edge because I can't handle a Casper moment right now. With one finger, she traces Mica's digits scrolled on her palm in his slanted print. He draws a line through his sevens the same way I do. She sets a pad of monogrammed stationery on top of her notes from last week and adds Mica's name to a short list of classmates, all of whom attended the party.

"This is your list of people you think might know something about my death, isn't it?" I ask her.

As I read the names, I think of Ethan in his bedroom. Alone. Even though I know what I'm in for when I see him, it remains the thing I want most. I feel it inside my chest where my heart used to beat—and still does when I'm with him.

I close my eyes and grasp at the tiny wisps of memories our relationship has been reduced to: his feet nestled between mine to keep me warm while we watched a movie on my couch, the way he always opened car doors for me, the feather-soft brush of his impossibly long eyelashes as he whispered my name in my ear. They seem so insignificant, ordinary, but I feel this desperation to hold on to them as tightly as I can or I'll disappear for real, forever.

When I open my eyes, I'm in Ethan's bedroom. I smile a little to myself for at last figuring out the ghost-a-porting thing. Evoke memories of the person I want to go to and *snap*, I'm wherever they are.

Yay me.

He's sitting at his desk again. He doesn't seem surprised to see me this time. Or happy.

"You're back." He sounds sad. I left him alone all day. I want to tell him why—that I couldn't face him after remembering being with Caleb—but I'm not sure yet if there's anything to tell.

"I was at school with Aimée and Madison. Aimée's convinced she can prove what really happened to me on the bridge. She has a list of people she thinks know something and—" I stop myself before mentioning he's one of Aimée's suspects. "I don't know. I thought they needed me."

"Did they?"

I don't answer right away. I'm not convinced there's anything I can do to help my friends. It's not like with Ethan. They can't see me or hear me. Everything I say and do merely filters through them. "I think I needed *them* more."

Ethan shifts his weight in his desk chair. "Maybe I should go back to school tomorrow so you can be with them *and* me. I missed you," he adds softly. "My parents got me excused from school until Friday, after the funeral"—he sucks in a deep breath—"but I could try to convince them to let me go back earlier."

"Do you want to go back to school?" I ask so I don't have to think about my funeral.

"I'd rather stay here with you."

I frown even though I'm happy to hear he wants to stay with me. It's getting hard to be around him with so many secrets between us.

He stands and walks to me. His fingers trace the curve of my mouth, until I can't help it anymore: I smile.

He smiles too. "I'm grateful you came back." *Grateful?* That's an odd word for him to use; it makes it sound like he asked for me back. He tilts my chin with two fingers so that we're at the same level and adds, "Gives us a fresh start."

I purposely avoid his eyes because even though I want a fresh start so badly I can feel it in my nonexistent bones, the only reason we would need it is that the first go at us went tragically wrong.

"This is probably a dumb question to ask," he starts, "but is something bothering you?"

There are countless things bothering me, but I decide to divulge the one that started the derailment of my life.

"I went to see my parents last night."

"That's good. Or not?" he amends after studying my expression.

I shake my head. "They were fighting."

"By fighting, you mean?"

"Arguing," I say in a rush. "They do that a lot."

"They do?" Ethan asks, surprised. "How long has that been going on?"

I take a minute before answering, "A couple months, I guess, but it got worse around my birthday."

Ethan rubs the back of his neck. "Wow, I can't believe they were acting like that on your birthday. That's, well, incredibly selfish. Is that why you didn't invite me over for your birthday dinner?"

I recoil from his comment, ignoring his question. "It's not about them being selfish, Ethan."

"That came out wrong." He holds up his hand. "Sorry. So, a couple months?" His concerned expression morphs into something else, something pained. "That's a long time. Why didn't you tell me?"

I chew on my lip, trying to find the right words. "I was worried you wouldn't understand, that you would see me differently if you knew."

"You honestly thought I would judge you that way? Because of your family?" His face screws up as he stares at me in wounded disbelief.

"Well, you sort of did a couple seconds ago."

"But I wasn't judging you."

"What, just my parents then?"

"No," he says in a less-than-convincing tone. "I just—"

"Don't have any clue what this has been like for me," I finish for him.

"Because you didn't tell me about it."

"How could I?" I retort. "Lately it feels like . . ."

My voice trails off, and his is a low murmur when he says, "Cassi, where is this coming from?" He squints at me, confused. "Cassi?"

I open my mouth to answer him, but my voice is lost even to me, floating beyond my range of hearing.

No! I don't want to remember anything else.

My hair melts into watery streamers, flowing off my shoulders and chest. I'm blinded by the glittering waterfalls until there's nothing left of me, and I'm gone again.

THE OTHER GUY

MY PUMAS WERE SOAKED through to my socks. The brown-and-purple suede looked almost black as I shook off a chunk of slush clinging to the toe. "This is ridiculous."

"Tell me about it," Caleb mumbled.

"I mean, if it's going to snow then snow. Enough of this melty-slush crap. The bottoms of my jeans are *always* wet and now my feet are icicles." I leaned back in the Adirondack chair on his mom's screened-in porch and showed him my wet shoes.

"Oh, that." He got up from the chair beside me. "Yeah, it's too warm for the snow to stick, I guess. But if you're cold, we can go inside."

"What did you think I was talking about?" I asked.

"Huh?"

"I said 'this is ridiculous' and you were with me, then I brought up the weather and you were all lost guy."

He sighed. "I'm cold too. You wanna go inside?"

"Isn't your brother home?"

Caleb's voice lowered. "What does that matter?"

"It doesn't," I backpedaled. "I just, I can't go home smelling like a hookah den again. My dad's going to start leaving those pictures of diseased lungs on the refrigerator soon."

"Then let's go to your house. Your parents don't get home from work for a while, right?"

"It's my birthday, remember? They'll be home early." I paused. "My mom's been staying at my aunt's house, but they agreed to spend my big one-seven together." I don't know why I kept dumping my familial dirty laundry on him. I guess I had to tell *someone*, and it seemed like he understood in a way my friends, with their perfect families, wouldn't be able to. "Plus, they'll no doubt be competing for my love with elaborate gifts that I'll have no choice but to resent. Can't miss out on that."

"Speaking of, I made you a little somethin' somethin'." He reached into his bright orange backpack and pulled out a brownie wrapped in pink cellophane and about ten different colors of ribbon.

"Caleb, you didn't have to do this."

"I wanted to give you something *special* to celebrate your birth."

I gave him a sideways look. "Is this . . . ?"

"You might want to eat only half since your tolerance is right around zero."

My mouth dropped open. "I'm not getting high with you. It's a school night," I added in an admittedly goody-goody tone.

He chuckled. "I know it's not your thing, but I thought it might help . . ." He stopped to scratch his head. "Never mind."

I twisted the curlicued ribbons around my fingers, thinking

about what Aimée would say if she knew I was considering sampling psychotropic baked goods. Then I thought how awkward and fake and unhappy my birthday would become as soon as I got home. I unwrapped a corner of the brownie and took a bite.

Caleb grinned when I offered him the rest. He finished it in two bites. "Y'know, living in a house with only one parental unit has its advantages. Certain freedoms." He pulled out a cigarette and lit it with a flourish.

I knew he was trying to make me feel better about my family falling apart, but his blasé attitude made my throat tighten. He must have noticed how uncomfortable I was because his expression changed and he snuffed out his cigarette in the ceramic candy dish he'd brought up from the basement to use as an ashtray. Our first-grade class made them as Father's Day gifts at the end of that school year.

"I can't believe you still have that." I pointed at the crudely formed heart, wondering why it was at his mom's house and not his dad's.

"I've learned to hold on to what I can."

My brain started swimming with images of Caleb holding on to every single childhood memento he owned like they were balloon strings in a windstorm.

"The idea of it sucks," he started again, snapping my mind back to reality. "Your parents don't love each other anymore, which makes you wonder if they could stop loving you too someday."

"Yes," I blurted, immediately feeling self-conscious about agreeing with him, followed by an intense urge to laugh.

He gave me a nod of commiseration and continued in this

voice that made my drug-induced giggles subside. "It took my friends ten days to stop inviting me for dinner and sleepovers like my house was the site of a bacterial outbreak. So you're probably looking at a full month." He picked up his cigarette like he was going to relight it, but smashed it into the dish. "My friends are emotionally inept."

"I haven't told—"

"Ethan?" I drew back at the way Ethan's name sounded coming from Caleb's smooth monotone.

I could almost see the letters disassembling as they rolled out of his mouth. E . . . t . . . h . . . a . . . n . . .

I blinked the image away and corrected him. "Anyone really. Especially Ethan. His family is *Brady Bunch* perfect. He wouldn't understand."

The quiet hum that only sounds in early spring filled the porch. It surrounded me like a fluffy white-noise blanket. I was perfectly content with letting it cloud my mind because I didn't want to think about my parents anymore and Caleb was one of the few people I knew that I could simply sit with, not having to fill the silence. He'd always been like that, even when we were little. I kicked at the pile of melting slush dampening the porch floor, wondering what he was thinking.

As if reading my mind he asked, "What are we?"

"Uh, humans?" I gave him a smile to cover the way I'd startled at his question. The look he gave me made my smile wither.

"Us." He ticked his finger between my chair and where he stood, leaning against the screen door. "Me and you. What are we?"

"Caleb." I turned my face away. I couldn't say what we were

because once someone said it out loud it would be real. I would be cheating on Ethan and there would be no going back. "Can't we, I don't know, hang out and not label this, or whatever?" I felt like the guy in this situation. I guess that made him the girl. I'd never been *that* girl, but Aimée had and Madison perpetually was. I understood how it felt. It was crappy. "I like you, but—"

"But you have to leave by five o'clock and I can't say hi to you at school."

"I never said you couldn't say hi to me." I jumped as my phone vibrated in my pocket. Pulling it out, I had to blink my slow-focusing eyes to see that I had three texts from Ethan. He wanted to know if my birthday dinner was still on.

I sighed. I'd been trying to figure out a way to politely uninvite him without mentioning my family drama for days, and now I was out of time.

Caleb waited until I looked at him. His face was as sober as I abruptly felt. "I'm not going to be the other guy, Cassidy. Not anymore. It was fine when we first started chillin' again. A couple kisses between old friends, I get that. But what we have now goes deeper than friends and you have a boyfriend. So what are we?" His voice sounded mechanical, like he'd rehearsed this speech before I showed up, like this was the hardest thing he'd ever had to say to anyone.

I tried to pull my eyes away, but his were like magnets holding me in their gaze, screaming *Answer me!*

I swallowed hard. "I don't know."

He looked at me expectantly.

"You want me to choose between you two?"

He put his hands in his jeans pockets and nodded once.

"Caleb, you know my choice. It's Ethan."

"Is it?"

"Of course."

His brown eyes flickered with an emotion I couldn't read. "Then why have you been skipping ballet to come here? And why do you slide me a secret smile every time we pass in the halls? You could be texting him back, but you're here *with me*." He exhaled a long breath and dropped his mechanical tone. "Why did you say yes to partnering with me for Wirlkee's class?"

"Because!" I stood, my toes digging into the soggy soles of my shoes. The fluffy haze from the brownie drained from my brain, leaving behind a sharp ache. "I said yes because everyone thinks you're this pothead loser and I know that's not you—not the real you. I thought you had changed when your parents split up and you started getting high all the time, but you didn't, and I feel awful for not being your friend when you needed me most. And I come here because—"

"Cassidy." He pushed off the door and walked toward me.

I held my hands up. "No. Let me finish." He stopped a foot away from me. My heart was beating so fast and hard I thought for sure he could hear it. I couldn't decide if the rise in my blood pressure was the brownie or nerves. "I come here because everything with my parents . . . you get it in a way no one else does."

"It isn't your fault we stopped being friends. I did more than my share to make that happen."

My mouth opened to tell him that even though he understood what I was going through, I couldn't be this person. I couldn't use him and hurt everyone else in the process. I didn't want to be this new liar-me anymore. But before I could say a word of that, my mouth closed around his and my arms dropped and he pulled me closer and I let him.

When he finally stopped kissing me, he whispered, "You're a good friend."

I meant to frown at him, but I smiled instead. "I thought you said we weren't friends anymore."

He let out a short laugh and bent down for another kiss. I closed my eyes and wondered how much longer I could keep this up, *why* I was keeping this up.

"You have to make a choice, Cassidy." His lips were soft against mine as he spoke, but his voice hardened. "I won't let you get away without making the right one."

13

I'M FROZEN IN PLACE EVEN though the memory has faded. I don't try to abate the sting attacking every inch of me because I deserve the pain. I kissed someone who wasn't Ethan—had been kissing him for three whole weeks. I can't hide this from him. I have no idea how I rationalized hiding it—or doing it!—when I was alive, but now that I'm, well, not, it seems utterly impossible.

The events of that day—my last ever birthday—are hazy and slow. Shaw had hurried home after his last class of the week for dinner, and he and Joules hung streamers across the archway into the living room. I remember feeling bad for making him wait to see me because I was late for dinner. They'd held off eating; the veggie lasagna was cold and the ice cream cake puddled around the edges of my dessert plate like a mint-green moat while Mom asked me over and over why I was being so quiet. I wish there was a dial I could adjust to bring things into focus.

I blink my eyes a few times and see Ethan sitting cross-legged in his desk chair, right where I left him. When he pushes his hand through his unwashed but still completely adorable spiky hair and rubs the back of his neck the way he always does when he sees me walking toward him between classes, I know I have no choice. I have to tell him. Besides, what's the worst that can happen? I'm already dead.

He uncrosses his legs and leans toward me. My resolve to tell the truth cracks around the edges.

"Ethan," I start. This is the part where I would take a deep breath if I were alive. But I'm not, and right about now, that police ruling on my death sounds pretty accurate. If I'd felt this deplorable on Saturday, I might have jumped. Maybe after I tell him I'll be gone for good. Maybe this is what I'm back to do: to tell Ethan the truth. I push forward before the consequences of that possibility can sink in.

"I have to tell you something," I start again.

"You already told me about your parents. Do you remember?"

I don't answer.

He rolls across the room in his desk chair and pulls me closer so I'm standing between his legs with his arms warm around my waist. "You're upset, I know. I'm sorry about what I said about your mom and dad. You're right, I don't know what it's like to have parents who fight, but—"

I interrupt him. "Ethan, that's not it." Closing my eyes, I press my hand over the spot where my horseshoe necklace rests on my chest. "I . . . I lied to you."

He drops his arms and waits for me to continue. The warmth from his touch slowly wicks away, leaving me cold and exposed.

"Do you remember our first kiss?" The words are out before

I know I'm speaking. Ethan nods slowly. "That was *my* first kiss. I told you it wasn't, but I lied."

He leans back so I can see his confused face. "Why are you telling me this?"

I hold my tongue even though I know exactly why I told him. I told him because I feel like I need to rectify every lie I've ever breathed. Even more, I want him to think back to that kiss on the covered bridge the summer before our freshman year and remember how we've been together ever since and realize that if he was my first kiss it means he was my only kiss. Ever. I want him to believe it no matter what it costs. I want that to be the one memory about me he never forgets his entire life and after. Even if it's not true.

"I know," he says.

"But how?"

"I know your tell, Cassi." He tugs on my bottom lip and offers me a small smile, then twines his fingers between mine. We both sigh at the rush of heat. "I was on my way to scrape together a late lunch. Want to come?"

I'm a little embarrassed to admit I don't eat anymore, so I nod instead.

From my perch on his kitchen counter, I watch him pour a bowl of Froot Loops. It's the closest thing to a multiple-food-group meal I've seen him eat in days. I keep trying to find lulls in his activity so I can tell him about Caleb, but there's a lightness to his movements that I haven't seen since before the party and he keeps smiling at me.

How am I going to do this?

He sets his bowl next to my crisscrossed legs and scoops up a bite. He hesitates between spoonfuls, lost in some thought I don't try to figure out because I'm lost in him. I'm lost in the deepness of his eyes, the natural shine of his golden-brown hair, the casual slant of his hips as he stands in front of me.

It's easy to get used to a beautiful painting hanging in a hallway after you've walked by it a few hundred times. The colors lose their vibrancy and the impact of the composition lessens, but I never thought that could be true for a person. Looking at him now, noticing how smooth his jawline is and how perfectly balanced his height is with his sort of smallish muscles that you wouldn't notice unless you were lucky enough to touch his arms or chest, I realize I let myself get used to his beauty. I was the lucky one, and I let myself forget.

I can't tell him.

I've already put him through so much, dying and coming back and all, and he finally seems comfortable with Ghost Me. Telling him would make things so much worse. And I would lose him all over again. A sharp stab of absolute terror cuts through me. I reach out for him, afraid he's already vanished.

Every time we touch, it's still this astonishing event. For a split second before I make contact, I always worry I'll melt right through him. I hesitate inches from his chest with my fingers spread wide. I glance up at his face to see if he notices how I've moved. He doesn't at first, but the second our eyes lock his back stiffens. I'm full of anticipation and fear and about a million other feelings I can't concentrate on because I can hear his heart beating through his thin T-shirt. He's holding his breath, but I can feel the slight rise and fall of his chest under the spot where my palm presses against his warm flesh.

He exhales the breath he was holding, and I breathe in his sweet air—really breathe it. The sensation tingles up my neck, out through my veins, to my arms and legs. I dig my fingertips into his muscles, double-checking that I don't slide through. I can feel my bones solidifying as he encircles me in his arms.

Behind my eyes, I see the time he hugged me in the center of the bleachers at the first football game of freshman year. That was always my favorite hug anyone had ever given me. It was before we were technically together but after our first kiss on the covered bridge. The giddy rush I felt when he picked me up and spun me around while the whole school watched was exactly how I wished every hug I received from that point on would feel.

This is so much better.

Too soon Ethan releases me, but he keeps hold of my hands. We both stare at my pearlescent skin against his. The way it glints in the sinking afternoon sun streaming in through the window makes the moment seem even more unbelievable.

Ethan tilts his head, looks down at me, and says through a crooked smile, "I don't think I'll ever get used to this."

A smile breaks across my face, too. This is us—how we're supposed to be, or as close as I can hope to get now. I can't lose it. No matter what.

I twist my fingers in his unstyled hair. It's incredibly soft without the pomade he usually puts in it to keep his bangs spiked.

"How hard is that for you to do?" he asks.

"What, this?" I comb my fingers deeper through his hair. "Not one bit. I don't even have to try." I give his sideburns a little tweak before pulling my hand back.

"That's good. That means you have the ability to touch things."

149

I shake my head. "Not things, *you*."

He lets go of my other hand and holds up his cereal bowl. "Wanna try to put this in the sink for me?" I give him a skeptical look, and he nods. "Too soon." He sets the bowl in the sink and offers me his hand.

I don't take it right away. I'm almost certain I'll never be able to open doors or hold a cereal bowl ever again, but he seems so excited by the prospect. It's enough for me to simply graze my fingertips along the back of his hand. When his fingers lace with mine, I wonder if I'll ever get used to the new heat of his skin against mine; if time will desensitize me again; if I'll have enough time in this afterlife to find out.

I float down from the counter and change the subject. "So we have another hour before your parents get home from work. What should we do?"

"That's probably one of the only advantages to our . . . arrangement. It doesn't matter when my parents come home. They can't see you."

"Yeah, but what are they going to say when they see you talking to appliances?" I gesture to the toaster sitting on the counter behind me.

He smiles a wry smile. "I think they'll give me some leeway for grieving. I should be able to get away with acting mental for a couple more weeks, at least."

I slip my hand out of his and fold my arms over my chest. "I'm making this harder for you, aren't I? It was bad enough that I—" He jumps in before I can finish.

"The first day . . . I didn't think it could get any harder. And then I saw you in my room that morning and I thought I'd dreamed you, but it felt so real." He pauses. "That was worse. Having you back for only a moment, then losing you again."

I look away from him. No matter how any of this turns out, I fear that exact thing will happen: he will lose me again. He smooths his fingertips across my cheekbone and my head lifts like he's drawn me up to him.

"But I have you back now."

"For how long?" I ask despite myself. "Neither of us knows what the rules are here, how much time I get. But even if I have forever, it's going to get real weird real fast being with someone nobody else can see." Ethan tries to interject, but I press forward. "Think about it. You'll be showing up at parties and tailgates and prom *alone*." I make finger quotes around the last word. "Eventually you're going to want a *real* girlfriend."

"You are real," Ethan says adamantly. I start to shake my head, but he presses a hand on either side of my face. "I can feel you and see you and smell you."

My expression softens. "Really? You can still smell me?" He nods. "I can't . . . not anymore." He doesn't say anything. "Do I smell different now?"

He smiles to himself. "It's you after you get out of your pool and the chlorine's worn off and you're wet and clean and the flowery smell from your shampoo and lotion is gone." He tucks my hair behind my ear and inhales. "It's you. Completely, purely you."

The only response I can muster is, "Oh." How did I ever take him for granted? Never again.

"That's how I knew you were real," he continues. "I could never mistake your scent." He looks down at my feet, positioned in a wide V, and smirks. "And that goofy ballet stance didn't hurt either."

I give him a playful shove.

"I have an idea for what we can do while we still have the house to ourselves," Ethan says with an excited grin. He looks over his shoulder and does one of those two-fingered whistles I've always wanted to be able to do. Wendell comes trotting up from the basement.

"Ethan, I've already tried to pet Wendell. It didn't work." I give the dog an apologetic smile. He shakes his head, leaving one ear flopped the wrong way.

"That's not what I'm using him for." He points to the front door and Wendell launches into full retriever mode. "Stand guard, Wend." Wendell obediently sits on the welcome mat, staring at the door.

I watch his bushy tail swish from side to side, remembering how geeked up the dog gets when Mr. Keys comes home from work. It's the only time he barks. "Okay. So whatever it is, you need a lookout to let you know when we're not alone anymore."

He nods but doesn't give anything else away. "Do you remember what we did the first time we were alone?"

"You mean like on a date?"

"No, like with no one else around."

My forehead scrunches up as I try to remember. I think I know, but it can't be what he has in mind.

"Mrs. Dunam's English block in eighth grade." I was right. "She was always late for class for some random reason."

"She smoked between classes in her car," I inform him.

"Seriously?" He laughs.

I nod. "I saw her once when my dad came to pick me up for a dentist appointment."

"Huh." He shakes his head. "Anyway, I was always early because my Social Studies class was right next door and you were early that day because you said you hadn't finished the homework, so I gave you mine to copy and you wouldn't use it."

"I didn't say no," I correct him, trying to figure out where he's going with this.

"Yeah, you took it, but it sat on your desk while you filled in your own answers and you never looked at it once."

I let out a short laugh. "How do you know that?"

"I thought you didn't like me or that you thought I was too dumb to copy off or something."

"I just didn't want to cheat." The word stretches between us, pushing us apart.

Cheeeeeat.

"So I did homework," I say to fill the gap, "and you watched me so we . . . ?"

"That's not the part I'm thinking about." I wave my hand for him to go on. "You changed two of my answers to make them correct."

"No, I didn't." He points at my face when the corner of my mouth twitches at the lie. "I thought I never looked at your paper."

He starts down the back hall, towing me by the hand. I feel unbelievably light knowing he can take my hand on a whim like that. "Before you handed in our assignments you pretended mine was yours and made the changes right on Mrs. Dunam's desk. It surprised me because you're usually such a terrible liar, but you made the changes pretty slyly."

"How did you know I was a bad liar? We didn't even talk back then."

He shrugs. "You pretended not to know the answers to a couple of Dunam's questions that week."

Luke Newman sat next to me that semester and soon became my "boyfriend," whatever that means in eighth grade. He was the first boy who said hi to me that wasn't a friend of a friend or knew my brother, so I said yes when he so eloquently asked me if he could tell his friends we were going out. I didn't want him to think I was a brain because I'd seen his less-than-stellar test scores, so I dumbed myself down in class. It was stupid. We broke up two weeks later.

Ethan stops in front of the den and turns to face me. "I told my friends I was going to ask you to the spring dance after that, but I knew you were on the dance team and I wasn't exactly light on my feet."

I cross my arms. Ethan is an awesome dancer and he never asked me to the eighth-grade dance. "None of this happened," I protest. There's a giggle in my voice from the walk down *happy* memory lane.

"It did," he says emphatically. "I didn't want to make a fool of myself so I took lessons from a friend of my mom's, but you already had a date by the time I was ready to ask you."

Stupid Luke Newman.

"So why didn't you cut in at the dance? I would've said yes."

"I didn't go." He has this look in his eyes like he wants to tell me something more, but the words won't come. I look down at our joined hands and try to remember what the answers were to the questions on that homework that I changed for him.

After a long minute he says, "Let's dance."

I laugh a little and look behind me down the hall to make sure Wendell is still on watch. Ethan's parents walking in on a seemingly solo slow dance would be beyond awkward. He lets go of my hand as he steps into the den and sifts through the vinyl collection stacked next to his dad's old record player.

John Lennon's raspy coo fills the room and after the first couple of lines a sweet harmony of voices joins him, accompanied by a laid-back drumbeat that triggers my memory.

"Remember this song?" Ethan asks.

"I remember you almost getting us kicked out of homecoming when the DJ refused to play it."

"I learned a whole routine to this song and I never got to use it."

As I stare at his outstretched hand a cloud passes in front of the sun, changing the light in the room from whitish yellow to gray. My skin goes cold. I have this vision of stepping onto the taupe carpet and turning around to a bricked-over doorway. No Ethan. No second chance.

He must sense my reluctance because he replaces the cover on the player and walks to me. "Dance with me?" He extends his hand with a slight bow like men do in old black-and-white movies. I lift my hand, then pull it back. "What's wrong?"

"I . . ." *I'm still terrified I might fall right through your arms, this moment, because I don't deserve you after what I did.*

Ethan takes hold of my right hand. He places his other hand low on my waist and my doubts float away. His feet step in perfect time with the music, guiding me in a loose box step. I think if I close my eyes it might feel like the last time I danced with him, before paper airplanes and basements and éclairs. So I do. I close my eyes and pretend I'm back there, but my muscles don't respond as effortlessly to music as they used to. When I rise up on my toes to pivot at the corners of his box step, my right shoulder drops, throwing off my balance, and I wobble on unsteady ankles. I grit my teeth at the unsettling feeling of being uncoordinated. It's an unwelcome reminder that *dancer* is on the depressingly long list of things I can no longer call myself. Along with *alive*.

"There are things I don't remember." Ethan's warm breath against my neck pulls me back. "Little details that sorta seemed insignificant at the time, but now I can't stop thinking about them." He lifts my arm and dips me backward.

I lean into his hand a little longer than necessary and hope he notices. I hope he feels how much I want to be here with him and no one else. Ever.

"Like the color of those striped shorts you wore the day I got my car," he continues.

"They were blue," I say.

"That's right." He leans away from me only far enough so that I can see his face. "The blue matched your eyes." He searches my face as if the color has leaked away and spilled across my cheeks.

"Are they still the same color?" I ask, suddenly nervous. "My eyes?" I glance down at my auburn hair grazing my shoulders. It hasn't changed color, but my skin has and maybe other things have too.

He locks my gaze. "Yes. They look exactly the same. Nothing has changed." He says it in a way that sounds like he wishes something had. "Cassi, I really am sorry about your parents."

"I know," I say definitively, truncating that line of conversation before it spoils this moment. "I remember the little moments," I continue. "It's the big ones that trip me up now."

Neither of us says anything for a long time. It's like the memories are so far off that they belong to two different people.

In the quiet, my thoughts drift back to my birthday party, trying to connect the bits of memory I have. I know Caleb was there, and that same week he made it very clear he wanted me to choose him over Ethan. Could he have been the person drinking schnapps with me on the bridge?

"Do you think the police are wrong about how I died?" I whisper to Ethan, thinking of Caleb and the silhouette standing over Other Me in the park.

Ethan's feet stop moving, but his hands stay on me. "Do you?"

"I know I didn't jump—*I know it*—but I've never heard a ghost story about a person who died accidentally. And I know I wasn't alone on the bridge."

"But you can't remember who you were with?"

I shake my head. "It's hazy. I can't see his face."

Ethan's forehead wrinkles. "His? You know it was a guy? Do you have *any* idea who it could've been?"

If I tell him I think I was with Caleb he'll definitely ask why. I'm not ready to go there with him. It'll ruin the small piece of us we've recaptured, and I can't bear losing that again.

Instead I say, "I know there has to be more to it than that I slipped."

14

WENDELL'S RAMBUNCTIOUS BARKING cuts through the silence right when Ethan opens his mouth to say something. He starts again, but the sound of the front door opening stops him. He steps around me to leave the den.

I follow close enough behind that I catch a glimpse of Mr. Keys hanging his coat in the front closet. He looks so much like Ethan. I've always been fascinated by the resemblance. It's like looking into a crystal ball at future Ethan. I used to imagine what I would look like at forty to see if we'd make as cute a middle-aged couple as we did high school sweethearts. I turn away so my thoughts won't veer down that never-to-be-traveled path.

When I get to Ethan's bedroom, the door is shut so I have to pass through it. Beautifully depressing music fills the room, and he's lying on his bed facing the wall. There's an inexplicable thickness in the air that keeps me standing in the middle of the room instead of next to him. It presses down on me. Makes me feel more real somehow.

I look at a picture of us that's taped to the square mirror hanging above his dresser. It's from last summer and I'm wearing those blue shorts Ethan talked about. My gaze wanders to my wispy reflection in the mirror. It's a pale shadow where a solid face should be. I lift my fingers to my face in the picture and trace the lines. I know the angle of my cheekbones and my small Haines button nose that both my brother and sister also have. The sharp arch of my eyebrows, the curve of my fullish lips, the violet flecks in my blue eyes, everything is perfectly preserved in my memory. Ethan was right; the sapphire color of every other narrow stripe in those shorts could've been sampled straight from my eyes. It's 100 percent me, but somehow me doesn't fit anymore.

Ethan's dad comes down to check on him, but he pretends to be asleep when Mr. Keys says his name.

After the door shuts, Ethan breaks the few seconds of silence between songs. "Sorry I shut the door on you. My dad," he explains.

I nod even though he's still facing the wall and I'm still staring at the Ghost Me that I can hardly see in the mirror.

He asks quietly, "How did it happen?"

"What?" I spin around to face him.

"On the bridge. You said you didn't slip."

"I don't know," I say slowly, trying to shake this eerie detached feeling.

"But you know it wasn't . . ." He doesn't say the word—suicide—and I'm glad of that.

"I only remember I wasn't alone." I take a minute to work up the courage to ask my next question, but my voice still shakes when it comes out. "Was I with you?"

Ethan presses his palms to his temples. "Drew told me where you were."

"Drew knew . . . and you were there?" Suspicion stirs my insides as Aimée's list appears behind my eyes, Ethan's name at the top. It feels acidy and wrong.

Ethan's voice is rigid. "We talked on the bridge. It was quick. I left, but you stayed."

"Why did you keep this from me?" I ask. He doesn't answer. "Why did you leave me there? What happened?"

He bends his legs up to his chest, braces his forearms on his knees, and drops his head.

"This is huge, Ethan. I can't remember anything and you were there? You have to tell me *something*."

"I wasn't—"

There's a knock on his door. "Ethan, sweetie?"

I ask him, "You weren't what?"

Ethan looks at the door. "I'm sleeping, Mom."

"I got off work early so you, me, and Dad could spend some time together."

"You have to tell me," I say again, unfazed by the proximity of his mom.

"I'd rather be alone," Ethan tells her while glancing at me.

"I know, sweetie, but I was hoping . . ." There's a long pause. "May I come in?"

Ethan locks eyes with me. When he doesn't answer, his mom opens the door. "Ethan?"

He releases a resigned breath. "You can come in, Mom."

She smiles and gives the room a quick Mom scan as she makes her way to his bed, tossing T-shirts in the laundry bin next to

Ethan's closet. I have this irrational urge to duck and hide—we're not allowed in his bedroom alone—but, of course, she doesn't see me.

She sits on the edge of his bed and pats his knee. "How was your day?" Her voice is so tender I don't know how he doesn't break down and tell her that I'm standing right next to her. "Did you make sure to eat a good lunch? There were leftovers in the fridge." Her lips press together as she joins him in silence.

There's no way I'm going to get any answers out of him with her here, and the helplessness in her expression reminds me too much of my brother and my parents.

"Ethan, you need to talk to her." He starts at the sound of my voice. His eyes dart to his mom, but her head is down and she's still patting his knee. "She's so worried about you."

He shakes his head almost imperceptibly. I move toward the door, making the decision for him.

"I'm going to leave." It sounds so normal saying that, like I merely stopped by to hang out and it's dinnertime. Except Mrs. Keys doesn't twinkle her fingers at me as she would if she could see me and there's no goodbye kiss from Ethan.

I step into the main room of the basement, thankful that she left the door open so Ethan won't have to watch me freakishly ghost through it. There's something materially different about the world outside his bedroom. Colors translate into shades of gray. The air is so much thinner that I can feel it slipping past me, gliding across my face like a remnant of silk. The differences intensify the farther away I get from Ethan.

I don't go home even though the idea of curling up next to Joules on the couch while she multitasks her way through cartoons, homework, and stretches is tempting. The beating in my chest draws me someplace else. I trudge an invisible path through the snow-covered woods that border Dover Park and end up in the only place that holds any hope of the answers to my questions, the questions Ethan was so hesitant to address.

I stare at the covered bridge, examine every inch of it. Every cracked plank of old dried wood, every fleck of chipped white paint on the exterior. Beyond that I try to *feel* this place. Something as severe as death should leave its mark; somehow I know this.

Death isn't what I sense though. The conflicted emotions trapped under the trusses are as alive as the fiery orange highlights streaking the violet sky. There's life in their silent invasion, not death. With each new emotion an image flashes behind my eyes. Temptation: a bare hand on my neck. Betrayal: shadows retreating across Aimée's backyard. Confusion: the heel of my Mary Janes lodged in a splintered piece of wood. Anger: eyes I can't place glaring at me. They're flat and dark and furious. With me.

I cover my face with my hands and curl into a tiny ball in the center of the bridge, rocking back and forth. I want to erase those eyes from my memory, but something tells me they're part of me, a part I can't rub out.

The bridge creaks the way it does in the wind. I concentrate on the sound, focus on the subtle swaying, try to match it to the shallow pulsing in my chest that led me here. When the board underneath me moves, I jerk out of my crouched position, whip around to see who's here, and end up smashing right into my sister—literally. My arms dissolve through her chest and appear out her back with a swirl of shimmery dust. I wince as the tiny wisps of me settle back into two "solid" limbs.

I feel snow on my face, resting on my cheeks, piling up so thick on my lashes that I have to blink. I'm sure I'll be pulled into another memory, but something keeps me here.

Joules sets her skate bag down and wraps her arms tight around her stomach. Not because she's cold—she has figure skater blood—but to ward off tears. She thinks it makes her look tough, but when she does it her bottom lip pouts out—always—and any hope she had of looking formidable is lost. Always, even here, alone, she's determined to act strong.

She's supposed to be at the ice rink. Her teammates and coach must think she's too grief-stricken to practice. She is. She just doesn't know it.

I stumble the rest of the way through her—cringing at the prickling pain—and watch her. She stands staring downriver from the opposite side of the bridge. She starts to glance over her shoulder to see where I fell but turns back before her peripheral can catch the broken railing next to me.

Suddenly she yells, "Goddamnit!" and I jump about a foot I'm so taken aback.

I have never heard my little sister swear. She says things like "bite me" and "forget you" with enough venom to get her point across, but she's ten. Ten-year-olds don't swear.

She continues through the alphabet like she's running down some vulgar list. Then she drops the big one: an f-bomb. And she yells it so loud that it reverberates off the roof.

I slap my hand over my mouth, stifling a laugh. It's so unexpected that I can't help myself. On top of the humor, I thought this would be a moment I would never get to experience. I'm so inexplicably elated to hear my little sister say the f-word that I could burst.

When she turns toward me, the last of my giggles tapers off. The humor is gone. Her blue eyes are rimmed in red. I can't believe I laughed at her—no, *with* her. If she knew I was here, she would've laughed too.

"This sucks," she says, kicking her skate bag. A metallic *clank* sounds from inside the black canvas, blades knocking together. As if the sun agrees, it sinks below the horizon at that exact moment, trading twilight for darkness. In a few hours the third day of my surreal afterlife will be over.

The spotlight at the end of the bridge that butts up to the Coutiers' property casts an unnatural white glow that only illuminates a fourth of the span. It's dark in the middle where Joules and I stand. Too dark. I'm glad she's not out here alone, but then again, she doesn't know she's not alone. And what could I do to help if something bad happened? It's an uncharacteristic risk for her to take. She probably had to guilt-trip Dad to get permission to go back to practice so soon. Then she walked halfway across town with her wrap skirt hanging over her warm-up pants, lugging her skates, to come to the bridge and stand in the cold and scream obscenities.

"It was stupid to come here." She says it very grownup-like, except for the "stupid." That part is said with a trademark stomp of her foot. She's always been a champ about taking crap for being the youngest because, in many ways, she's more mature than me or Shaw, but that stomp nullifies any maturity she's earned.

"Yes, it was," I tell her. "Mom and Dad are going to erupt when they find out you lied and ditched on practice to walk here of all places." It dawns on me that she came here like this—alone and without permission—on purpose, not only to vent some verbal anger, but to cause a distraction.

She's used this tactic before, whenever Shaw or I got caught breaking curfew or taking the car without permission. The discussion about punishment would inevitably lead to Mom and Dad screaming at each other about conflicting parenting styles, and Mom would segue into "This is why I need my nights away." At that point, Joules would do something off-the-wall like walk across Mom's Persian rug in the living room with her skates on, guards off. Damage would be minimal, but my parents would be so distracted that the argument would fizzle.

Mom and Dad must be fighting again.

A shift in the shadows pulls my attention to the broken portion of the bridge. In the distance I see an elongation of darkness spilling over the riverbank in an unnatural arc. The image of Other Me bent and broken on those rocks, being swallowed by that same silhouette, jolts me.

Afraid the silhouette has come to claim my sister, I rush to her side with every intention of begging her to leave, but the silhouette is gone before I can speak my plea. She sits with her hands folded in her lap, facing the damaged side of the bridge, like nothing happened. Maybe nothing did, but her eyes are closed. She still hasn't looked at the broken rail.

I blink rapidly, making sure the invading darkness is gone, before pushing down my fear and sitting beside my sister. I cross my stretched-out legs to match her position. Our shoes almost touch. Her lashes flutter, and I can feel her building the strength to look at that forbidden spot.

"It's okay, Jouley." I place my hand above hers and curl in my fingers as if I'm holding her hand. "We can look together."

She takes a deep breath, and I artificially match the rise and fall of her chest.

"Ready? One. Two." I hesitate until her eyes start to open. "Three." We turn our heads and see the yellow caution tape hung taut across the break in the rail. Almost immediately, she starts shaking. I snap my head back to her and frown. "Oh, no, Jouley."

Her cheeks are soaked with tears, eyes even redder. My fingers grasp at air as I strain to comfort her. I ignore the pain stabbing my insides and squeeze so hard I can almost feel the heat from her hand transfer into my floaty flesh.

After several minutes that feel like hours, Joules gets to her feet, wipes her face with the back of her sparkly glove, and slings her bag over her shoulder. "I really miss you, Cassidy-dee. It sucks that you're gone . . . really sucks." She takes a few steps toward Aimée's house, then stops. "I hope you don't mind, but I've been pretending that you're not gone." She lifts her chin. "Shaw gets it . . . I know you would too. So I'm gonna keep doing it, 'kay?"

My mouth opens with a silent reply. *I'm not gone, Jouley. Please don't stop pretending. I'm here!*

As she disappears into the trees beyond the bridge, darkness creeps after her in a now-familiar unnatural arc. The sharp pain returns as I yell her name. "Jouley!" I can't let the darkness fall on her like it did on me. I appear beside her in an impossible instant. "Jouley, it's not safe—" I start, but her expression makes me look up.

"Joules? What are you doing here?" It's Madison. "Are you alone?"

When Madison steps closer, Joules bursts into sobs. She's wearing a stubborn frown as she nods. "I'm supposed to be at practice."

Madison stands watching my sister cry for a moment and then wraps her arm around Joules's shoulders. "It's okay. I'll drive you home and make up something about seeing you at the rink while I was at Drew's hockey game."

My relief at seeing Madison is slightly diminished by her forcing a lie on my sister, but I'm starting to realize sometimes a lie is worth avoiding the pain of the truth.

After Joules and Madison are inside her car, I look back at the spot where I last stood alive. The darkness is gone, but the ache from walking through Joules still lingers. I focus on it for a moment, hoping the stinging under my skin might make me feel "not gone" like Joules said. It doesn't. Guilt replaces the pain. Everything I did Saturday night—whatever I did Saturday night—not only took away my life, it took away so many irreplaceable things from my sister and brother and parents, my friends, Ethan. They'll never be the same and it's my fault.

This is why consciousness is supposed to disappear when you die, I think. The wreckage is too much to bear.

My hands begin to drip like melting icicles, and for the first time, I'm relieved when I slip away.

DIVORCE

WHAT ARE YOU DOING with my suitcase?" I stood in my bedroom doorway and watched my mom stuff her toothbrush into the toiletry kit she always packed for our family road trips.

"This isn't *your* suitcase, Cassidy."

"Yes, it is," I insisted.

"Honestly"—Mom sounded tired—"the family shares a set."

"Yeah, and mine is the medium-size one. I always use that one. Besides, that's not the point. What are you doing with a suitcase?"

Mom's blue eyes flicked to Joules's open bedroom door. My sister was filling up her Hello Kitty backpack for the school day. "I'll call tonight." Mom raised the roller handle on the suitcase and hurried down the hall.

My heart clenched behind my ribs, keeping me in my doorway for a short minute. Then I followed her down the stairs.

She pulled her long wool coat from the front closet in a quick jerk, knocking Joules's skate bag from the hook on the door. She swore under her breath as she gathered up the bag and tossed it onto the bottom stair. I looked down at it from two steps up and gripped the banister when my heart clenched again.

"Mom, where are you going?"

"Work," she snapped.

"With a suitcase?" I hated how young my quiet voice made me sound.

She exhaled a sigh as she slipped into her coat. "Your father and I want to wait to tell you kids together."

"Tell us what?" My mouth kept asking all these questions I didn't even want the answers to.

"Shaw's coming home for your birthday weekend. I know it's bad timing, but he's taking twenty credit hours this semester and it's the only time he could come up for a visit, so we decided—"

"You decided to celebrate my birthday by announcing you're moving out?"

Mom held up her hands. Her purse swung from her arm like an off-balance pendulum. "One step at a time. It's only a separation."

"That leads to a divorce," I added, swallowing hard. "That's what steps do, right? They lead to something." I walked down the remaining stairs and held my arms out to exemplify my point.

Mom softened her tone. "Cassidy." She reached for me, but I pulled back. The muscles in her neck were visibly strained as she steeled her face and shook her hair out from under the collar of her coat. "We'll discuss this tonight."

Heat crawled up my arms and neck like a million long-legged spiders. I'd never felt so angry in my entire life as I did watching her wheel my suitcase out the front door and down the sidewalk to her stupid new car. She'd been parking outside the garage ever since she bought the sky-blue Beetle two months earlier. I'd guessed it was for a quick getaway, but Dad joked that she wanted to show off her "midlife-crisis mobile." Mom never laughed at any of Dad's jokes anymore.

I ran after her into the snow in my slippers and yelled, "Whenever you decide to come home, I want my suitcase."

I didn't notice Madison's teal Jetta parked beside Mom's Beetle until Mom backed out of the driveway. I held one finger in the air to let Madison know I needed a minute, then ran inside. As I traded my wet slippers for my Pumas, Joules came down the stairs.

"Why are my skates on the steps?" she asked.

"Mom put them there."

"Why'd she do that?"

I grabbed my backpack and said tersely, "Because she doesn't think about anyone but herself."

Joules's face scrunched up. She looked so old, like I'd taken away her whole childhood with that one sentence.

I opened my mouth to apologize, but I knew if I started explaining she'd ask more questions. This was not my job. How was I supposed to avoid my sister until Mom and Dad decided to buck up and be honest with the rest of their children?

Joules tugged on my wrist as I started for the front door. I didn't turn. My face was too hot with anger I didn't want her to see.

"I didn't mean that about Mom, Jouley." The lie came out surprisingly easily. "I'll see you after school, okay?"

"But I have practice today, and you have ballet."

"Then at dinner." I waved over my shoulder as I made a break for Madison's Jetta. I slammed the car door shut and slouched into the passenger seat, crossing my arms.

She greeted me with an air-kiss on each cheek and peered at me over the top of her tortoiseshell sunglasses. "Wrong side of the bed today?"

"More like wrong family today," I muttered.

Madison kept her eyes on me for another second before sliding her sunglasses back up the bridge of her nose and putting the car into reverse. "So," she asked hesitantly, "what was that scene with the suitcase about? Mom going on vacay without the fam?"

I stared out the frosty window at the tire tracks Mom's car had left in the snow. I could feel Madison's eyes on me, but I stayed quiet.

"I bet you can talk your dad into extending your curfew. If you want to meet up with the boys tonight for a movie or something, I'm in. While Mommy's away, the kiddies will play," she singsonged.

"She's moving out," I blurted.

Madison slammed on the brakes at the stop sign at the end of my road. The car skidded a little before stopping mere inches from the intersection. Madison tore off her sunglasses and turned in her seat to face me. "No. Way. For how long?"

"I don't know, for good."

"Oh, Dees," she gushed, "I am supercrazy sorry. What happened?"

I shook my head. "I didn't ask—not like she would have told

me if I did. They fight constantly. I guess I should've seen this coming." I bit my bottom lip, shutting myself up. I hadn't told anyone about my parents fighting or how much it was eating me up inside, making me feel like an outsider around my friends and Ethan.

Despite the national average, every one of my friends' parents were still happily married and taking second honeymoons like Aimée's mom and dad. The first thing Ethan's dad did when he got home from work every day was pull his wife into his arms and kiss her—deep, passionate, make-your-son's-girlfriend-uncomfortable kiss her. None of my friends would understand what it was like watching the two people who were supposed to love you more than anything else fall out of love with each other.

"Wow. Your parents are like my backup set. I can't believe . . ." Madison's voice trailed off, and she was quiet so long I finally turned to face her. She was staring out the windshield with this curious expression on her face.

I cleared my throat and pointed at the stop sign we'd been sitting at for several minutes now.

She shook her head and turned off my street. "Now we're definitely going out tonight. My treat, wherever you want to go. My mission is your happiness."

"Thanks, Mads, but I'm not really in the mood."

I could tell Madison was disappointed and hurt I had turned down her help, but I didn't have the strength to pretend to be okay. I leaned my head against the cold window.

Madison fiddled with the radio. "Parents always screw up families."

"I've never once seen your parents fight."

"That's because Helen reserves her negativity *pour moi*." Madison grinned sarcastically.

"At least your parents still love each other."

"Yeah, my parents love each other," Madison replied, "and that's about it."

"They love you too, Mads."

"My dad hasn't been inside my bedroom since I stopped shopping at Baby Gap, and my mom can't even look at me without mentioning how the way I'm wearing my hair these days makes my face look 'round.'"

"I like your new hair," I said in a lighter tone, fluffing my similar style. She didn't laugh. "Hey, you're beautiful and lovable. Stop it."

"That must be why it's so easy for me to keep a steady boyfriend." She pouted. It was so Madison to turn my parents' separation into a pity party for herself—the product of a lifetime of psycho overanalyzation by her psychiatrist dad—but I welcomed the diversion, and she knew that. This was her upended way of making me feel better.

I put my hand on her arm. "Drew will come around."

A sharp laugh jumped out of her mouth as she turned into the block-long line to get into the school parking lot. "Drew is so not—" She shook her head. "Sometimes I wonder why I even bother with him. I don't feel like we're getting anywhere. Like, the things I have going on are so far away from him that it makes absolutely no sense whatsoever being with him, you know?"

Without realizing it, I nodded, saying, "Yes." My chest tightened again, but this time I was thinking of Ethan and how what

I had going on at home, and in my head, was not something I could—or wanted to—share with him.

The shrill sound of Madison's car horn made me jump. She jammed the heel of her hand into the center of the steering wheel a second time as she yelled at a group of stoners loitering in the middle of the school driveway. They tossed her peace signs and chuckled to themselves while they casually strolled out of her way. "Move along, half-baked little ducklings." Madison made a shooing gesture with her hands at the windshield.

Caleb looked up to respond to her second honk, but when he saw me in the passenger seat, he turned tail and separated from the group.

"Didn't you use to play doctor with that one back in pre-school?" Madison pointed at Caleb. "He'd be kinda cute if he washed his hair, like ever."

I watched as he shuffled through the thin layer of snow covering the lawn that bordered the quad. He bent to tighten the laces on his black Vans, not bothering to actually tie them, then kept shuffling. He looked about as alone as I felt. I couldn't help thinking how I had been the one who didn't understand back in eighth grade when his parents split up. Ironic how now our situations were so closely related.

Madison bumped me with her elbow and smirked. "Am I right? He has potential, no?" She eyed him like he was a quaint fixer-upper. I tried to nod, but my brain was preoccupied. "At least Drew has the decency to shower and wear clothes that don't make him look like a homeless skate rat, I guess."

I forced a cheery tone. "That's because he knows you wouldn't accept any less."

"I don't know," she replied gruffly. "My standards aren't exactly Eiffel Tower–high these days."

"He adores you," I assured her, guiltily feeling better about my own situation knowing her life wasn't as perfect as it seemed.

Madison waved her hand at her face like I was making her cheeks hot with a blush and pulled into her parking spot.

"Hey," I began when she turned off the engine. "Don't tell anyone about my mom and the whole suitcase thing, okay? Even Aimée." I dropped my head, feeling shameful for wanting to keep anything, especially something this big, from my oldest friend.

Madison turned toward me with a stunned expression and leaned over to hug me. I tightened my arms around her shoulders, wanting to feel comfort in her gesture, but my stomach wouldn't stop roiling.

"Don't worry, Dees," she said. "Your secret is safe with me."

15

WHEN I OPEN MY EYES, I expect to see Caleb because that's who I saw after I got out of Madison's car that day. I went into school, sat in my assigned seat in Mrs. Wirlkee's class, read Caleb's paper-airplane note, and talked to him for the first time in three years. Did I set my death into motion that day, three weeks before it happened? Was opening Caleb's note and talking to him some test of character that I failed? Did fate send him to the bridge the night of my birthday party with schnapps and an angry heart as punishment?

I've always believed in fate, but in a meant-to-be kind of way. Like the way I was fated to be with Ethan forever. I still believe that—even more now—but I don't understand how cheating with Caleb and dying fit into any sort of logical plan that fate might have for me. Right now it doesn't feel like fate is watching out for me one bit. I feel as alone as I did that day in Madison's car.

A distant light flickers beyond the darkened woods, past the end of the covered bridge. As the towering form of the Coutiers' home slowly emerges, I place the light; it's coming from the third-floor window. Relief rises in me. I close my eyes and think of nine-year-old Aimée dressed in gold sequins, strutting around the playroom while Madison and I laughed into our matching feather boas. "Dress-up," I whisper to myself, hoping the memory will take me to her.

Instantly, I'm standing next to the rack that used to hold rows of Mrs. Coutier's discarded dresses and my and Madison's old dance costumes. Aimée's standing right next to me, hanging her royal-blue peacoat on the rack.

Her dark hair is windblown but still in the tight French braid she wore to school today. She sighs heavily when her cell phone echoes an insultingly cheerful tune through the room.

"You really should change that ring tone," I tell her.

She drops her keys and kneels, dumping the contents of her messenger bag onto the floor. I expect to see her patchwork makeup bag and red leather planner, some notebooks and folders, but none of the typical stuff falls out. It's full of random throwaways like dull pencils and old folded notes, probably from me or Madison, and an empty water bottle. The contents of her bag are the one thing she's let take on the state of mind I imagine she must be in: confused and overloaded.

She unzips the front pocket of her bag, releasing the full volume of pep her phone is delivering.

"Hi," I hear Madison say through the speaker before Aimée has a chance to talk.

Aimée replies with a hi so short it makes Madison's seem like a full paragraph.

"How was the rest of the day at school?" Madison's usual

sugary voice sounds strained and tired on the other end of the line.

I can't help feeling responsible. She found Joules on the bridge with me—or alone, as she would've seen it—and drove her home, which probably ended in a conversation with my parents. I can imagine how that went: Dad squeezing her in an awkward hug while Mom asked a bazillion accusing questions. I lean toward the phone and thank her for putting up with them. She hasn't mentioned to Aimée being here earlier or finding Joules on the bridge. Probably to save her the worry of knowing Joules was out at night by herself.

"I'm not mad that you went home early," Aimée says to Madison.

"I didn't think you were." The long silence that follows tells me they're both lying.

Finally, Madison asks, "So did you talk to him?"

I lean in close so I don't miss who they're talking about.

"He didn't answer his phone. I'm going to stop by his house tomorrow after school if he doesn't call me back. Do you want to come?"

"No," Madison replies firmly. "He must be completely destroyed. I can't see him like that."

"If Caleb would sober up I could at least talk to him at school."

"Good luck with that," Madison says with a verbal eye roll. "I'm telling you, it's a waste of time trying to get information out of him. Even if he saw something Saturday night, he probably wouldn't remember it. Did you find out anything else? Any new leads?"

"Maybe." Aimée thinks a minute. "I might have another angle to explore."

Madison's voice is a mix of eagerness and nerves. "What is it?"

"Mica Torrez. He practically begged to walk me to class today."

"Sounds pretty standard to me."

"Exactly. Everyone else tiptoed around me like I was explosive lava. Mica jumped right in."

I look at Aimée and say, "So that's why you softened up on him."

"Keep your friends close," Aimée says.

"And your enemies closer," Madison finishes for her. "Do you really think he saw something at the party?"

"I'm not sure yet, but I'm going to find out."

"So you didn't turn up anything else today?"

Aimée grumbles a quiet no. Then she clears her throat and asks Madison if she's coming back to school tomorrow.

"Doctor Daddy thinks I won't be able to function in society anytime soon—side effects of the 'scrips." Madison's voice cuts short at the end, and I imagine her clamping her hand over her mouth for revealing too much.

"Mads, you're not . . . you're medicating?"

"It's only to help me sleep," Madison says dismissively. "I keep having these dreams . . ."

Aimée slumps against the mattress. Her whole demeanor changes. So does mine. "How long do you plan on being out? I need you back at school with me."

"I don't know, Aims." The line goes quiet. "I kind of think it might be a good idea for me to stay away from . . . things right now. My dad's full of BS most of the time, but I think he's right on this one. I need to grieve in my own way—and you should in yours."

During the long pause that hangs on the line, Aimée lets silent tears fall. She thinks there's no one here to see them. I'd give anything for the ability to wipe her cheeks dry. Sadness rolls over me, knowing that I'll never again be the person she turns to for comfort.

"I'll call you in the morning if I decide to go back."

"Bye, Mads," Aimée and I say in the same distant tone.

After she hangs up, Aimée reaches across the floor and pulls her bag onto her lap. She digs out a handful of notes, her pad of stationery jumbled in with them. I'm sure that's what she was digging for, but she sets it aside, studying the notes instead. One in particular: a yellow one folded into the shape of a star. It reminds me of the notes everyone used to pass in middle school. Her forehead creases with tense lines and her green eyes look darker somehow as she carefully unfolds it.

Her eyes grow to the size of dinner plates as she reads what's printed inside.

I cross the room and stand behind her so I can read over her shoulder. There's only one sentence, written on an upward slant across the middle of the page in those irritatingly large Sharpied letters that psycho killers always use to taunt their next victim in horror movies. Nobody actually writes like that unless they're trying to hide their penmanship.

I reread the sentence, hoping it will say something different this time. No such luck. It glares back at me screaming its all-caps truth: IT'S EASY TO JUMP WHEN YOU GET A PUSH.

16

THE RIDE TO SCHOOL with Aimée the next day is so déjà vu, I can't even think. The only difference from the last time we drove together is that she's not talking my ear off about early admissions to Ivy Leagues and where she's planning to intern in the summer. I never thought I'd be nostalgic for morning over-achiever reports. Then again, anything would be a welcome distraction from the nonstop loop of the same nine words in my mind:

It's easy to jump when you get a push.

When she pulls into her assigned parking spot, a feeling of utter helplessness smacks me in the face. I spent the entire night with her, worried that whoever slipped that note into her bag meant what they wrote as a threat, but the reality is I wouldn't be able to protect her from anyone or anything. I can't even warn her if someone is coming, same as when I was on the bridge with Joules. I am totally, infuriatingly helpless. Even so, I feel responsible for her safety. She wouldn't be receiving cryptic notes if it weren't for what happened to me.

Everyone stares at Aimée as she walks across the quad to the main building. On a regular day, she'd relish the every-eye-on-her arrival, but this morning she's scrutinizing everyone back. Her stare lingers on a group of guys sitting on the low stone wall that runs along the brick walk. They seem impervious to the early-spring chill that everyone else is bundled up against as they casually talk about whatever it is guys like that talk about. My eyes focus on the dent in the group's nonchalant armor: Caleb.

His arms are crossed so tightly around his middle that it looks like he'll collapse in on himself. His breath puffs around his flushed cheeks and he's shaking slightly. He looks like he belongs in one of those videos we had to watch in health class about CPR and hyperventilation. For a fraction of a second, I feel bad for him. Then I remember what he did—might have done—to me and how it's a very real possibility he wrote that note to Aimée to try to scare her off investigating. He's not worth my pity.

I rise up onto the low wall to avoid ghosting through anyone on my way to him. I bend down right in front of him, meaning to study his face for some proof of guilt, maybe attempt a ghostly trick to will a writing sample out of his obnoxious orange backpack, but the only thing I can think about is his mouth closed around mine. My eyes wander to his lips. They're trembling and look about as cold as mine feel. Pity seeps back into me.

Without thinking, I trace the outline of his lips, awaking the memory of his kiss against my mouth. I yank my hand back, wincing at the dusty pain. He reaches into his pocket and pops one of his Tic Tac pills before crossing his arms tighter with a shudder.

"I must have been out of my mind to kiss you," I growl at him.

He shudders again.

As soon as the first bell rings, he bolts for the door like he's superconcerned with arriving to class on time. That would be a change. I stand, watching him pinball through the crowd, and realize Aimée's not part of the crowd anymore. I pull the first Aimée memory that pops into my head to the front of my mind. She's arguing with Madison about who will get to ride shotgun. It's last year, my first day with a driver's license, and even though it's March, I'm wearing those shorts I wore when Ethan got his car.

I appear beside Aimée as she enters the commons. She cuts a path through the cluster of student councilites standing to the left of the main office and takes a stance in front of their queen bee: Nancy Yeong.

Nancy halts her mile-a-minute tongue to give Aimée an awkward hug. Aimée shakes off the gesture and glares at her.

"It is so brave that you're here," Nancy says to Aimée with over-the-top amazement.

Aimée rolls her eyes. "Whatever. You and I need to talk."

"Agreed." Nancy nods once. "I've taken on the responsibility of organizing a *real* memorial service for Cassidy, and I would appreciate having your input on the photomontage."

Oh no. I've become *that* girl, the one with a photomontage. I loathe photomontages because no matter how cheerful the

184

circumstances, I cry during them. If I really pay attention and let myself get into it, I cry. It's probably the most embarrassing thing about me. That is, before I went all undead.

I tried to explain it to Aimée a few weeks before my birthday because Madison wanted to make me a montage for my party and I wanted Aimée to talk her out of it. Madison has this massive stockpile of photos going back to elementary school that she keeps in a moss-green satin-covered box under her bed. She never fully embraced the digital age and has printed every photo she's ever taken; that decorative box is stuffed full of them.

One night last summer Aimée and I slept over at Madison's house instead of our usual hangout, the playroom at Aimée's. Madison fell asleep before we did, so, naturally, we went searching for deep dark secrets lurking under her bed. Instead we found the box and started going through it, giggling at how terrible Aimée looked with a perm in fourth grade and the way I was always in the middle of pictures of the three of us. We found a stack of yearbook pictures of the boys in our class. Madison had marked the backs with rows of hearts according to how she ranked them. Aimée snorted when she found Ethan's picture in the stack with a perfect five hearts on it, waking Madison. She acted pissy and grumbled something about privacy, then stuffed the box behind her pillow. She slept with it there the whole night. The next morning she acted like nothing had happened.

I bet Nancy has already e-mailed her a bazillion times about photos of me. I really hope Madison pitches a fit and refuses.

"For music," Nancy is asking, "do you think mellow-inspirational pop or classic instrumental?"

"They both sound equally repugnant," Aimée grumbles. I want to hug her for attempting to save me the inevitable humiliation.

Nancy continues, totally not registering Aimée's boiling irritation at the idea of a memorial service. "I was envisioning—"

"Listen," Aimée interrupts, "I didn't come back to school to help you pick out some Taylor Swift song to play at an assembly to make you feel better about my best friend dying."

Nancy and her student council cronies stare at Aimée with gaping mouths. "W-w-why are you here then?" Nancy sputters.

"To find out who's responsible."

The girl next to Nancy says, "We don't judge Cassidy for taking her life. That's why we're putting together the memorial."

"Well, I'm judging you if you buy that craptastic story the police are shopping around," Aimée replies.

Nancy glances nervously around the group and starts toward an empty alcove of lockers. She nods for Aimée to follow. She stands with her back to Aimée for a second, then turns. "This must be extraordinarily hard for you, being here, but we're trying to be respectful during this tough time by honoring Cassidy's memory."

"Spare me the PC rundown. Why are you really putting together this memorial?"

Nancy hesitates. "Principal Dewitt's assembly was a generic school-board handbook speech that didn't speak to the heart of this issue. I'm only trying to unite our devastated student body through healing. In fact, I think it's unhealthy for you to go around accusing everyone who was there."

Aimée arches her perfectly tweezed eyebrows. "How many

points do you plan on getting when you write that healthy-little-healer speech for your college apps? Not a bad plan, mooching off a classmate's tragedy to land yourself in the Ivy—not the classiest plan, but a workable one nonetheless. You should've stopped at the memorial assembly though. The photomontage is a bit much. Looks like you're trying too hard, like you have more at stake here than admission to Yale."

Nancy tries to put up a confident front, but the effort seems too much and her shoulders sag. "I'm sorry," she says, suddenly close to tears. She's been captain of the debate team since sixth grade and I've never seen her back down from a challenge. "I know I showed up even though I wasn't invited to the party, but I didn't drink any of your alcohol and I don't know anything about what happened to Cassidy except what the police released. In fact, I wish I'd never gone to that party."

That makes two of us.

Aimée folds her arms. "Why did you?"

"My brother called me to be his DD. I was waiting for him in the park since the party was invite only." Nancy relaxes some when Aimée nods, but it's premature.

"You're not getting any Brownie points from me for pretending to respect my party rules when clearly you violated them the second you showed up. I already knew you were in the park when Cassidy fell, but I want to know what you saw."

Nancy smooths the front of her pleated skirt, trying again at a confident front. "I told you before, I don't know what happened. Now, if you'll excuse me, I have music to select for a memorial service and—"

Mica walks up behind Aimée and interrupts Nancy. "Don't

you think someone who actually knew Cassidy should make those decisions?"

Aimée spins around quickly to face him. I watch her expression closely, waiting for her suspicion to show through. She's too poised to let it though.

Nancy bristles. "We had English together."

"Two years ago," I retort, wishing she could see my annoyed expression.

"I think an actual friend might need to be involved," Mica replies.

"Her friends seem to be unstable with grief." She looks pointedly at Aimée. "I happen to think I'm the exact person who should be handling this delicate matter."

"Well," Mica counters, "I happen to think you're in the lead for most-annoying girl in the junior class."

"This type of harassment is unhealthy." Nancy tugs down the bottom of her shirt as she turns her chin up at Mica and walks away.

"Aimée, hey," he says, like the whole throw down with Nancy didn't even happen.

"I was talking to her," Aimée replies sharply.

"You were scaring the crap out of her. I thought I was going to have to referee a chick fight." He glances back at Nancy. "Not complaining, but . . ."

"Depending on what I uncover," Aimée says, "you might find yourself stuck in a real fight."

He claps his hands, grinning. "Challenge accepted." The amusement on his face fades when he realizes Aimée isn't kidding. "Let me walk you to class, Million Dollar Baby."

I arch my eyebrows at him.

"Again with this?" Aimée speaks my disapproval. "And don't call me baby."

"I could use an escort if she's not into it," a brunette flaunting pigtails and a detention-worthy skirt coos from behind Aimée.

Mica gives her a halfhearted smile noticeably lacking his usual innuendo. "Not on duty today, Sara. Sorry."

One corner of Aimée's mouth teases into a grin when the girl sulks like a two-year-old and stomps off. Aimée steps around Mica and starts across the commons. He follows. Aimée gives him a sidelong glance. "You sure are persistent."

"And you're stubborn."

"Bad combination," Aimée replies.

"So you've thought about us combining?" Mica smirks as Aimée fumbles for a response.

I laugh a little at Aimée's visible discomfort with Mica's pro flirting. Their awkward back-and-forth makes me temporarily forget our suspicion of him.

Aimée tells him, "I actually have to take care of something. I need to get going so I'm not late for class."

"None of your teachers are gonna mark you late this week. Not even Rosenberg."

I turn to face Mica, trying to get a read on him. He's been on the hunt for Aimée's affection since she turned him down for a dance at freshman homecoming and he realized she was the only single girl in the tri-city radius that didn't turn to gooey butter before him, but I had no idea he was dedicated enough to know her classes. If he knew her schedule, he could've slipped the note into her bag anytime.

"How do you know what I have first hour?" Aimée echoes my concern. "Have you been following me?"

"Only if you're into that kind of thing." Mica winks at her suggestively.

Aimée opens her mouth to say something—from her expression, something harsh—but she lets out a self-deprecating laugh instead. "I don't actually think you've been following me, but people I haven't said one word to since fifth grade, like Nancy Yeong, keep trying to comfort me, which has the exact opposite effect, and everything seems to mean something that it doesn't. And I have to see that bridge every time I go into my bedroom, so I don't anymore, which means I'm not sleeping much, which has me on edge and . . . I'm rambling."

Mica waits for Aimée to look up at him. "It was a cute ramble." It's probably the most honest attempt at a compliment I've ever heard him make even though he was still clearly flirting.

Aimée's face runs through several emotions, like she's not sure which one to feel. She shakes her head. "I'm going to go. The first bell's about to—" She points at the ceiling when the bell rings. "Bye." As soon as she clears the corner, she drops the flirty mask she was wearing for Mica.

"I sure hope you know what you're doing, Aims." I keep walking when she stops to straighten the cuff of her jeans over her black ankle boot and end up facing a wall of lockers. Staring at Caleb.

He's sitting with his back against the maroon metal doors, pulling the drawstrings on his bright blue hoodie so it cinches in around his face, hiding his half-closed eyes. He should be in Mrs. Wirlkee's class sitting two seats behind my empty seat. He reaches his arm up like he's stretching after an exhausting spell of sitting on his butt ditching class, letting his fingers linger on the small number plate on the locker behind him.

Number 200E. My locker. The slightest twinge of nostalgia pricks at me before it dissolves and re-forms into suspicion.

He reaches into his pocket with his other hand and fishes out a gum wrapper, some lint, and fourteen cents. He leaves that stuff on the floor and pulls out a small paper airplane.

Water splashes onto the wrinkled, yellow paper as I reach for it, melting through. I kneel next to him, ignoring the growing puddle of me, and stare at the familiar double fold of the wings.

"Where did you get that?" I ask him, assuming it's one of the notes he passed me in Psych.

One side of his mouth lifts like he's suppressing a laugh or maybe a scream as he flattens the airplane so it will fit through the vent on my locker door. He taps the end of the airplane with his thumb, sending it into my locker with a shallow *plunk*.

Aimée's head snaps up at the sound. I get to my feet and step away from Caleb. It's a reflex I'd developed for when my friends saw me with him. Of course, Aimée can't see me now, but old habits never die.

"You shouldn't be here." When Caleb doesn't so much as open his eyes, Aimée adds, "Kind of tasteless hanging out by her locker after what you did." She puts on a cool expression when one of the few stragglers left roaming the halls looks over at them. After he turns down the math hall, she kicks at the locker bank, sending a reverberating rattle five doors down. Caleb opens his eyes in a lazy, delayed reaction that tips me off that he's high. Again.

His head lolls to the side as he looks up at Aimée. "You girls always seem to track me down."

"What is that supposed to mean?" Her mouth quirks in disgust. "Whatever. How did you know where Cassidy's locker was?"

"Who said I knew?"

Aimée lets her glare burn into him. "I don't believe in coincidences." She waits for him to react, to give some small inkling of guilt. He doesn't. She changes tactics. "I saw you two at her birthday party. What were you doing together?"

"Talking."

Aimée flouts at his response. "I gathered that much from your mouths moving. Listen, I know my friend, and she never lied to me until you came along. So what was your angle? How'd you lure her to the bridge?"

Caleb's eyes suddenly focus and go wide. "I didn't lure her anywhere."

"Then what's the nonincriminating reason you two were on the bridge together?"

"We were friends."

"So you admit you were on the bridge?" It sounds more like an accusation than a question.

Caleb's voice lowers. "I didn't admit anything." He stands.

"You were there," Aimée persists. "I know it."

"Do you? Did she tell you that? 'Cause I was under the impression her lips were sealed."

Aimée starts to shake she's so mad. "That is not funny."

"Am I laughing?" Caleb gestures to his austere expression. "She's dead, Aimée. Is she feeding you lines from beyond the grave?" He looks in my general direction and adds under his breath, "She can't."

Tears fill Aimée's eyes. She swipes them away before they can fall. "She's not even *in* her grave yet. Get away from her locker. You don't belong here. She didn't care about you—you weren't friends anymore. You were nothing to her."

"Aimée," I begin to interrupt her, but she yells at Caleb, *"Leave!"* and I flinch because it feels as much for me as for him.

Caleb lifts his orange backpack onto his shoulder, shoves his hands into his pockets, and does what she told him to do. He leaves.

She digs her chipped manicured nails into her palms as she balls her hands into tight fists. Now that she thinks she's alone, Aimée murmurs to me, to no one, "Don't worry, Dees. I won't let him get away with this."

I step between her and my locker, willing her to see me. "Aimée, there was more going on with Caleb and me than you think." I hate that she doesn't know this, that we have this lie between us for all of eternity. So I tell her everything—at least the parts I remember—about flirting with Caleb in Psych class, and him remembering that I love éclairs, and feeling like he was the only person who understood my parents' separation, and what happened on his porch when my shoes were wet with slush and I didn't push him away. "I don't remember who I was with on the bridge," I tell her, "but I know I was with *someone*."

Maybe she's right to suspect Caleb. He said he wouldn't let me get away without ending my relationship with Ethan. Is he really capable of murder though? The Caleb I remember definitely isn't, but that's not saying much these days.

Aimée gives the dial on my locker a spin before measuring out my combination. She opens my locker and immediately starts straightening my haphazard stack of books. She adjusts my mirror so it's perfectly centered on the inside of the door, then reaches into her messenger bag and pulls out a canvas grocery tote. She stares at the reorganized space, smiling wistfully at her handiwork for a brief moment, then grabs my Psychology book. She flips through the pages, tipping it upside down like she's expecting some explicit clue to fall out. She does the same for my American Lit, Trig, and Spanish books. When nothing reveals itself, no clues, she frowns.

I look down at Caleb's airplane lodged between two binders at the bottom of my locker. "Aimée," I say very slowly as if overenunciating will allow her to hear me, "look under that binder." Even if Caleb didn't sign the note, she'll know it was from him. He was just here. She'll figure it out; she has to. If she would look . . .

Instead she pulls down the group picture we took on the first day of school this year that's taped above my mirror. Drew and Mica are in the back, not smiling and grinning ear to ear, respectively, and Aimée's next to Madison, who's striking one of her eyes-diverted-from-the-camera poses toward the center, where I'm standing with Ethan hugging me from behind. She studies the picture awhile then removes my mirror and other random magazine cutouts from the inside of the door and places them in her tote along with the denim jacket I keep hanging in the back in case the temperature decides to drop unexpectedly, which it frequently does in Crescent Valley. My locker is almost empty.

Finally, she reaches for my binders, and I'm sure she'll see the note, but the paper airplane glides to the floor as she stacks them on top of my jacket. She doesn't see it.

I futilely try to grab the airplane, then straighten with a frustrated grumble. "Aimée, please, *look down*!"

Her face lights up like she has remembered something she forgot, and she bends to retrieve the note. I smile to myself, half believing I got through to her. When she sees what's written on the inside flap of one of the wings, she gasps, and my smile disappears.

It says: *I'm sorry.*

Caleb's apology stirs the image of the silhouette on the riverbank passing off excuses for apologies. "I didn't mean to . . . This is *her* fault."

Aimée reaches into her bag and pulls out the note she found there yesterday. The folding job is similarly precise, and the handwriting is close enough, large and written in Sharpie, that the same person could've written both. Caleb could've written both.

Aimée kisses her fingertips and presses them to my locker door as she shuts it. Her arm is sticking right through my middle, stirring up glittery dust around us. I don't even flinch. The iciness clogging my throat and soaking through my leggings already has me numbed.

"He's going to pay." Her voice echoes like the ripples of the current pulling me under.

BETRAYAL

I DID IT FOR YOU—it was for your own good." Madison's pathetic and completely untrue excuse unleashed a sickening pang in my stomach.

"You don't do anything for anyone but yourself, and I can't believe it's taken me this long to figure that out." I whipped my head around to address Caleb. "And what about you? Did you have an elaborate plan for my own good too?"

"No," Caleb insisted. "I only came here because she told me you would need me."

"He's high, Cassidy. He doesn't—"

I shoved my hand in Madison's face to stifle her lies and turned back to Caleb. "What did she tell you?"

He leaned against the thick oak tree that was hiding the three of us from the party and pressed his hands to the sides of his head like he was literally holding himself together.

"Well?" I snapped at him, taking one step closer and stopping, my arms stiff at my sides while I swallowed down the quaver I felt creeping up my throat.

He met Madison's eyes with an expression somewhere between surprise and insult, then looked at me. "You want to know why she invited me here? She and I share a common goal."

"He's lying, Dees."

I narrowed my eyes at him. "I can't believe you set me up like this—with help from my friend." I bit back the last word, blinking away tears. Madison was not my friend anymore and there was no way I was going to give either of them the satisfaction of making me cry. "How could you?"

"How could I?" Caleb's brown eyes widened, and he dropped his hands. "You're cheating on your boyfriend. I'm a free agent." He crossed his legs at the ankles, resting his full weight on the tree.

I coughed a short breath. "Yeah, and what's your specialty? Freelance betrayal? Do you charge per day or is there a flat rate for breaking up happy couples?"

"You and Ethan aren't happy together," Madison cut in. "If you were, you wouldn't have stooped so low behind his back."

I tried to speak, but nothing came out. She was right. Something was off with Ethan and me. We weren't happy the way we used to be, but that didn't mean I'd stopped loving him or wanting to be with him. There were other factors that had nothing to do with him for why I was unhappy. It just felt easier to push away someone I knew wouldn't leave than to face the real problem.

"I never would've even talked to him if it weren't for my paren—" I leveled a death stare at Madison. "You've known this whole time, haven't you? And now you're using it against me? I trusted you." She broke into sloppy tears in response. I turned to Caleb. "I thought you understood what I was going through, but I guess that was a big act."

His expression softened. "I do understand, Cassidy. She told me, but I didn't expect to . . ."

"To what?" I spit at him. "Betray our friendship with an ultimatum?"

Caleb looked away from me into the woods that hid Aimée's house from the rest of the world and quietly answered, "To care so much to take it that far."

A frigid breeze swept through the lifeless branches hanging above us, causing goose bumps to prick my legs. Even if he was telling the truth, no matter how he felt about me, the damage was already done. He was nothing more to me now than a mistake I couldn't take back.

"You're not caring, you're inebriated, remember?"

"So that's how it is now?"

I squared my shoulders and inched up my chin as if I was above his affection. I wasn't, but I was so mad I wanted him to think I was, to feel bad about it.

His expression changed, like he was finally going to get serious. He pushed off the tree, glanced over my shoulder, and leaned forward to whisper against my hair, "I'm not the only person who wants you to choose me."

Snapping my head away from him, I forced down the anger burning under my skin and met Madison with the unguarded eyes of a friend. "Why would you do this to me?"

Tears streaked her reddened cheeks. The more she cried, the

more I couldn't stand to be near her. After what she'd done, she wouldn't even give me an explanation.

I turned on my toes to leave but stopped when I saw Ethan walking toward us. I grabbed Madison by the arm and pulled her in the direction of Aimée's house. "You're coming inside with me."

Caleb took hold of my other hand and pulled me back behind the tree. "Cassidy, I can explain." He flicked a look at Madison, who'd conveniently stopped crying so she could eavesdrop, then lowered his voice. "But not here. Meet me on the bridge?"

I peeked past the tree again. Ethan was only a few feet away now. "Fine. I'll meet you there, but later. You need to leave *now*. And don't tell anyone where you're going."

Caleb nodded. "See you on the bridge."

17

THE PHRASE "THE TRUTH HURTS" is so literal right now it could be my theme song. Whoever is in charge of the universe's sound track should cue it up every time I float through a wall or talk to someone who can't hear me. I don't bother shaking out the pain stinging me from my scalp to my toes; I hardly feel it. I'm too numb.

Madison helped Caleb try to break up Ethan and me. The thought is so absurd I can't even begin to process it. And Caleb asked me to meet him at the bridge. I agreed, and I definitely went, but was he there? Was he the guy with the schnapps? Did he push me off the bridge?

I start walking even though I haven't gotten my sight back yet. The sense of normality that putting one foot in front of the other brings me is worth not knowing where the preternatural force is guiding me. It seems to be growing stronger, harder to resist, the more I remember. Part of me is relieved to have some direction, albeit involuntary, but a larger part is terrified of where it might lead me.

Along the way I tilt my head back and blink into focus the leafless trees towering above me. The snow on the sidewalk doesn't crunch beneath my feet the way it should, but there's a woman walking a pug two houses up; her steps could be mine. If I close my eyes, I can pretend I'm me—Alive Me—taking a leisurely stroll for no particular reason, enjoying life.

The pulsing draws me toward a hunter-green house that I know almost as well as my own. I try to resist the pull, but I feel so weak from shouldering the weight of what I last remembered. The best I can do is pause for a moment next to the car parked at the top of the circular driveway: Madison's car.

That teal Jetta has been a fixture in her driveway since the summer before fourth grade, when her family moved to town. It belonged to her mom back then. We used to sneak out with the cordless phone and climb into the backseat to prank call boys in the middle of the night. It was Madison's favorite sleepover activity since it would've mortified her mom if she'd found out we were breaking the no-calling-boys rule—in her car nonetheless; gasp!—that she'd implemented after Madison got sent home for kissing boys on the playground in fifth grade.

Mrs. Scott was always very concerned with what everyone else thought: the neighbors, her friends, other kids' parents. All her worrying had the opposite effect on Madison. I wonder what Mrs. Scott would think if she knew her daughter was a relationship-sabotaging frenemy.

I uselessly try to dig my heels into the snow as I'm drawn

through the perfectly sculpted bushes flanking the Scotts' front door, hoping the pulse isn't guiding me where I'm sure it is.

As soon as I'm inside Madison's bedroom, I go on hyperalert, overwhelmed by paranoia, because I don't trust her anymore. Even if she can't see me, merely being near her now feels like walking into a trap.

She's sitting at the desk that lives in the alcove surrounding her dormer window. She has pictures scattered haphazardly across the L-shaped white work surface, and her moss-green satin photo box is on her lap.

"Looks like Nancy got to you."

Short little whimpers shake her shoulders every couple of seconds. I step soundlessly across the pink rug in the center of her wooden floor and see a picture of the two of us on the desk in front of her. In it, she's leaning into my shoulder with her hip popped out, flashing her fake camera smile. The picture is off center so it looks like the woods are posing with her. I'm looking off to the side.

Another whimper breaks the heavy silence that feels so out of place in her bright and girlish room.

Seeing her cry makes my anger fade some. Whether it's about my death or what she did, at least she feels remorse about *something*. I bend down to get a closer look at the picture and glimpse her face. It's as white as a candlestick, not red and blotchy like I'd expect from someone crying so hard. A twinge of sympathy rises in me, but I push it down.

Madison traces the tiny oval of space between our necks where she's propped her head against mine in the picture. Our shoulders are smushed together and I'm holding a red cup full of grape jolly vodie. We could pass for sisters with our matching hair. We seem so in the moment. Well, she does. I look like I'm being pulled out of the moment. I can see that thick oak in the foreground to my right, where Caleb promised to tell me the truth she was too cowardly to admit.

This was taken right after I heard those girls, Carly and Megan, gossiping at the party about Ethan breaking up with me. When I left my friends to find Ethan and ended up finding Caleb instead. Somewhere between posing for this picture and dying I found out one of my closest, most trusted friends had betrayed me.

I rip my eyes away from the photo and force myself to look at Madison. A tear drips off her cheek onto the image of my face in the picture. She uses her thumb to wipe it away, but she's pressing too hard and the glossy image starts to smudge. The ink spreads across my face, almost as if a strong wind has picked up in the snapshot of a world that doesn't exist anymore and blown my hair awry.

Madison reaches across the desk with her free hand and begins to methodically fan out the photos like she's searching for a specific shot.

When her cell chimes somewhere in the room, she drops the picture of us and pushes her chair back so quickly that I almost don't have time to move out of the way. She grabs her car keys, halfway through replying *Not home* to whoever texted her, and whips open her bedroom door.

"Omigod!" she yelps. Her cell clatters to the wooden floor when she sees Drew standing there. His face gets this sad light about it when he bends to pick up her phone and sees what she's typed. She says, "I was just on my way out."

"Where to?"

She ignores his question. "What are you doing here?"

"Your mom let me in."

Madison sighs. "Of course she did."

He hands her her cell. "Thought I'd skip out on lunch to see why you weren't at school again."

"I didn't want to see *anyone*," she adds with a biting connotation toward him.

He pretends not to hear it and steps around her into her bedroom. "Don't worry. I made sure nobody talked about the fight you had with Cassidy at the party."

"That's not why I didn't go," Madison says in a defensive tone, watching Drew closely as he wanders her room.

He stops in front of the desk and picks up a photo of her reading *Cosmo* next to my pool during last spring break. She's wearing a green-and-pink striped bikini with a gauzy sarong wrapped loosely around her hips. Aimée took the picture while Madison wasn't looking and ended up getting dunked in the deep end for it. It's one of the best pictures of Madison I've ever seen. The way she has one leg bent up accentuates her curves and her hair is flowing down her back in its natural straight style. This was before she dyed it, so it's that cheerful shade of strawberry that always reminded me of summer. The main reason she looks so good is she didn't know her picture was being taken; she wasn't *on*.

Drew points at the desk. "When did you take these? There must be a hundred pictures here."

Madison snatches the picture he's holding and throws it into the satin box. "I hate how I look in that picture."

"I think you look phenomenal, but if you don't like it, why'd you print it?" Drew asks.

Madison draws her arm across the desk and bulldozes the rest of the pictures into the box, undoing the organized line she'd fanned out before he arrived. "I print everything within twenty-four hours."

"Like Quik-Sav's lab," Drew says, trying to make a joke and failing miserably.

Instead of answering him, Madison stares at Ethan's yearbook picture, which is resting on top of the overflowing stack; it's the one she drew the hearts on the back of. I watch her staring blankly for a long time, wondering why she wanted to break up Ethan and me. Had I upset her somehow?

"You printed the ones from Saturday night already?" Drew's voice is low as he picks up the picture of Madison and me that's still on the desk, knocking the one of Ethan off the stack and upside down. The Magic Marker–hearts on the back of Ethan's picture have been rubbed out, like my face in the picture Drew's holding, and an answer to my breakup question begins to form in my head.

It takes Madison a second to pull her eyes away from the stack. "I'm supposed to be getting pictures together for some school thing. I thought there would be more of Cassidy, and I could . . ." She shakes her head. "I guess it's my fault there aren't more. I spent half the party inside."

"I know," Drew says intently. "I did too. Remember?"

Madison murmurs, "Not so much."

"Hey, don't feel bad. She was drunk." Drew's tone is blunt. It stings—not in the physical, ghostly memories way, but in a hurtful, emotional way. "It doesn't even look like she knew you were taking this one." He studies the picture of me, of the woods and the tree. "Are there any of me in here?"

"No." Madison shuts the box on his hand as she wipes at tears sneaking out of her eyes.

Drew's mouth curves into what I think he means to be a sexy smile, but it looks more like a smirk. He walks to her side. "Don't let what happened with her ruin what happened with us. We're finally together—officially. No more breakups and makeups." He wraps his arms tight around her waist and leans in for a long kiss that she cuts short. His expression tightens. "Maddy, you promised."

"I know," she interrupts, "but I think that maybe I need, like, time or . . ." She pushes her fingers through her half-curled, half-fallen-straight hair and claws at her scalp where her strawberry roots are growing in.

He bends to whisper something into her ear that I can't make out. Her blue-gray eyes flood with an unidentifiable emotion. She leans away from him, reaching for the door. I'm sure that she will open it wider and shove him out in their usual off-again style, but she quietly shuts the door instead and leaves her hand pressed against the door frame.

Without facing him she asks, "You would tell me if you knew something about Cassidy's fall, right? Like if you'd heard something from someone?"

"Of course. I tell you everything. Besides," Drew coos, "none of this is your fault, babe."

"This is *completely* your fault!" I yell at Madison. "You're the one who's always hot and cold, not Drew. You faked all those times he stood you up, didn't you?" I choke out a laugh of disbelief.

Before Drew can say another word, she abruptly turns from the door and throws herself at him, smashing her mouth against his. He stumbles back a few steps and rights his footing in a way that tells me he's used to the spontaneous tongue assault.

I *so* am not.

"Seriously?" I gawk at them. "You're going to fool around *now*?" I don't even bother telling her how repulsed I am by her actions. What's the use? She can't hear me, and she's obviously not the person I thought she was.

When Madison reaches for his belt, he tilts his head back and moans, "Maddy." That one word stops her cold. She looks past his shoulder at the stack of pictures now spilled out of the box on the floor. When he follows her eyes, she grips the sides of his face and pulls him into one of those desperate kisses that you see in movies when someone's about to go off to war. The raw emotion of it is palpable. Something feels off though. Maybe it's the fact that her eyes are still open. I've never seen anyone kiss with their eyes open.

My eyes squeeze shut because I can guess where this is going and I don't want to be around if Madison decides to give Drew what she "promised." Before I can think of a specific person like I usually do when I ghost out of a room, the air shifts, inexplicably thickening, and the pulse in my chest slows to a steady, repetitive beat. I open my eyes to the glow of a fish tank.

"Ethan?" My voice dithers. I'm not sure I'm ready to see him, knowing what I now know.

He sits up in his bed, a smile playing at the corners of his mouth when he sees me. It makes me feel like the worst person in the world. "Cassi. I thought—" He pushes the covers back and stands.

"Wait." I hold up my hands. It's so dark in his room I can hardly see them in front of me. "We need to talk."

"Shh." He silences me with one finger on my lips. "Don't ever leave me like that again," he says softly.

"Like what?" I ask, momentarily forgetting what I needed to tell him.

"Without saying goodbye. Dealing with that once is enough for a lifetime—too much."

My head drops with what's left of my heart. Would he still want me to stay with him if he knew how I'd abused his trust? He lifts my chin and gazes at me. Having his skin against mine feels so incredible I can't imagine how I stayed away Tuesday night and most of today. I almost forget why I did. Almost.

"Ethan, I'm sorry I didn't come back yesterday, but I had to go to school with Aimée again."

"Why?"

"I'm worried about her. She's on this mission to find out who was on the bridge with me, and she got this threatening note."

His brow furrows. "Threatening?"

"Well, sort of. Someone put a note in her school bag that said, 'It's easy to jump when you get a push.'"

"Is that supposed to be about you?"

"I think so because she found another one in my locker." I take a second to search for the right way to say what I need to ask. "What did we talk about on the bridge?"

His face does this tightening thing that looks both agonizing and wistful. "Cassi, can we not . . . It's like this miracle that I get to have you back. I don't want to drag up stuff that reminds me of how I lost you." He gently rests his hand over the place where my heart once lived. An echo of a beat awakens with the heat of his touch.

I back away from him even though it's the last thing I want to do. Ethan takes hold of one of my hands and sets it on top of his heart. When his palm presses against the back of my hand, there's a tingling right beneath my skin that reminds me of being alive. I look up at him through my eyelashes and my heart flutters up into my ears. It pulses there for real! I can feel it!

He leans forward, his lips inching toward mine, so close I can feel the warmth of his breath on my tongue. Our noses nuzzle each other, and I'm sure he's going to kiss me. My ears are on fire. I can't even remember what we were talking about twenty seconds ago. I hold my impossibly real breath . . .

Then sharp bites of pain nip at my ankles, stinging up my legs, gnawing away the sensation of our almost kiss and replacing it with the ache I felt at the river when I first awoke to this new ghostly existence. I pull away.

He steps back quickly. "I'm sorry."

I touch my lips where the shadow of his almost kiss lingers, trying to capture the heat wafting off me as it floats away with the sense of realness in my phantom pulse. My skin goes cold, suddenly unsubstantial.

I shake my head wearily. "How weird is it that kissing has become this off-limits thing for us? We used to kiss, like, thirty times a day—and it felt amazing."

"Is that what—does it hurt you being so close to me?" I don't answer. He turns his face away from me. "I suppose things are different now."

"Yeah." I tuck my hair behind my ears. Things are different now. *We're* different. In the nearly three years we've been together, I've told Ethan everything, even things Aimée and Madison swore me to secrecy about. Not because he asked me to or anything, but because I wanted him to know. I trusted him with every part of me, knew he'd understand better than anyone else because he and I were meant to be, true love revealed on a sunny day on the reflective river.

I didn't even realize I'd stopped telling him everything until he asked to come over one night to watch a movie. I knew both my parents would be home—and predictably acting out their own drama—so I told him I'd rather see a new movie in the theater instead of admitting why I hadn't invited him over in a month. Avoiding my house meant less privacy, which meant less making out. At first we'd say extra-long "goodbyes" in his car when he dropped me off, but the thrill of that wore off after a couple weeks and we sort of became . . . boring.

But now when we're together—even when we're not—he brings a small piece of me back to life. And that kiss, even if it was only an almost kiss, was the definitive opposite of boring.

"Ethan." My voice comes out gravelly. "I need to know what happened on the bridge."

He grips the back of his neck with both hands. "I told you. We talked."

"You mean we argued. I remember you were mad at me about . . ." I open my mouth to say the words I've been dreading since I remembered kissing Caleb, but I have this flash of me stumbling into Ethan and being pushed off him. "Did you push me?" I ask, still half consumed by the image.

"No!" Ethan takes a step back, shocked. "I can't believe you asked me that."

I hold my hands up. "That's not what I meant. When we were arguing, I stumbled into you and got pushed away, right?"

He avoids my eyes. "Oh. That was—that wasn't me."

"Someone else was with us?" I bite my bottom lip, bracing myself to hear Caleb's name.

"Mica thought you were trying to hug me or whatever and stepped between us."

"Mica?" I struggle to fit him into my memory of that night.

"Yeah, he's the one who found you two on the bridge."

"What do you mean 'you two'?"

He stares at me expectantly. "You really don't remember?"

"No. Not a thing." That's a lie, and I can't bring myself to lie to Ethan. I start over. "I don't remember our argument."

"Do you remember leaving Madison with me before you went to the bridge?" he asks. I give him a blank look. "She was upset and crying?"

I recoil at the thought. "I would never leave Madison like that," I protest. Unless it was after I found out she'd invited Caleb.

"Guess you had someplace more important to be," he replies derisively. "Drew told me you wanted to meet me at the bridge. So I went and . . . you weren't alone."

"I wasn't alone," I reply, hoping saying the words out loud will shake some small bit of memory loose. I touch my lips, stirring the syrupy taste of schnapps. "Ethan, I—I wasn't with him like you think. We were just . . . having a drink," I finish lamely.

"Yeah, so was the rest of the party, around the bonfire. Why did the two of you need a private drink on the bridge together?"

I can't speak. There are no words to make anything that I can remember about what happened sound acceptable. There's no way to explain what I did.

"Why did you have Drew tell me to meet you? Did you want me to see that?" Ethan's voice gets louder with each question. "What would've happened if I hadn't shown up? How many *drinks* would you two have had together?"

"No, I didn't want you to—I don't know why. I don't even remember talking to Drew."

He laughs a harsh laugh and pushes his hands through his hair. "You can only play that card for so long, Cassi."

Anger fills me. "Maybe if you tell me what you know I could remember more." He shakes his head, and I grit my teeth. "I don't understand why you're keeping the truth from me. Do you want me to stay like this forever?" I gesture to my iridescent freak-show body. "I'm not me anymore. This isn't how I want to spend the rest of my li—" I throw my hands up. "Whatever this is. Why won't you help me?"

Ethan's Adam's apple works up and down his neck as he swallows hard. "You think I want to relive the most painful night of my life? Sometimes I tell myself I never even went to your party so I can avoid thinking about it."

"Well, it's the last night I have, Ethan!" I struggle to lower my voice. "I know I did something . . . something bad happened and I need to make it right. I need to find out the truth so I'm not remembered as some drunk girl who was desperate enough to jump off a bridge instead of facing her mistakes. I know it hurts, but you're the only person I can ask for help."

"It's not only that *I* don't want to hurt." Ethan hesitates. "I don't want to hurt *you* again."

"Again?"

"After what I saw . . ."

"Ethan, there's more to that than you know. Someone was trying to break us up."

"Y'think?"

I shake my head. "You don't know."

My chest feels like it's cracking under an enormous icy weight. Moist flakes of snow sprinkle my face, gathering at the corners of my eyes, blotting my vision.

"No. You can't do that now!" Ethan shouts at me. "You can't leave like this again." All the guarded tension in his voice gives way to frustration and pain. The pain is so intense I wonder how he's not falling to pieces.

I am. I'm falling away into tiny drops and the last thing I hear before I'm gone is my wavering voice asking him, "Again?"

THREATS

SAY THE WORD, E. A few bloody knuckles won't hurt me. Wouldn't mind rearranging Stoner Boy's face." Mica was pounding his fist into his palm like an absolute barbarian.

"You have some nerve, Mica. Back off." A board creaked under my foot as I stepped in front of Caleb. He scowled at me through the darkness of the bridge like I'd taken away his manhood by sticking up for him. Fabulous. One more reason for *everyone* to hate me.

"Is Cassidy your little bodyguard?" Mica taunted Caleb, reaching over my shoulder to shove him away from Ethan.

"Who's the 'little bodyguard' again?" Caleb jeered with a smirk that looked nothing like his usual laid-back expression.

"Little?" Mica puffed his chest out, cockier than usual. "Are you having problems seeing? Do I need to shine up your eyes for you?" He clenched his right hand into a fist, extended it toward Caleb, then turned it sideways like he was aiming a gun.

"Enough with the threats!" I turned toward Ethan to plead

with him, but my drunken feet slipped on a patch of ice and I stumbled into him instead.

Right when I thought I felt Ethan's arms tighten around me, Mica drove his hands between us and pushed me backward. "Hands off my boy, bitch."

I recoiled at his harsh tone. No one had ever called me a bitch before.

"Mica, stop." Ethan put his hand on Mica's shoulder.

"No way." Mica looked at Ethan with wide eyes. "We can't leave this unsettled."

I sputtered out some weak defense that only seemed to hurt Ethan more.

His brown eyes turned cold when he said, "It's pretty clear this is settled." He started back toward Aimée's house. I wanted to follow him, but my Mary Janes felt nailed to the boards beneath me.

Mica stopped him. "You're going to let them get away with playin' you like this?"

I stammered something else, but it was too late. Ethan's stare cut through the shadows that possessed the covered bridge and bore into me. "It's not worth it." Before I could react, he was gone.

My heart evaporated from my chest. I no longer had a use for it. "It's not worth it." *We* are not worth it. My. World. Over.

Mica scowled at me, then jogged after Ethan.

I couldn't breathe. My head felt light in the frantic, self-implosion kind of way. In my mind I shouted the perfect apology, one that made Ethan come back. I swallowed hard, but only got out, "Sorry," after Ethan had disappeared into Aimée's backyard.

"I'm sorry too, Cassidy."

I whipped around to face Caleb. Hot anger flooded my veins. "I wasn't talking to you. Why would I ever apologize to you?" I threw my hands up and let them fall on top of my head. "Everything is destroyed. *I* destroyed everything—how stupid could I be? Everyone is going to hate me when they find out."

"Hey," Caleb said sweetly, "I don't hate you."

"No?" I swiped at my tears. "Well, I plan on never having anything to do with you ever again. How about now? Hate me yet?"

Caleb's voice hardened. "Don't I get a say in that?"

"No." I stomped away from him and turned toward the frozen river so he couldn't see the tears burning my cheeks. Chunks of ice knocked against one another in the sparse patches of thaw with no place to go.

"That's the way it always is with us, right, Cassidy? I put myself out there and you reel me in or toss me out whenever you feel like it."

"Oh, shut up. This thing is over."

"'This thing'?" he asked, looking wounded.

Maybe it was all the schnapps I'd drunk, but his question was infuriating. I turned to face him. "Us." I ticked a finger between him and me, almost yelling. "*This* is your fault."

He stepped toward me. "I care about you and maybe that's on me because you have a boyfriend, but at least I was honest with you. How many people have you been honest with in the past three weeks?"

I clenched my teeth, swallowing down the abhorrent truth:

I'd become a very good liar since I spent that first afternoon in Caleb's basement. "You took advantage of me."

"No, I cared." He reached for my hand in a gentle, concerned gesture that he had no right to make.

My voice came out as cold as the wind cutting through the cracks in the bridge walls. "You are the biggest mistake I've ever made in my entire life." I looked down at his hand on top of mine, wrenched free, and started toward the park side of the bridge. I would walk home in the freezing cold in my totally not-snow-proof Mary Janes. I didn't care. I needed to get off that wretched bridge.

"Cassidy."

The chill in my bare hands spread up my arms until they were so cold I could barely lift them to show how completely done with the situation I was. I got them up in an exasperated flail, but they didn't drop back down. Instead they were gripped and I was hauled back into the shadows.

18

WHAT DID I DO? *What did Ethan see?!*

For once, I'm not relieved to be back in the present. I'm grasping the snatches of images left spiraling around in my mind, hoping, longing for answers, but they tumble away from me before I can make sense of them. The knot I'm left with is nothing compared to the ache in my chest. The pulse has slowed to a hollow tremble that leaves me feeling so far from alive that I'd rather not feel anything at all.

The setting sun casts a golden hue on the powder-blue walls of my bedroom and my pearlescent skin, melting away some of the chill that lingers there. I'm so relieved to be in my own room, where I lived my normal life, alone and not with Ethan. Each recaptured moment from that night makes it harder to face him, which is terrifying because he's the only person I can face. No one else even knows I exist; maybe I don't. Maybe this is my punishment for the bad choices I made and the hurt I caused. Maybe I'm in some sort of purgatory.

Then why can Ethan see me?

I bow my head, feeling even more confused and defeated, and see a sliver of light shining from under my closet door. On the other side, my sister is sitting on the floor with her head resting on a stack of sweaters near my shoe wall of fame: her favorite hiding spot. She pulls a pair of turquoise wedge sandals from the bottom shelf. They're way too big, but she slips one on her left foot anyway. Her flowered pajama pants get twisted in the tie. She rolls them up, reties, and starts on the right one.

She looks absolutely ridiculous in baggy pj's and my three-sizes-too-big shoes, but it's Joules so it works. She twists her ankles from side to side, checking out her new footwear. I feel a twinge of comfort knowing that she'll inherit several years' worth of mall trips and allowances well spent.

"Those go with your eyes." I bend down to get a closer look at my sister's eyes, to memorize them so the image will stay with me always, and I'm struck by their vivid indigo.

Mom used to brag to anyone who would listen about how "thoughtfully" blue my eyes were, whatever that meant. Joules's were always more of a baby blue. It's like I've passed on some of my color to her. I wonder if her color will intensify even more when I'm not a ghost anymore, when I'm for-real dead, if that ever happens. That's weird to think, but kind of nice too. I like the idea that I'll be with her, especially in her eyes—pointing her in the right direction, guiding her when she's lost, helping her avoid my mistakes.

She picks at my white mohair sweater, which is on top of the pile she's leaning on. Before long, she has a fluffy pile of fuzzies that resembles freshly fallen snow in her lap. It reminds me of so much that I want to forget. Her eyes glisten, and I wish I could hug her and let her know I'm here.

"Jouley, do you think I was a good person, like . . . did you trust me?"

She gathers the fuzzies into her palm, making a faux snowball.

"I don't know if you should have. I lied to you." I stare down at her, waiting for some small sign that she can hear me. She keeps rolling the faux-ball between her hands until it's small enough to mistake for a cotton ball. I continue. "A few weeks ago when I missed your skating competition and said it was because I was cramming for a Psychology test, I wasn't at the library—nobody studies at the library pretty much ever. I can't believe parents still buy that." I shake my head at how easy it became for me to fabricate the truth once I had something to hide. "I was with a boy and it hurt a lot of people when they found out. You wouldn't have approved."

Joules got her first crush a month ago, on Hunter Farlow, and suddenly became very puritanical about the ways of love. Her eyes were only for Hunter. She started asking me questions about what to say to him at recess and what to wear to the Crescent Valley Elementary winter art show, where his paintings would be on display. She was so nervous I had to go with her to the show. His paintings were surprisingly trippy with neon swirls and black waterfalls. Deep for a fourth grader. She said they were "epic." I'm not sure she knows what *epic* means, but I knew what she meant.

"Have you talked to Hunter yet?" Of course she doesn't answer me. "You should invite him over. And when he inevitably says yes because you're so irresistible, it's vital you tell Dad you're working on homework together. Mom doesn't care as much, but Dad turns warden the second he figures out it's a date—even an elementary-school date would wig him out."

I know she can't hear me, and I'm the last person who should be giving relationship advice, but I need to tell her this. It's the good stuff we never got to. Saying it now, I hope it reaches her somehow even if it's only subconsciously. There are so many things I need to tell her about dodging curfew and boys and sex. I feel guilty thinking of Mom telling her instead of me. I remember how mortifying it was when she gave me "the talk." I was supposed to save Joules from that.

I rub my horseshoe pendant, wondering where to start. "Never kiss a boy until the third date—but if you don't want to kiss him on the first, don't even bother. And wait as long as you can for that first kiss." I pause. "You should save your kisses, Jouley. I didn't, and look where it got me."

I press my cold fingers to my even colder lips and gaze at my sister, who is gathering more white fluff from my sweater and spreading it over her lap, creating a protective barrier of warmth against her grief. I think about when and where her first kiss will be and who it might be with. She still has every one of her kisses left. So many possibilities. So much more time . . .

"You're the best sister ever, Jouley. Promise lah-miss." I laugh a little at our rhyme and poke her on the tip of her nose. It stings, but it's worth it to feel normal.

I wish I could take back lying to her, maybe most out of

everybody. Until recently I had never lied to my sister, even when she asked me if the tooth fairy was real. But I had never needed to. I had never had anything to hide from her until Mom moved out and Caleb . . . I grit my teeth, wanting so badly to blame Caleb for what happened between us, but he isn't solely to blame. And despite whatever insider information Madison gave him, she's not to blame either. I was the one who agreed to go to his house.

I sit with Joules, hoping to offer some form of comfort, but the memory I recently came out of infects my every thought. I can't get it to match up with my memory of drinking schnapps. The faces were so clear during the argument, but the schnapps memory is full of shadows and the voices are distorted. The drinking had to have happened before Ethan found Caleb and me. I can't imagine hanging around with him to finish off a bottle *after* I told him he was "the biggest mistake I've ever made in my entire life." I'm not sure why it's so unclear though. Maybe because I was drinking?

You're not ready to know. The thought is a faint echo, but it rings through loud and annoyingly clear. If I'm not ready now, when will I be, and how do I get to that point?

The closet door opens. It's Mom looking tired and relieved. "She's in here, Rodger," she calls to Dad. He rushes into my room from the hall and kneels next to Mom. "She was in here the whole time. Can you believe it?" She gazes over at Dad like they're two comrades back from battle. "Our baby is safe."

Dad wraps one arm around Mom and gently shakes Joules's shoulder with his other hand. Joules stifles a yawn, pretending to be asleep. When Dad scoops her up into his arms, the strongest dose of jealousy imaginable fills me. He'll never carry me like that ever again. I try to pull the six and a half years I had as his only daughter to the front of my mind so I can remember the piggyback rides and upside-down hugs I had completely to myself before Joules was born and not feel this festering envy for my little sister, but it's not working. The memories are too distant. I know they happened, but I don't get a replay.

"Hey," Joules protests, landing a weak punch on Dad's chest. "I want to stay."

Dad stops walking. "I miss her too, but your mom"—he glances down at Mom, picking up the fluffy mess Joules made—"she can't exactly handle anyone being in here right now."

"Well, I can't exactly handle *not* being in here right now." I'm sure she meant it to sound snarky, but it came out dispirited. Mom stands, clasps my turquoise sandal that's dangling off Joules's foot, and gives her a wistful smile.

"Jouley," Dad starts, but Mom stops him.

"She can stay in here if she'd like. If that's what she needs."

Dad bends to kiss Mom on the cheek, and she wraps her arms around him and my sister. Part of me wants to be mad at Mom for waltzing back into their lives like she didn't leave with my suitcase three weeks ago with every intention of never coming back, but a bigger part oddly understands how she must have felt when she decided to leave. After remembering what happened between Caleb and me, I get how life can stumble so far off track that you don't know how to live it anymore.

As they walk out the door, something cold and comforting fills me at seeing them together, really together and solid like a family should be. No more fighting. Mom takes hold of Dad's hand as she closes my bedroom door. They're a family. Without me.

The quiet of my room surrounds me. I feel so utterly alone. The prospect of roaming aimlessly, ghosting through all of eternity, is unbearable. Even though the pulse in my chest guides me more strongly than ever, I have no idea where it's pointing me. I feel so completely lost.

I close my eyes and let go of everything. I push back my questions and half-remembered moments and succumb to the pulse, concentrating on its slow beat, letting it pull me where it wills.

A slow chill creeps up my arms and legs. When I open my eyes, I'm standing outside in a white plume of smoke. The dense air shifts as it dissipates, then re-forms into a new puff.

Caleb is leaning against a tall wooden fence with his head tilted back and his hood pulled down over his eyes. I'm not sure if the vapor coming from his mouth is his breath or smoke from the joint pinched between his thumb and middle finger.

"This is where I end up? With *you*?" I point at Caleb, shaking my head, then mutter, "Thanks a lot, almighty pulse." The fact that I haven't seen Caleb sober once since I ghosted back to life doesn't help much with rationalizing why I risked everything I had with Ethan to be with him. I want to leave, but the pulse within me has grown too strong to fight. I'm trapped here with my mistake.

"So Aimée was right. It was you on the bridge." I stare at Caleb, waiting for his eyes to open or for him to talk, some kind of a response.

Nothing. He merely kicks at the snow that's piled high along the fence.

"Why were you even at my party? You knew I didn't want you there." I clench my teeth. "Madison." Everything was planned: him showing up at my party, those girls gossiping about a breakup . . . I look down at Caleb, rubbing my forehead as my thought veers off. Madison must have been very persuasive to get him to listen to her over me. "Why would you write that note? You've already gotten away with whatever you did. Why incriminate yourself by confessing to the one person who doesn't believe I jumped? Do you want Aimée to know it was you? Is the guilt getting to you that much?"

Caleb starts digging around in his baggy jeans pocket for his cell. He texts *Refill* to a contact saved as *Doc*. I frown at the obvious code for someone who must be his dealer.

I jump when he abruptly flicks the remaining nub of his joint to the ground. It sizzles as it sinks into the snow. I can't look away from the wisps of smoke escaping the melted hole. They look like tiny rivers rushing upward to join the lingering haze covering the sinking springtime sun.

His cell chimes, pulling my attention from the tiny smoke rivers. When I look up, he's gone and there's a trail of footprints leading to a loose board at the far end of the fence.

I close my eyes and think of Caleb doing cannonballs at my seventh-grade swim party, and suddenly find myself in a squishy pile of melted snow underneath someone's swing set. Yuck. At least my feet don't feel the wetness. I scan the yard and spot Caleb speed-walking under a row of pine trees alongside the house with the swing set. I join him on the snow-free path, but

I keep my distance, studying the houses. This neighborhood seems familiar.

Caleb hops a low picket fence that I walk through and stops behind a small cedar gazebo I recognize. He digs his cell out of his pocket again and texts: *Outside.*

This must be a meeting place, a coincidence. No way it's what I think it is.

"Doc" takes her time quietly shutting the back door to her hunter-green colonial and wraps her arms tight around her stomach when her furry white boots crunch into the snow covering her backyard.

Neither of them says a word, but I'm screaming. "Madison! Oh my god! First you're hooking up with Drew, now this?"

Madison holds out her hand like she's waiting for test results. Caleb pulls out that Tic Tac container he's been carrying around and hands it over to her. She holds it close to her face to see what's inside.

"I gave you enough to last at least a month. Where'd the rest go?" she asks.

"My bloodstream."

I gape at her. "Are you some sort of high-end drug dealer now? And for *him*?" I'm right up in Madison's face and beyond fuming because she doesn't even blink at my yelling. I let out an exasperated scream. "Somebody answer me!" Caleb's eyes are glued to the ground, but Madison is staring right at him with the strangest combination of triumph and regret.

She purses her lips. "You would've had to take five a day to get through the whole bottle already." Caleb shrugs and Madison's eyebrows spike. "You'd be dead to the world if you took that many."

"Not dead enough." Madison starts to say something else, but he cuts her off. "I need more, okay?"

"What, do you have a tab with her?" I scoff.

She tells Caleb, "I didn't agree to helping you OD."

"Yeah, well, I didn't agree to Cassidy dying."

Silence hangs heavy in the air. I can't get any words out. I can't think.

Finally, Madison slips the container up the sleeve of her cashmere sweater and hands Caleb a small packet of what looks like pill samples from her front pocket. "That's the best I could do on short notice without my dad getting suspicious, and this is the last time you come to my house." She points at the little white ovals inside the packet that Caleb is examining. "So you better make those last." Madison bounces anxiously on her toes. "Aimée said you were messed up at school again."

"Yeah, well, you can tell her and the testosterone twins to lay off the verbal assaults."

Madison cringes for the smallest second, then resets her expression. "Aimée's über suspicious of everyone who was at the party—especially you. You're going to make yourself look guilty if you keep this up."

Caleb looks up, meeting her eyes for the first time. "Go ahead, ask me if I did it."

"If you had anything to confess, you would have already." Madison starts toward the house.

"If it was as easy as turning myself in, I wouldn't need to

down a horse's dose of these." Madison turns to see Caleb shaking the packet of pills she gave him. He clasps it between his palms, pleading, "Ask me what I saw."

"Ask him," I yell at Madison. I turn to Caleb. "Tell her."

Madison coils a lock of her hair tight around her pinkie and glances nervously over her shoulder. "I better get back inside." She takes one step toward the house but turns back. "I didn't agree to that either—Cassidy . . . That's not why I invited you."

"But you *did* invite me," he retorts. "And lied about her relationship status that day outside Wirlkee's class before all this began. Isn't that why you told me she was still into me? You wanted me to do your dirty work for you, and I was chump enough to fall for it. If I knew I could've been getting quality pharms out of the deal, I'd have started having anxiety attacks sooner."

She exhales a ragged breath. "I only wanted Ethan."

"Guess it was an all-around loss then." Caleb pulls the drawstrings of his hood tight and heads back the way he came, making sure to step in the exact prints he made on the way here. "See ya 'round." He holds up the pill packet. "Or not."

So Madison invited Caleb to crash the party because she wanted Ethan. I almost laugh because he's still mine, even in death. She doesn't have a chance in this life or the next.

I storm after her, beating her to the back door. "Explain. Now." She walks through me into the mudroom. I bite back the prickling pain and frustration as I wait for the dusty particles of me to settle. As soon as I'm whole again, I turn on my toes. "Tell me now, Mads, or I'm going to suspect the worst." I already do.

"There you are," Madison's mom says from the kitchen. "Why

are you wearing those god-awful boots?" She leans against the rich mahogany cabinets with two apples in her hand, glaring disapprovingly at Madison's favorite boots.

Madison pretends to struggle with the laces as she wipes her eyes dry. "I went to check the mailbox," she lies flawlessly.

"I already got the mail today."

"Probably why it was empty." As she walks into the kitchen, Madison forces a smile and grabs a Chips Ahoy! from the pantry, ignoring her mom's offer of the second apple.

Mrs. Scott snatches the cookie out of Madison's hand and replaces it with the apple. "Did you see today's newspaper?"

Madison shakes her head at her mom's question, twisting the stem of her apple until it snaps off.

"There's a tasteful announcement in the obituaries for Cassidy."

"Tasteful?" A short laugh hiccups out of Madison. "Good word, Mom."

I'm so confused and angry right now that I read an array of terrible things into her sarcastic laugh.

"Well, considering how she died, *intentionally* and *drunk*." Mrs. Scott whispers the last word like it's dirty and shudders. "Her family must be so disappointed."

I glare at her over the center island. What a hypocrite. She has half a bottle of wine with dinner every night.

"Yeah, I'm sure they're overcome with *disappointment* about Cassidy's death." Madison slams her apple into the fruit bowl next to the sink. "I've lost my appetite."

"Madison Rose, I think you're overreacting a bit."

"Oh?" Madison stops at the top of the stairs and spins to face her mom. "And what would be the acceptable way to react to my best friend's suicide, Mother? Sending flowers? A *tasteful* wreath of greens for her grave?"

"Well," Mrs. Scott sputters, crossing her arms.

"Yeah, Mom. *Well.*" Madison laughs again, but tears shine in her eyes. Once inside her bedroom with the door shut, she shakes out her sleeve and whips the Tic Tac container Caleb gave her across the room. She slumps against the door and lets out this frustrated growl of a sob.

I struggle to keep my voice even. "What is going on with you, Mads? You're dealing pharmaceuticals that I'm sure you got from your dad by faking symptoms, and you obviously have some secret vendetta against me. How long has this been going on? Does Aimée know?" I hesitate. "What did I do to make you hate me this much?"

Madison reaches under her desk and fumbles through several messy piles of photos. They seem to be sorted into two categories: my birthday party, and everything else. She pulls out one of her, me, and Ethan from an everything-else pile. Aimée took it at her first bonfire, the week before we started high school. It was supposed to be of Ethan and Madison together, but Ethan pulled me over and insisted I be in it too.

The memory of the bat crashing into the bridge comes back to me. Madison invited Ethan to that party. She'd practically declared him her future boyfriend, but right after this picture was taken Ethan asked me about the bats and we ended up having our first kiss together on the covered bridge.

I remember being scared to tell Madison that we'd kissed. I made it through the party, but the second I saw her and Aimée at breakfast the next morning, they called me out on hiding something. I practically bit off my bottom lip trying to stay quiet. I never gave the fact that Madison had invited Ethan for herself another thought after that since she smiled and teased me along with Aimée.

That was almost three years ago. Had Madison seriously been harboring a crush on Ethan and a grudge against me that long?

She grips the picture in her hand so tightly the corners fold in. When she starts to tear it, I'm sure she'll lob me off, but she separates herself instead, crumbling her smiling face. She sniffles and clears her throat before grabbing her cell off her bed. She dials a number and says, "I need to see you . . . I'll explain when you get here."

She hangs up and immediately strips off her dingy yoga pants with the stain on the knee from when we tie-dyed a couple summers ago and reaches into her dresser for a pair of skintight black jeans like this is a drill she's practiced: In case of emergency, dress slutty to distract a boy from seeing the real you. She twists so she's facing the gilt-framed mirror behind her and swoops her hair up into a messy bun with tendrils hanging around her face.

I'm so bewildered by how quickly her mood has shifted that I don't notice the chill climbing up my arms until it's liquefied my fingers.

I try to focus on staying in the present by following Madison around her room as she prepares for whatever she has to "explain" to whoever she called, but it only pisses me off more. Every little Madisonism reminds me of a time I laughed with her or shared a private moment, the years she pretended to be one of my closest friends when in reality she resented me. When she sprays her bare chest with her signature body mist, I back away. The spray lingering in the air reminds me too much of my dusty glitter, and the weirdness of not being able to smell it creeps me out. The scent used to remind me of Grandma Haines's rose garden. Now the memory of the sickeningly sweet aroma carries the effluvium of a funeral.

Madison opens the bottom drawer of her jewelry box, where she keeps her many necklaces in an impossible tangle that only she can ever undo. When she pulls out the knot of silver and gold, two prescription bottles roll to the front of the drawer. They're both prescribed to her.

"Doctor Daddy sure has you stocked," I say with faux congratulations.

I lean forward to read the labels: Percocet—contains oxycodone, empty. That's definitely what Caleb was popping like candy. And Xanax. I've seen commercials for Xanax; it's an antianxiety drug.

I straighten, watching Madison's fingers weave an impossible path between two silver chains that don't so much untangle as knot together in an aesthetically pleasing way. I wonder what to say, how to respond, how to feel about her taking—or judging by the fullness of that bottle, not taking—antianxiety drugs.

As she picks the bottles up to put them back in their hiding spot, I notice something rattling inside the empty one. She opens it and gazes at the single aquamarine stud—*my* aquamarine stud that I thought I'd lost the day after I received the earrings for my sixteenth birthday.

I reach out to reclaim it, but my hand slides through and a knock on the door forces Madison to cut the moment short. She closes the drawer, pill bottles safely hidden away, slips the knotted chains over her head, and opens her bedroom door.

"I was hoping you'd call," Drew says, grinning. "I haven't been able to think about anything but you since lunch."

Madison mumbles, "Must be nice," but it's so low there's no way he heard her.

Drew steps inside, shutting her door, and pulls her close. She gives him a quick peck on the lips, then pushes his groping hands off her body.

"Drew, we can't. My mom is home."

"That didn't stop you earlier." He lets out a conspiratorial laugh.

Madison steps back and straightens her sweater. "Well, I'm not like that anymore—or I don't want to be." She takes in a deep breath. "I need to talk to you about what happened with Cassidy. I did terrible things, and I need to know if—"

Drew closes the space between them. "The only thing you need to know is how perfect I think you are."

"Really? You think I'm perfect?"

"You know I do. I love you." Madison relaxes from her tense position, and Drew takes the opportunity to cuddle close. "Nobody blames you, so you shouldn't blame yourself."

"The only reason they don't blame me is that they don't know the truth."

"And who's going to tell them?"

Madison searches Drew's face. He leans back, seeming lost in her heavy-lashed eyes, unfazed by the tears moistening her cheeks. My eyes are fading in and out of focus, making this conversation even more unsettling.

I blink to stay in the moment, determined to get answers. "Madison, what is he talking about? What did you do?" My voice gets buried in the icy downpour swallowing me. I catch a glimpse of Drew wrapping his arms around Madison before my eyes wash out completely.

TRAITOR

CASSI! WAIT UP."

I flinched when I heard my nickname—the one that only Ethan used. The mixture of adrenaline and anger shooting through my veins had made me forget anyone else was in Aimée's backyard. I glared at Madison as I blotted the tears threatening to spill over my eyes.

"I'll go inside with you," Ethan finished when he reached me, a little out of breath. He squeezed me around the waist and whispered in my ear, "It'll be cold out here without you."

I leaned into his kiss on my cheek, temporarily forgetting the crushing truth I'd learned minutes ago about my *so-called* best friend. I eyed the thick oak tree to make sure Caleb had done what I asked. Relief poured over me when I saw that he wasn't in sight.

"Why did you leave the bonfire?" Ethan asked.

I went into insta-blasé defense mode. "I was on my way to

find you. Someone told me a lie that you were inside." I glared at Madison again. She covered her face with her hands.

"Oh, Madison." Ethan looked up like he'd only noticed her there that second. He probably had. He never paid anyone else a drop of attention when I was around. His voice lowered with quiet concern. "Are you okay?"

Madison dropped her hands, letting her arms dangle weakly at her sides. She wasn't only crying, she was bawling. I bit down on the inside of my cheek and swallowed back the venom I wanted to spit at her.

"What's wrong with her?" Ethan asked me.

"The usual drama," I replied in the most even voice I could manage.

"Is it Drew? He said he had something to tell me after the party." He gave Madison a sympathetic smile. "Another breakup?"

"No one's breaking up," I blurted. "I mean, he's her ride. He needs to take her home now." My voice went flat. "She's sick."

A whimpery sob sputtered out of Madison. I rolled my eyes. She had no right acting like the victim here, but I couldn't get into it with her again, not with Ethan around.

Ethan looked at her, and she bowed her head. He must've known something was up, but he didn't question what I'd told him. He never did. I savored that small moment of trust, knowing if he found out the real reason I wanted Madison to leave, it would be gone forever.

"I'll get Drew." He started toward the bonfire, but I grabbed his hand, suddenly terrified about him rejoining the party where rumors of our breakup were running free on who knows whose lips. I racked my brain for an excuse to keep him near me, but everything I came up with sounded like a transparent lie.

Then Madison squeaked out, "Ethan, I'm sorry." I threw her a look that could've iced over hell.

Ethan turned back to us and furrowed his brow in the adorable way he did when he tried to conjugate Spanish verbs. "About what?"

I stepped toward her and hissed between my teeth, "Don't, Mads."

Madison gnawed on her pinkie fingernail and looked away.

The lines in Ethan's forehead deepened. "Are you sure she should leave with Drew? If they've broken up . . ." His voice was timid, releasing his first inkling of doubt in me.

I wanted to answer his pleading eyes, but a few feet away the spotlight on the covered bridge flickered as if it were reminding me of where I'd said I'd be. My eyes skittered between Ethan and the bridge and Drew standing by the bonfire a few million times before I locked my gaze on Ethan's warm eyes.

"Wait for me inside. I'll get Drew and make sure he's okay to drive. It'll only take a few minutes."

I grabbed Madison's shoulders and mimicked her signature air-kiss goodbye, using the closeness of the gesture to whisper, "Not a word or I'll make sure Ethan hates you every bit as much as you want him to hate me."

"Are you sure?" Ethan asked me. There was the doubt again. A pang of guilt stung me.

I nodded emphatically. "You know how they are with each other. I should explain things to him before he sees her like this. I'll meet you inside, but . . . promise you'll wait for me."

He leaned forward and kissed the crown of my head. I wanted nothing more than to forget about Madison's betrayal and how easy it had become to lie to Ethan, ignore the nagging light on the bridge, and tilt my face up so I could melt into Ethan's soft lips, but I couldn't get my lips to relax. They were frozen in a thin line.

He pulled back and smiled a small, almost-sad smile at me. "I promise." His expression shifted to a more playful one. "As long as I'll have you all to myself when you come back."

I placed a hand on each side of his face. "Always. All yours." My lip didn't even twitch when I said it.

19

I COME OUT OF THE MEMORY with this unsettling feeling that I don't truly know anything about anyone I care about. The pain thrashing inside me isn't from ghosting into my past; it's from accepting the truth that one of my best friends has secretly hated me for almost three years. But the worst part about Madison's lies and scheming is on me. I was so preoccupied with my own crap that I didn't even notice a change in her. I spent three days a week at ballet practice with her, and two shared classes and lunches at school, and weekend nights, and countless moments in between. How could I have missed her vying for the decay of what meant the most to me?

I try to think back to any moment that I ignored or wrote off because I stupidly trusted her, but the only things I can see are flashes of Madison crying and me yelling at her after discovering her betrayal. I can't make them stop.

I blink the watery haze from my eyes and see Ethan sitting at his kitchen table with his hands wrapped around a steaming mug of the herbal tea his mom is always trying to get him to drink.

"Ethan." I say his name with relief until his eyes meet mine. They have a new sharpness to them. Fragmented pieces of what I've remembered since the last time I saw him fill my mind. Caleb and the argument on the bridge. Ethan has known about Caleb this whole time. My mouth opens and closes a few hundred times as I try to decide how to deliver the biggest apology in the world when I'm not 100 percent sure what exactly I need to apologize for.

"You've gotta believe me, E."

My mouth clamps shut at the sound of the unexpected voice. I turn my head and see Mica pressing his hands on the kitchen table.

"You're not alone," I say to Ethan, and he nods once.

Mica continues. "I followed your girl because she looked tipsy in an unsafe way, and you weren't around."

"She told me to wait for her inside," Ethan replies distantly. His eyes fix on the ribbons of steam floating above his mug. He won't look at me.

"See, dude? She was hiding something. Not saying I knew"— Mica holds his hands up and moist imprints of his fingertips evaporate slowly, one by one, disappearing from the tabletop— "but come on, we were both there. I mean, nobody could've known what would happen after, but you did the right thing breaking up with her."

Ethan's eyes flick up to me for a second, then back to the ribbons. "I didn't break up with her."

"You don't need to feel guilty about it, E. She cheated on you."

An airless gasp escapes my lips. Ethan steals another look in my direction. The sad-confused look from Saturday invades his face.

He straightens in his chair. "She never got a chance to tell her side of the story."

"Kissing another guy speaks for itself, don't you think?"

Ethan looks right at me. I don't know what to say, but I do know I can't bear him looking at me with those guarded eyes and that frown. I pull the first non-Ethan memory I can think of to the front of my mind. It's long past our bedtime and Aimée and I are using her mom's good mixing bowls to microwave way too much cheddar for our "homemade" mac 'n' cheese. Eleven-year-old me squeals when the cheesy goo bubbles over, and Aimée clamps a hand over my mouth so I won't wake her parents, but her loud laughing takes care of that.

Right when I'm about to close my eyes and escape to the comforts of my *real* best friend, Ethan's voice holds me here. "How do I know the kiss was mutual?" he asks Mica. "You can't prove she wanted it. Can you?"

Mica grinds his jaw from side to side as if the words are stuck between his teeth. He says, "I know you don't believe me, but I won't hold it against you."

Ethan barks a curt laugh.

Mica shakes his head. "Do you want me to leave?" He's already halfway to the front door.

Ethan looks up at the broad line of his friend's retreating figure. "Why won't you hold it against me?"

Mica stops like he's come to the edge of a cliff. He turns slowly and flashes a smaller version of his usual wide smile. "You've got enough going on without worrying if your friends have your back. Call me if you change your mind about talking." Mica snaps his letterman jacket closed and leaves. The kitchen is so quiet I can hear the clock above the stove measuring the space between Ethan and me. *Tick, tick, tick. Lies, lies, lies.*

"I wasn't going to tell you I saw," Ethan says at last.

"Oh." The clock ticks some more.

"Since you didn't remember, I wasn't—" He rubs the back of his neck. "I didn't want to remember that part of us."

My arms go cold in a slow spread, like someone's pouring ice water over my shoulders. I look down and it's dripping from my fingertips onto my leggings and puddling at my feet.

"Neither did I," I realize. My voice shakes with the cold.

Ethan looks at me for a long minute, until he gets up and walks to where I'm standing at the other side of the round table. I lift my hands to stop him but drop them back down, afraid I'll splash him. He stops close enough that the puddle surrounding my Mary Janes is dampening his socks—or at least it should be—and wraps his hands around mine, instantly drying the puddle.

"You remembered?" His voice shakes as much as mine did, but I know it's not from the cold. Both our feet are dry now.

I answer him in a rush in case I melt away again before the words can make their way out of my mouth. "I didn't at first, but I'm starting to piece it together."

"And?"

I almost wish the chill of the water was back to numb the pain swelling in me. "Ethan, I don't want to hurt you—I *never* wanted to hurt you." Snow gathers at the corners of my eyes, melts down my cheeks. "I don't know why I went to the bridge that night—I only wanted to get back to you—but first I had to clean up the mess Madison had made."

"Madison?"

"That's what I was trying to tell you the last time I saw you, before I—" I search for the right words to describe how I travel into my memories.

"Before you left me again."

I say in an adamant voice, "Before I remembered. Madison invited Caleb that night for one reason: to break us up."

Ethan's face lights with surprise. "Why would Madison want to break us up?"

"She wants to be with you. Always has, I guess."

"That's crazy. She's going out with one of my friends."

"Yeah, I'm guessing in hopes of making you jealous or maybe to keep you close." I pause. "I saw her this afternoon dealing pills to Caleb as some sort of payment for coming to the party. They were prescribed to her, and seeing her when she thinks no one else is around has been . . ." I cringe at the idea of her hoarding other possessions of mine. "I think she's depressed or something. Maybe that's why she planned everything." I sigh. "I don't know."

Ethan thinks a minute. "How did she know what you were doing?"

"Maybe she saw me at his house," I say, rubbing my horseshoe pendant for any shred of luck it might still hold. "I went there a few times."

"When?"

I force myself to look at him. I want to look away, but he

deserves more than that. He deserves the straight truth—or at least the parts I remember clearly enough to give him. "That time when I told everyone I was at Joules's skating competition . . . and last week when I said I was working on my Psych project. And on my birthday."

"Your birthday?" He shakes his head, bewildered. "What happened?" I can *feel* the hurt in Ethan's voice—it suffocates the pulsing in my chest. I don't want to tell him any of this. I don't want to have done any of this.

"It was over before it started, Ethan. It wasn't like it is with you—I didn't feel the same." I pause a moment to gain the strength to continue. "We used to be friends when we were little, and it was easier to talk to him about everything going on with my parents. I guess he knows me in a different way than you do."

Ethan's eyes flicker. "How well does he know you?"

You can do this. "We kissed—I promise that's it."

"Sure there isn't anything else you can't remember?" He says "remember" with a spiteful bite that stings.

I reply firmly, "Yes. I may not remember every detail, but I'm *certain* I love you—*only you*. I know how backward that sounds right now, but it's the truth."

He studies my face, waiting for my lip to twitch. It never does. He says, "It must be so strange not remembering what you did."

"You have no idea."

"No, I don't. *I* remember." His words cut me in short jabs. He kneads the back of his neck, thinking for so long I wonder if I've gone invisible to him, full-on ghost as punishment for my cheating and lies.

"I know I don't deserve any favors from you," I start slowly, "but I need to find out what happened to me. How I . . . died. And I can't do it without you."

Ethan lowers his head, shaking it. "Cassi, I don't know what happened—I wasn't there. I'm no help."

"When you talk, people can hear you." He tilts his head up, giving me a careful look. "Every question I have is going to stay unanswered forever unless someone asks for me."

Ethan's jaw drops. "You want me to be your medium?"

"No. Medium sounds so hokey. More like"—I meet his eyes when I find the right word—"translator."

He doesn't say anything, but he doesn't look away from me like I expected him to either. I decide to take that as a good sign.

"You have every right to say no, but I think this is the only way to get the truth."

"And what happens then?" he retorts. "Once you know, what would keep you here?"

I look away from him, not wanting to think about what will happen once I complete my ghostly task. That's truly what I'm afraid of, what makes the pulsing in my chest quicken. If the reason I'm here is to discover how I died, and I solve the mystery, complete my unfinished business or whatever, I could lose everything a second time. I can't lose Ethan again, but . . . I need to know how I died.

"This is what I have to do, Ethan," I tell him in a whisper. "Find the truth, clear my name, *know*." The warm, solid feel of his hand on mine makes me turn to face him again.

"I'll help," he says.

20

OKAY," I SAY SLOWLY as Ethan pulls his car into Aimée's driveway, "if this is going to work, you should probably leave out the part where you can see me."

"You want me to lie?" Ethan takes the keys from the ignition and rotates in his seat to give me the same judgmental look he's been giving me since yesterday.

I lower my voice. "No. But I think this will be a lot easier for her if she doesn't have to deal with believing in a ghost she can't see. I mean, you had a hard enough time with it and we can touch each other."

Early-morning sunlight catches the shimmery glints dancing off my hands, temporarily softening his expression. He lifts his hand like he's going to brush my hair away from my face, but instead he switches off the radio.

"Fine. I'll play puppet then. Whatever you say, I'll repeat—or translate." His tone lets me know he's still angry, but then, with a small smile, he reaches across the passenger seat to push open the door for me like he always does.

I can't keep up with him. One minute he's so mad about Caleb that he can't look at me and the next he's opening doors for me. I motion toward the door handle, and he stops.

"I'm guessing it's going to come off as strange if you open the door and no one steps out."

He shakes his head. "Habit. Sorry."

I shrug, playing it off like this happens every day. "I don't need it opened anyway." I swing my feet toward the door, place them on the cobblestones on the other side, and stand.

"Right," he says hesitantly. He opens the driver's-side door and steps out.

I begin to apologize for the confusion with the door, but he's halfway through his next sentence. He gestures for me to continue, but I gesture back, insisting he finish first. "I was going to ask you not to do stuff like that when we get inside."

"S-sure," I stammer, holding my hands up. "No more going through doors—or walls—no freaky ghost stuff of any kind." He gives me this inexplicable look that makes me feel totally self-conscious. I hate how awkward we are now, stepping on each other's words, not knowing the right thing to say. It makes it seem like every intimate moment we've shared never happened.

Aimée's sister, Bridgette, opens the front door with a toothbrush in her mouth. She wipes her face with the back of her hand, surprised. "Ethan? What are you doing here?"

A slight blush colors Ethan's cheeks. "Sorry, I know it's early."

Mrs. Coutier looks up from the newspaper she's reading and

pushes off a stool at the marble kitchen counter. She straightens her dark hair as she hurriedly swallows the bite of croissant she took before she saw us—er, Ethan. "Oh, Ethan, never mind what time it is. You are always welcome in our home." Mrs. Coutier nudges Bridgette, who nods sheepishly and ducks into the hall bathroom. Mrs. Coutier places a gentle hand on Ethan's shoulder. "How are you holding up, dear?"

Ethan hesitates, staring at me. After a long minute, Mrs. Coutier pulls her hand back, folding and unfolding her arms nervously.

"Say something to her, Ethan," I whisper, even though she can't hear me. He looks at me expectantly. I purse my lips. "You're taking this translator thing a bit too literally, don't you think?" He doesn't budge. I heave a sigh. I asked for this, right? "Tell her you tried calling Aimée earlier, but her cell went straight to voice mail."

Ethan repeats what I said, word for word, only switching the "you" for "I."

"Real mature, Ethan." He opens his mouth, and I quickly add, "Don't say that to her!" He snaps his mouth shut, waiting for his next line. "Tell her you hope it's okay that you stopped by because you really need to talk to Aimée." He does. Word for word. Again.

"Of course." Mrs. Coutier looks relieved. "Maybe you two can comfort each other." She pauses. "Aimée's in the playroom. Go on up."

"Thanks, Mrs. Coutier." He came up with that one on his own.

I follow him up the back staircase and wait by his side as he knocks on the door. After a few seconds he knocks again. "Maybe she's still asleep," he whispers.

"Aimée? No way, she shares an alarm clock with the sun. Let me go inside and check."

"Wait—" Ethan grabs for my arm, but I'm already halfway through the door. "So much for no freaky ghost stuff," I hear him mutter on the other side.

"Oops," I say halfheartedly. He deserves a little jolt after what he pulled downstairs. My amused expression fades when I see Aimée sitting in the window seat, bent over that yellow note she found in her bag.

"Knock again," I tell Ethan. He does, but Aimeé doesn't even look up. She simply keeps reading the note over and over in a soft murmur: "It's easy to jump when you get a push."

Ethan knocks a third time. "Just come in," I call to him.

He slowly pushes open the door. "Aimée? It's Ethan. Can I come in?"

Aimée quickly refolds the note and stashes it under a throw pillow when she sees him.

"Tell her you called and you need to talk to her about me," I instruct before he can ask what to say.

Ethan slides his hands into his jeans pockets as he walks toward her. "Sorry I didn't call you back."

I snap my head to look at him. "When did she call you?"

Ethan ignores me, eyeing the corner of yellow paper poking out from under the pillow behind Aimée. "I thought talking in person might be better. I know it's early, but I wanted to catch you before you left for school."

"I was up," she says, looking exhausted. "How did you know I was back at school?"

"Why didn't you tell me she called you?" I interrupt.

"Um." He sneaks a look at me before answering Aimée. "I guess I heard you went back."

Neither of them says anything for a long time. I'm sure Ethan's waiting for me to feed him his next line, but I'm a little pissed he didn't tell me about Aimée's call. "You should find out why she called you," I finally say, hoping to satisfy my own curiosity.

He says, "You know Cassidy wasn't alone on the bridge, right?"

Aimée narrows her eyes at him. "How do *you* know that?"

"I met her there."

Aimée studies him, sussing out why he'd admit this to her. She glances over her shoulder at the pillow that's covering the note. "Did you tell the police that?"

"Of course."

Aimée waves her hand at him. "Sorry. That came out . . ." Her voice trails off with a sigh.

"It's okay. I get why you'd ask."

"So why don't the police suspect you?" Aimée says, then backpedals. "Sorry."

"You better give her your alibi before she turns you in," I tell Ethan.

"It's okay," he says again, and this time I'm pretty sure it's directed at me. "Once the cops read that note, suicide was pretty much the only option they considered. Plus, my dad vouched for me that I was home by 11:45. And Mica saw me leave before she died." We both flinch when he says "died."

Aimée nods. "Mica told me you left."

"Aimée's finally warming up to Mica. They've been quite friendly at school," I fill Ethan in.

"That's not a good idea."

Aimée tilts her head to one side at his odd response. "What's not a good idea?"

I can tell Ethan is straining not to look at me. He says to Aimée, "Hanging out with Mica. He's not—he only wants what he can't have. As soon as he snares you, he'll turn his back on you. That's just how he is with girls."

Aimée's expression shifts. "I know how he is, Ethan, and I'm a big girl. Trust me. I don't want a guy complicating my life right now."

"He can be very persuasive."

"I'm not easily convinced." Aimée pauses. "Harsh analysis of your best friend, don't you think?"

It takes Ethan a second to swallow whatever it is he wants to say but won't. And I'm no help with lines because I'm trying to figure out why his friendship with Mica is in shambles. "Guess I know him too well."

Aimée's upper lip stiffens. "You're going to have to give me more than that if you want me to stop hanging out with the only person at school who doesn't give me sympathy eyes."

"Okay—" Ethan says.

Aimée interrupts him by pointing at his "sympathy eyes."

He blinks. "Mica was on the bridge with Cassi."

"So were you," Aimée shoots back. Then she asks, "Were you the last person to see her alive?"

Ethan waits for me to give him the answer that he must know

by now I don't have. He shakes his head. After a silent minute, he says, "You don't believe me?"

"How do you know you weren't?"

"Because she told—I left her with Mica." He glances at me out of the corner of his eye, jaw tight.

"What?" I ask, stepping in front of him so he can't avoid my question. "Tell her why he was there. I want to know!"

"Why don't you trust him anymore?" Aimée asks, saving him from having to answer me—but her question is just as loaded.

Ethan responds slowly, "You and I both know she didn't take her own life, and he was there."

"That doesn't prove anything. He could have left after you were gone. It was a party, Ethan," Aimée reasons, "and Mica enjoys a good drunken walkabout. You know that. Last year you had to pick him up at 7-Eleven after homecoming. Besides, he was with Drew when it happened. There are more logical suspects than your best friend."

"Sounds like you've been convinced."

Aimée narrows her eyes at him. "You were the last person *I* saw with her. Why should I believe you?"

Ethan's voice hardens. "Do you honestly think I'd be here if I was guilty?"

Aimée doesn't answer.

"Don't challenge her, Ethan," I warn. "It'll make her suspect you more."

"I want to help, okay?" he tells her. "And you're right, there are other suspects."

"Someone else was there too?" It sounds more like a statement than a question. "Was it Caleb Turner?" Aimée asks.

Ethan's eyes widen. "Good guess," he says.

Snow falls onto my hands, sending a chill up my arms. As if he senses me fading away, Ethan shifts his stance so our arms touch. His warmth spreads through me, drying the snow.

"What happened when you found her with him?" The way she asks makes Ethan—and me—aware that she knows there was something going on between Caleb and me.

Ethan risks a glance in my direction. "I didn't push her."

"I didn't say you did. Guilty conscience?" she says, and Ethan grimaces. "I know you two fought at the party and that's why you left early."

"That doesn't mean . . ." Ethan's voice wavers. "I left before she fell, but you were there. It happened at your house—"

"*I* wasn't on the bridge with her," Aimée interrupts. "If I had been, she'd still be alive." Her words hang in the air, sprouting between-the-lines meanings. She grips the pillow beside her so tightly that her knuckles turn white.

Ethan holds up his hands. "No one's accusing anyone here. Right?"

Aimée stays quiet.

I put my hand on Ethan's shoulder to stop him from saying anything else. "Give her a minute."

Aimée straightens the elastic holding her side ponytail in place and clears her throat. "Are we really going to do this?"

"Do what?"

"Team up to figure out how our girlfriend died?" Aimée has been referring to me as her girlfriend since middle school when we set the class record for being each other's consecutive dance dates. She used to tease Ethan that I'd been *her* girlfriend longer than his.

"You need to do this," Ethan replies.

Aimée crosses her arms indignantly. "How do you figure?"

"You love Cassidy as much as I do, and I know that if I don't do this for her I'll regret it for the rest of my life." He pauses. "You will too."

Aimée flinches at his use of *love* instead of *loved*, but her expression relaxes. She takes a deep breath and reaches under the pillow beside her. "I found this in my bag after school on Tuesday." She hands Ethan the star-shaped note.

He unfolds and reads it. "Who wrote this?"

"I think Caleb Turner did. I found another note in Cassidy's locker," Aimeé says.

Ethan glances at me as he hands the note back to her.

"Sorry about the third degree," Aimeé goes on, "but I have to exhaust every possibility if I'm going to prove Caleb's guilty. I showed the police both notes. They're not going to be any help. According to them, Cassidy's blood-alcohol level combined with her supposed suicide note makes 'foul play unlikely.'" Aimée harrumphs. "They're lazy dolts who don't want to do their job. That's why I went to school on Tuesday and Wednesday. I'm going to prove them wrong. If you want to help, you have to come back too. Today."

Ethan thinks for a minute. "You're convinced Caleb's to blame?"

"Is there someone else you suspect?"

"It doesn't make any sense that Caleb would give you that note to, what, brag? Turn himself in? Why not go straight to the police?"

Aimée thinks a minute. "I know he put the other note in Cassidy's locker. I saw him there."

"Did you tell Madison about the notes?"

"No. Why?"

"I think she has something to do with this."

"And I think you're not telling me everything you know, but what choice do we have? Everyone else is happy to sweep Cassidy's death under the rug as a cautionary tale. We're the only ones who want to find the truth. So are you coming to school with me or not?"

Ethan curls his hand around mine. "Will you be there?"

"Do you mean me?" I ask.

He tightens his grip, and I hope Aimée assumes he's making a fist to fight back some emotion.

"Of course I'll go with you," I answer on top of Aimée's yes.

Ethan squeezes my hand tighter and looks at Aimée. "I'm in."

21

ARE YOU SURE YOU'RE READY FOR THIS?" I ask Ethan as we cross the school parking lot. "Everyone's going to ask about me and how you're doing."

"I'll be fine," Ethan reassures me, adjusting his backpack, which, thankfully, he had in his car. "You'll be here to keep me sane whenever someone asks me what it's like to lose my girlfriend and I have to pathetically pretend I know what to say, right?"

"A ghost only you can see is your source of sanity?" I jeer, feeling unbelievably good about him calling me his girlfriend and not his *ex*.

"As long as you do the same for me, I'm up for the job." From behind him, Aimée answers Ethan's question, which she thinks was for her.

He spins on his heel and lets out a nervous laugh. "Oh, thanks, Aimée."

I say, "We should definitely work out some form of nonverbal communication. That was a close one."

"I'm on it." Ethan looks at Aimée but nods to me. I smile at his effort to co-communicate.

Aimée says, "You're calmer than I was on my first day."

"I guess it's easier knowing someone has my back."

Aimée starts toward the school. "Yeah, I thought Madison had mine."

I grimace at hearing Madison's name.

"Where is she today?" Ethan asks, falling in step beside Aimée.

"She didn't even make it to lunch on Tuesday, and now her dad has her on new meds for nightmares or something." Aimée shakes her head, looking disappointed, then peers over at Ethan. "Don't go reading into that though. She didn't have anything to do with whatever happened to Cassidy."

"Did you ask her about it?" Ethan replies.

Aimée fidgets with the strap of her bag before she finally admits, "Her cell has been off since yesterday."

Ethan throws me a pointed look.

"That doesn't mean what you think it means." Aimée kicks at a piece of loose gravel. "She was deep in issues even before Cassidy . . ."

She knew about Madison's depression and didn't tell me? No, I realize. Madison probably asked her not to tell and she kept her word. There's a difference.

Ethan gives her a second. "Yeah, she was crying at the party. What was up?"

Aimée shakes her head again. "What else? Drew."

"She told you that?" I ask, and Ethan repeats it for me so Aimée can hear.

"She didn't have to."

Aimée stands between Ethan and me inside the doorway, taking in the audience of shameless gawkers who aren't even pretending to be on their way to class like they did when she was alone. Now that Ethan's here too, it's a full-on spectacle.

"Not much for subtlety, are they?" Aimée deadpans.

"I'm so glad you're here," Ethan murmurs. I'm not sure if he means me or Aimée.

"Are you going to be okay on your own?" Aimée asks him. He leans his shoulder against mine and nods. She nods back and hands him a page of her monogrammed stationery.

"What's this?" he asks.

"Your assignment. It's a list of people who were at the party and who also had access to my bag on Tuesday. One of them had to have either written the notes or seen something Saturday night that we can use."

"I thought you said Caleb wrote the notes."

"I *think* he did, but I need proof for the police. Plus, you brought up a good point. I'm still trying to figure out why he'd incriminate himself that way. So far the only explanation I've come up with is his irrational stoner logic, which is obviously not solid proof of anything, except Caleb's lack of willpower." She points at the list. "Try to get through as many of them as you can. We'll reconvene at lunch."

Aimée watches him walk away toward his first-hour Econ class with a wary expression. I get her suspicion. There's no way she doesn't notice how he's always looking slightly past her (to me) or how weird some of the co-communicating stuff he says comes off as. And the fact that she saw us arguing at the party is going to keep him guilty until proven innocent in her eyes unless she finds proof someone else is to blame.

When the bell rings, Aimée rushes to Physics, and I make my way to Ethan's class.

"C." I turn instinctively at the sound of Ethan's voice. He's motioning for me to join him in the boys' bathroom at the end of the hall. He lets the door fall shut after I walk in.

"Why'd you call me C?" I ask, scrunching up my nose at the dingy olive-green tile as I dodge the urinals—a big *ew* to ghosting through a urinal cake!—and stand in the middle of the room, glad, for the first time, that I can't smell anymore. I don't want to be near anything in here regardless of how immune I am to germs now. That very human, alive, reaction lightens my mood.

Ethan explains, "In case someone heard me—'C' could be interpreted as the word *see*, as in 'Did you *see* that?' or '*See* what I mean?'"

My mouth curls into a smile. The sense of relief from being around him—feeling the pulse inside me steady—makes me forget how much things have changed between us.

"Why didn't you follow me when I headed to Econ?" Ethan asks, reaching for my hand. "I wanted to turn around, but I thought that might freak Aimée out."

He pulls me close the way he always does before a casual kiss at school, with our hands clasped between us. I savor the borrowed warmth I get from his hands. Maybe being here has reminded him of how we used to be. My eyes travel across his face to his lips. I lean in, but he steps away and lifts himself onto a sink.

"It's weird being in school. Everything's so . . . normal."

"Yeah, normal can get weird when you're used to this." I extend my arm and rotate it so it sparkles in the fluorescents. My weak attempt at a joke falls flat. "Do you want me to go to class with you?" I ask.

"I'd rather get started on Aimée's 'assignment.'"

"You don't mind?"

"Well, technically I'm excused for today, so none of my teachers will be expecting me. Plus, this is important to you. I can surrender to Aimée's demands if it means making things right for you." Ethan walks toward the door and pushes it open.

"And for you," I add as I pass by him into the hall. "This is important to you too, right? You believe I wasn't alone—that I didn't mean to die, don't you?"

Ethan turns his head from side to side to make sure we're alone. "No question. But you need the truth way more than Aimée or me. You have some kind of fated mission to accomplish."

I start down the hall, avoiding the "fated mission" comment because I don't want to think about what will happen to me when I complete this "mission." "So who's first on that list?"

Ethan pulls the page of stationery from his pocket and reads the names very formally. "Carly Davies, Megan McCuller, Nancy Yeong, Jacob Yeong, Drew Ridelle, Mica Torrez"—Ethan clears his throat uncomfortably—"and Caleb Turner."

"I don't even know half those people."

"Makes sense, I guess."

"No, Ethan . . . I knew him. The guy I was with on the

bridge—from what little I can remember—he seemed to be a friend."

"Hmm." Ethan focuses back on the list, holding his thumb over Caleb's name as if he can erase Caleb's entire presence from my life if he covers his name on that list. "Nancy is an office assistant first hour. We should start with her."

"I think Aimée may have already burned that bridge." Ethan gives me a crooked look at the unintended and completely inappropriate pun. I wave a hand at him. "What I mean is, she called out Nancy in front of her friends about some lame memorial she's putting together for me."

Ethan cuts through a bank of lockers as he heads toward the main office. "Trust me. We should start with Nancy."

"Fine, but you're flying solo on this one."

I hesitate in front of the glass wall that separates the main office from the commons. The wide central hall looks endless without the clusters of cliques spotting the brown-brick perimeter. Ethan walks inside and leans his elbows on the reception counter while he asks the secretary if she can get him an excused-absence form. One shoulder sits higher than the other as he shifts his weight to his right foot.

He used to lean on the hood of his car like that while he waited for me after school. I'd take the long way around the lot so I could enjoy the view and his effortless turnabout when I called his name from behind. His hair always did this golden-sparkle thing in the sunlight even though it was more brown than blond. When the sun reflected off the Sebring's hood and hit his highlights, they shined the same golden-brown color in his eyes. My hair did the same thing—turning golden in the sun. Now it looks rainbow-y in sunlight along with my skin and clothes. We've lost that physical sameness I always secretly thought proved we were meant to be together.

The secretary stands and disappears around the corner. Ethan does a played-down version of the turn and tilts his head toward the door. I enjoy the view for another second before stepping through the glass wall. He stares at me with big eyes, and mouths, *Showoff.*

I stand next to him, feeling a smile coming on. The anger I was afraid would ruin what time we have left together seems to have lessened some. He glances up at me as he absentmindedly traces the multihued prisms my skin casts on the gray laminate counter in the morning light pouring down through the skylights. Maybe he's ready to forgive me.

"You needed an excused-ab—" Nancy Yeong holds her hands out, waving the paper for emphasis. Her usual "uniform" of crisp white shirt, cardigan, and pleated skirt is uncharacteristically wrinkled and untucked. Her eyes look tired too, as they rove over Ethan's face like she expects gnarled emotional scars to magically reveal themselves. Aimée must have really gotten under her skin yesterday. "Mrs. Graham didn't tell me the form was for *you*. I'm sorry."

"It's okay." He gives her a small smile when she hands him the form over the counter. "Thanks, Nancy."

"I can't believe you're back already. I'm only here because I'm lead organizer for Cassidy's memorial. Any requests for remembrances? I'm asking her closest friends." Nancy twirls her sleek black hair around her finger like she's wringing out the over-flowing concern in her voice.

When he answers with a simple no, I say, "Aimée didn't take that question as well as you." He presses his lips together, fighting a grin.

Nancy continues. "Student council teamed up with the counseling office to offer extended hours at lunch for anyone who needs to talk through the loss the student body has suffered. I'll be there for sure."

"Is she for real?" I jut my arm out, hand palm up, toward her. "She didn't even like me."

"Cassidy had more friends than she knew," Ethan says. "But I don't actually need this form."

Nancy looks mortified. "Oh, did I bring the wrong one? I thought Mrs. Graham said—"

"You gave me the one I asked her for," Ethan says, "and I'm sure my parents are supposed to fill it out since I missed Monday, Tuesday, and Wednesday, but I actually wanted to talk to you." He turns the excused-absence form under his finger and looks away shyly like he doesn't notice her checking him out.

"Can you ask her if she saw who pushed me so we can get out of here already?" I say brusquely.

Ethan doesn't seem to notice the venom in my voice or how Nancy is strategically leaning toward him. "Do you mind if we talk?" he says.

Nancy untangles her hair from around her finger and flattens her hands on the counter. "Sure, Ethan. Whatever you need." Her fingers spread so that she's touching pinkies with Ethan.

I grit my teeth. I don't know what it is that makes me want to materialize for the sole purpose of irrevocably spooking her—actually, I totally know what it is. She's flirting with my boyfriend in front of me! Okay, I get that she can't see me and I'm not technically his girlfriend anymore unless you follow the whole love-never-dies *Romeo and Juliet* credo, but we've been together for close to three years and he's a widow . . . ish. Where's the respectful student council president who organized special counseling for "the loss the student body has suffered"? Or was that a cheap ploy to catch him on the rebound?

"It's been hard for me not knowing how Cassidy"—Ethan swallows hard—"died."

Nancy straightens and crosses one arm over her stomach in a rigid twitch. "Did Aimée Coutier put you up to this?"

I look at Ethan. "Told you. Bridge burned."

"No," Ethan says. "I thought you might have seen something at the party. And"—he pushes his hands through his hair and rests them back on the counter—"I don't think I can move on until I know what happened."

"On the news they said there was a possibility the railing on the old covered bridge gave out, but I was under the impression that it wasn't an accident. Everyone knows about her note." Nancy's voice is guarded, but I can tell she feels bad for Ethan. Maybe she will tell him something useful.

"Did you see anything that might help me understand why she was on the bridge?"

Nancy shakes her head real quick. "No—well, I saw her, obviously, but only from the park. I was waiting for my brother. I was supposed to be his designated driver," she adds quietly.

"Around what time were you there?"

"Oh, I don't know." She replies so fast it sounds like one long word.

"Could you maybe check your phone to see what time your brother called for you to pick him up?"

"Um." She narrows her almond-shaped eyes and knots her black hair between her fingers again.

"Oh, she totally knows something," I say. Ethan kicks my heel and clears his throat simultaneously.

"I'm trying to figure out what time Cassidy went to the bridge." Ethan picks up a calm, reassuring tone. "So if you saw her there at a certain time it would be a big help."

"I'd like to help you, Ethan, but . . ."

"Anything you can remember." He gives her an irresistible pleading look.

She hesitates a second, then confesses she was supposed to drop off her brother and come back at midnight to drive him home but instead stayed without telling him. I can't blame her for cracking after Aimée's display yesterday. Plus, Ethan can be very disarming simply by being in the room, and he was actually trying with her. "It was 12:12 when we got to the park. I remember because my brother told me to make a wish. He's superstitious."

"Did you see anyone else in the park? Footprints in the snow, maybe?"

"No. But when I was still in Aimée's yard, I overheard a girl saying something about getting Cassidy away from the party so she could explain."

"Explain what?"

Nancy pulls up an apologetic smile. "I didn't hear anything else."

Ethan's eyebrows scrunch into a thick line. "Well, do you know who she was?"

"She had her back to me, so I couldn't see very well, but she had on furry white boots that made her look like a polar bear. I definitely remember those. And the boy she was talking to is on the hockey team."

"Mica Torrez?"

Nancy shakes her head. "No, the name embroidered on his hat was Ridelle."

Ethan turns his head and stares straight at me. "Drew."

"And Madison." I ask, "Have you talked to Drew since the party?"

"He called me on Sunday, but I didn't answer," Ethan co-communicates.

"He was at Madison's yesterday," I tell him.

Nancy begins talking again and Ethan nods like he's listening, but I can tell he's homed in on my words.

I continue. "And she was acting superstrange, like she didn't want him there at first but then he mentioned a promise she'd made and they started making out. Something was off though. Maybe he knows something she doesn't want anyone else to find out. Maybe inviting Caleb wasn't the only thing she did and he's protecting her," I offer, playing my own devil's advocate.

Nancy sits in Mrs. Graham's chair, wheels herself to the computer, and maneuvers the attendance software like a pro. "Drew's in Wood Shop this hour." She points to his schedule displayed on the screen.

"Drew takes Wood Shop?" I ask.

"Figures," Ethan says distantly, "his dad's a mill worker." Nancy nods, trying to seem interested in the random factoid that wasn't even meant for her.

"He is?" I ask, surprised. I always figured Drew's dad was a lawyer or something highbrow like that considering his Ralph Lauren–sponsored wardrobe and precious BMW. Although now it makes sense why he has a "vintage" model instead of something new.

"I could write you a pass if you need to talk to him," Nancy offers, and Ethan accepts. "I wish I could help more." Nancy hands him the pass, then crosses her arm over her stomach again. "Let me know if you need a shoulder or an ear. I'm an excellent listener."

"Can you believe her?" I say as Ethan pushes open the side entrance to the main building that leads to the quad. "'A shoulder or an ear,'" I mock. "Could she have been any more obvious?"

Ethan stops in front of the arts building, pulling the sleeves of his black thermal down over his hands. "She was being polite."

"Right."

"Are you jealous?" he asks.

"The only thing I'm jealous of student council queen about is the fact that she's breathing."

"You sound jealous."

I pretend not to hear him. "She was totally hiding something. Did you hear how fast she was talking and that move with her arm over her stomach?"

"What do you think she's hiding?"

"I don't know, but she pulled up Drew's schedule suspiciously fast. She could've looked up Aimée's schedule too and slipped that note into her bag."

Ethan squints at me. "Is this about protecting Caleb?" His question jolts me.

"No. I don't trust her."

"You mean you don't like her."

"She was flirting with you in front of me. What do you expect?"

"She couldn't see you."

I harrumph. "Still."

"Guess some people don't care about that kind of thing." Ethan's expression shifts, and I realize he wanted me to see Nancy fawn over him. But I can't even be mad about it because he knows exactly how I feel, only worse. He saw another guy's lips flirting with mine.

"I think she knows something," I say, refusing to let Nancy off the hook. Anyone who flirts with a dead girl's boyfriend deserves the most thorough of investigations.

"Cassi—"

I cut him off. "We—you—should tell the police to question her again."

"Cassi."

"What?" I snap, still ripe from the scene in the office.

"She found you." Something inside me sinks. "After you fell . . . she's the person who called 911. That's why she's on Aimée's list." Ethan lets his backpack slide down his shoulder.

The image of a silhouette looming over Other Me at the riverbank floods my mind. It doesn't resemble Nancy—she's far too petite—but if she found me . . . My thoughts jumble. I can't process this. Ethan shivers.

"You must be freezing," I say. "We should get inside."

"I'm fine. Out here I can talk to you without worrying about anyone thinking I should be institutionalized."

I'm not sure I want to talk now. "You don't have your coat on and it's about thirty degrees."

"You're not cold—I mean you can't get cold, right? What do you care?"

Maybe the weather doesn't affect me anymore, but I suddenly feel drained of the warmth I usually get from him.

The door swings open and two guys step around Ethan. One of them gives him the guy nod, but the other one recognizes him and shoves the nodder. They both stutter out a "S-sorry about your girl" and hurry off.

"That was awkward," Ethan murmurs.

"Ethan," I start tentatively.

"First hour is almost over. We should talk to Drew."

"But." I open my mouth to continue, but Ethan's already inside. I pass through the door and a couple classroom walls to meet him in Wood Shop. He looks surprised when he sees me waiting next to Drew at the band saw.

"E?" Drew yells over the hum of the saw. He flicks the power-off switch, chucks the piece of wood he was cutting into the scrap bin, and brushes sawdust off his red Polo V-neck. "I didn't know you were back today. Jesus, man, how are you?"

Ethan averts his eyes in my direction, silently asking me what his response should be. I don't answer, and neither does he.

Drew gives Ethan another second to respond, then shakes off

his befuddled expression. "What are you doing in Wood Shop?" Ethan follows Drew to one of the beat-up worktables in the center of the room and watches as he cleans sawdust off his leather loafers.

I look around the room at the other T-shirt-clad woodworkers and wonder if Drew's dad made him take Wood Shop the way my mom made me take Trig or if he actually enjoys building birdhouses.

Ethan holds up the pass Nancy gave him. "Thought I'd skip Econ today. Wanna join?"

Drew examines the pass, then stands up from the stool he was sitting on. "Sure, man." He shows Mr. Gower the pass, grabs his backpack, and follows Ethan into the hall. "I've gotta say, I didn't think you'd be back to school this soon."

Ethan expels a humorless laugh. "I've been getting that a lot."

"So where we off to?"

"Someplace private. Any ideas?"

"Yeah, I know a place." He leads Ethan across the quad. "Is everything cool with us?"

"Why wouldn't it be?"

Drew slips on his fleece. "I wasn't sure after what happened with Mica. I thought you might think I knew what was going on—I didn't though."

"It's cool," Ethan replies quickly.

Drew drops his head with a weight-of-the-world sigh. "Have you talked to him yet?" he asks. Ethan gives a stiff nod. "That's big of you, man. Forgiving and forgetting like that."

I step between them and look at Ethan. "What's he talking about?"

"I haven't forgiven or forgotten anything," Ethan says through clenched teeth.

"But you talked to him. I wouldn't be able to be in the same room as him if it were me," Drew says. "What'd he say?"

"Ethan, what's he talking about?" I ask again, louder.

Ethan tilts his head toward me. "Now's not the best time to get into it."

I respond with an audible huff.

Drew stops in front of a rusty maroon door on the side of the gym and pulls hard a couple times before it jerks open with a metallic scrape. The sound loosens something at the back of my memory. A chill stings my arms.

Ethan pokes his head into the dark room. "What is this place?"

"Private." Drew steps inside and turns on the overhead light. It flickers and buzzes for a second and then settles into a dim glow.

Ethan pulls the door shut after I join them in what looks like a storage room. The metal shelves are empty except for a couple old deflated basketballs in the back and a disassembled volley-ball net.

"Wait!" Drew thrusts his foot at the door, stopping it seconds before it shuts. The gesture is eerily familiar. "You can't let it close or we'll be locked in." He slips a thin wedge of wood that looks like the one he was sawing in Wood Shop between the door and the wall. "Learned that one the hard way," Drew continues. "Luckily, Maddy had her cell."

"Did she say anything to you about wanting to get Cassidy away from the party on Saturday?"

"Let me think, um." Drew tilts his head up and squints

like he's sorting through the vast amount of information Madison has shared with him. The effort is almost comical to me since I know the truth is that she tells him only what she wants him to think he knows. "Well," Drew says, "they had some massive fight at the party, but you know more about that than I do."

Ethan gives Drew an expectant look.

Drew asks, "The fight is why you took her inside, right?"

"I knew she was upset about something, but she was crying too hard to explain." Ethan glances at me. "What was the fight about?"

Drew shrugs and leans against the small sink in the corner. There's something I recognize in the repetitive *plunk, plunk, plunk* of the dripping faucet. The sound is echoed by the droplets falling from my fingertips onto my shoes. I stare at the growing puddle, unable to move.

"Who knows," Drew answers. "Girls *always* fight when they're drunk, right?"

Ethan thinks a minute. "What did Cassidy say when she talked to you at the party?"

"That Maddy drank too much and needed a ride home. Then she sort of told me quick to tell you to meet her on the bridge, and she ran off. Mica and I went inside to find Maddy after that, so I guess that was the last time I saw Cassidy." Drew's eyes widen. "It's so weird that nobody will ever see her again. Right?"

"I never asked him to take Madison home, Ethan. I was going to after I went to the bridge, but I never got a chance." My words sound echoey, like distorted ripples underwater.

"You're sure that's all?" I don't know if Ethan is talking to me or Drew, but he seems too far away to ask.

"Yeah," Drew replies.

I struggle to move my feet, but they're stuck in thick, wet snow. I sink deeper into the wetness that puddles and piles around my feet, the *plunk, plunk* filling my ears, until my leggings are soaked up to my skirt. I try to clear away the snow with my hands but they sink through the white mound, farther and farther, until it swallows me.

NO PLACE TO JUDGE

I CHEWED ON MY THUMBNAILS as I walked across the quad. I looked down at the chipped, uneven edges and frowned. I'd painted my nails an extra-fabulous shade of hot pink the day before, for my birthday, and now I'd have to redo both thumbs before my party tomorrow.

I don't even bite my nails. This is not me!

I shoved my hands into my jeans pockets, staring at the faded maroon door in front of me. The handle was crusted in rust and scratched like someone had taken a crowbar to it. The door didn't budge when I pulled on the handle, so I knocked. No answer. I leaned on the cold brick wall of the school gym. When my toes were cold enough to make me wish I'd worn boots instead of my mesh Pumas, I gave the door another pull. I might as well have been trying to yank a tree from its roots.

"Ugh." I kicked at the door, sending a shooting pain up my frozen foot. How had I gotten myself into this situation? Skipping Creative Writing—my favorite class—to freeze my toes off because I received a text from an unknown number saying: *We need to talk. 4th hr east entrance of the gym.*

Could you get any more cryptic? If I didn't have such a guilty conscience, I would have ignored it. But with what I'd been up to the past few weeks, I could read exactly what was written between the lines. I kicked the door again with my other foot to balance out the pain.

"There's a trick to it." I spun on my toes to identify the voice. Drew brushed his brown curls out of his eyes and slipped his backward Crescent High Hockey cap back on. "Both hands, pull hard to the right, and"—he yanked hard on the handle—"open-says-a-me." The dark room reeked of old rubber and sweat.

"What are you doing here?" I asked, hoping I wouldn't have to go inside that ancient sweat box. "I wasn't expecting . . ." I wasn't sure how to end that sentence.

"You know why I'm here."

I reached into my back pocket and pulled out my cell. "You texted?"

"Inside." He nodded toward the room, which, from what I could tell, was an old storage closet.

I sucked in a long breath of fresh spring air so I wouldn't have to smell any more of the old-sweat stink than humanly necessary. He thrust his foot against the door while he propped it open a crack with a thin piece of wood, then lifted himself up on the edge of the utility sink in the corner. He didn't say anything for a long time, and I sure wasn't going to be the first to talk. He might not know about Caleb and everything in Mrs. Wirlkee's class. Anything I said would be self-sabotage. So I stayed quiet.

The sink's drippy faucet kept track of our silence. *Plunk, plunk, plunk.* With each drop a new bead of sweat moistened the back of my neck.

He finally said, "You're awfully quiet."

"You're the one who wanted to talk. I don't even know why you asked me here. Is something up with you and Madison?"

He snickered as he gripped the edge of the sink and leaned forward. "Last chance to come clean."

"About what?" I asked. What good would selling myself out do? If he knew, he'd tell Ethan and probably Madison too, which meant Aimée would know in under a day. I might as well stay silent until I found out what Drew knew.

"You're going to make me say it, aren't you?" he asked. I stared at him, eyes unblinking. He said, "I know you weren't at your sister's competition like you said you were."

"What are you talking about? I was at the rink that entire week—"

"No," he interjected. "*I* was at the rink that entire weekend, working the peewee hockey camp. I didn't see you sitting with your dad."

"I—I was with my mom."

Drew narrowed his eyes at me. "No you weren't."

The last wisp of clean outside air I'd managed to hold in my lungs came rushing out. A gasp pulled in the rank odor I'd been avoiding. It filled my lungs, seeped into my veins. It ran through me and I instantly felt disgusting and dirty inside and out.

"Do you have any idea how much E loves you?"

I set my jaw, on the defensive. "Of course I do. I love him too."

"Then stop what you're doing. Now. Before someone gets hurt."

"I'm not doing anything."

"I know what's going on with you and that stoner kid." He paused. "What's off in your head that you'd cheat on E with someone like that?"

"Caleb and I are only friends. It's not what you think."

"I think you're making a sucker out of my friend. He deserves better than that."

"So does Madison," I threw back. I couldn't stand this lecture coming from Drew.

"What's that supposed to mean?"

"Half the time you're smothering her, making sure she calls you before she makes plans to do anything, which doesn't make any sense because the other half of the time you're standing her up."

His face flushed deep red. He opened his mouth twice, then pressed his lips together. "You don't know what you're talking about, and you're in no place to judge anyone's relationship."

He pushed off the sink and crossed the cramped room in one step. His shoulders broadened as he closed me into a corner. My throat tightened up, trapping the vile grossness of the room, this moment, inside me. A rush of heat filled my cheeks, making my head feel too heavy to hold up.

"Caleb and I were only—only working on our Psych project," I stammered. "I didn't want to tell anyone that's where I was because . . ." A million believable, totally true reasons why I lied about going to Caleb's that weekend ran through my brain, but none of them would come out. Instead my mouth betrayed me. "It's over now. Please don't tell Ethan. Let me do it."

Drew's face slowly returned to its natural pale color, but his eyes were still fiery. He thought awhile, then tugged open the door and gestured sharply for me to leave. I turned my head away from him as I left the wretched closet.

"Cassidy." I reluctantly turned back. "If you don't come clean by this weekend, I'm telling E."

It was a punch to my stomach that knocked the air out of my lungs. The party on Saturday, Madison's and Aimée's planning, everything would be ruined if I told Ethan the truth this weekend. I crossed my arms tighter against my chest as the door scraped shut and Drew passed me on the sidewalk. I stood there beside the gym numb to the biting wind. My eyes spilled over with tears of regret while my world slowly began to implode.

22

MY EYES BLINK BACK INTO FOCUS as my limbs tingle painfully. I turn my head from side to side and realize I'm in the girls' bathroom at school, the small one in the foreign-language hall with floor-to-ceiling mauve tile. For some reason, the sight of it makes me want to scream. I'm so sick of not being able to control when I fall into a memory or where I end up afterward, of being in bathrooms and closets, and of people harboring secrets.

It seems everyone I know holds captive some piece of my past. I want the pieces back no matter how much they'll hurt. They're mine and only I deserve to hold them.

I stare at my reflection in the mirror above the row of sinks, desperately searching for clarity, but I don't recognize myself. Not because the iridescent glow of my skin shimmers insubstantially where a solid face should be, but because something is missing. Something I need to get back.

I squeeze my eyes shut and try to focus on a truly me moment, something that can bring me back from this place where I'm a stranger in my own mind, but I'm so mixed up that I can't even differentiate one memory from the next. It's a fast-forward reel of dance recitals and family road trips and afternoons spent playing Chinese checkers with Joules. I look so young. It's like my memory is telling me I haven't been myself since fifth grade and there's no going back.

The sound of a stall door unlatching makes my eyes open. A small piece of me locks into place when I see my best friend reflected next to me in the mirror.

I turn to face her, then lift my hand to replace a rogue hair that's escaped her royal-blue knit hat. She catches it before I can, turning my fingers to dust. I snatch my hand away from the prickly shock and wait for the dust to settle into ghostly flesh.

Aimée and I sigh at the same time. I lean into the warmth I know her breath must carry even though I can't feel it. She's wearing the super-low-cut black sweater that I bought her for her sixteenth birthday last year. She hasn't worn it since the day one of Shaw's friends teased her about being able to see her bra under it. I saw her hide it in her sock drawer that night. She must have dug it out.

"You know, Meems, I'm pretty sure Kyle Daley was flirting when he told you you needed a license to wear that thing."

Boys was always the one subject Aimée was slow in. She never picked up on the way their teasing was flirting or their staring was admiring. That was probably why she'd been able to fend off Mica's advances for so long.

I smile to myself, remembering the time Kyle and Aimée joined my family on a trip to Niagara Falls. *Three times* he "accidentally" walked in on her changing in the back of the RV

Dad rented. Once, I can give him. Twice, maybe he forgot to knock. But three times? Shaw's friends never once walked in on me like that, let alone three times.

"He totally thought you were hot," I say, pretending things are normal and she can hear me.

After a few seconds of digging around in her messenger bag, she slams it onto the sink in front of her and starts pulling textbooks out and tossing them on the floor—the floor! It's so not Aimée to bend the rules of hygiene like that.

"What are you looking for?" I ask, wishing I could help.

"You have to be kidding me." Aimée groans. She turns the bag upside down in the sink and rummages around in the pile of pencils and assignments. Finally, she pulls out a small tub of vanilla lip balm with a flourish.

"That's empty," I tell her. It's Madison's favorite. She used the last of it when we were at Ethan's house for a movie night a month ago and put it back so Aimée wouldn't notice. Anger rises in me, thinking how she must have primped like that in an effort to impress *my* boyfriend.

Aimée's addicted to lip gloss the way some people are addicted to coffee or cigarettes or crack. The problem with Aimée's addiction is, she never has any lip gloss with her. She frowns when she opens the tub.

Out of habit, I reach for my coat pocket because I always carry my watermelon lip gloss with me in case such an Aimée emergency arises, but I'm forgetting, I don't have access to ordinary things like pockets and zippers anymore.

My eyes jolt from my one-dimensional, freak-show outfit when Aimée's arm whips past my face. The glass lip-balm tub shoots across the room and cracks in half when it makes contact with the tile wall. The pieces clatter to the floor and the metal top rolls its way back to the sinks. Aimée kicks it so hard with her pointy boot that it ricochets off the door and disappears under one of the stalls. She leans against the wall and slides to the floor.

I sit next to her. "If it makes you feel better, I'm pretty sure my lip gloss wand would poke right through my mouth."

She tilts her head back and closes her eyes. "If you were here my stupid lips wouldn't be chapped because you'd have that watermelon crap"—I say, "That you hate," at the same time as she says—"that I hate, but sort of obsessively want now because you aren't here to lend it to me." She exhales. "I'm a mess. This is a mess. I need some friggin' Bonne Bell post-friggin'-haste!"

A girl with mousy brown hair opens the bathroom door. "Everything okay in here? I heard yelling."

"Having a mental meltdown here. Do you mind?" Aimée waves her hand at the girl, who looks quizzically at the busted glass on the floor.

"What's going on?" A second girl peeks her head past the door; her blond ponytail swishes across her neck. As Aimée looks up, a wicked smile curls her mouth because two people from her list have offered themselves up for questioning.

"You know who I am, right?" Aimée asks them as she stands.

Carly and Megan nod in unison as they step inside. "We're really sorry about your friend," Carly says.

"I'm sorry too—for you," Aimée says with faux sincerity, hand over her heart.

Megan tilts her head to the side, clueless. "Why?"

"You must have been close with Cassidy, seeing as you were

at her *invite-only* birthday party. You lost a friend too, right?" The girls look at each other, scrambling for a response. "Have you told the police you were uninvited guests at a party that ended with a body count?"

Megan and Carly flinch at Aimée's harsh tone. I do too.

"We were invited—honest," Megan says.

Carly elbows her.

"By who?" Aimée asks.

Megan looks at Carly, who flicks her ponytail when she turns to Aimée and says, "I'm getting a little tired of taking crap for a rumor I didn't even start." Aimée arches one eyebrow, challenging Carly. "I don't care if you don't believe me. The person who told me is a reliable source."

"Of course." Aimée steps toward Carly. "And I'm going to assume that 'source' is yourself and pass my suspicions on to the police unless you tell me what you know right now."

"M-Mica Torrez," Megan sputters. "Carly hooked up with him last week, and he told her Ethan and Cassidy were going through a rough patch, about to break up or something."

Carly's eyes practically pop out of her skull. "*Megan*. Shut. Up."

Megan looks at Carly. "What? It's not like he ever called you back. *He* can deal with her." She lowers her voice so only Carly will hear. "She's scary."

Judging by the smirk Aimée turns on, she heard. "Did he invite you to the party?"

"Chill, I'm not scammin' on your man," Carly says in a rush, cutting Megan off. "We were invited by Madison Scott like everyone else."

Of course. Madison invited the freshman gossip twins to

spread the word that Ethan and I were breaking up, probably as backup in case her original plan fizzled.

"Mica is *not* my man," Aimée insists.

"Whatevs. I didn't even see him at the party. And he didn't tell me anything about Cassidy. I sort of read his texts while he was in the bathroom." She pinches the top of her nose like telling the truth has taken this enormous toll on her nervous system. Or maybe lying has. "I truly am sorry. I wouldn't have said anything if I'd known Cassidy was going to take it so hard. You're not going to call the cops on us, are you?"

The genuine look of horror on Carly's face reveals her role in what happened to me: pawn. Aimée sees it too and answers no. The girls leave before "scary" Aimée has a chance to say anything else. As soon as they're gone, her tough façade fades.

That rogue piece of her hair falls again, and I mimic her movement so it seems like my hand tucked it under her hat, not hers. She reaches into the sink for her bag and starts replacing her textbooks inside. She hesitates, holding the star-shaped note. She carefully unfolds it and reads, "It's easy to jump when you get a push."

I run my finger just above the large print. "We need to find out who wrote this, Meems."

Aimée checks her watch, then gets to her feet. She stuffs—or rather, very quickly reorganizes according to height—her pencils under the front flap of her messenger bag and dashes out of the bathroom to class.

. . . . .

AT LUNCH, Aimée waits for Ethan at a small table in Fresh-man Bottom-Feeder No-Man's-Land on the clear opposite side of the cafeteria from our usual crowded table. I follow Ethan through the lunch line, where he purchases a supremely nutritious meal of Powerade.

"How's that liquid diet treating you?" I ask as we cross over into No-Man's-Land.

Ethan holds the bottle up to his mouth and pretends to take a sip as he answers me. "Those who don't eat don't get to judge the dietary choices of others."

"Ha-ha."

"I didn't expect to see you smiling," Aimée says to Ethan as we reach her table. "Do you have good news?"

Ethan's head snaps up. "No, I was, um, superthirsty. This Powerade really hit the spot." He holds out the red drink for Aimée to see.

"Dork," I say, and laugh.

Ethan pulls out the chair across from Aimée, purposely bumping into my leg, and I stumble. He takes a drink to hide his smirk. I poke him in the ribs as I sit beside him.

For a moment, this feels so blissfully normal that I forget I'm invisible to Aimée and the rest of the world and that there's another me in the morgue somewhere. For a moment, I'm back to being me. Good old normal alive Cassidy.

"Do you have any ChapStick on you?" Aimée asks Ethan as she rubs her red lips.

I open my mouth to answer, but Ethan beats me to it. "That was Cassidy's job."

"That's the problem." Aimée slouches in her chair. "Every little thing that pops up feels like it's a Cassidy job. Talking to people, being friendly so they'll be willing to tell me what I need to know. My tolerance for fake sympathy is too low. I get annoyed. And I feel like no one's telling me the whole story."

"Well, you are pretty intimidating, Aimée." She angles her chin upward like it was a compliment. He spins the cap of his drink like a top and it goes rolling along the table—through my arm.

That moment of normal passes.

Ethan stares in awe at the cap as it slowly wobbles in a progressively smaller circle until it stops flat under my elbow. Aimée reaches across the table, snatches up the cap, and replaces it on the bottle.

"Ouch!" I hold out my arm until the dusty bits of me reshape. When I look up, Ethan's jaw is on the floor. "Pull yourself together," I whisper to him.

"Sorry," he whispers back.

"What?"

Ethan turns away from me quickly and looks over at Aimée. "Don't feel bad about getting frustrated with people. No one in this school knows what it's like to lose someone they love as much as you loved Cassidy."

"Except you," she says quietly. Ethan drops his eyes to his lap, and I wrap my fingers around his hand, ignoring the rift between us because he's the only thing I have left and he knows it. "So," she asks, "what did you find out?"

"I talked to Nancy."

"She has an alibi." Aimée pushes her tray of untouched nachos aside and folds her arms on the table. "I talked to her brother. He said he was with her when she found Cassidy."

"He could be lying for her," I say.

"She used his cell to call 911," Aimée adds before Ethan can translate for me.

"Yeah," Ethan replies, "I didn't get the feeling she had anything to do with what happened."

"I talked to Carly and Megan, too. Not much there to work with either."

"Maybe." Ethan pauses. "Maybe we're talking to the wrong people."

Aimée perks up. "Who do you have in mind?"

"Nancy told me she overheard Madison at the party telling Drew she wanted to get Cassidy alone."

"Your point?" Aimée says with a challenge.

Ethan glances at me before continuing. "I talked to Drew. He said Madison and Cassidy got in a big fight that night."

Aimée instinctively starts to defend Madison, then sinks back in her seat. "I wouldn't doubt it. Madison was avoiding Cassidy for most of last week. I asked her about it, but she told me it was my imagination."

"Madison hasn't mentioned anything about a fight?"

Aimée shakes her head. When Ethan glances at me again, I tell him, "She needs to know what Madison did."

Ethan looks squarely at Aimée. "I know about Caleb. I found out at the party courtesy of Mica, but it was a setup. Madison was trying to break up Cassi and me."

Aimée straightens. "I don't believe that."

"Cassidy saw her dealing pills to Caleb. Didn't you say Dr. Scott made her stay home because of the meds he had her on?"

"That's absurd." Aimée's voice shakes, making her confidence in Madison seem tenuous. "She would never do that, and her dad didn't write her 'scrips for anything remotely recreational until after the party."

Crap. I scramble for a believable excuse for how I told him about the pills *after* I died.

Ethan says without missing a beat, "That's what Madison told you. Doesn't mean it's the truth."

Aimée's eyes go wide. Her voice is hard and flat. "Are you suggesting Madison killed her best friend over *you*?"

"No, actually, I have absolutely no idea why she'd want to hurt Cassi. Do you?"

Aimée gathers her hair into a knot at the nape of her neck and grips it with both hands. "I'm calling her." She digs her cell out of her bag and discreetly holds it to her ear. Aimée groans when Madison's voice mail picks up. She hangs up and puts her thumbs to work speed-texting *We need 2talk!!!* before looking across the table at Ethan.

"Now what?" he asks.

"We run through the rest of the list."

"Between the two of us, we've already talked to everyone."

"My list has a few more names than yours." Aimée reaches into her pocket and flattens the folded page of stationery between them. Ethan frowns at the inclusion of his name. Aimée's voice holds a note of apology when she says, "I had to include everyone who was alone with her at the party."

"Then you better re-add Mica. Why did you cross out his name?" Ethan jabs his finger at her list.

Aimée snatches it up and narrows her eyes at him. "Because I put him on your list. It's a moot point anyway though because he wasn't on the bridge with Cassidy. He was in my house with Drew and about five other people who vouched for him."

Ethan shakes his head. "I knew he'd get to you. Let me guess, those five people are girls he's hooked up with?"

"Why don't you trust him? He's supposed to be your best friend."

"Was."

Aimée and I both stare at Ethan, waiting for an explanation he doesn't offer. "You do realize what you're doing here, right?" Ethan doesn't answer. "You're focusing on two ridiculously un-likely suspects so you won't have to admit who Cassidy was ac-tually with on the bridge."

"If you don't believe me, ask Madison about the pills. Skip the rest of the day and go to her house. I hear she's a mess." He glances at me out of the corner of his eye. "She won't be able to pull off lying to you anymore."

"If you're right . . ." Aimée thinks a minute. She stands. "I'll call you after I talk to her."

He half stands when she passes him to leave, and I take an involuntary step toward her. Warmth travels up my arm when his hand finds my wrist, tempting me to stay with him, but the pulse in my chest is pulling me toward Aimée. I place my other hand on top of his. "Ethan. I have to go with her."

He opens his mouth again, maybe to stop me, but he stays

silent, releasing his hold on me. I don't want to let him go, but indomitable forces are making that decision for me.

I catch up to Aimée in the parking lot in what feels like a single blink. She's so worked up from arguing with Ethan that she can't seem to find her car keys. She digs through her coat pockets three times each, then shoves a hand into her messenger bag. Right when she clutches her rhinestone *A* key chain in victory, she bumps into the tailgate of a yellow pickup truck. "Son of a—*ow!*" She bounces on her good leg and groans.

"Aimée, hey." Mica pokes his head out of the driver's-side door. "Are you here to bust me for skipping?"

I stare hard at him, struggling to awaken some fragment of my memory that knows whether he's responsible for my death. I try to figure out what Drew and Ethan were talking about earlier and how Mica knew about Caleb and me before Ethan did, but it's no use. That part of my memory is blank.

Aimée hobbles around the side of the truck, rubbing her knee. "I'm skipping, too." She stands as best she can despite her hurt knee, defiant and proud.

Mica nods. "I'm impressed. Not sure you'll be able to outrun the law with that injury though." Aimée smirks at him, but stays quiet. "Is something wrong?"

"Why?"

"You look like something's bothering you, I guess."

She rubs her visibly chapped lips. Then she asks abruptly, "Did you go out with Carly Davies?" Mica appears confused. "Freshman. Blond. IQ of a mentally challenged unicorn."

"I know who she is."

"Okay. Did you go out with her?"

Mica scratches his smooth cheek. "Maybe once, I think."

Aimée narrows her eyes at him. "How long ago?"

"Is that what's bothering you? Carly wasn't anything serious. You don't need to worry about her." Mica reaches for Aimée's hand, but she backs away.

"Can you get over yourself for one minute? I couldn't care less about how many V-cards you've swiped—quite the opposite, actually," she says a little too insistently. "I'm more concerned about you starting rumors about Cassidy and Ethan breaking up."

"It wasn't a rumor. They did break up, at the party. You knew that, right?"

Aimée shakes her head, losing some of her attitude.

"Yeah," Mica says, "E walked in on her making out with that Caleb kid and ended it. Was pretty brutal."

Hearing him sum up the worst moment of my life in twenty words or less does painful things to my ghostly insides.

"Ethan said you were there when he found Cassidy with Caleb. He was really pissed about it, actually. Why didn't you tell me you were there?" Aimée asks.

Mica scratches his cheek again. "E blames me, y'know, 'cause I'm the one who told him what was what. Guess I didn't want to be the one to have to tell you, too."

"How did you find out?" Aimée's expression tenses as she waits for his answer.

"Well, Drew told me a few weeks ago that Cassidy was steppin' out on E. I didn't believe it though. Not until I caught her with him at the party."

"You must've been angry with her for cheating on your best friend," Aimée says, assessing his reaction.

Mica pulls up his playboy grin. "It would be pretty two-faced of me to be angry with someone for sleeping around."

"Cassidy didn't sleep with Caleb," Aimée says with quiet confidence even though she has no way of knowing whether it's true; she simply trusts it. So do I. She looks up at him. "Did Drew tell Madison about Caleb, too?"

"No," Mica says with genuine surprise in his voice, "not that I know about anyway. Drew's always crazy careful not to have to break bad news to her. He's paranoid she'll take it out on him, finally dump him for good. He'd never risk it."

Aimée hesitates a moment, and I can tell she's trying to make sense of what Ethan told her about Mica being alone with me at the party and Madison inviting Caleb so she could set me up, deciding if she believes any of it.

"You still look like something's bothering you," Mica says.

Aimée bites down on her bottom lip. "Actually, I am in dire need of lip gloss."

Mica digs into his truck's coin tray and pulls out a Chap-Stick, the original kind with a black label, the kind that smells like grandpas. "Will this work?"

"Oh, thank *god*." She lunges for the stick and smiles deliriously as she rolls it over her red lips. She sighs and hands it back to him.

He laughs and sets it in her palm without letting go of her hand. "You clearly need this more than I do. Keep it." He leans forward. "You still haven't told me what's *really* bothering you."

"I don't . . ." Aimée stares at Mica's tan hand wrapped around hers for a moment before tightening her fingers around his. "Do you know where Caleb Turner lives?"

My head snaps up at her unexpected question.

"Yeah," Mica says slowly. "I've been to a few of his parties. Who hasn't?"

"Me," Aimée answers. "Can you tell me how to get there?"

Mica peers over his shoulder, scanning the parking lot. "I'll do you one better and drive you there." He reaches for Aimée's bag.

"Give it back." She grabs for her bag, but he's already tossed it behind his seat. "I don't need a ride."

"This is about what happened to Cassidy, isn't it?"

"Stay out of this, Mica." Aimée tries to push past him to retrieve her bag, but he's too big to get past.

"No way. If you're right about her death not being suicide, someone is obviously hiding something dark. Asking questions might get dangerous. Besides," he says, adopting a lighter tone as he steps out of the truck, "you'll definitely get caught skipping if you're alone." Aimée begins to protest, but Mica silences her with a raised hand, waving his fingers. "Don't worry. You're in good hands."

Aimée hits his hand away. "Keep your hands to yourself."

"For now, right?" Mica teases. Aimée laughs despite herself and lets him hook his arm with hers as he leads her to the passenger-side door.

A thousand repetitive memories flicker behind my eyes. Aimée and I walking to English together, sharing a blackberry frozen yogurt at the mall, both of us sprinting for the elementary-school door after the rest of our class was already inside after recess. Our arms were *always* hooked. Now she can't even tell she's walking through me.

I try to follow her into Mica's truck, but my legs won't move. I call out to her that it's not worth it—revealing the truth, clearing my name. None of that's worth anything if she gets hurt—but as my lips form the words, I know they're not true. It's how I feel deep down, but keeping her safe isn't why I'm here.

I'm here because I lied. To everyone. I even lied to *me*. Somehow I managed to convince myself no one would get hurt, that I had control, that Caleb was nothing more than a friend, that kissing another guy wasn't wrong.

No.

I never convinced anyone that what I did was right. But I did it. I let it happen, and now I'm dead. Does that mean it was all my fault?

The éclairs, the leaning closer, the kissing, the lying, the avoiding, the fighting, the schnapps, the falling . . .

My skin burns cold from the regret building inside me. No matter what Madison did to push me into Caleb's arms, I shouldn't have fallen. This is my fault, and it's up to me to fix it. I close my eyes and welcome the hurt that's rooted in my unreal bones. It holds me to this place, this life that's no longer mine. The pulse throbs beneath my chest, and for a second time, I let go of everything else and allow it to guide my path. I sense this time it will finally lead me to where I need to be—to answers.

When I open my eyes, I'm on the bridge. With Madison. She's wearing a rose-pink peasant dress with tiny blue flowers and loose sleeves that are being ravished by the wind tunneling through the bridge. She must be freezing. Her hands are cradling her cell in front of her face. Aimée's text is illuminated on the screen: *We need 2talk!!!* The screen changes, alerting her of an incoming call from Drew. She hits ignore.

I stand with her in the cold, watching her hair twirl wildly around her face and stick to her cheeks in places where tears have fallen. She looks so young, so small and alone. From under her sleeve, she pulls out one of the pictures I saw in her room. It's a random group shot from the party with the bridge looming in the background. She looks at it with this strange longing.

"I'm sorry I took Ethan, Madison." The apology slips out before I can stop it, but once it's said I realize I mean it even though taking him wasn't so much a choice as an inevitability. I can't count how many times I hugged Ethan in front of her or talked about some romantic gesture he'd made when her heart must have been silently breaking. It's not that I think she was justified in plotting to break us up—especially since it landed me in the morgue—but it's too late for grudges; I know that now. For me, there is no point.

As she tucks her long bangs behind her ears, I realize the toes of her tan cowboy boots are dangerously close to the exposed edge where the caution tape used to be. A flash of yellow catches my eye, and I see the torn tape gripped in her left hand.

I turn my head toward Aimée's house. The lights are off. Her family isn't home yet and Aimée's at Caleb's house with Mica when she desperately needs to be here.

Madison rocks back on her heels, then onto the balls of her feet. I want to stop her, but there's nothing I can do if her balance wavers. I don't know exactly how much she had to do with my death, but I can't let anything happen to her. Especially not here, like this.

I rub the spot where my horseshoe pendant rests, hoping for some otherworldly luck. She steadies herself with a hand on the broken wall for a moment. Then she lets go.

23

LITTLE LATE FOR LUCK, isn't it?"

My eyes fly open. I'm in Ethan's car. He's sitting with one hand on the ignition, the other pointing at my necklace.

I look down at it. "It's not for me. It's for Madison." I open my mouth to explain, but he gives me a smile so small and weak that it stops me.

"You're on Aimée's side now?"

"Ethan, there aren't any sides. Madison's unstable. I'm worried about her."

"What did you remember earlier when we were with Drew?" He pulls the key from the ignition and turns to face me.

"That's not important right now."

"I want to know," he insists, almost yelling.

I lean away from him. "I'm sorry about leaving you at lunch, but I wasn't picking Aimée or anyone else over you. It's not like that."

"I'm getting used to you leaving," he murmurs. The awkward

silence that follows makes his Sebring seem the size of a Smart car.

It takes me a second to find my voice. "That room Drew took you to . . . I've been there before."

Ethan's eyes narrow, widen, and narrow again. "With who?"

My words feel trapped behind my suddenly taut lips.

When I don't answer he says, "Please don't lie to me anymore."

I force myself to look at him. His eyes are glistening and his mouth is slightly open. I think of the hundreds of times I've kissed those lips and touched them with my fingertips. It should've been enough; it would be now.

I want to wrap my arms around him and take away everything sad and replace it with warmth and pleasure. I want to kiss him so much my lips burn. I lost track of our hundreds of kisses a long time ago, but now I can feel each and every one of them rising to the surface. I look down, half expecting to see them marked on me.

"The day before my party," I answer, "Drew asked me to meet him there. He said he knew what I'd been doing."

"You mean with Caleb?" Ethan says. I nod. "Did you invite Caleb to your party?" he presses.

"No," I insist.

Ethan throws his hands up. "You're such a liar."

"No." I shake my head. "I suck at lying to you. You know that."

"You must be pretty good at it if you convinced me to take care of your drunk friend while you met up with some other guy."

"It wasn't like that. Madison—" *Is teetering on the edge as we speak and needs your help*, I finish in my head, but before the words can form, I'm making excuses, explaining why I went to the bridge. "She planned the whole party as a setup." My entire body is shaking and it's like my mouth isn't attached to any logical part of me, like something supermundane is choosing my words for me. There's no way I'm going to be able to help Madison if I can't even speak for myself. "I needed to end it with Caleb before . . ."

"What?" Ethan asks in a harsh tone. *"Say it."*

The words come rushing out as if he pulled away a twig at the crux of a dam. "Drew threatened to tell you about Caleb if I didn't. I was going to wait until after my party so I wouldn't ruin it for everyone, but Caleb showed up because Madison invited him and I . . . I didn't have a choice."

Ethan arches his eyebrows. "You were the only one in any of this that did have a choice, Cassidy, and you chose to lie." I want to scream at him that he lied too, about Mica and Nancy and being on the bridge, but I don't because he's right. And he doesn't even seem angry about it, which makes me feel worse.

I don't know what to say, so I don't say anything.

"Well," Ethan continues, his voice so even it makes me feel like a total creep, "did you do it?" I look up at him, still unable to answer. "Did you really sit him down in the middle of your birthday party and explain how it was fun while it lasted, but it was over?"

I blink back tears. "It wasn't fun—that's not why." I start over. "I met him on the bridge to end it because I didn't want to make a big scene."

Ethan laughs a humorless laugh. "I don't know who's worse,

you or him." Me. It's me. "The part that gets me the most is I can't even be mad at you."

I turn sideways in my seat, facing him. "Yes, yes you can. You *should*."

"Cassi, you're dead." He lets that sink in. "What's the point?"

I ignore the pain attacking my insides. "You have every right to—"

"To what? Hate my not-so-dead girlfriend?" He slips his hand underneath mine, and despite the overwhelming pain and self-loathing I feel, his warmth makes the corners of my mouth turn up. "What you did hurt. But you didn't deserve to die for it."

I shake my head. "I can't believe you're not mad at me."

"Oh, I'm definitely mad at you. And at Drew for knowing and not telling me, and at Madison for setting you up, and at Caleb and Mica—even at the friggin' bridge for being old and brittle. I'm so mad at so many things I don't even know where to start."

"Start with me. Why have you been so nice?" I ask.

"Because we fought, okay!" I wince at his outburst. He slams the heels of his hands into the steering wheel, then pushes them through his disheveled hair. "The last thing I said to you was 'Leave me alone,' and then you were . . . gone. For good." He looks over at me with some unidentifiable emotion burning in his eyes. "But you came back."

So that's why he agreed to help me remember. He felt guilty for yelling at me before I died. None of this was his fault and he felt guilty—*I* made him feel guilty. And now I wanted to ask him to help Madison. Would I ever stop hurting him?

"You told me to leave you alone and I did the complete opposite," I say, astounded.

"It's not like you had control over it."

"Didn't I? You said it yourself, I had a choice. Maybe . . . I can't believe I cheated on you and then forced my way back into your life when you should've been left alone to grieve and get over me." I blink, expecting tears to fall, but my eyes are dry. I turn to leave.

"No!" Ethan cries out desperately, grabbing my arm. "Cassi, I don't want you to go. I'm mad, but I still love you. We'll find Aimée and figure everything out. Please don't leave. What if you don't—" His voice catches. "Please. Stay." His expression crumbles. I want to pick up the pieces, comfort him, take away his pain, but my being here is why he hurts.

"This isn't fair to you, Ethan. I'm not alive. It's . . . not right." His grip tightens as I pull my arm away from him, but the smooth texture of my new skin slips away easily.

"Cassi." Once I'm out of the car, I turn to look at him from the other side of the passenger window. He says "I love you" softly behind the glass, but I hear him clearly.

I love you too, I reply silently. That's why I have to leave.

24

MADISON IS STILL ON THE BRIDGE, but she's not teetering over the edge anymore. She's leaning against one of the main supports that hold together the remaining shreds of the wall, with her arms pinned to her sides. She looks frozen, as if someone clicked the pause button on her emotional collapse to keep her safe. For now.

"Aren't you cold?" I ask her. "Your mom would flip if she saw you were wearing that dress."

Last month when Aimée, Madison, and I were shopping at the end-of-winter sales at Anita's Closet, this fabulous high-end consignment shop on the south end of River Road, Madison found and fell deeply in love with the dress she's wearing. Mrs. Scott agreed to buy it for her as an early birthday present with the stipulation that she not wear it until her birthday. In July. It's been hanging on the back of Madison's bedroom door ever since, taunting her.

With what I've learned about her these past few days, Madison finally putting on that dress seems to mean something fateful and life changing, but I'm not sure if it's for the good or the bad.

"It looks nice on you," I tell her, resorting to small talk. It's my most futile attempt yet to convince her to go inside. I even considered leaving to find Aimée and coercing her to come home to help before Caleb or Mica—both?—can hurt her, but the pulse holds me here. I'm beginning to wonder why I'm bothering to try, to care.

Then Madison starts to hum our favorite song. Hers and mine.

Aimée and I may have been friends since before we could say our own names, and we agree on everything from skinny jeans versus bootcut to who has the best pizza crust in Crescent Valley, but the only thing we've never agreed on is music. She likes hard-hitting dance music that sends me into a sensory overloaded seizure and I like basically anything that *isn't* hard-hitting dance music that sends me into a sensory overloaded seizure, including pop-country. Aimée *loathes* pop-country. I thought we were doomed to a battle of the bands for life until Madison moved into town. That's actually how Madison and I became friends. Aimée and I were arguing over which song to listen to at the bus stop the first day of fourth grade and Madison offered a tiebreaker vote in my favor.

A million insignificant but priceless memories of my friendship with Madison play behind my eyes.

"Remember that day last summer when Aimée refused to get in your car because you had the Band Perry cranked," I say to her, "so we drove off like we were going to leave her at the movie theater, and she went back inside and saw a second movie alone?"

The laugh that rolls up my throat is cut short by something

dark creeping over the hill in Dover Park. A chill crawls up my back as it merges with the shadows of the trees lining the riverbank. I walk to the bridge entrance to see who's there, but when I step off the wooden planks I'm not in the park. I'm standing next to Aimée in Caleb's bedroom. I recognize the room by the *Jungle Book* wallpaper border that no one bothered to take down when he grew up.

The animals look so sad trotting along beside his stashes of backlogged homework and stacks of well-worn sci-fi paperbacks and piles of unfolded clean laundry. Kind of like Caleb himself, sitting at the foot of the twin bed that we used to play dragons and fairies underneath, staring at Aimée in awkward silence, out of place in his own bedroom.

How did I get here?

I haven't been inside this room since I was twelve years old, but something about it feels like home. Maybe it's the fact that he and I never met up here under the guise of working on our Psych project. That was limited to his basement or back porch. This space was off-limits, kept safe behind the veil of memories of the past.

"I don't have the answers you're looking for," he says to Aimée like he's finally answered some question she asked hours ago.

"But you do have answers?" There's an intimidating tone to her question.

I move to stand next to Caleb. "You better not lie to her."

Caleb glances out the window beside his bed. I follow his gaze and see Mica's truck parked in front of Caleb's mailbox. Looking behind me, I notice for the first time that Mica is leaning against the closed door. That veil protecting my good memories starts to unfurl.

Aimée exhales an exasperated breath. "I know you wrote me that note."

Caleb's expression contorts in either confusion or denial, I can't tell which. "What note?"

"Acting coy won't do you any good. I know you were writing Cassidy notes. I found your paper airplanes in her Psych binder and the one you put in her locker on Tuesday."

"Okay, so I passed notes back and forth with her, but I didn't write *you* any note." He shakes his head, looking bemused. "I didn't think Cassidy kept those airplanes."

Mica snorts. "Don't go getting sentimental about it. Those notes prove you were scammin' on Cassidy. It's a motive."

Caleb sneers at Mica, then says to Aimée, "You're right. Cassidy wasn't alone on the bridge."

"Is that a confession?" Mica asks tauntingly.

Aimée throws him a you're-not-helping look. She turns back to Caleb. "Who was with her?"

Caleb hesitates, his eyes skittering around the room like he's looking for hidden cameras. "I can't tell you."

Aimée purses her lips, frustrated. "Why not?"

"I'm gonna have to plead the Fifth on that one."

"You know enacting the Fifth Amendment is basically an admittance of guilt, right?" Aimée glowers at him. "Or did you sleep through that day of Government class?"

"I manage more asleep than half the jocks in my class do taking notes."

"Hilarious," Mica deadpans. "Keep it up and you'll be explaining to the cops why you can't tell us."

"Oh?" Caleb laughs darkly. "I'll be sure that ends in your favor."

Mica makes for Caleb, but Aimée stops him with a raised hand. "I think you should wait in the truck."

"But," Mica says, stepping toward Aimée, "I'm not leaving you alone with him."

Aimée lowers her voice. "What could he do to me here, with his mom eating lunch downstairs?"

He grinds his jaw back and forth a couple times before reluctantly opening the door. "I'll be right outside."

"Got it." Aimée nods at Mica with a taut smile. "Thanks." After he's gone, she closes the door, drops the smile, and meets Caleb's tired eyes. "I know you've been in love with Cassidy since middle school."

Caleb reaches for a can of Red Bull on the floor next to his nightstand-less bed and sloshes it around instead of drinking it. The sound of splashing liquid pulls my thoughts to the river, to chunks of ice shattering on impact then crashing back down with an incredible *whoosh*. His raspy voice brings me back. "Is that so?"

Aimée nods confidently. "And when she agreed to work with you on that Psych project, you got your hopes up. Problem was, she had a boyfriend, and you got jealous."

"I've always known what my chances were with Cassidy." He holds up his hand and makes a zero with his fingers. I give him a sympathetic look. He continues, "My jealousy didn't kill her."

Aimée asks him, "But someone else's did?"

"Careful how close you get to the truth, Aimée. It won't be as satisfying as you want it to be."

She slams her hands on her hips, stepping on the sleeve of one of Caleb's hoodies on the floor as she moves closer. "I know you know. The only question I have left is, are you protecting yourself or someone else?"

I say, "He's telling the truth, Aimée." I don't know how I know, but suddenly it's very clear to me that Caleb isn't the bad guy here. She stares at him, waiting.

Finally he answers, "That's not the question you should be asking."

"So what is?" Aimée asks, impatient.

"It's not about who was on the bridge. It's about why they were there in the first place."

"Who?" I ask Caleb. "Who else was there?"

His mouth opens, but instead of answers, sparkling bursts of light shoot out around him. They hit my eyes, causing me to blink over and over. I raise my hand to block the painfully bright light and realize it's coming from my arm. Rainbows are glinting off my not-so-real skin in the high-noon sun.

I'm back on the bridge.

I rub my eyes, trying to regain hold on my suddenly errant surroundings. As the wooden walls and sunlight dull around me, Madison comes into view. She's still standing in the spot she was in when I ghosted away, the spot she's been in for hours, a shivering statue.

I watch her for a long time, thinking about what Caleb said. "Why didn't you tell me you liked Ethan?" I ask her. "I can't say it would've changed things, but at least I'd have known. You didn't have to put yourself through that." I hesitate. "Were you with me on the bridge, Mads? Did you . . . did we fight or something?" I stupidly wait for her answer. She remains staring at the picture in her shaking hand, the random group shot.

This is insane. I can't hang out on the bridge and talk to my friend who isn't even my friend anymore like she can hear me, like I'm alive. If there's one thing reliving my memories has taught me, it's that none of it can be redone or changed. I made my choices, good or bad, and I need to face the very real consequence: I died.

The long, broad shadow engulfing the hill has grown so big that there's no way it can belong to the trees. As I watch it undulate and grow, the pulse inside me shudders, sending another chill through me. I glimpse Madison's expression to check if she sees it too, but she's staring straight down at the slowly thawing river below us, rocking back on her heels again in front of the exact spot where I broke through.

When she rocks forward, I instinctively reach for her, but Aimée's voice stops her from leaning too far over. "Madison? I've been looking for you everywhere." Madison doesn't even blink at Aimée's arrival; she's still staring at the river. Aimée takes a cautious step toward her. "What are you doing out here in your birthday dress? You're going to go into hypothermic shock."

"I wanted to look nice."

Aimée's eyebrows knot together as she walks to Madison's side. "For what?" she and I both ask.

Madison finally looks up. "I should have been here for her."

"I know. I feel the same way." Madison flinches when Aimée takes her hand. "God, Mads, you're freezing. Let's get inside and warm you up. We need to talk."

Madison shakes her head again, refusing to move. I follow her blank gaze out to the riverbank where the shadow is bending unnaturally over the rocks and crawling up toward the bridge. "I don't want to talk. Talking isn't going to change anything."

"I know," Aimée says intently, "but you have to tell me what happened. No more lies."

Madison's mouth opens and shuts, searching for an excuse, but as soon as she meets Aimée's eyes, she falls apart. "You don't know what I did." Her voice is muffled by the tears streaming down her flushed cheeks.

Aimée clasps Madison's hand between both of hers and pleads, "Then tell me."

"I had to. It was the only way I'd get my chance with Ethan."

Aimée sighs. "Mads, you didn't."

"I had to." Madison's voice cracks. "Cassidy swooped in and stole him from me before I got my fair chance. But they were inseparable for so long and they seemed happy, so I stepped aside for the sake of our friendship, tried to move on. I've never loved Drew, but I *tried*. For Cassidy. Then her mom moved out and she got distant."

"Mrs. Haines moved out? When?" Aimée asks, shocked and probably a little hurt that I didn't confide in her. I should have.

"Ethan needed to know about Cassidy's betrayal." Madison continues as if Aimée didn't speak. "So I put out the word to a few eager listeners that their perfect relationship wasn't what it seemed and hoped Ethan would get wind of the rumors and confront her. But he believed every whopper she told him. I had to do something—she didn't deserve him anymore."

"So it's true. You planned the party to stage their breakup." Aimée hesitates. "Mads, please tell me you didn't pay Caleb to show up?"

Madison pulls her hand away from Aimée. "Who told you that?"

"If it's true, does it matter?" The hurt in Aimée's eyes burns through me.

Madison cups her hands over her face as her entire body visibly shudders. "I didn't mean for her to die. I just needed to be alone with Ethan, to explain so he would know I did it for him— and for Cassidy. They weren't right for each other. They deserved to be with someone they love so much there would be no lies."

I don't hear Aimée's response because I'm shouting, "But you've been lying to both of us!"

Madison chokes out a sob at whatever Aimée said to her. I hope it was harsher than what I said. "That's why I wrote that note."

Aimée's eyes go wide. "*You* wrote the note?"

"I had to. Cassidy wouldn't take my calls. It was the only way I could apologize to her."

"Apologize?" Aimée looks curiously at Madison. "What note are you talking about?"

"The one I never should have written during the party."

So Madison wrote my presumed suicide note. But how did she get it to me and when?

"Mads, she had that note with her when she fell. Everyone

thinks she committed suicide because of your apology. Why didn't you tell the police you wrote it?"

"If I did, everyone would've found out I was responsible for my best friend jumping to her death . . . Ethan would've found out."

"There you are." All three of us snap our heads toward the Coutiers' side of the bridge.

"Mica," Aimée says like she forgot he drove her here. "Listen, we might be awhile. You should go. I'll ask my mom to drive me back to school to pick up my car when she gets home from work."

"Okay, but Drew called a second ago asking where Maddy was."

"You didn't tell him I was here, did you?" Madison asks anxiously, turning the picture over in her hand. Her voice is startlingly clear for someone who was crying two seconds ago.

Mica answers, "Didn't know you were." As he walks closer, Madison inches toward the exposed edge. He cranes his neck to peek down at the river. "That's not as high as I thought."

"It's high enough," Madison says, moving another precarious inch forward.

Aimée takes a quick step forward and offers Madison her hand. "Come away from the edge, Mads. You don't want to hurt yourself."

Madison looks back at Aimée's outstretched hand. "Maybe that's exactly what I want—maybe it's what I deserve."

"Don't talk like that. Mads, please, come away from there."

"You could tell everyone I slipped on the ice. Or you could each tell a different story and my fall would be a mystery like

Cassidy's." Madison's voice has this eerie amusement to it, like she wants to have *everything* I had, even my death.

"Not unless you're drunk." My vision goes blurry at the sound of Mica's voice.

"Cassidy was a ballerina. She didn't randomly slip on some ice. And she wasn't even that drunk," Aimée adds haughtily. "The jolly vodie I made her barely had any vodka in it."

"But she had a lot of peach schnapps, too," Mica replies.

"Schnapps?" Aimée asks, confused. "Cassidy didn't drink any schnapps."

"Sure she did," Mica says automatically, then backtracks. "I mean, I think I saw her from across the bonfire. She slammed back probably half a bottle on her way to the bridge."

"I didn't have any schnapps until after I was on the bridge," I protest. "From the bottle that Caleb—" I stop myself, searching my memory. Maybe Mica saw me with the bottle when he and Ethan came to the bridge. No, that can't be right because Caleb threw it into the river before they found us . . . or did we drink it after they left? The timeline is jumbled. Faces don't match up with places and events, and I have this feeling I didn't drink a drop of schnapps with Caleb.

"Whatever she drank," Aimée says, "her fall wasn't intentional. Caleb confirmed that."

Madison finally steps away from the edge and faces Aimée. "You talked to Caleb? What did he tell you?"

"That Cassidy wasn't alone when she fell."

"So he confessed?"

"Pretty much," Mica answers before Aimée can. "There's no way he'd know she wasn't alone unless he was the person with her."

Aimée's expression tightens as she thinks. "That's not enough. There's no proof, and he's high most of the time lately. The police aren't going to believe him unless we have something solid."

"Do you believe him?" Madison asks.

A hollow ringing in my ears drowns out their voices. Through a murky curtain of gray, rows of desks appear. Posters of ancient Egypt and maps of the Eastern Hemisphere are tacked to the walls slowly forming around me. Mr. Scarsoonie is pointing at me and grumbling about something I can't hear. Everything looks opaque and temporary as the memory takes shape around me. This strange sense of being in two places at once grips me as a gust of spring air blows my hair across my cheek. The tie-dyed backpack that I had in seventh grade materializes in front of me as my hand reaches into the front zipper pocket of its own will. "Need a pencil?" a voice asks me. I turn and see thirteen-year-old Mica in basketball shorts lighting up the room with his garish smile.

The sounds of the river flowing and the bridge creaking in the wind come back to me in a vacuum, as if the past has been sucked away. I blink as the posters and desks dissolve. It's a frantic blinking, like someone's flipped on the lights and my eyes can't adjust quickly enough to the brightness. Mica was in Mr. Scarsoonie's class with me. He loaned me pencils. But then that means . . .

Oh no.

"I was in charge of supplying alcohol for the party," Madison is telling Mica. "I only got vodka and beer. I didn't buy any schnapps."

"Y'know, Drew said he saw those stoner guys bringing in

their own booze. Maybe they brought the schnapps," Mica suggests with a raised finger, like *Ah-ha!* What a complete fake. He turns to Aimée. "If Drew saw Caleb with schnapps, that's proof, right?"

"Possibly," Aimée says hesitantly.

"I'll text him." Mica pulls out his cell and begins typing. A reply beeps within seconds. "He says he'll meet us here in ten."

Madison looks down at the picture she's still holding, then grabs both of Aimée's arms. "Let's talk—like you said. Let's go inside. I need to explain about my *other* note."

"Other note?" Aimée's face lights with understanding. "You mean . . . ?"

The star-shaped note. So Madison wrote that too. She knows what Mica did—she must. But why wouldn't she tell Aimée straight out? Why be so cryptic? And why wait so long to come forward?

The pulse in my chest quivers as something desperate slowly turns in Mica's dark eyes. The emotion is surprisingly familiar and it pulls the jumbled pieces of my memory into terrifying order. My toes sink into the wet soles of my Mary Janes as I start to slip into that night. I tighten my fists, fighting to stay in the present.

Aimée's expression runs through several emotions before she turns her head to look curiously at Mica. "How did you know the schnapps was peach flavored if you only saw Cassidy drinking from across the bonfire? The only way you could know something so specific is if you were drinking it with her here. On the bridge." She takes Madison's hand and shifts her weight to her back foot, subtly stepping away from Mica.

He clenches his jaw and narrows his eyes at her. I remember that look.

Oh. No.

Snow gathers at the corners of my mouth, filling up my throat so I can't warn her. It melts down my neck and arms in ice-cold streaks, soaking my coat. I call out to my friends, but the snow muffles every sound until I'm drowning.

BLACKMAIL

GIVE ME FIVE MINUTES TO EXPLAIN, please," Caleb said.

I crossed my arms, shivering when a gust of chilled wind blew through the bridge from Aimée's backyard and past Caleb, carrying with it the sounds of the party going on without me. "You have three."

"Oh, a minute for each year you pretended I didn't exist. How fitting," Caleb quipped back.

I scowled at him. "That's not fair and you know it."

"Sorry. Forget I said that." He dropped his head. "I had a ton of stuff planned out to say, but now I'm screwing it up. I don't want you to go back to hating me."

"I never hated you, Caleb, but I didn't know what to say to you or how to act. You were so sad back then and I didn't know how to help you. Things are different now, but that doesn't mean I've changed my mind about us."

"Do I at least get a chance to bribe you with more chocolate?" he joked weakly.

I offered him a small smile that got lost in the shadows between the bridge walls. "Chocolate's what got us into this mess."

"Actually, the letter *b* is patient zero in our little epidemic," he said. I stepped closer so he could see my questioning look. "In kindergarten I used to mix up my *b*'s and *d*'s, so the teacher sat me next to you because you were an expert speller. I never did thank you for the help," he explained.

I laughed a little remembering five-year-old me helping five-year-old Caleb with his alphabet. "Well, I never would have learned how to draw a tree with finger branches if it weren't for you, so we can call it even."

"Not yet we can't. I owe you an explanation for showing up here tonight."

"I don't need an explanation but, Caleb, not to be a jerk, I need you to leave."

"Maybe *you* don't need an explanation, but I need to give you one." He closed his eyes and tilted his head back slightly, breathing out puffs of hot breath, before starting. "Looking at you reminds me of who I used to be, the good I had in me that I've smoked out over the past few years. But *being* with you"—he smiled to himself—"it makes me feel like the good's still in me, like I have a shot at turning my life around."

"You do have a shot, Caleb, but you don't need me to take it."

He lifted his hand to my cheek and met my eyes; his looked like glistening black marbles in the moonlight. I placed my hand on top of his and held it there for a moment. Then I curled my fingers in and moved his hand away.

"You can't have me, Caleb."

He looked down at his empty hand. "I know," he said in a soft, dejected tone. "Was worth a try anyway though, right?" When he took my hand, pulling me close, I didn't lean away because I knew this last kiss was a goodbye.

I eased away from Caleb's kiss and watched as he walked out of my life and into the trees beyond the bridge in the park. A strange sense of foreboding, not the relief I had expected, filled me. The bridge was so dark it felt like I was in another world, another life. Separate from my mistakes and lies. I leaned my elbows on the railing and looked down at the moonlight reflecting off the river. Sparse patches of ice stirred ripples in the thaw, disturbing the shape of the reflections, distorting the memory of Ethan's face next to mine.

I heaved a long sigh and flinched, catching my breath mid-exhale, when someone said, "You look like you could use a drink."

I straightened with a jolt to see Mica standing at the end of the bridge, illuminated by the spotlight. "What are you doing here?" My voice was harsher than it should have been, but I had no idea how long he'd been standing there, what he'd seen, and I couldn't ask without stirring up suspicion.

I brushed the snow from the railing off my sleeves and buried my wet hands in my coat pockets, nervously shifting my feet through the basic ballet positions: first, second, third . . .

"I could ask you the same thing. E know you're out here?"

A sinking feeling opened a pit in my stomach. "Why? Is he

asking for me?" I craned my neck to see past Mica to the house, but I couldn't see a thing through the shadows cast by the bridge's roof.

As he walked toward me, he waved his hand, revealing the bottle of peach schnapps he was holding. "Relax. He went inside a while ago. Probably getting a refill."

"He wasn't drinking." My voice was a distant whisper. Ethan was waiting for me with Madison, and I was out here freezing my toes off for my lies that she was probably gleefully divulging to him this very minute. What was I thinking leaving him alone with her? I needed to tell him the truth and apologize before he heard a skewed version of it from someone else—especially Madison. I started for the house, but Mica stepped in front of me.

He cocked his head and tapped the bottle against his leg. "You feelin' okay? You look a little wasted, and not in the good way."

I raised a hand to my forehead. "Yeah—no. I came out here to . . . sorta clear my head." More like clear my conscience. Again, I wondered how long he'd been standing at the entrance to the bridge before he spoke up.

"Have a drink with me then. Your head will be swiped clear in no time."

I looked past him, watching shapes emerge and fade in the shadows. "That's not really what I had in mind. I have to get back to Ethan."

"Y'know I've known you longer than E has?"

I shuffled my feet restlessly. Every second I spent here with Mica was another opportunity for Madison to tell Ethan her version of the truth. "What are you talking about?"

He ignored my tone and smiled at me with dizzy eyes. "We had Scarsoonie's class together in seventh grade, remember?"

I did remember. Something about a gangly seventh-grade Mica Torrez who wore basketball shorts to school every day, even in winter, stirred a giggle in my stomach. Mica knocked my knee with the bottle. It hurt more than I expected because I was so friggin' cold. I bent down to rub my knee, and Mica squatted in front of me with the bottle raised between us.

His tone softened. "Come on. E's not goin' anywhere. Stay. Have a drink with me. I feel like chattin'." He nudged me with the bottle and a smile.

I straightened, hesitating for a second, but I was so cold and nervous about talking to Ethan that I'd have done basically anything to calm my shivers. Plus, drinking more meant liquid courage that I would definitely need if I had any shot at being honest with Ethan tonight. I took one last glance at the bridge's entrance. Caleb would be halfway across Dover Park by now if he'd kept walking, or at the very least passed out on a bench. He wouldn't come back, not after saying goodbye.

That rush of relief I was waiting for finally kicked in. So I took the bottle from Mica and drank.

Mica started reminiscing about how Mr. Scarsoonie used to whistle his *s*'s. He laid his arm across my shoulders. My head buzzed with warmth as the old, innocent memories pushed the new, destructive ones back. I looked over the railing at the river below as he said something about green pens and "contrast ratio." *Oh god, that's funny.* This was good. The alcohol was definitely taking effect.

He offered me the bottle again, but I shook my head and slid out from under his arm. "I'm good. Seriously, no more."

He guzzled the rest of the bottle and chucked it off the bridge. I looked over the railing to see where it had landed and told him he'd have to pick up the bottle before Aimée's parents saw. He gave me this sly look that made goose bumps form on my arms.

"I should get back to the party. Birthday girl and everything. Why don't we walk and talk?" My voice shook, shattering the casual veneer I was trying to put on.

As I started toward the house, he said, "I don't think you want to have this conversation in front of everyone."

I stopped, rubbing my chilled arms. "What?"

"The party's here." He pulled a flask from the pocket of his letterman jacket and sloshed it around.

"That's not what you said."

He didn't seem to hear me. "Everyone says I'm a loose drunk." He snickered at some unspoken joke I didn't bother trying to get. "Wouldn't want to let something *you'd* regret slip out."

Without thinking I said, "There's a lot I regret." My heartbeat raced up my neck to my ears. I peered skeptically at him. "What did you say you wanted to talk about?"

"I didn't." He took a swig from his flask, and something inside me knew, right then, before he told me. I knew what he wanted. His teeth looked glaringly white in the shade of the covered bridge. I looked away from the shine for a moment and when I turned around, he was practically on top of me.

"Hey, bubble space much?" I forced out a short laugh, trying to downplay my nervousness. I shoved him away.

Mica licked his lips and pulled up a crooked grin the way he always did when someone complimented him after a hockey game or mentioned how he was Top Teen Athlete in the local newspaper for the millionth time. Then he leaned forward and smashed his mouth into mine. Except he was so drunk that he missed, smearing my lip gloss with his chin.

"Ew!" He leaned in for another go. "Stop it!" I turned my head away, threw both my hands onto his chest, and pushed him as hard as I could. The momentum from the effort rocked me backward and the heel of my Mary Jane rolled as I stumbled into the railing. Pain shot up my right ankle.

I wiped my face with the back of my hand and looked at him with incredulous eyes. "What are you doing?"

"What," Mica slurred, "I'm not your type?"

"My type? Are you *that* drunk? Remember Ethan—your *best friend* and my *boyfriend*?"

"Funny, that's exactly what I thought about when Drew told me. What about E?" His words crawled across the shadows masking the bridge and wrapped tight around my neck like slimy tentacles.

I opened my mouth to speak, but the tentacles tightened their grip. I swallowed hard, fighting the constriction. "I don't know what you're talking about."

"Don't be modest, Cassidy. You and that stoner prick put on quite a show. Good thing I came back to recycle that bottle of mine or I'd have missed out on the action."

"Mica, please, you don't know what you saw. I ended it. That's why we were on the bridge." I swallowed again. "Please don't tell Ethan."

Mica bowed his head so we were eye to eye and met me with a look that didn't suit his round baby face. "Who said anything about telling?"

I took a step away, ignoring the pain in my ankle as I did. "We should go back," I said in a shaky voice.

His lazy smile warped. "What's the matter, Cassidy? Afraid E will think you're with your little stoner boyfriend? And your friends too? Do they know what those lips of yours have been up to?"

"You wouldn't."

"I could help you cover this up, even get Drew on board or . . . I could make it worse."

"You can't blackmail me. *You* are the one who tried to kiss me."

"Hmm, not sure that's how E will see it."

I *hated* that he had this thing to threaten me with. I tried putting weight on my ankle again; the pain was less, but still sharp. I stumbled toward the park side of the bridge and the heels of my Mary Janes hit the railing again.

An overwhelming urge to run as fast as I could to Aimée and tell her everything so we could come up with a solution together, like we always did when anything was wrong, filled me. I tried to push past Mica, but he grabbed my shoulders and held me against the railing.

I squirmed under his strong hands. "I have to get back."

He nodded, leaning closer, swaying drunkenly. "Right, we should go. Tell the truth. Crush E's little heart."

"Yes." I shook my head. "I mean, no. I don't—you know I—I," I stammered. "We should go back."

"Or we could work out a deal and make this trouble go away."

"Deal?" The word felt sticky on my tongue, but Mica could help me keep Drew quiet if I agreed.

The adrenaline running through me made my throat dry. Of course I didn't want to hurt Ethan, but the lies I'd told him were stabbing at my insides. I had to get rid of them. Am I really going to tell Ethan? "Yes," I answered my own question.

"Yes?" Mica perked up and leaned toward me again. He brushed his fingers along my jawline.

I looked away from him as I thought about how Ethan would react if he found out I'd been lying about where I was for three weeks so I could sneak off to be with Caleb.

The only thing Caleb and I did was kiss, I rationalized. *They were only kisses and so could this be . . . meaningless kisses—a kiss. One kiss and I'd swear Mica to secrecy and this would be over. I could go back to normal with Ethan—only Ethan. Forever.*

That was all I had to do. One kiss to end everything.

25

I TURN MYSELF AROUND in a disoriented blur. My mind is shards and fractures between the past and the present. When my eyes finally focus, I see Mica shadowed from the sun on the covered bridge. He's still trying to pin the schnapps on Caleb, and Aimée's only half listening because Madison is backing away, toward the house, not so subtly gesturing for her to follow.

I want to look away, but my eyes won't break their frozen glare on Mica's sharp-lined mouth. My jaw aches at the memory of his wide chin smashing hard against it.

I find my voice. "Aimée. Grab Madison and leave. Now!"

"She was drunk," Mica is saying to Aimée, a hint of disapproval in his tone.

I sneer at him. "How much schnapps did *you* have?"

"E had broken up with her," he continues, playing the calm, rational guy. "She was probably a wreck and didn't think things through before jumping." He's wearing this consolatory expression that makes me wish I could touch him for just one second so I could punch his phony face. He puts his arm around Aimée's shoulders the same way he did mine in my last memory, and I throw that phantom punch.

Flexing my dissolving hand, I yell, "Oh, *come on*, Meems. Ignore the dazzling smile and get out of here!" She doesn't move. I turn to Madison, who looks like she's about to bolt any second. "Say something, Mads." Nothing. At least Drew's on his way. Mica wouldn't do anything violent with him here, right?

"We can't assume anything," Aimée says, finally looking as uncomfortable as I'd expect her to be under Mica's arm. "The only way to know is to question the person who was with her. Don't you agree?" She peers up at him. His smile falters.

"Please, Aims." Madison anxiously glances in the direction of Aimée's driveway. "Let's go inside."

"Yes!" I interject. I can't believe I'm on Madison's side. "Do what she says, Meems."

"I'll tell you everything," she promises.

"What do you mean you'll tell me everything?" Aimée slips out from under Mica's arm and steps toward Madison.

Madison wrings her hands like she's digging for the courage to come clean. "In my other note"—she glances warily at Mica, then continues in a slower, more cautious voice—"I was trying to let you know someone was lying about where they were when Dees died."

"Why didn't you tell me in person?"

"Because I wasn't sure *which* someone."

Mica pats Aimée's arm. "How 'bout we wait and see what Drew has to say about the schnapps?"

Aimée exchanges a look with Madison and nods at Mica's suggestion.

"Aimée." I step between her and Mica. It means one of my arms is inside her torso, but I ignore the pain. "Wake. Up. Mica tried to blackmail me. You have to get how bogus that Colgate smile is." Mica flashes her another smile in response to whatever she's saying. I don't hear her. I'm screaming too loud. *"Listen to meeee!"*

I can't believe I was relieved that Aimée had him to talk to before. How did I not sense that he is the reason I'm dead? And where is Drew?! I want to scream so loud that the entire earth shakes with my frustration. Instead, I squeeze my eyes shut and concentrate all I have on the one person who can help me, can help Aimée.

"Ethan." I shout before I know where I am. The door to his bedroom flies open.

"Cassi?" He pulls me inside, quickly shuts the door, then encircles me in his arms. He's so warm and comforting. I wish I could stay like this, in his arms, for whatever is left of my time in this world. My chest aches with each throbbing beat of the steady pulse that links me to him as my head nestles in the hollow spot below his shoulder.

An image of Aimée smiling up at Mica, taking false comfort in him, flashes behind my eyes. I press my lips together, fighting the desire to forget everything but Ethan and me in this fading moment.

I unlock his arms from around my shoulders and look at him. "Ethan, you have to help Aimée and Madison."

"Why? Did something happen to them?" He rubs his tired eyes. His sleeping schedule must be thrown off from hanging out with a ghost into the wee hours of the night. Even with everything that has my mind running on overdrive, I notice how completely adorable his confused blinking is.

Focus!

"They're with Mica. I remembered what happened on the bridge with the schnapps. It was Mica, not Caleb and—"

"Whoa, slow down. What did you remember?"

"Mica—he was on the bridge with me."

"I know."

"No, Drew must have lied for him about them being inside together. We were alone and he tried to kiss me."

"What?" Ethan's eyes flash with anger.

"He told me if I made a deal with him he wouldn't tell you about Caleb."

Ethan paces the room twice. He wraps his hands around my arms. "What else did he do?"

My hands start tingling with the chill of snow. "He . . ." I shake my wrists, trying to stop the wetness. The carpet under my feet creaks as it morphs into ice-covered wooden planks. "Crap!"

"What's wrong?" I can barely feel Ethan's hands on me as the snow piles high on my shoulders and the sound of the river whispers across my skin.

"It was him . . . on the covered bridge . . ." As I say the words, splintered crossbeams replace the walls of Ethan's bedroom and wind blows the corners of his posters up.

He's saying something, but it's muffled like when someone calls your name as you sink to the bottom of a swimming pool.

I manage to say "The covered bridge" once more before his room completely fades away.

THE PUSH

GET AWAY FROM HER!"

Mica turned to see who was behind him. "Ha! Stoner Boy to the rescue? This I have to see." He let go of my shoulders and tossed his head back, chortling.

Caleb slowly walked toward me, his sober eyes solidly on Mica. "Cassidy, are you okay?"

I closed my eyes and sighed. Could this night get any worse? "I'm fine. Let's go back to the bonfire and forget about it." Caleb's eyes darted to my right foot as I limped toward the distant sounds of the party.

He glared at Mica. "What did you do to her?"

I answered, "Nothing, I twisted my own stupid ankle on one of the splintered boards." I wiped the smeared lip gloss off my mouth as I struggled to keep the adrenaline shake out of my voice.

"You twisted your freakishly muscular dancer ankle? By accident?" Caleb eyed me skeptically.

A tiny sprig of comfort that he knew me well enough to question an ankle injury sprouted in me. I stomped it flat. "Yes. Now let's leave."

"No," Caleb insisted. "You're hurt." He couldn't have picked a worse time to become chivalrous.

"I'm fine."

Caleb stepped between me and Aimée's yard and gently placed his hand on top of mine. "Cassidy, if you're hurt"—he looked past me to Mica—"if he did something to you, I want to help. I'm still your friend, y'know."

The tears I'd been holding back burst out with a loud gasp. I dropped my head onto Caleb's shoulder and cried. I was so done with the lies and the mistakes and being forced to choose when no matter what I decided someone I cared about would get hurt.

My hair fell around my face as I shook my head. "I can't. I can't with you anymore—not even friends."

"I know," he said softly.

An enormous weight lifted from my chest, like I'd been trapped in a tank of water for days and had finally been given fresh air to breathe.

"Cassi?"

I tore away from Caleb and spun on my toes. "Ethan." I couldn't get anything else out. The words backed up into each other, clogging my throat.

"I thought you were . . . Why are they here?" Ethan pointed at Caleb and Mica, confused. "Cassi, are you crying? What's wrong?" He took an automatic step toward me, but something stopped him. "What's going on?"

I cringed when Mica's deep voice sounded behind me.

"Dude, I'm sorry you had to walk in on this." I flicked my eyes at him as he moved past me, blocking my view of Ethan.

"On what?" Ethan asked.

I stepped away from Caleb and Mica, as if I could distance myself from the truth.

Mica glanced back at me with pitying eyes. It made me nauseated. "Cassidy was making out with this prick." He threw the last word at Caleb.

"Right," Ethan said, and laughed. In the quiet that followed, Ethan's eyes ticked curiously between Caleb and me. Ethan pushed past Mica and took my hands in his. My cold hands burned as they thawed with the warmth from his gloves. "Cassi." He waited until I met his gaze. "Just tell me the truth, like always."

I chewed on my bottom lip. The truth would take away his best friend and his girlfriend and forever taint everything we had or might've had together if I hadn't fallen for Madison's little scheme. I couldn't hurt him like that even if he asked for it.

"Is Mica right? Did you send me inside so you could"—his throat worked as he swallowed—"meet up with this guy?"

Tears pooled deep in my eyes until they were too heavy and spilled over. I couldn't move, couldn't blink or speak, but my answer was in my silence.

"You said you were going to get Drew, that you'd come back to me." Ethan's warm eyes turned to ice. "You . . . lied to me."

"I—I didn't mean to. There was so much going on at home. I needed someone who understood—but that's not even it." He dropped my hands and started to walk away. "Wait! Please give me a chance to explain."

He stopped but didn't turn to face me. "Why should I give you one second to explain?"

"Because this isn't what it looks like. Caleb and I aren't—"

Mica interrupted me, cocky and spitting threats, his chest puffed out. I'm sure he would've been happy to beat Caleb to a pulp so he wouldn't talk, but now that Ethan was here and I could see the pain invading his perfect face, I knew the only way to stop his—and everyone else's—hurting was to tell him the truth.

"Enough with the threats!" I yelled at Mica. I turned toward Ethan to plead with him, but with my weak ankle I slipped on a patch of ice, and I stumbled into him instead.

Right when I thought I felt Ethan's arms tighten around me, Mica drove his hands between us and pushed me backward. "Hands off my boy, bitch."

I recoiled at his harsh tone and sucked my raw lips into my mouth, tasting the slight remains of my watermelon lip gloss mixed with dried tears. I could see a sheen smeared under Mica's bottom lip. Evidence.

"Your boy?" I jabbed my finger at Mica. "Now who's the liar? Ask him why he's wearing lip gloss, Ethan." Ethan's eyes darted to Mica, who was wiping at his mouth. "Go ahead, lean in; he smells like watermelon."

Mica held up his hands. "No shame in some game, right, E? I was with Carly earlier."

"Can you tell he's lying?" I asked Ethan. "He's better at it than me."

Ethan glanced at me and back at Caleb. He focused on Caleb's lips, then my lips and Mica's chin and their shared sheens.

"E, dude, she's making this up to save her own tail. I saw her with Stoner Boy."

Ethan brushed a finger at his chin and looked pointedly at Mica. "You've got something there, *dude*."

Mica's eyes burned into me.

"Ethan." My voice cracked. The farther he backed away the harder it was to lift my feet. *"Please."*

Tears filled his eyes, staining his beautiful, sad face. "Leave me alone." His voice reverberated off the wooden walls closing in around me.

I watched him disappear through the watery curtain covering my eyes. Mica's broad shoulders trailing after Ethan interrupted my view and anger boiled inside me, drying up the tears and lighting a fire under my skin. Caleb was apologizing now, but I didn't want to hear it. He was the only person left to burn.

I whipped around to face him. "You are the biggest mistake I've ever made in my entire life." My words entwined in the wind as I stomped toward the park side of the bridge, ignoring my throbbing ankle, abandoning Caleb and the lies.

Above the sound of ice-crusted snow crunching under my Mary Janes I heard my name.

Strong hands clasped my wrists behind my back. Too strong for me to wriggle free from. Too strong to be Caleb's. They hauled me away from the park, and I caught myself with a few staggering backward steps, barely managing to turn forward to see Mica.

"What was that back there?"

I opened my eyes as wide as I could to see past Mica, to call Caleb for help, but I couldn't see him.

"We had a deal," Mica added.

I threw knives at him with my eyes. "I didn't agree to anything. And even if I had, you told Ethan—no, you lied to him. There is no 'deal.'" I looked away and muttered, "At least this is over. Now let me go." I yanked my hands, but he pinched my wrists tighter. "Mica, you're hurting me." My voice was high and uneven.

He glared at me for a moment, then ripped his hands away. The motion thrust me forward, and I barely caught myself on the snow-covered rail before my hands slipped and my stomach slammed into it. I wasn't sure if it was the schnapps or the horror of what had happened, but I caught a woozy rush from leaning too far over the rail and had to close my hand over my mouth to hold in the bile rising up my throat.

"Whoa, Cassidy, I'm sorry. Are you okay?" Mica reached out to help me, but I didn't want his help—I didn't want anything from him except for him to leave. I knocked his arm away from me, then shoved him hard.

Caught off guard, he stumbled back into the railing. The old wooden support responded to the force of his hulking body with a sharp *crack*. He gaped at the splintered wood for a second, then turned to me so fast I didn't have time to raise my arm to protect my face.

The sting in my cheek was so intense I thought for sure it was split open and raw. I touched the spot where the back of his hand had landed and drew my hand away. There was no blood, but the salty taste of it filled the inside of my mouth and dripped down my throat. I doubled over and gagged.

"Mica. Not smart, man."

I lifted my head to see who'd spoken. "Drew." I braced my hands on my knees, feeling an irrational surge of relief. Drew had already proved he wasn't on my side, but at least he'd stopped Mica from taking another swing at me.

Drew walked to the center of the bridge where Mica and I were and bent down close to me. "I take it it didn't go too well fessing up to the boyfriend," he said in a low voice so Mica couldn't hear. Any shred of relief that I'd grasped when he'd arrived evaporated.

I straightened, giving Drew a wary look. "I have to go."

Mica took hold of my elbow, stopping me. He stammered, "Cassidy, wait. I—I didn't mean to hit you—stupid reflexes. I'm sorry."

I wrenched free. "Don't touch me! I'm telling Ethan *everything*."

Drew stepped forward when I started to leave again. "E left. And I wouldn't advise going back to the party looking like that."

I turned away, subtly wiping tears dry as I touched the tender skin of my cheek.

"Mica, why don't you go get her some ice," Drew suggested. "Least you can do, right?"

Mica murmured another apology before leaving Drew and me alone. I pressed my palm to my cheek, letting my cold skin relieve some of the lingering sting, and took a deep, ragged breath.

"You don't cry much, do you?"

I looked up at Drew's bizarre question. "Why are you out here?"

"Maddy asked me to give you this." He handed me a piece of the floral notepad paper that sits next to the Coutiers' landline phone in their kitchen, then continued like he'd already forgotten he'd passed along her message. "I can tell you don't because your eyes are puffy—from crying, I mean. Do you have any idea how many times a day Maddy cries?"

My face scrunched up. "What?"

"Try ballparking it," Drew added. I stared at him, thoroughly confused. "Twelve." He let out a low cackle. "I thought that was an impossible number for anyone, even a psychiatrist's daughter with body-image issues, but she sneaks in a cry, like, every half hour."

"What are you talking about?" I asked. "Madison doesn't cry that much. I'm with her almost every day."

"And she's usually wearing those huge sunglasses or flipping her bangs down over her eyes, right? Especially when Ethan's around?"

My heart sank at hearing Ethan's name. "Look, he knows about Caleb now, okay? You win."

"Y'know, when Maddy started hanging on me at parties and at school in front of everyone, I thought I'd won the hot-girl lotto. Then she started asking me if E was going to be at the places I invited her. I saw the way she looked at him, but every girl in school looks at him that way. You have to know that, right?"

I crushed Madison's note in my fist.

He continued. "I thought if I pretended I didn't notice, gave her everything she asked for, eventually she'd get over him and we'd be together, officially, but then she started obsessing over the piddly things you kept from him, the lies you told to keep him."

"Wait." I held my hands up. It was like he was having a

conversation with himself suddenly. "Madison told you about me and Caleb? That's how you found out?"

"Not exactly. See, when I told her you weren't at the rink that weekend like you said you were, she got curious." He tilted his head toward me. "You're the one who said you're with her every day. Did you honestly think she wouldn't find out?"

His lips kept moving, and I'm sure words kept coming out, but I couldn't hear them. I looked down at the wrinkled paper in my hand. Madison's high voice filled my mind, as if she were reading her note to me: *What I did was unforgivable. I want to go back in time and erase everything I did, but I know I can't. This is the only way I can tell you I'm sorry because I am, so sorry in every sense of the word.*

Madison got Drew to give me an ultimatum that would make Ethan hate me no matter how I responded, and, in case I didn't take his threat seriously, she invited Caleb here to ensure I was forced into coming clean. Sorry didn't even begin to cover it, and there was a definite theme here.

"Don't you get it?" I interrupted Drew's rant. "She used you to get with Ethan."

"The only reason she wants him is because you have him— like everything else. Her hair, ballet, that terrible music she listens to; she does everything to be like you." He scowled. "It's pathetic."

I didn't want to believe him, but Madison did dye her hair to match mine, and she hated ballet. I always thought she kept going to appease her mom, but she had way too much fun ruffling Mrs. Scott's perfectly primped feathers for that to be the reason. Plus, she always took my side over anyone else's . . . except Ethan's. A chill crawled down my arms. I started toward the Coutiers' side of the bridge.

"Where are you going?" Drew asked.

"To find Ethan."

"I told you, he left."

"Then I'll find Madison and tell her what a loyal little doppelgänger I think she is," I responded sarcastically.

"No! You can't tell her I told you." He grabbed the sleeve of my coat and pulled me back before I reached the crescent of light at the end of the bridge. I glimpsed the wild desperation in his brown eyes.

Adrenaline shot through my veins, willing my legs to sprint as I tugged my arm free. My already-injured right ankle sabotaged my getaway, twisting painfully as I slipped on the ice. A strained shriek escaped my lips as I fell to my knees and grasped my ankle.

My heart quavered against my ribs as heavy footsteps approached me. "I can't let you leave this bridge, Cassidy," Drew said. The boards beneath me bent and creaked under the weight of his snow-smudged loafers as he strode closer. "You know this is your fault. Ethan's never going to forgive you. So let it go."

I refused to believe that.

As I hobbled away from him, I spotted a shaggy head of hair in the thicket of trees lining Dover Park.

"Caleb!" I meant to scream, but my throat was dry and suddenly hoarse. Drew appeared before me, and I turned to run in the opposite direction, toward the party.

He clamped his hands down on my arms, forcing me against the splintered railing; it cracked and bent under my back. "You can't leave."

My heels slipped like I was on a treadmill coated with ice as I struggled to regain my balance. "Is that what Madison told you? Drew, she's using you—" The word caught in my throat as the fractured rail behind me gave out. I desperately clutched the collar of Drew's jacket before the rail collapsed completely into jagged splinters floating down to the frozen river.

For a relieved moment I clung to him, thankful I hadn't fallen over with the rotted wood. Then he whispered against my ear, "She never would have wanted Mr. Perfect if you hadn't dangled him in front of her. How's it feel to be the one being dangled now?"

I gripped his jacket tighter, holding on for dear life. So tight, my fingers ached when we were wrenched apart, away from the edge. Someone told me, "Get out of here."

"What?" I blinked, trying to comprehend who was there and what had nearly happened. *Did I almost fall off the bridge?!*

"Go!" Caleb shouted.

My mind clicked into awareness. *Right. Get out of here. Find Ethan and apologize—go!* I ran toward Aimée's backyard, not even feeling the sprain I'm sure was stabbing at my ankle, but the *thud* of fists on flesh stopped me.

I looked over my shoulder and saw Drew putting years of hockey brawls to use on Caleb's body, knowing that each shoulder jab and punch he threw was because of me. In the past three weeks, I'd made a career out of keeping my secrets so no one would get hurt and now *everyone* was hurt. I needed to stop this.

By the time I reached Drew and Caleb, they were staggering around each other near the broken rail. My eyes flicked to the exposed spot, and then to Caleb, who was ducking and dodging Drew's wild arms with surprising agility.

"Drew, you're mad at me," I said in the most controlled voice I could muster. "Leave Caleb out of this."

Drew's eyes went flat as he landed a powerful elbow in Caleb's ribs. Caleb collapsed into a heap of moans. Fear clenched my stomach at the change in Drew's expression from desperate to eerily controlled.

"You can have her to yourself now," Drew spat at Caleb. "You're welcome."

"That's not what this is about," Caleb groaned, holding his side and peering up at Drew. "Your girl set this up tonight. You think Madison's not running after Ethan right now? You think it wasn't part of her plan the whole time to occupy you so they could be alone?"

Drew grabbed Caleb by his hood and heaved him upright. "Take that back."

"Cassidy never would've made a big scene of things like this. She's too good for that, for me."

"She's a liar."

Caleb laughed a low, rumbling laugh, smiling through a wince. "Every one of us is a liar. At least she has a conscience about it." Caleb turned his head to look at me. "You are. You're too good for this."

My heart slid down my spine to the soles of my shoes. He was right. The boy that I had lost myself with was, impossibly, the person who had brought me back. The real me—the *me* me who would never in a thousand years end up on a dark, broken bridge fighting, and kissing a boy who wasn't her boyfriend—was better than this. I picked my heart back up and stepped into *my* shoes.

"Drew, this is crazy. Let Caleb go."

"Not until he takes it back."

Caleb kept his eyes on me, not even acknowledging Drew's demand. He'd gotten high after I yelled at him. I could tell by his hooded eyes. Why did he always have to be so out of it? The laid-back stoner act was only going to piss off Drew more.

Sure enough, Drew shook him. "Take it back now!" Caleb casually turned his head to face Drew and stared, defiantly speechless. Drew shook him harder and whipped him around so his back was to the new hole in the wall of the bridge. "Say it." Drew shoved Caleb's shoulder. "Take back what you said about Maddy."

After everything, Drew being so infatuated with Madison that he was willing to beat the honesty out of Caleb over it, he still called her Maddy—a nickname she despised. He didn't know anything about her. Each of us was doing terrible things for unbelievably misguided reasons. Everyone was so guilty that no one was to blame; our compounded guilts canceled each other out. This needed to end before someone did something that couldn't be taken back.

I walked slowly toward Drew, careful not to spook him into a rash decision.

Caleb glanced over his shoulder down at the river. "Easy, easy. I—I'll back off. Chill, okay?"

Drew kept jabbing with his fingers until Caleb was so close to the edge he had no room left to escape. "Say it."

Caleb stole another nervous look over his shoulder. Drew raised his arm to push Caleb again, and I lunged between them, absorbing the force of Drew's anger—it was for me anyway.

I didn't think about the broken rail or how far the fall was or how hard the rocks and ice in the river would be. None of that crossed my mind until I was falling and it was too late, but in the split second before I crashed into the rocks and the river swallowed me in its burning cold water that wasn't what I thought. The only thing I could focus on—the only thing I could see or hear or feel—was Ethan. I never got a chance to make things right with the only boy I would ever love.

I allowed myself this one last secret, a promise that even death couldn't deny me: I would make things right with Ethan.

26

THE SECOND ETHAN'S BEDROOM materializes around me, I search for some hint of how long I'd been gone this time. His light is still on and his closet door is open with a trail of pajama pants and socks leading into it. The hook his coat usually hangs on is empty, but his wallet and cell are sitting on his dresser. It's clear he left in a hurry.

The covered bridge. Aimée and Madison and Mica—Drew!

My feet are moving before the weight of those words can sink in. *The covered bridge. Drew.* I told Ethan that Mica was with me on the bridge before I was sucked into that last memory, but that wasn't the part he needed to know. I have to get to Ethan before he accuses Mica of killing me in front of my friends and Drew verifies the theory with a fake eyewitness account or something that will leave my death forever unresolved.

Would Drew do that though? Would he hurt his friend that way? *He hurt me.* I can't stop the thought from running on repeat in my mind: *Drew hurt me. Drew killed me.*

The pulsing in my chest falters for a beat and I feel it weakening, slowly releasing its hold on me. I close my eyes and think of Ethan's smile right before he kissed me on the bridge that first time. I blink and I'm at the river—no, I'm *in* the river. My leggings are soaked up to my knees in the bitter cold water. The temperature isn't what is stabbing at my insides though; it's the voice I hear echoing under the canopy of trees that line the river, floating through the narrow windows in the wooden bridge walls, streaming into the gaping hole that my body made when I was pushed—not when I jumped or slipped.

When I was *pushed.*

I know that's what happened to me now and it makes my arms and legs feel floatier than usual, like they're unhinging at the joints and stretching away from me by the force of some inexplicable sideways gravity. The silhouette that was standing on the riverbank the night I died looms over me again, its shadow stretching and bending in irrational response to the low afternoon sunlight reflecting off the ripples of the thawed river.

The voice fills my head, startlingly clear, as if I'm back in that moment: *I didn't mean to. This isn't how it was supposed to go—this is* her *fault.*

Madison's voice replaces the silhouette's. "How do you know Mica went back to the bridge?"

"I thought you were gone by the time Cassidy fell," Aimée adds, her tone curious, but with the barest hint of accusation.

"Trust me on this." Ethan's voice wavers the way it does when he talks to teachers. I wish I'd had the chance to tell him the rest of what I remembered before he came here. There's no way he'll be able to hide his reaction when I tell him about Drew, and Aimée and Madison will know something's up.

A raspy voice dissolves that thought and sharpens the edges of the looming silhouette. I need to get on that bridge.

I close my eyes and think of the one time Aimée beat me in a race across the bridge to see who got to eat the last red Fla-Vor-Ice, but nothing happens. I recall the first time the three of us camped overnight on the bridge and the day we found the bats roosting in the trusses. Still nothing.

I open my eyes and push my legs through the unseasonably turbulent river, but it's as if I'm trudging through frozen pudding. The water suctions around my legs and drags against my movements. The faster I rush toward the bank, the thicker the substance seems. A glossy film begins to form around the rocks like an impenetrable bubble, like the force field that surrounded Other Me at the morgue.

The pulsing in my chest weakens as I grow more and more frantic about what's happening on the bridge especially because I can't see. It's the opposite of how my body should be reacting— how an *alive* body would react. My heart should be rabbiting against my ribs, not lulling to a weary whisper.

I open my mouth to call Ethan's name, but my voice comes out a strangled squeak. I grasp my neck and try again. The effort feels like razor blades sliding down my throat.

"Mica was with me, E," a new voice that cracks my insides says. "In the house looking for Maddy."

The black of the silhouette standing over me on the river-bank falls away, revealing Drew's flat brown eyes and matching hair curled out around his wide, pale face, making excuses and twisting facts without hesitation to conceal what he did to me.

Liar! I scream at Drew in my mind. That alibi wasn't to cover for Mica, it was to keep suspicion off himself.

I thrust my body forward, gasping for air that I don't need as the river pulls me down. I sink like a warped pebble, shifting in the current, left to right, farther down with each sway. My hands claw at the rocky slope that connects the riverbank to the park above, but the force field keeps knocking me back. The urge to give up—to let my arms and legs float away, drift off with the current—is strong and alluring. I close my eyes and imagine that I've disappeared without a final thought . . . or promise.

Pain strikes my chest like a sharp piece of flint reigniting my purpose here. My eyes fly open and through the murky waves I see Ethan's sad-confused face from Saturday night. I close my eyes again and visualize the bridge: every flake of white paint chipping off the walls, the splintered corners of the rails and beams, the rusted bolts connecting them, the way the sun cuts through the flaws in the wood and illuminates jagged patterns on the boards. The scene brings on a rush of memories that I've been fighting against for almost a week, but I don't fight them now. They're exactly what I need to get on that bridge.

The watery curtain clears, and the vivid images in my mind dull into flat, gray reality. I'm next to Madison, who is standing with her arms crossed over her chest like she's protecting herself from some unknown threat. She has no idea. Her body is angled slightly toward the wooden wall on her right side where Mica stands in front of the broken rail. Ethan's next to him, and Drew is a couple feet away, closer to the park end of the bridge, an arm's length away from Aimée.

"Get her away from him!" I tell Ethan without looking away from Aimée. I'm terrified that if I lose sight of her I'll never see her again.

Ethan shoots his eyes in my direction for a split second, then steps between Aimée and Mica.

"Not Mica, Drew." My voice shakes so much I'm not sure he understands me.

He takes a quick step toward Drew, shifting his weight to make the movement seem less obvious. It has the opposite effect. The four of them stare at him.

"Are you okay?" Aimée asks.

Ethan answers automatically, "Sure." Aimée scrutinizes him.

"Be more convincing," I tell him.

"Being on this bridge is really creeping me out," Ethan says in a run-on line. "Can you and I go inside and talk—Madison too?"

Madison turns away from Ethan. Her cheeks blaze as she chews around each of her fingernails.

Aimée smooths a hand down her long ponytail and glances at Mica. "You saw Ethan leave before Cassidy fell, right?"

"Yeah," Mica answers. "I tried to go with him, but he wouldn't let me in his car."

"Why not?" Aimée turns a skeptical eye on Ethan.

"You're accusing the wrong person," I tell her in a voice so quiet even I have a hard time hearing it.

"Because he tried to kiss Cassidy," Ethan finally admits. "I didn't want to be anywhere near him. Still don't."

Aimée's and Madison's heads snap toward Mica, mouths gaping open. "You made a move on Cassidy?" Aimée shouts.

Mica lowers his head, cracking his knuckles one by one. "It wasn't like that. I walked in on her kissing some other dude and it seemed like a clutch idea at the time to test the limits of her trifling so that when I told E about the other dude I would have solid proof that she was cheating. I was drunk, but, no excuses, I took it too far." He pauses and faces Aimée. "I didn't actually kiss her."

Aimée glares hard at him, then asks Ethan, "Why didn't you tell me about this sooner?"

Ethan throws me a pleading glance and his answer becomes clear: me. He didn't tell her because he didn't want me to hear. He didn't want me to remember the bad bits and taint what time we had left together. I wish I could tell him what I remembered, what Drew did, but an intangible force is pinching my throat shut. I can't seem to form the words: *It wasn't Mica. Drew pushed me!*

"He didn't tell you because he believed Cassidy's lies," Drew sneers. "She cheated on him with that stoner kid Caleb—*and* Mica evidently."

Mica looks between Ethan and Aimée, insisting, "Nothing happened. I swear." Then he glares at Drew in disbelief. "Dude, what gives?"

"Actually"—Drew perks up—"I saw that stoner kid run into the park after I delivered a note to Cassidy. Remember, Maddy, you asked me to give her that note?" Madison nods unheedingly. Drew continues. "I didn't think much of it, but if he was drinking that bottle of schnapps with Cassidy on the bridge I bet he did something to her."

Madison finally lifts her head, eyes fixed on Drew. I step in front of her. "Tell them what you know, Mads."

"Where were you when you saw Caleb running?" Aimée asks Drew.

"With Mica, inside. I already told you that."

"At what time?"

"We went in after E left, so around 11:30."

"And you didn't come back outside until after Cassidy was found?" Aimee asks, thinking out loud. Drew nods. Aimée squints at him. "But the only window in my house that over-looks the park is in the playroom."

"Right." Drew struts to Madison's side and hooks his arm around her waist. She doesn't move, still staring at him. "That's where I found Maddy," Drew says.

There's only one reason to go to the playroom during one of Aimée's parties, but Drew wasn't up there with Madison. He was too busy beating up Caleb and killing me to force Madison to *physically* prove they were "official" like she promised they would be after he helped her with my breakup.

"So you guys were . . . while Cassidy was . . . ?" Mica's mouth pulls down in an exaggerated grimace. "That's messed up."

Aimée watches Mica closely as she asks, "If they were on the third floor, where were you?"

"With us. Right, Mica?" Mica doesn't answer. "What, you don't remember? You had what's her name with you—ponytail girl."

"Carly?" Mica asks.

"Yeah."

Aimée's eyes flicker, and I'm sure she's remembering what

Carly told her about not seeing Mica at the party. She asks Drew, "Why didn't you tell the police you saw Caleb running away?"

He scratches his head. "I was pretty drunk. I forgot."

"You weren't drunk," Madison finally speaks up. Drew bends his neck to look down at her. "You *never* get drunk," she continues, suddenly strong. "You walk around with the same beer the whole night pretending you've downed a six-pack." She meets his glare. *"You pretend, Drew."*

Drew pushes his curly hair back, and for the first time, I realize he does that so it will fall onto his face and cover his eyes, which are so devoid of emotion that looking into them makes me tremble.

"What are you doing?" he says through clenched teeth, barely loud enough to hear.

"I can't let Caleb take the blame for this—it's too big. I can't lie for you anymore," Madison replies at full volume.

Aimée straightens to attention. "Lie about what?"

"He wasn't inside with me or Mica. I sent him to the bridge to give Cassidy a note telling her how sorry I was about Caleb and everything. I told him we could go upstairs when he got back so he'd hurry. But he never showed."

"Why didn't you tell the police?" Aimée asks Madison.

"Because I didn't know for sure what happened. It could've been Caleb or Drew or an accident or suicide like the police said, but, either way, it was *my* fault. And Drew knew everything— he'd helped me, so I had to lie for him. It seemed like a better option than admitting I'd killed my best friend." She stops. "Until you started investigating Ethan. I knew Drew was on the bridge, but I didn't know if that had anything to do with

351

Cassidy's death. Then I found out he was threatening to frame Caleb. That's why I wrote you the *other* note."

Drew interrupts with a sharp, "Ha! You lied for *me*?" He lets go of Madison and takes a wide step toward the center of the bridge. "So we're telling the truth now? How about we start with you moonlighting as a recreational pharmacist or how much you hated Cassidy."

"I didn't hate Cassidy!" Tears flood Madison's stormy eyes. "I—I . . ."

"Wanted to ruin her life?" Drew retorts.

"No! I didn't ask you to hurt her."

"What did you think was going to happen when she found out?"

"I don't know, that you'd be a rational human being. Guess that's too much to expect from you."

Drew grabs for Madison's arm, but Ethan blocks him. Drew's eyes flare with anger, and he pushes Ethan hard. Fear stabs me as he stumbles dangerously close to the edge.

Mica steps between his friends with a hand raised to each of them. "Chill. Fighting about this won't help."

"*You're* preaching peace now," Drew scoffs at Mica. "That's rich considering where the back of your hand was Saturday night."

The memory of Mica's slap stings my icy cheek.

Mica steps forward, momentarily shutting Drew up. He turns to Ethan. "E, I'm sorry about trying to kiss your girl—really, I am—but I wasn't the only person making bad decisions with her that night. What she went through would've been enough to push a sober person overboard, but drunk . . ."

352

"She didn't jump," Ethan says confidently, and turns to look at me. "You were pushed, weren't you?"

My throat might still be clenched shut, but I can nod.

A tear draws a line down Ethan's face. "I am so sorry I left you."

It's okay, I tell him silently. Tears seep into my mouth when I smile at him. I can't feel the warmth of his touch as he brushes his fingertips along my cheekbone to dry them.

Mica turns his head to investigate the empty space where I'm standing. He cocks an eyebrow at Ethan. "Dude, what are you talking about?"

Ethan doesn't respond, but keeps looking at me, as if tiny windows have been carved into my middle and he can see through them to a different time and place, one where I can touch and talk like everyone else and none of this has happened. Where I'm not fading away.

"Ethan?" Aimée places a hand on his shoulder, pulling him back to the present. He blinks, focusing on her. "What are you looking at?"

"Cassidy." Everyone goes silent at the shock of my name. There's no sound but the wind whistling through the cracks in the wooden walls.

When he meets my eyes, I try to shake my head, but I'm not sure I manage it. My movements feel slow and detached from my mind. I hold his gaze, hoping he'll understand what I'm telling him in my head: *I'm only yours.*

Finally, he turns back to the group. "This bridge—what's here—is everything that's left of her."

"Tell him the truth, Drew," Madison demands. "He deserves to know what happened. Everyone does."

"I was with Mica. How many times do I have to say that?"

Mica shakes his head. "Tell us."

Drew looks frantically between the friends he's been fooling for days. "It was an accident. I was supposed to give her that note, but Caleb showed up and started talking trash about Maddy." He gazes desperately at Madison. "I had to defend you. I lost it. Cassidy got in the way."

Ethan's lip curls up in disgust; he's seething. "She got in the way?" He charges toward Drew, and Mica pulls him back. Ethan's arms quickly break free, but Aimée stops him.

"Not like this," she says. "Not like he did to Cassidy."

Mica takes a step forward to help support Ethan's weight as he crumbles into Aimée's arms, the immensity of the truth finally hitting him.

"You better lawyer up," Aimée growls at Drew. "You're going to need one to explain your 'accident' to the police."

"N-no," Drew stammers. "I didn't do this—it was Maddy's idea—it's *her* fault. And Cassidy was drunk. She fell on her own." He takes hold of Madison's arm, but she yanks it back and pushes him away. "If it was such an accident, why didn't you call 911?" Madison asks.

"Why didn't you *help* her? She might still be alive if you hadn't left her for dead."

"You can't prove I did anything," Drew declares. "You can't even prove I was on the bridge."

"Caleb can," Aimée says fervently.

Drew laughs nervously. "Like anyone's going to take his word over mine. There's no proof."

Madison holds up the photo she's been concealing under her

arm since Drew arrived and explains, "I left my camera on the drinks table when I went inside and it must have gotten passed around the party because a bunch of random shots ended up on my memory card."

"Is this going anywhere?" Drew asks in a short snap.

Madison's voice steadies, more confident. "When Nancy asked me about pictures for the memorial, I started looking through them, and I noticed this." She points at a figure in the background of the smiling group: it is, distinctively, Drew leaving the bridge at 11:59 p.m., according to the time stamp printed in the bottom corner.

That's thirteen minutes *before* Nancy found my body and enough time after Drew pushed me for him to threaten Caleb into keeping quiet. And for me to drown.

Aimée leans in to examine the photo. "You can see the bridge in the back. Is that . . . ?" She turns to Drew in amazement. "That's you. This is proof that you lied about being in the house." Her expression hardens. "You told Caleb you'd tell the police he pushed Cassidy if he talked, didn't you? That's why he was acting so cagey. You were threatening to frame him for murder." Aimée adds furiously, "*I* almost helped you do it."

Drew grabs for the photo, but Mica stops him. "It was an accident," Drew repeats numbly.

"You pushed her," Madison says. "It was not an accident."

"And it wasn't your fault," Aimée says to Madison. "Or Caleb's." The outlines of their bodies start to blur as she places her phone to her ear.

The distant sounds of sirens and muffled voices that I don't recognize float in and out of me. Aimée must've called the police.

She thinks of everything. I'm really going to miss that about her. *Thank you,* I whisper to my best friends—both of them—in my mind, because my mouth won't move. My death will no longer be a mystery that haunts the people I love after I'm gone. Since that's what I am.

Slowly . . . fading . . . nearly gone.

27

I CAN'T TELL WHERE I AM. Everything is white and blotchy and cold. I think of Joules and Shaw and my parents, and how I would've said goodbye to them if I'd had the chance. I imagine them happy to have had the time they had with me instead of sad to lose me, but I'm not ready to let go yet.

It takes all that I have left to blink away the light blinding me—lifting a single eyelid seems like moving an eighty-story building—but then I see him. And it's worth every second of the struggle.

Ethan.

His face is the only clear image I know now. I reach for him, but I'm not sure whether he can still feel me until glittery bits of dust float before my eyes, and I know he can't.

He pulls up a rueful smile. "I'm here, and so are you." He must not see the dust taking over my hand, spreading up my arm and across my chest. He says something else I don't hear.

I wonder what it was, but it's just as well not knowing. I can tell I don't have much time left, so I say the two things I've been meaning to tell him since the first time I knew he could see Ghost Me. "I . . . love you and . . . I am so sorry."

"I know. I love you too," he replies against my hair. "No more sorrys." He leans away from me so I can see his face again. "Do you know what I see in the river?" He waits a moment, then continues. "You. Always you."

Every inch of me sings. My lips manage one last word, one last promise. "Always."

His head tilts toward mine, and I squeeze my eyes shut, terrified my face will melt through him. But I can feel his mouth close around mine and the warmth of his tongue as it smooths along my bottom lip and slides into my mouth. I pull him closer, but my fingertips sink into his too-soft flesh as I slowly fall forward. The air around me thickens as I pass through him, like the cool rush of a waterfall.

My entire body seems to open up and release any pain and guilt and confusion. I sense the world is slipping away from me, but I'm still anchored to Ethan—not the way I once was, with a pulse, but by a new connection that is unfaltering, endless.

Then I'm gone and I'm here, and I'm everything and nothing. And all the choices I made, good and bad, when I was alive seem to make perfect sense because they led me to this freeing moment, this peace.

The whole world feels as if it has restarted and my journey has only begun.

ACKNOWLEDGMENTS

There are a lot of people I need to thank considering there's a very real possibility I died during the revision process and they brought me back as a storytelling ghost(ish) to finish Cassidy's tale. Here goes my attempt to remember you all!

The first thank-you goes to my agent, Stacey Glick, for believing in my worth as an author and for being generally awesome on all fronts. Next, I must thank my editor, Janine O'Malley, for using phrases like "fantastic" and "perfectly creepy" in editing notes. Also, to Elizabeth Clark for designing a *gorgeous* cover and everyone at FSG Books for Young Readers / Macmillan who worked on this book. Another huge debt of gratitude goes out to the incredibly generous Lauren Oliver for saying she'd be happy to read my manuscript, and then actually doing it! I'd also like to thank the band Metric for the inspiration of their music. If this book finds its way into their talented hands, they may recognize a few names . . .

For most, writing is a solitary process, but I'm lucky enough to have the AAAWG to keep me company when I venture out of the confines of the Writertorium and into the land of the living. Thank you all for welcoming in a wide-eyed newbie way back when. Your weekly input and encouragement is invaluable and usually quite fun. Special thank-you's to: Karen Simpson for writing "I love this" on my pages when I was ready to throw in the metaphorical towel and for cheering when it was my turn to read and sighing during first-kiss scenes. You have been an invaluable mentor, and I will never be able to pay you back for all your guidance, wisdom, and pound cake. Patricia Tompkins for weaning me off adverbs and always commenting on my over-the-top manicures. Stephanie Feldstein for saying, "I wish I had more to pick on," and demanding gossip sessions about our fictional characters. Shelley Schanfield for calling me out on inconsistent ghost "rules"—'cause those totally exist!—and your enthusiasm for finding out who done it. Kim Peters Fairley for needing Bubble Wrap that day in Staples so I could vent to you in line. Robyn Ford and Stephanie Feldstein (again) for being my badass betas—vive la YA! Also to Ellen Halter, Karen Wolff, Shannon Riffe, Skipper Hammond, Dave Wanty, Yma Johnson, Elli Andrews, Fartumo Kusow, Rachel Lash Maitra, Naomi Petainen, Leslie McGraw, Kay Posselt, Matt Bliton, Ray Juracek, Natalie Aguirre, and Connie McQuade.

Thank you to Stephanie S., Christina M., Lauren "the Duke" M., Allison A., Sam P., Lizzie K., Marianne A., Gretchen P., the Insane Soccer Posse, and all my other Ann Arbor friends for "forcing" me out of the house. A double, sparkly sprinkles-on-top thank-you to Christina M. for being an enthusiastic reader and keeping me vigilant against the dreaded pitfall of battology. Renae Reisig for driving with me to Grand Rapids in a monsoon and agreeing that Rendezvous is an acceptable name for a child given the right circumstances. Stacey Hahn for being my first *ever* reader and partner in absolutely fabulous crime. Caitlin Mary for just being you. And, of course, Pig-bomb and F.C.

To Christopher Barkham for embracing all my shades of crazy and for constantly reassuring me I'm only "seventeen years old with a few years' experience." You answer all my random questions with zeal. You listen when I need to talk out where my insane pantser stories are going. You discuss the myriad ways to kill and consequently stash a body with me like it's talk of the weather. You give me *Castle* references to ensure my mystery-solving skills are on par. You are my rock-solid alibi—if anyone asks. I will stand with you for all of ever . . . as long as you behave.

Mom, this book may not be dedicated to you, but it couldn't have been written without your support and encouragement. Thank you, and I love you a bushel and a peck and a hug around the deck. Dad, your enthusiasm for my girly pursuits, from synchronized figure skating to writing books about kisses, is awesome. Thank you for always letting me know how proud you are of me. To *all* my family and friends: you have no idea how much your support means to me.

Saving the best (and, let's face it, hottest) for last, it's your turn, dear reader. All this superfuntastic, amazingly shiny book goodness would not be possible without you. Thank you, thank you, infinity thank-you's!

GOFISH

BETHANY NEAL

© Bethany Neal

What sparked your imagination for *My Last Kiss*?

My Last Kiss started out with Cassidy alive and her boyfriend Ethan as the mysteriously "dead" character, but the story was just the saddest thing you've ever read (and not in the good feels way). I knew something needed to change, but I couldn't quite figure out what. Until I got in the car for a mini roadtrip to see my family for Thanksgiving that year. Driving always seems to clear my head and listening to music is a big part of that. That day I was listening to one of my favorite bands Metric's album *Fantasies* on repeat, and when it got recycled back to the lead track "Help I'm Alive" something clicked in my writerly brain. I thought, *What if being alive was a problem and you—i.e. Cassidy—needed help to figure out what'd gone wrong?* I instantly pulled a napkin out of my glove compartment and began writing chapter one . . . on my steering wheel as I maneuvered the highway. (Not recommended!) It was one of those genius-had-struck moments that I savor more than chocolate. There's a line in the song that goes "My heart's still/Beating like a hammer/Beating like a hammer," and that was when I knew that Ethan would be the only person who could see Cassidy and he'd enliven her still heart so it could beat again for him.

Since this is your first novel, what challenges did you face during the writing process, and how did you overcome them?

The biggest challenge writing this novel was hands down the nonlinear structure of the plot. Cassidy has a touch of postmortem amnesia, as one does, naturally, so the details and clues vital to solving the mystery surrounding her death are presented to her and the reader out of order. It makes the novel very exciting to read because every flashback chapter ends with a cliff-hanger, and it was actually quite fun to write the first draft that way, as well. I got to solve the mystery right alongside Cassidy. Then came the revisions. It was an epic headache making sure all the flashbacks lined up properly and nothing was inconsistent, so I ended up organizing the flashbacks in a separate Word doc and wrote out the full chronological version of the night Cassidy died. That way, when I reinserted the flashback in their out-of-order order, they were seamless.

What were your favorite scenes to write?

Anything featuring Caleb. I just love that little stoner with a heart of gold! He's so funny without trying, and I think I appreciated the comic relief in writing an otherwise dark tale. Everyone thinks I'm nuts, but I also have a soft spot for Madison. Her scenes are so layered with emotions brimming below the surface of her dialogue and body language. She was a lot of fun to create.

If you could, what advice would you give Madison after she finally confesses the truth at the end of the book?

Oh, Madison. I would tell her so many things, but I think the most important would be to never underestimate her friends' ability to forgive. So many times we have one fight with some-one or make one bad decision that puts strain on a friendship and we assume he/she can't possibly be our friend anymore. So we walk away for good. Humans are social creatures, so that never works. We all need someone to confide in and lean on. Madison's lucky that she has Aimée for that (even though she doesn't always realize it). I wish for Madison that she eventually can find the strength to forgive herself, as well.

The mystery and intrigue of this book is so great, we're constantly kept on our toes guessing what really happened at the end of Cassidy's life. How did you come up with and then keep track of all the different threads of the final story?

I didn't do a pre-writing outline for this novel. Instead, I did that pretentious writer thing where I let the characters "talk" to me. Not every story allows me to write that way, but I was lucky in that I felt a very strong connection to Cassidy and her emotions. I experienced everything as she did, which meant at times I, too, was on the edge of my seat wondering what would happen next. One thing that helped keep things straight was making individual timelines for each character detailing what each of them knew set against the timeline of what ac-tually happened the night Cassidy died.

Did you always know how the book was going to end, or did you ever change your mind about what the truth was going to be?

I always knew how Cassidy died. The malleable element then became *why* she died. The original ending in the first draft of *My Last Kiss* featured someone other than you-know-who-that-we-all-want-to-punch as the bad guy, but as soon as I wrote it, I knew it was too obvious. So I revised making that person merely a suspect, which was actually a blessing because I ended up with all these red herring clues scattered throughout without having to think about it. Writers love any opportunity to not have to think! (Or at least I do.)

Which character do you relate to the most?
I think there's a little piece of me in every character in *My Last Kiss*, especially the three girls. In a way, Cassidy, Aimée, and Madison are like the embodiment of the various facets of my personality. With that in mind, I think I relate most to Cassidy. I lived in her head for nine months writing her story. How could I not?!